PUBLIC AND PRIVATE

Maggie Sommers was beautiful, bright, witty,
unflappable—the sharp-edged picture of a perfect TV
reporter going where the action was and focusing in
on it unblinkingly no matter how brutal it turned out
to be.

But now Maggie was in love and she alone knew how
soft she could turn, and how ripped apart she could
be, when she let a man into her heart. For Maggie
wasn't afraid of flying. She was afraid of falling in
love.

**This profoundly moving, deliciously witty novel
captures all the exhilaration, intelligence and
passionate fury of a smart woman in love . . .
as it takes a piercing look at romance in
today's perilous world. . . .**

ABSENCE
OF PAIN

"A winner . . . made me laugh and cry."
—*Boston Herald*

"Novels as entertaining and compelling as this
don't come along often enough."
—*Shreveport Journal*

ABSENCE OF PAIN

A NOVEL BY

BARBARA VICTOR

A SIGNET BOOK

NEW AMERICAN LIBRARY

A DIVISION OF PENGUIN BOOKS USA INC.

In memory of a *Tat Aluf*

SIGNET TRADEMARK REG. U.S. PAT. OFF. AND FOREIGN COUNTRIES
REGISTERED TRADEMARK—MARCA REGISTRADA
HECHO EN DRESDEN, TN, U.S.A.

SIGNET, SIGNET CLASSIC, MENTOR, ONYX, PLUME, MERIDIAN, and NAL BOOKS are published by New American Library, a division of Penguin Books USA Inc., 1633 Broadway, New York, New York 10019

First Signet Printing, October, 1989

1 2 3 4 5 6 7 8 9

PRINTED IN THE UNITED STATES OF AMERICA

ACKNOWLEDGEMENTS

Absence of Pain is a book of fiction and therefore no research was done except if living can be construed as research. In this vein, there is the common notion that any first novel is at least slightly autobiographical, condemning the author to an inability to invent incidents, characters, and scenes. The only truth here is that *Absence of Pain* is set in geographical locations that are familiar to the author although each and every character is fictional and bears no relation to anyone—whether living or dead.

The only nonfiction portion of this book is the people who have given so generously of themselves to make my life so much richer. They are listed not in alphabetical order but rather in the order of their appearance in my life.

Dmitri Nabokov
Lucy Jarvis
Walter Weiner
Michel Alexandre, for always arranging the impossible
Jean Rosenthal, for the very beginning
Therese de St. Phalle
Brigitte Jessen
Jacques Bodenheimer
Elaine Markson, for getting me out of the trenches in every sense of the word
Geri Thoma
Bernard Mocquot
Abigail Moss
Lawrence P. Ashmead, for his warmth, patience, humor, brilliance and for knowing when fast is sometimes good
John Michel

PROLOGUE

The year is 1982. Two months of fighting between Palestinians, Lebanese and Israelis in Lebanon has produced a level of suffering that is incomprehensible to me. I am sitting on the ground somewhere near Sabra Camp in Lebanon, examining a guarantee that came with Joe Valeri's battery-packed Walkman. The screaming of women and children is only interrupted by the moaning of the sick and the wounded or the steady hum of bulldozers removing the dead. One year in the Middle East as a correspondent for an American television network and I am still unable to understand the reasons for so brutal a war. Yet, I am here to give explanations for the human carnage, the rubble-strewn refugee camps—to cover the story of this chaos that was once a society, to show the drama of human beings who once carried on the mundane functions of everyday life. I stand before the camera each day, backdropped by wide-eyed Palestinian children rummaging through the debris for a possession from the pile of ruins that was once their homes.

Sweet, frightened Joe Valeri, the man who produces the audio portions of my stand-ups in these war torn areas of Lebanon, listens as my voice drones on reciting the various features his guarantee offers. He presses me to continue, to speak louder, for he needs the reassurance of my words to block out the sounds of pain, grief and hopelessness. As I begin to read about a guarantee for life, I glance up and notice that Joe Valeri's head is no longer on his shoulders. Lifetime guarantee—the words barely leave my lips when I realize that my sound man is dead. Bits of what were once his head and neck are now scattered all over the ground and on my white T-shirt. I can't even scream. I can't seem to register anything that might even remotely connect me to what just happened.

"Lifetime guarantee" I repeat to no one in particular over and over until someone finally picks me up—arms under my arms and around my chest. A blurry image of a uniform is lifting me off of Joe Valeri. Looking down at myself, I see that I am covered by Joe. The uniform takes shape—a familiar Israeli general is holding me tightly and stroking my head. Burying my face against his shoulder, I can think of nothing until suddenly the nightly newscast flashes before my eyes. I will go on the air, bloodstained and covered with Joe. "Look what you've done to my sound man—you the American people who demand grisly reports of the suffering only for the purpose of recording the visual—never for an instant do you really comprehend the reasons for so senseless a war." Joe Valeri's Walkman is guaranteed for life. Why? I wonder, did Joe have a will? "I, Joe Valeri, hereby bequeath my guarantee for life to my friend Maggie Sommers since my life ended rather abruptly one morning near Sabra Camp in Lebanon and the guarantee still has about forty years to go."

Several hours later, in the bar of the Commodore Hotel in Beirut, the usual group of journalists are gathered around a table drinking themselves into a stupor. The Israeli general has still not left my side—a man I have known casually since the war began. Avi Herzog's hand is resting lightly on my shoulder, and while I am only vaguely aware of his touch, I am acutely aware of a pain inside of me that I can't quite locate. There are suddenly remote voices around me, drawing me into the conversation. "Pretty awful about Valeri—wasn't it? Brains blown out. A random RPG caught Valeri's head and suddenly no more Joe Valeri," someone says, snapping his fingers. Avi squeezes my shoulder reassuringly.

Much later, alone, nibbling a fingernail and staring at the peeling ceiling that is illuminated by one low watt light bulb, I remember my only session with a psychiatrist. Thirty minutes of the fifty-minute hour passed with only the sound of my muffled sobs.

"What do you want out of life, Maggie?" he asked.

"I want to be happy," I answered simply.

He didn't hesitate for a moment. Leaning forward, he said, "I can't promise you happiness, but if you maintain your dignity, I can guarantee you an absence of pain."

CHAPTER ONE

It was a Sunday afternoon in June 1969, when seventeen white doves flew out of their gilded cages in the grand ballroom of the Pierre Hotel. My wedding to Eric Ornstein was not only an important social event but also a guarantee to Father that he would continue to receive his yearly retainer as counsel to the prestigious Wall Street brokerage firm of Ornstein and Ornstein. Flowers were everywhere the day I walked down the aisle on Father's arm. "Smile, Maggie," he muttered. "This cost twenty grand."

He was still so bitter. He never forgave me the bad grades, the stolen lipstick from the dime store, the pregnancy that forced me to San Juan—oversized sunglasses and khaki army jacket—protesting the war in Vietnam but also protesting what was happening to me. The women's clinic in the suburb of San Turce with the porcine doctor who charged one hundred dollars per week of unwanted fetus after a hurried examination, remained a vivid memory.

Father and I were halfway down the aisle when he suddenly whispered, "Do you really want to go through with this, Maggie?" There was a glimmer of hope that he would spin me around so we could walk back up the aisle together and pretend this had never happened. Instead, Father said that after a while, a short while, passion died, and it was better to be well provided for, given my tendency to get fat. The man who had given me life, apparently without benefit of passion, was delivering me under the *chuppah* to a man I believed would rob me of my soul.

I concentrated on the *chuppah* because I was confused—my Jewish father, Russian Orthodox mother, baptism in the Episcopal Church, and now this—the *chuppah*. Standing underneath the elaborate canopy that was part of the ritual in any Jewish wedding ceremony, I noticed that it was less a symbolic roof than one of the most ostentatious overhangs I ever saw. Rows of white garlands were interwoven with tiny springs of baby's breath and delicate rosebuds, all intricately arranged on a seventeenth-century embroidered tapestry that depicted cherubic infants spraying water into the open mouths of voluptuous virgins. Not particularly representative of Mr. and Mrs. Eric Ornstein's junior four-room apartment with eat-in kitchen and eastern exposure near Gracie Mansion—my new home.

Eric took my arm and gave it a squeeze. This stranger standing next to me, the man whose name was already on my passport, had clammy hands. Looking up at him, I hoped that we would never have daughters, but if we did that they wouldn't have his nose. I wanted to scream that this was some kind of terrible mistake, but the rabbi was already speaking in Hebrew. Perhaps I could claim that I never understood what he said, and the contract therefore wasn't binding. "Had I known, Your Honor, had I understood that this was forever, I never would have stood there while the doves flapped around in their cages, their excrement dropping precariously near to Eric's mother. And something else, Your Honor: I'm an Episcopalian."

I think I might have lost consciousness, became suddenly it was over and the rabbi was saying something about man and wife. It dawned on me that only seconds before, I could have simply walked away, apologized to everyone and exercised other options, but now it was too late—I was Sadie Sadie Married Lady. I might not get fat, but I would have to account for my every move to someone named Eric Ornstein. I was doomed to a life without passion.

One of Eric's hands held me firmly at the waist, while the other began to fumble with my tiara and veil. My sister Cara, Eric's accomplice, was grabbing at my lace train—trying to reach the white taffeta and get it out of the way so my husband could kiss me properly. My own sister, a traitor, married with one child and currently swollen with another. Misery loves company, I thought as I twisted away from her nimble fingers, her tight grip on my shoulder. "Maggie," she whispered, "everybody is waiting for you to kiss him, untangle yourself."

Eric's wet mouth was pressed against mine, which was clamped shut, not allowing his tongue between my lips.

Everybody was waiting. Suddenly I was an actress, and this was my Academy Award performance: My entire career hinged on this particular scene. Letting the tiara and veil fall to the floor, I shook my head ever so slightly, causing my hair to tumble from its chignon and cascade down my back. Give the people what they want, I thought, as I kissed Eric, my husband of thirty-five seconds, passionately on the mouth. The crowd cheered. "More! We want more!" I imagined wriggling out of my Bendel wedding gown, strap by spaghetti strap, until I am completely naked except for a white garter belt, lacy white stockings, and high-heeled white shantung shoes. Lying down, I prop my legs up on the platform, knees apart, and watch as the doves fly excitedly around the grand ballroom. Copulating under the *chuppah*. The guests are in a frenzy, clapping to the rhythm of Eric's strokes into my body, as the ice sculpture drips symbolically over the chopped-liver mold.

My fantasy ended. Holding on to Eric's arm, I walked slowly up the aisle, my hair in disarray, my train held by Cara's tiny daughter and an unidentified child from the Ornstein side of the purple velvet rope. I heard a rip as one of the children stepped on the material, but it didn't matter. That dress would never be worn again.

Mother had accomplished her self-proclaimed mission in life. She successfully married off her daughters to two unsuspecting wealthy Jewish men. The Sommers family conveniently forgot about the baptism at St. Andrew's, neglected to mention that Mother's side of the family was guilty of stomping on the faces of the Ornstein clan in czarist Russia, and never did inquire if Maggie really wanted to marry this man.

Peter Duchin and his orchestra were playing "Fascination" when we finally stepped away from the receiving line. Holding me tight and breathing heavily in my ear as we danced our first dance together as man and wife, Eric whispered, "I'm going to fuck your brains out tonight."

Everyone watched approvingly as we pretended to dance. Mother with her diamonds, Father with his bad cigar, Eric's mother with her heartburn, his father with the lecherous leer, and all the friends, the pillars of the Jewish community, celebrating what to me was a bad dream. Even Father's tennis partner was there, the ambassador from Thailand, who had voted against Israel in the United Nations that year; inviting him had been a democratic gesture on the part of the Sommers family. The other democratic gesture was to seat Jonesie, our beloved black housekeeper, in the front of the banquet room. And there I was—Marguerite Sommers, twenty-one, college degree in English Literature, aspirations of being a journalist—dancing with a man who not only wanted my body but was also intent upon eliminating my brain.

Two days later, Eric and I arrived in Munich, where our honeymoon was about to begin, a planned tour of the concentration camps throughout Europe. Sitting in the hotel room that first morning, I thought about the horrors he wanted me to witness and wondered why I had accepted his decision. Munching on cakes and sipping *Kaffee mit Schlag*, I contemplated the insensitivity of the man with whom I now shared a bathroom. I was ashamed that I hadn't protested that decision, disturbed that it had never even occurred to me to try.

Eric hadn't yet fucked my brains out, because I was still able to think more or less clearly. His penetration of my body had, however, left me feeling nothing more than several moments of discomfort—similar to Dr. Drysdale's pelvic examination two weeks earlier to fit me with a diaphragm. In response to my cries of pain, Drysdale used a virgin speculum—another sham, since my abortion was a matter of record in my file. Eric's response to my cries of pain was only more heavy breathing and a

strange guttural noise that alerted me to the explosion he
was about to have—the one that caused his unborn children to slam up against the rubber wall of Dr. Drysdale's
diaphragm. "Was it good, sweetheart?" he asked on six
different occasions—six being the number of times that
Eric released his fluid inside of my body.

"What's good, Eric, and how would I know, when my
only experience with sex was with Skip Hillingsworth at
college?"

"What happened with Skip?"

"It was after an anti-Vietnam protest rally, and we were
dancing to the Platters—"

"Why?" Eric interrupted.

"Because they were singing 'I Am the Great Pre-
tender.' "

"No," he interrupted again. "Why the hell did you
go to a protest rally?"

So the conversation ended there, and I never did finish
telling him how outraged we were by the war, furious at
school policy and drunk on cheap sangria from a cracked
punch bowl that had rotten fruit floating on top. It was
just so natural to follow Skip up three flights of stairs to
his cramped room in one of the Harvard dormitories,
where he placed me gently on his small, rumpled bed. It
would be a lie to say that I had no idea what was about
to happen, but it would also be a lie to say that I understood that "putting it in a little" was far enough. Two
months later I was in Puerto Rico and Skip was gradu-
ating from Harvard. I hardly recognized him a year after
that, when he grabbed my arm at the notions counter in
Bloomingdale's. I hardly remembered it was his baby I
had murdered that rainy morning in Puerto Rico.

Eric walked out of the bathroom where he had just
taken a shower, a towel wrapped around his waist, and
sat down. His chest and shoulders were covered with
curly black hair, his olive skin still glistened from the
steaming water and his face a mass of red blotches all
over it. Looking at my husband, I could objectively admit
that if he had a chin and if his nose were shorter, he
wouldn't be that bad. It was just all that hair. He rubbed
his hands together vigorously and proceeded to devour

his breakfast. I was wrapped in a pink silk dressing gown, my left breast slightly exposed each time I reached for something on the tray, and my legs tucked up underneath me.

"Go easy on the cakes, or you'll get fat," he cautioned, and then added, "Can you be ready soon? I want to catch Dachau while the sun is right."

I looked at him in disbelief and tried again to understand why Dachau meant more to me—a technically non-Jewish fraud—than it did to my observant Jewish husband. But if Eric understood how inappropriate it was to view Dachau as anything other than a historical shame, he would have surely been my husband for life.

"I'm going to take a bath," I said, stretching.

Eric was studying me in that particular way he had that meant at any moment I would be facing the ceiling—a fish out of water, a caught flounder. Hunching over, I tried to invert my chest so my breasts, Eric's admitted weakness, were not standing straight out. But he wasn't fooled. He caught me by the wrist, pulled me over to the bed, and pushed me down. Murmuring several sentences I didn't quite catch, he proceeded to stroke my breasts and pop one nipple in his mouth while instructing me to hold his erect appendage in my hand. I didn't protest, because protestation took more energy than participation in Eric's assault on my body. I felt his thing, as he taught me to call it, pulsating within my grasp.

"Let go," he ordered, "or I'll come too quickly."

But I kept touching him, having caught on that coming meant going. Then, just as he was entering my body, I realized that I hadn't put in my diaphragm.

"Stop!" I cried. "Wait, I'll get pregnant."

"Never mind," he said between gasps. "So we'll have a baby. I can afford it." And then he listed in the space of time it took him to have his orgasm, exactly how much a baby would cost—including a maternity wardrobe for me, hospital, insurance, a nurse for the first six weeks, and tuition at a decent prep school and college.

How did this happen? I was trying to escape him by affecting my hunched-over pose when he somehow managed to impregnate me in the Three Ostriches Hotel in

Munich, Germany. Stumbling into the bathroom, I could feel his warm liquid dripping down my thighs and knew that whatever hope I'd had to escape this life with him had just been dashed. I felt pregnant. There was no doubt in my mind, as I stepped into the bathwater, that I was two beings. There was no possibility that I had avoided those thousands of sperm that were, even as I scrubbed, swimming frantically upstream to trap my ovum. The desperation I felt at that moment was even more acute than my despair while listening to the words of the rabbi at the Pierre Hotel, only several days earlier.

Eric was whistling tunelessly as I walked back into the room, stark naked—brave because it was too late. He stepped behind me, his reflection visible in the mirror, and smiled. "Hurry, Maggie. I have a car waiting to take us to Dachau."

It was the first but not the last time I resisted him.

"I'm not going."

"What you mean, you're not going? It's all arranged."

"It's just too awful to turn something like that into a celebration—our honeymoon. I can't."

"You'll do what I do," he answered. "We're one."

He was wrong. He was one. I was still zero.

"Maggie," he whined, "I wanted pictures of you there to remember." And who would get custody of those pictures, I wondered, during our divorce settlement?

"It was my camera," Eric would argue.

"Yes, but it was my smile frozen on my face in front of that memorial." We would battle it out right down to the last orange juice glass in the kitchen cabinet. It occurred to me that even though I was sure I was pregnant, there would never be a custody battle over the child. Somehow I knew there would never be a child.

He went alone to the Dachau that day while I stayed in the room, trying to piece together a clue—anything that could explain how this had happened to me. I remembered the large house on Long Island where I spent my summers as a child—it seemed so easy then. Mother printed those adorable invitations—"Summers at the Sommers' "—for all her extravagant garden parties. It was several hours before one of those events that they had one of their famous arguments. Maybe it wasn't so easy after all.

o

Cara and I were eating sandwiches under a large striped umbrella—on the patio behind the kitchen, while Father and Mother were inside, fighting. The sandwiches were piled neatly on a platter and placed in the center of the redwood table. The crusts were removed, and peanut butter and jelly, yellow American cheese, and tuna fish peeked out from underneath the usual Pepperidge Farm bread. Cara seemed oblivious to everything except licking the rim of jelly from around the sandwich she was holding. Straining to hear their angry words, I managed to catch the gist of what it was all about—a secretary who worked for Father in his law office. Mother was upset, threatening that if he continued whatever he was doing, she would leave. Not a word, I noticed, about us. Fins I wanted to yell. Who gets us? I was terrified by this mysterious intruder, who seemed to be suddenly very important in my life. Glancing at Cara, I noticed that she was still busy nibbling the sandwich from the outside in so that there was only a small circle left, which had barely any peanut butter or jelly on it.

"Cara," I whispered, "did you hear that?"

"Yes. So what?" she said, popping the circle of bread into her mouth and following it with one index finger, which would liberate the peanut butter that was sticking to her gleaming braces. I didn't realize then that Cara was in as much pain as I—that she was as frightened but had other ways of coping with that fear. Neither of us knew how to give the other comfort or strength, because there was no one capable of teaching us.

Mother stumbled through the kitchen door just as I was about to reach for a tuna fish sandwich. Father followed.

"Dumb shiksa," he screamed.

"I love you, Mother," I said, without even thinking.

She was blinded by her own tears as she ran toward the tennis court—never once looking back. Father sat down, and I marveled at Cara's ability to engage him in conversation about plans for the second half of the summer.

But individual survival was an integral part of living at the Sommerses'—every child for herself.

"Could I take tennis lessons at the club?"

"Yes," Father answered distractedly.

I interrupted then, because at nine years old I was not terribly well versed on the subtleties of male-female relationships.

"Why are you and Mother fighting?"

"We're not fighting," he snapped. "Grownups sometimes have disagreements—it's not fighting."

"But," I persisted, "what's a shiksa?"

"A shiksa," he said, without the slightest hesitation, "is someone who is stupid."

Even at nine, I did not accept either explanation. Years later, however, I learned that I had been mistaken—grownups *frequently* have disagreements; and to men like Father, shiksa *does* mean stupid.

○

When Eric failed to return to the hotel for dinner that night, I had that same gripping fear in the pit of my stomach that I remembered from my childhood—every time that Father turned his key in the front door to reenter my life at the end of a day. I never knew what would happen and when the fighting would start. I thought about what I endured at his hands—my father, who was Jewish when it suited him and non-Jewish when he mingled in Mother's world of displaced but titled Russian aristocracy. Jewish when he proudly pledged money at charity benefits in New York, where his valued colleagues reserved seats for him at their ten-thousand-dollar tables. Non-Jewish when he visited his oil-rich clients in Texas, who slapped him on the back at the end of an anti-Semitic joke.

There was some kind of connection between all of that and what happened to me as a child in that insulated apartment house on Fifth Avenue. I grew up surrounded by doormen and elevator men whose faces I learned not

to recognize on the street when they were out of context
and dressed in civilian clothes. I saw them as only ser-
vants of the rich—of my family and others like us and I
was ashamed when they greeted me on Madison Avenue.
Yet, I spent many more hours in their company than most
tenants on those numerous occasions when Father refused to allow me into our apartment if I returned home
past the designated curfew. I shared my shame and disgrace of having to sit on that tattered leather sofa in the
lobby with the late night doorman. The disgrace of doz-
ing as the sun came up over those impenetrable buildings
facing Central Park. Should I have tried to explain to
Otis, the doorman, that it was perfectly natural for a
young woman of my class to sit in the lobby all night?
Should I have tried to explain that it was actually being
done for his benefit—a sociological study in how the rich
treat their offspring? Otis watched me sitting huddled in
a corner of that tattered couch and looked pained. He
would shake his head as he peeled an orange that he
produced from a brown paper bag that Mrs. Otis packed
for him. Otis would sometimes share his orange or even
his Twinkie with me—chatting pleasantly until Father
rang downstairs and instructed him to send me up. Upstairs before the neighbors who walked their dogs in the
morning saw me. Upstairs before the mailman who carried the large leather pouch noticed me wilting in the
lobby. Inside the apartment before the morning shift
doorman came on duty and gossiped to the others in the
building. I sometimes contemplated the actual extent of
Father's cruelty—whether his opinion of the night doorman as the lowest form of life was worse than the fact he
closed his youngest daughter out of his home because she
returned ten minutes late from a school dance.

Waiting for Eric to return that night in Munich, I decided that Father's treatment of me had something to do
with his own torment—that much I knew when I finally
grew up and became Mrs. Eric Ornstein. But, how could
I ever explain it to Eric—the man who bought the sham
and facade of my rich and socially acceptable family—of
the conflict and pain of this gilt-edged girl he had married? It was then that I had a vision that would haunt me

for the duration of my marriage. I saw my tombstone clearly before my eyes—"Here Lies Marguerite Sommers, Beloved Wife of Eric Ornstein." Later, I learned to think of it as the final credit roll, then it was simply The End. Yet, I knew even then that I wanted more than Beloved Wife.

It began to make sense. I had always functioned as the abused child who defends her parents and denies that they were the ones who had inflicted the bruises on the frail and defenseless body. The ongoing battles with Father that I waged while protecting his motives, rewriting history because there was no other alternative. And Mother with her cold analysis of what life had dealt her, never hid her indifference and disapproval of me. Poor Eric Ornstein. And that was exactly what I said to him when he finally returned that night. But he never understood.

"Poor Eric."

He looked bewildered, his hand still on the doorknob.

"It's not fair, is it?" I said softly.

"Many things aren't fair, Maggie," he finally answered. "But choosing not to be with me on our honeymoon comes under the heading of unacceptable behavior."

Although Eric finally stopped viewing the remnants of a gruesome period of history, I continued to ponder the memories of a gruesome childhood. We finally ended up at the Connaught Hotel in London, where my first impression of that city was the one that would remain with me always. I felt as an intruder in an exclusive men's club, crashing the gate into a world where thick cigar smoke, brandy snifters, and financial sections of newspapers excluded me from the mainstream of what was Eric's life. He had come to London to see people in the investment business and had made it very clear that I was to occupy myself during the daytime hours. And it was during one of my diversions that I wandered into the Scotch House looking for a kilt and met Quincy Reynolds.

She was everything I wasn't, the complete physical opposite, beginning with her petite frame, red hair, freckles, sparkling green eyes, and a tiny voice. And she was deceptively tough, living proof that people could survive anything. Quincy had buried a child who began dying of a degenerative disease from the moment he exited her body. It was Quincy who finally made the decision to cut off the life-support system when her son lay in an irreversible coma—brain dead—for twelve weeks. And if that wasn't enough to endure in one lifetime, Quincy also survived a husband who informed her, after she had miscarried a replacement baby, that he was leaving her for someone he had met on an airplane.

Quincy viewed life as an obstacle course and managed—managed to be one of the most successful television agents in the business. She worked with her second husband, Dan Perry, a well-known tax accountant, who was also smart enough to realize that grief does strange things to people. He understood her need to succeed, sometimes to the exclusion of everything else. "Reynolds and Perry" was painted on the door of their office, and someone once wrote "Forever" in lipstick underneath. Neither Quincy nor Dan ever washed it off.

Quincy maintained that people could survive anything as long as they had a sense of humor. That was what brought us together that day among the piles of Shetland sweaters and cashmere cardigans. As I rummaged through the merchandise spread out on one of the sale tables, I thought about my marriage. Eric had already grown weary of my lack of enthusiasm for anything he offered me as a reward for being his wife. Tears ran down my face as I realized that my marriage had already failed. He had even ceased asking me if the lovemaking was good, having understood that I endured his ardor rather than craved it. Quincy noticed me immediately. Ignoring my tear-streaked face, she said, "They ball up."

Glancing first at her face and then at the left ring finger of her hand, I saw with relief that she was wearing a gleaming gold wedding band. She had a husband—proof to me that she hadn't failed as a woman.

When I didn't answer her, she added, "Nobody is worth crying over."

"How do you know it's a nobody and not a something?"

"Because only a nobody can make a woman cry like that when all the cashmeres are on sale for half price." She smiled.

"What balls up?"

She looked puzzled for a moment. "The cashmeres. It's better to get wool blends."

We both laughed as we wandered through the wool blends, past the acrylic sweater vests, and finally outside to get something to drink. We found a small café, where we sat down and began to talk.

"What are you doing in London?" she asked.

"I'm on my honeymoon. We've just come from—" And I stopped, because how could I tell her what Eric chose for us to do as a celebration of our marriage?

"Were you crying over him or just because it's all so new to you?"

"I suppose I was crying because I just wasn't prepared for this. And now I don't think I'll ever be anything else but this: I can see the writing on the tombstone."

"You mean the wall."

"No, I mean the tombstone."

Quincy must have understood, because she didn't bother correcting me again or even asking what I meant.

"I'm in London," she offered, stirring her drink with a straw, "with a client. I'm a television agent and my client is doing a documentary on Windsor Castle. Everybody said it was impossible, since everybody's been trying to get permission for years."

I was fascinated. I had never met a woman who not only wore a wedding band but who also had a job.

"It turned out to be one of the most unpleasant experiences I ever had," she continued. "I managed to get permission from the Royals, marched my client into the American Broadcast Network studios here in London, and some bastard executive vice-president ranted and raved for an hour."

"I don't understand," I said.

"Simple. He was jealous, enraged that I got permission, when he'd been trying for two years."

"Why?"

"Because," she said impatiently, "that's what women endure in this world of male supremacy, and television is about the worst. What do you do?"

"I'm married."

"We know that." She grinned. "Remember I was the one who found you crying over the cashmeres. But what do you do for work?"

"Nothing."

"Well, that's ridiculous. Marriage isn't enough, especially when you're not happy. It's only two weeks, and already you're wondering what it's all about."

"And if I knew what it was all about, would that make it better?"

"Probably not. You should really think about doing something else. Are you interested in anything?"

I started explaining, slowly at first, because I was so unsure, but then the words began to tumble out. "I think I want to be a journalist—but world events. I think I want to be based overseas, where I could report on international politics or even cover wars."

She listened very carefully, taking in everything I said. "Do you want to write or do television?"

How did I know? It was the first time I'd even really talked about it, or made it enough of a reality to actually put all of those dreams into sentences.

"Television," I blurted out. The irony was that it was absolutely true—that was exactly what I wanted to do.

"How do you know you could do that? It's not easy."

"I don't know," I answered defensively—for I was already fighting for a career that two minutes ago I didn't even know was possible. "But I'm sure if someone gave me a chance I could learn."

Quincy smiled again. "It's a tough business—probably the toughest to break into. I know because that's what I do, and I'm only on the other end of it."

So there we were, having a conversation that began innocuously enough but was suddenly touching on something as monumental as what I had secretly been dreaming of doing with my life.

"I have to go now. I promised Eric I'd meet him at

five, and it's already five." I didn't add that Eric Ornstein didn't like to wait for anything. And I also didn't add that I was clever enough to know that because I gave him little of what he demanded from me as a wife, the least I could do was not inconvenience his vertical existence with me.

"Let him wait," Quincy said. "He'll wait for five minutes, even fifteen, I promise."

Shaking my head, I stood up and tucked her card safely away in my wallet. "I'll call you when I get back to New York," I said.

I felt light-headed walking back to the Connaught, almost as if I had just committed an act of adultery. But what I had done was worse, because it was something that could alter my fate. And unlike adultery, it might not have that inevitable ending.

Eric was waiting for me in the lobby, sitting at a table and drinking tea. It was obvious that he was anxious, for he kept craning his neck in the direction of the entrance—waiting for me to appear, expecting me to be contrite when I finally did appear, almost fifteen minutes late.

"Marguerite," he said sternly, "never keep me waiting. I pay the bills in this family."

Two weeks and four concentration camps later and my husband already knew the rules of the game. I was only vaguely aware of being on the losing side.

CHAPTER TWO

The cargo-transport plane is parked on a deserted strip of tarmac at Ben-Gurion Airport in Tel Aviv. My hand rests on the lid of the gray metal casket that is about to be loaded into the gaping hole underneath the craft. I did another stand-up yesterday, amidst renewed shelling of Sabra Camp, where many more people lost their lives. Facing the camera, I recounted the situation of the war and how it affects the Israelis, Palestinians, Lebanese, and countless other factions that have joined into what is the most spectacular hostage drama ever recorded. It is doubtful if the American television audience really understands that an entire country has been taken captive by groups of desperate combatants who are fighting for their survival.

Tears gathered in my eyes and my voice broke during the broadcast as I described how Joe Valeri's head had been blown off by a random rocket-propelled grenade only several hours earlier. My producer waved me on, refusing to stop the camera when I signaled that I needed time to compose myself. He was only sorry that the tape wasn't running when it actually happened, as it would have guaranteed an Emmy-winning nomination. But he assured me that the piece was terrific—the next-best thing to a live shot of the episode. Joe Valeri is now an episode.

Avi Herzog is still with me, the same *tat aluf*, or two-star Israeli general, who was there when Joe was killed. He is holding my arm to steady me while several military officials check the necessary forms that will accompany Joe's body back to the States. Perhaps I should try again to call Joe's parents at their home on Staten Island, even

though the studio in New York has already informed them
of their son's death. Maybe they would like to hear from
someone who cared—someone who appreciated Joe's
stories of his youth and what it was like to be the son of
the neighborhood policeman. Joe, the tough kid whose
father sometimes arrested his friends when they were all
teenagers, a lifetime ago. Mrs. Valeri might be touched
to know that Joe was sorry for telling her once to shut
up, there was no God. Joe imitated her wide-eyed expression, her hand clamped over her mouth in shock and
disbelief, when her son uttered those words in their very
Catholic home. It's probably better if Mrs. Valeri didn't
hear that again—best to let her forget and be assured that
Joe is with her God now. Only, perhaps she might want
to question Him in His infinite wisdom, as to why He
robbed her of her only child.

Tears are streaming down my face as I recall that Joe
invited me to his house for Thanksgiving, which is less
than one week away. I should tell Mrs. Valeri: "I don't
know you, but I knew your son—I loved your son, and
he invited me home for Thanksgiving because he said
that at your house you care how your child feels rather
than concentrating on topics that will enrich his mind.
You see, Mrs. Valeri, at the Sommerses', mind enrich-
ment is the main course, nurturing the soul is not
included on the menu."

Tat Aluf Herzog silently hands me a crumpled handkerchief from his pants pocket as my weeping becomes
more audible. I take it without even glancing at him and
wipe my eyes and nose. I can't move now because four
men are lifting the gray metal casket onto a mechanized
dolly that will hoist it up into the guts of the plane. Joe
Valeri is going home for Thanksgiving. I wonder if he
would feel better knowing that there are people who are
grieving, who love him and are even anxious to receive
the little that is left of him. Thirty-seven Palestinians lost
their lives yesterday at Sabra Camp—six of them members of the same family. There is no one left to mourn
them. Eight Israeli soldiers died somewhere in the southern sector of Lebanon this morning. Their deaths pierced
the heart of the entire nation of Israel. Tonight I have to

do another stand-up in front of the Israeli Ministry of Defense concerning the latest position of the Israel Defense Forces and the repercussions of the current Palestinian stronghold in the Shatilla refugee camp.

My hand is crammed into the pocket of my blue blazer, squeezing the balled-up piece of paper that is Joe Valeri's lifetime guarantee for his battery-packed Walkman. It's all over now, the plane's cargo doors are slammed shut and people are beginning to disperse. Backing away slowly, I am determined to etch in my brain the image of that box as it disappears forever from my sight.

My producer is running toward me, calling out over the roar of the engines as the plane taxis down the runway. "Maggie, it's for the evening news. You're live at one A.M. in front of the ministry."

I nod—a live remote about the dead remote. Which is more remote? I wonder. Will they allow me to describe why all wars hurt all people—even those of us who are here simply to record the insanity of this bloodshed?

"Our survival is part of the everyday routine of living." I can't remember who said that to me—an Israeli, a Palestinian, or Quincy. Thinking of her now, I smile because she would undoubtedly have a funny remark, a comment so absurd that I would laugh in spite of my inconsolable grief. Quincy . . . How long since we shared a dinner in the Russian Tea Room and laughed until we cried? Quincy, who was there through it all, including the night that I finally left Eric Ornstein. I remember how she sat and listened to me while I listed all the painful truths that were part of my marriage to a man Quincy only tolerated because he was my husband. "There are worse things in life than divorce," Quincy had said matter-of-factly. And she was right.

"I'm going to drive you back to your hotel," Avi says, taking my arm.

"No, you don't have to, someone from ABN can take me back."

"I know I don't have to," he answers, already leading me toward the parking lot, "but I want to—very much."

Looking at him, I know why I have studiously ignored this man for the past six months. The countless times

that I saw his tall and muscular figure racing around the
Defense Ministry, I always pretended not to notice him.
Each time he tried to speak to me with his lilting foreign
accent, I pretended not to hear. I eventually learned to
recognize him from a distance—his unruly hair and peculiar walk, with his shoulders hunched forward and his
hands crammed into his pockets—so I could flee before
he had a chance to corner me. And once when we came
face to face, careening into each other from around the
corner of a corridor, I had to restrain myself from smiling
back into Avi's amused brown eyes. His handsome face
stunned me into an awkward silence as I was only able
to mutter something inane before stepping quickly around
him. He was so attractive—just too dangerous not to ignore.

"You're at the Golan Hotel at Tel Aviv, aren't you?"
Avi asks.

"Yes. How do you know?"

"I just do," he says softly.

The car is an indescribable sedan, which has four tires,
two doors, and one steering wheel. It makes sense—cars
should be like this, just as *tat alufs* should wear black
boots and khaki trousers. I let myself into the passenger
side, seasoned in the social customs of Israeli men, who
are not known for helping women in and out of auto-
mobiles, lighting their cigarettes, or even letting a respectable amount of time pass after making love before
they are hunting around under the bed for their socks,
underwear, and other belongings. Sneaking a look at him
as he starts the ignition, I judge him to be forty, quickly
calculating the disparity in our ages to be about six years.
Only, tonight, Maggie Sommers, Middle East correspondent for the American Broadcast Network, doesn't feel
thirty-four. She has seen enough to be ancient, yet understands so little of what she sees to remain a child. I
feel drained.

Avi guides the car onto the highway that separates Jerusalem from Tel Aviv and points out the various land-
marks along the way where Jordanian soldiers once held
strategic positions before the 1967 Six Day War. He
shows me the spot where Jordanian troops, with the aid

of field glasses, could have looked into the windows of the Knesset and seen if the Israeli prime minister had shaved that morning. I have heard that justification one million times—the excuse for the thousands of Palestinians who continue to rot in abhorrent conditions in the camps. Leaning my head back against the seat, I shut my eyes. My head is throbbing and my body is racked with a pain that is more severe than anything I have ever felt.

"Why have you ignored me for the past six months? I've seen you almost every day, and you refused to speak to me." Avi is concentrating on the road.

Opening my eyes, I noticed his incredible hands on the steering wheel. If they just brought me those hands, I'd know they were his.

"Quite frankly, I'm terribly nearsighted. I probably didn't see you."

He turns his head to look at me, and I automatically turn mine to gaze out the window.

"I've spoken to you on several occasions, and you've walked away, sometimes in the middle of my sentence." He is smiling.

"I'm really sorry," I stammer. "I probably didn't hear you."

"So," Avi says, "not only are you blind, but you are also deaf."

I try not to, but I laugh. "That was rude, wasn't it? I'm sorry. Could we pretend that we just met today for the first time and start again?"

He takes my hand, which has been resting on the seat between us. "Yesterday would be more realistic, since I doubt that either of us will ever forget what happened."

Closing my eyes again, to block out the pain, I know he is right.

We ride in silence until the car finally swerves into the circular driveway of my apartment hotel in Tel Aviv.

"I'm going to take you upstairs. I don't want you to be alone," he announces.

"No, really, I'm all right, and—"

"Under no circumstances. I want to make sure that you're safely settled and have everything you need." He touches my cheek lightly with his hand. "I don't want you in the elevator alone."

This must be a new social practice of Israeli men—never under any circumstances do they allow their women to brave an elevator unassisted. There is no discussion when it comes to other things: in battle, yes; in bed, absolutely; in the *mikvah*, without question—but never, never in elevators.

We walk into the lobby, where Gila, the hotel manager and my closest friend in Israel, immediately calls to me. "Maggie, you've got a message from New York. Wait." Walking out from behind the reception desk, her hourglass figure stuffed into a clinging blue jersey dress and her blond hair pinned back from her attractive face, she hands me the pink slip of paper.

"Thanks. It's the third one this week, isn't it?"

She smiles and glances over at Avi, who is engaged in conversation with someone he must know.

"He's still with you?"

"I guess so."

"With someone who looks like that, you shouldn't guess, you should be sure. I can tell you that he's definitely with you. Are you going to be all right because I'm on duty tonight if you need me."

"Don't worry about me. I'll be fine."

"I'm sure you will," she says, glancing over at Avi again.

" 'Thanksgiving yes or no,' " I say, reading the message. It's from Mother, who's been trying to reach me to know if I intend to come home for the holidays.

"Are you going home?" Gila asks.

"I hope not. I hope I can avoid it," I answer, determined not to endure another painful holiday with the Sommerses.

o

It was Thanksgiving 1961, and Cara and I were giggling at each other over the cornucopia that spilled dried corn, grapes, persimmons, and sprigs of holly. Grandpa Malkov was sitting next to me, beaming because he had just won the marathon chess competition at the Russian Immigrant Chess Club. He kept patting my knee, trying to make me stop laughing. Grandma Malkov was going on about the indignities she was forced to suffer at the Metropolitan Museum of Art when she tried to view the display of artifacts from czarist Russia. "Imagine making me stand in line to see what those thugs stole from our family."

Jonesie, my minder and friend, who once helped me finish a crossword puzzle in my third-grade grammar book by telling me that the word for *more*, four letters beginning with an *a*, was *agin*, brought in the turkey, perfectly roasted, on a cobalt-blue platter. Jonesie who had not yet been enlightened about Brown versus the Board of Education, the civil rights of movement, or that her counterparts on the trains—those ever so polite Pullman porters—were now running for political office. Poor Jonesie somehow got trapped in a time warp, ever since she came up from Alabama and began working for the Sommers family. Rose, Jonesie's helper, carried in two other cobalt-blue dishes, spilling over with wild rice and baby peas—indigenous to the neighborhood Gristede's. Father was about to carve the turkey, when Mother cleared her throat loudly several times.

"Grace, dear," she said.

"Who's Grace?" Father asked and then promptly remembered, but not before Cara and I giggled at his initial response. It sounded like a bad joke from grade school. We weren't surprised when he adjusted his silk ascot, brushed a speck of lint from one shoulder of his brocade dinner jacket, lowered his head, and recited, "Thank you, Father, for what you have so generously bestowed on this family, in the name of Jesus Christ our Lord. Amen."

So grace was said by Father, who, a mere twenty years ago, was wrapping tefillin in the Bronx. But it was Thanksgiving, a tribute to the Pilgrims, the founding fathers of our country, which meant that tonight the family was Episcopalian. It was New Testament night at the Sommerses'.

Father picked up the mother-of-pearl carving set and

was about to dissect the turkey, when he stopped. Looking at me sternly, he said, "Maggie, I'm granting you amnesty—it's Thanksgiving and I'm going to grant you amnesty."

"Thank you, Father," I mumbled, not exactly sure which father I was addressing. And then, after a slight pause but right on cue, I asked, "What's amnesty, Father?" I already knew the definition, even if I didn't know the angles of an isosceles triangle, but I realized even at thirteen that it was adorable to play dumb and much better for my chances of actually receiving the reprieve that was being offered to me.

Mother was smiling, proud that her husband and father of her two children was after all a benevolent dictator who was about to grant her second-born child amnesty. Maggie Sommers could have her privileges back, even if she did have the distinction of getting the lowest grade in math ever recorded in the history of Miss Harkness' Classes.

"Go and get the dictionary, Maggie," Father instructed me.

Getting the dictionary was merely a figure of speech, since it was an enormous antique book positioned on an old English stand on top of an eighteenth-century Chippendale desk located in the foyer of the apartment. Standing up, I was very careful not to scrape my chair on the highly polished white marble floor. Walking solemnly to the Webster, I flipped through the thin parchment pages, searching for the word *amnesty*. I was terrified that I wouldn't find it because my spelling was so terrible. And if I couldn't find it, I wouldn't be allowed to answer the phone, watch television, listen to my record player, and apply a dab of Tangee lipstick to my mouth on weekends and other school holidays. "God, whoever you are," I prayed, "Father, Son, or bearded Jewish man, please let me find *amnesty.*" One of three people I addressed must have heard me, because there it was: "Amnesty—noun, general pardon, for political offenses."

Walking slowly back to the dining room, I mouthed the definition over and over as I slipped back into my chair. Cara had already started to cry, and Grandpa seemed to be trying to make her laugh by moving his dentures around in his mouth. Grandma was shaking her head, and Mother was sitting on the edge of her chair, her strand of opera-length pearls clanking against her dinner plate.

"Maggie," Father said, "what is the definition of *amnesty?*"

I recited the words, not forgetting to include that it was a noun and carefully remembering to finish with a "Thank you Father I appreciate it" in the same tone, as if that were also part of the definition I had just found in the dictionary. Father appeared to be satisfied, because he immediately turned his attention back to the turkey—the one lying on the cobalt-blue platter. But suddenly Cara excused herself and ran from the table, sobbing uncontrollably, with Mother right behind her.

"Why do you do that to her?" Cara cried from the other room. "Why do you insist upon humiliating her like that?"

There was a strained silence in the Sommers dining room, as the family made another feeble attempt to celebrate yet another joyous holiday meal. When Cara finally returned, I smiled at her gratefully. Still, I couldn't help but feel personally responsible for the tension that permeated the room.

○

Avi Herzog is standing on the terrace of my living room, overlooking the sea, with an expansive view of the coastline of Tel Aviv below. Facing him, I am huddled in one corner of the sofa. He has been questioning me about my life—cleverly, for he is practiced in the art of interrogation, having practiced it regularly with the many Arab prisoners the Israeli army has captured during the last three wars, wars that made him a *tat aluf*.

"You're a strange combination of sadness and humor," he says. "Why do I feel that about you?"

I don't respond right away, because I would like to avoid the subject of Maggie Sommers. How can I explain

to him that I am willing, in principle, to allow him inside
of my body if he would only skip the preliminaries of
delving inside my mind. Words escape me—a satisfac-
tory explanation that will convince him I am nothing
more than what he sees, or even a flippant response would
be helpful if it would make him get down to the business
at hand.

"I suppose I can't be happy all the time," I say, and
immediately wish I hadn't, because it sounds so dumb.

"There's more to it than that, Maggie. I watched you
for months and wanted to know you, but you were harder
to approach than Arafat. Yet I used to see you laughing
and joking with the other correspondents, or even with
some of my staff at the ministry. Why were you so afraid
to talk to me?"

I find it difficult to look at him now because he almost
has it all figured out—that the others were safe. Instinct
told me from the beginning that he wasn't. Shifting my
position so my head is resting on my arms, I say, "Please,
Avi, talk about yourself—tell me about you."

And clever as he is in the art of interrogation, he pro-
ceeds to do just that because that's how they make people
talk, by putting them at ease.

"I was born in Russia and came here, which was Palestine, when I was four." Another victim of Vera Malkov's family and their version of justice during the
pogroms.

"I have a tremendous pride in this country because I
watched it grow from nothing—a dream that nobody really thought would come true. Yet a part of me is still
very Russian. I speak the language and I love the music,
the songs my parents used to sing when I was small."

"Did you always want to be in the army?"

"No," he answers, smiling slightly. "I wanted to be
a doctor, but then things happened." He pauses.

"What things?"

"You sound as if you're interviewing me."

"No, I just want to understand how people can go
from wanting to be part of the healing process to suddenly becoming part of the killing process."

He looks pained. "I grew up on a kibbutz in the Emek

Hasharon region of Israel, living side by side with Palestinians. Then in 1947, before the war of independence,
it began, the killing process, as you call it. The British
were the occupiers and the Arabs were beginning to feel
threatened, so the raids on the Jewish kibbutz began. I
suppose they believed if they drove us out, then the British would be anxious to leave. When I was five, the Arabs
raided our kibbutz and my father was killed. That caused
me to change any notion I had of peaceful coexistence.''

There is no doubt that Avi touches something deep
down inside me, something that undoubtedly began happening during those months while I ignored him.

''During the 1956 Sinai campaign,'' he continues,
''when I was fourteen, my older brother was killed. That's
when I gave up any idea I had of going to the United
States to study medicine. I knew I belonged here. Only
my mother was left, and I couldn't leave her.''

At this very moment, it is more than a sexual attraction
that causes me to suppress a desire to take him in my
arms. I want to comfort him with my mouth, my body,
for his father, brother, those lost dreams, and anything
else that hurt him over the years. But I am not about to
do that without waging my own kind of battle—constructing a barrier between my head and my heart so that I
won't become too much a part of him. ''I'm sorry,'' I
say quietly, ''about your brother.''

It was a natural course of events that led Avi to make
the army his career—a combination of anger over his
brother's death and the realization that in Israel, a military life was a safe and vital profession: safe because he
would never be out of a job, and vital because it was
crucial to the continued existence of the state.

''Do you have any regrets?'' I add.

''I suppose if I had, my father and brother would have
died in vain.''

''It's a full-time job, a commitment, isn't it? I mean,
it doesn't leave you time for a lot of other things.''

He shakes his head—the conversation about him is
over. ''Now you, Maggie. Tell me about yourself other
than you're beautiful and have a successful career.''

It would be so easy to tell him everything about myself

from the very beginning, to pour out my heart to this stranger. But instinct tells me that it would be more prudent to let my body relate to him, safer for me in the long run not to open up my heart.

"Well," I say, "the army certainly keeps you in good shape."

That same amused expression crosses his face. "I swim in the mornings, or try to when I'm not in the field."

He's humoring me, playing my little game.

"And you," he says, "how do you keep in such good shape?"

But he really doesn't care about my muscle tone. He is much more interested in knowing why I haven't had children by the age of thirty-four. The details of my pregnancy, almost twelve years ago, when my baby was born with the umbilical cord wrapped tightly around its neck, is something I still can't talk about. It's impossible to explain that had that not happened, it would have been a terrible mistake, because I felt trapped from the moment Eric Ornstein's sperm penetrated my body.

"My marriage ended six years ago. Since then there's been nobody I wanted to be with enough to have a child."

"And you never wanted a baby with him during the years you were married?"

"No, never," I answer. "It was all wrong from the beginning. Do you have children?"

"No."

And before I can continue that line of questioning, he interrupts. "Do you see your parents often?"

"I try not to." I laugh. "My childhood was sufficiently awful that I stay away, but I have a sister I see when I go back."

"There's that pain again," he says, lighting a small black cigar. "The other half of that wonderful humor you have." He looks at me tenderly.

"I remember when I first saw you," I say quietly.

He looks surprised. "You do? Then why . . . ?"

"It was the day the war began, June fifteenth, and we were in Marjayoun—"

"You were with your ABN crew, trying to get an interview with the head of the Southern Lebanese Army, Haddad,'' he interrupts.

''And I didn't get it,'' I say, laughing.

''No, but if you hadn't ignored me, I probably could have arranged it for you.''

''I'll remember that for the next time.'' Now it's happening, and there isn't much I can do to postpone the inevitable. I'm not sure anymore that I want to.

''You were so professional that day. Everybody was watching you because you looked so out of place—a woman war correspondent.''

''I felt out of place, it was very frightening. But I suppose the first time always is.'' I glance at him and see that he is looking at me very seriously.

''I wanted to protect you. It sounds foolish, doesn't it?''

I nod, thinking how very appealing it really sounds.

Avi extends his hand to me and invites me to stand next to him and look at the beautiful view of the Tel Aviv coastline. I am about to get up, although I feel so terribly tired that I'm not sure if my legs will carry me the six feet to the terrace. I am somewhere between sitting and standing when he suddenly says, ''If you get up, Maggie, I'll kiss you, and if I kiss you I'll make love to you, and when that happens, I won't let you leave Tel Aviv.''

I am calculating very quickly—still somewhere between sitting and standing—that it is already the twenty-second of November and Thanksgiving is a mere three days away. My bureau chief offered me a leave of absence at Quincy's request so I could return to the States to have Thanksgiving with my family. Thanksgiving—the tradition that to most Americans conjures up images of laughter, fires stoked in stone hearths, sweet potatoes, funny stories about childhood, and memories that evoke tears and sentimental embraces, as people gather together to validate their love form one another. There is no decision, as far as I'm concerned. The telegram I compose in my head reads: MOTHER FATHER STOP HOW MUCH I WANTED TO SPEND THANKSGIVING WITH YOU AND CARA STEVEN LISETTE MUFFIN AND BRAD STOP UNFORTU-NATELY TAT ALUF AVI HERZOG THE COMMANDER OF THE

NORTHERN FRONT AND THE PRIME MINISTER'S ADVISER
ON LEBANESE AFFAIRS HAS DETAINED ME INDEFINITELY
IN ISRAEL STOP WILL BE IN TOUCH AS SOON AS I HAVE
FINISHED INSPECTING THE COASTLINE OF TEL AVIV STOP
MAGGIE.

Avi kissed me and went on kissing me, before he finally took my hand and led me back to the couch in the
living room, holding me in his arms even as he lowered
me onto the cushions.

"I want you, Maggie. I've wanted you from the first
moment I saw you." Avi reaches over my head and tosses
the pillows on the floor. The only lights are coming from
the reflection of the cars and streetlamps outside, near the
coastline of Tel Aviv. I remember him in Marjayoun, in
Metulla, Tel Aviv, Beirut, and today at the airport. His
arms are around me as he lies down next to me on the
narrow sofa, his body pressed tightly against mine.

"I've gained a little weight," I say, feeling suddenly
awkward.

Avi doesn't answer but just pulls me even closer toward
him, almost to keep me from trembling, to make it his
so it will stop. It occurs to me that this is exactly why I
ignored him for all of these months—because I knew it
would be like this if it ever happened, and I knew it
would eventually happen.

"I fell in love with you in Marjayoun that day," he
whispers.

I press my fingers to his lips, touch his face and feel
that he hasn't shaved. At least this wasn't completely pre-
meditated. Taking my hand away from his mouth, he
draws me into him, kissing me again and again.

"Let me make love to you," he murmurs. "Come to
bed."

What would Quincy say if I told her this—a man fell
in love with me the first time he saw me, on a battlefield,
over the border in Lebanon. She would probably never
believe it. And right then I couldn't figure out why I did.

Avi caresses every part of my body with his tongue
and I resist, but only for a moment. I have bought in
bed, sold in bed, even traded in bed, but I have never
ever been had in bed. Not ever—until now. When it hap-

pens with him, I close my eyes, bite my lip, and mourn my loss. He kneels next to me as he switches off the light that is glaring in our eyes, and then starts all over again, in case I might have forgotten the story so far. Kissing and touching me in a now familiar way, he always comes back to my eyes—looking into them as if to reassure me that it is still him.

He was the best even before he went inside me—the one perfect and elusive lover that I never had, the one I had been trying to find ever since I started out. And I'm involved in this particular act, a full partner participating with my eyes wide open, aware of the *person* who is currently inside my body rather than just an unconnected organ filling an aperture.

Avi takes my face between his large and tender hands and says, "Open your eyes and look at me, Maggie. I love you."

And as my body falls over that mysterious cliff, I know that this relationship could cause me a great deal of pain when it inevitably ends. I think *when* and not *if* because my level of optimism has been more than slightly tested over the years. But the feeling still won't stop again and again, as he holds me in his arms—and somewhere in the back of my mind, I hope that it isn't because of a need to blot out the pain of Joe Valeri. I don't want this to be my way of assuring my existence in the face of death.

"Please stop, please. I can't anymore," I cry.

"I love you," he says again, wiping the tears from my face. And I'm not sure whose tears they are. For the moment I believe they are ours, because he's a part of me. At least for the moment.

It is over, but we haven't moved. Stroking Avi's hair, I contemplate asking the fatal question—the one that has been on my mind for the past several hours. I have hesitated asking it, afraid to spoil what has just happened and well aware that Avi avoided the subject. I am suddenly angry, because I am entitled to this minimum amount of pleasure. I want to believe that life goes on.

"Are you married?"

"That is very complicated," he responds, pausing.

I am not exactly aware that I asked a multiple-choice

question: a simple yes or no will do, and by the way, it's too late now, because I already made love to you. I'm just indulging my fantasy that I would have to stay in Tel Aviv and not go home for Thanksgiving. You see, Avi, it's not all that serious—how silly of me to have believed you when you said you loved me. But I did, and I believed what you said on the terrace too—that you would keep me in Tel Aviv for all eternity, millions of light-years away from the reality of spending the holidays with the Sommers family. But you wouldn't understand that, Avi, because in Israel everybody is family, except for your Palestinian cousins. And something else: I fell in love with you, too, that day in Marjayoun, the day your army slammed across the border into Lebanon.

Finally, he adds, "My marriage hasn't been a marriage for years."

"Then why do you stay married?"

"Because I'm afraid if I leave Ruth she'll fall apart. She's fragile."

I understand the entire unspoken story of Avi and Ruth Herzog. Ruth is a fragile woman who is only too happy to accept Avi's duplicitous life. She would fade into oblivion if he picked himself up, thank you very much, and put his dirty clothes in someone else's hamper or dropped his stray hairs on someone else's sink in the morning. That's what he wants to believe. On the other hand, Ruth Herzog is probably trying to find the right words to explain to Avi that she would really be much better off if he simply took his business elsewhere, which is what he is in the process of doing right now. But that's what I want to believe.

"Things change, Maggie," he says. "Now that I have you, things are different."

And since when do you have me, Avi Herzog? One time in bed with Maggie Sommers does not constitute a necessity to reevaluate one's life. I glance at my watch, which is lying on the night table, and notice that it is almost eleven o'clock. Avi is lying on his side with his head propped up on one arm, and watching me. I notice that he doesn't appear to be rummaging around on the floor for his garments, which were strewn about in the frenzied passion of foreplay. Avi doesn't seem to be in any hurry to go anywhere. It is I who am in a hurry.

"Avi, I have to bathe and dress. I have a stand-up at the ministry."

"I know," he says, without moving, "I'm going to drive you there, wait and then come back with you so I can hold you all night." And what about fragile Ruth— the one who wouldn't survive if he left her? I don't dare to ask the question, because I've learned that prolonging any happiness, even for a few additional hours, is too precious a gift to spoil.

While I am soaking in the bathtub, Avi wanders in and leans against the sink. "Tell me about your marriage, why you got divorced."

"It's too complicated to explain away seven years in a few minutes."

"I have all the time in the world," he says quietly.

"Well, I don't," I snap.

Avi Herzog has suddenly become the enemy, and while I was prepared to give tacit approval to something I don't fundamentally approve of—specifically, sleeping with a married man—I am not prepared to give that enemy any knowledge of my private past. I feel an inexplicable kinship with Ruth now—a kind of guilt in having contributed to anything that prolongs the agony of her relationship with Avi. I see myself as merely a viable diversion, a pleasant sensation that allows Avi to sustain that other thing, keep it going, make it easier for him to bear. And what about her? And what about me? Avi who has been inside my body, and who has already penetrated my heart, now wants a piece of my mind. And so I decide to give it to him. "What makes you think that we are intimate enough for me to tell you about my marriage or anything else about my past? I mean, just what gives you the right even to ask?"

He smiles slightly. "When do I get that right?"

But any response on my part would be less than truthful, dishonest even, for Avi Herzog already owns a part of me.

"Don't be distant now," he says tenderly. "You just happened, I need time to change my life."

He doesn't understand. He interprets my silence as disappointment that he is not yet free to make a life with me. But perhaps I have also misunderstood, interpreting his words as a desire that I change my life for him. Yet, I am not at all certain that either of us is prepared to change our lives for anybody.

But now he's kissing me, my soapy face sliding against him. "I love you, Maggie," he says, "I'm not going to let you go."

He follows me out of the bathroom and pulls on his socks, steps into his khaki trousers, and laces up his shiny black boots. Sitting down in a chair after he is dressed, he watches me carefully applying lipstick to my mouth with a brush. Inspecting my eyes, I rub in the dark green shadow—careful that it is not too bright for the camera—and bend my head forward to brush my hair. I flip it back so the final effect is wild and manelike around my face. There is a natural glow to my skin that I haven't seen in many months. Finally, I put on my tortoise shell-framed glasses and study my total image in the mirror.

"Do you wear glasses, Maggie?" Avi asks me cleverly.

"No," I answer without thinking. "The glass is clear, but they make me wear them so I appear more intelligent on the air—you know, more believable." And then I suddenly remember, *"I'm nearsighted. I never saw you, Avi Herzog."*

He gets up and takes me in his arms. "Why did you waste these six months? We could have been together six months longer."

I stand up to my full height of five feet seven inches and look Avi Herzog straight in the eyes. "Why . . . Why?" My hands are clenched into fists at my sides. "Because I was probably trying to do the smartest thing I've done in years—saving myself an extra six months pain being involved with a married man. That's why."

"You're not giving me a chance," Avi says calmly.

"You'll have to take your own chances," I say softly, and then add, "I did."

"What are you trying to prove, Maggie?" he asks sadly.

○

"What are you trying to prove, Marguerite?" Mother asked.

Lying on the king-size bed, I looked up into her worried face, while the air conditioner groaned laboriously in the background, pumping cool air into my Wedgwood-blue bedroom. Although it was only nine-thirty in the morning, Mother had already managed to look like the older half of the Ivory soap commercial. She was immaculately dressed in a crisp white linen outfit, with a colorful Hermès scarf draped casually around her shoulders. Her makeup was flawless, her hair caught in a chic bun at the nape of her neck, and she was even wearing stockings in the ninety-degree heat. I marveled at her ability to suffer for the sake of propriety.

She sat down on the edge of my bed, her brow once again furrowed in concern and near panic as she watched me sob uncontrollably. I had the feeling that she was less moved by my tears than she was annoyed because I had created enough of a problem to merit Eric's calling her to come right over.

"Vera, could you get over here and do something with your daughter?" I automatically became Vera's daughter when I was not behaving correctly as Eric's wife—much as I became Father's daughter when I did something to displease Mother.

When my tears wouldn't subside, her manner changed rather suddenly to sympathy—undoubtedly she had summoned up everything she had ever read on the subject of child psychology. Gesell and Ilg, *The Child from 20 to 30*, the sequel somebody forgot to write. "The child from twenty to thirty suffers from a confusion about death and deity, alternating between accepting death as a welcome end to a miserable existence and viewing God as a traitor for causing a profound disappointment with life."

"Mother, I don't want to live anymore. I hate my life."

"Maggie, Maggie, you have a beautiful life, with all—"

"Oh, Mother," I snapped, "what kind of beautiful is this? I weigh one hundred and seventy pounds."

"But, Maggie, look at your lovely view of the East River. Now, how many people have that?"

"Mother," I moaned, "I want to work, and he won't let me. I feel useless."

"Does Eric have financial problems?" Mother was horrified at the unmentionable possibility that she had miscalculated Eric Ornstein's earning power. Had she erred? Had she sold her daughter to a fraud?

"No, Mother," I answered, wearily. "I just want to work for me. I want a career—why did you send me to college?"

Mother looked at me sadly and shook her head. "I sent you to college to have a wonderful time and marry a wonderful man like Eric."

Lying there that morning with my swollen face, and obese body, my pudgy fingers still wrapped around a crystal glass half-filled with orange juice, I was certainly living proof that things were not the way they were supposed to be. That crystal glass, once part of a set of twelve, was the reason Eric had summoned Mother. I had deliberately dropped eight of them on the kitchen floor earlier during our routine morning argument.

"Please, Eric, could we talk for just a minute? I promise I won't cry and I won't raise my voice. Please, Eric. I just want to ask you something. Put your paper down for just a minute, Errrric," I whined.

My voice reached a crescendo that could be heard three floors below us and three floors above us in our luxury apartment building on East End Avenue.

"I refuse to listen to you, Maggie," Eric answered, peeking out from behind his *Wall Street Journal*, "if you cry and scream."

"OK, Eric," I whispered. "I'm not crying anymore; see, I'm not screaming. Now will you talk to me?"

"What is it, Maggie?" he finally said, appraising my body from head to toe with a look of disgust. "Are you hungry again?"

"Please, Eric," I pleaded. "I want to get a job. Please let me work." Most women were fighting for equal pay and job opportunities; I was begging for permission to get a job, any job.

"I make enough money, Maggie. I don't want my wife working. There's enough to do right here at home, taking care of me."

I heard the words, but I couldn't understand the reasons. I had a college degree and had even passed a typing course after graduation. Mother had the foresight to enroll me in a school that was run by Princess Ragda, the eldest daughter of the deposed king of Libya. Mother told me that no matter what might happen in life, at least I would have that to fall back on. She still had the victim mentality caused by the Russian Revolution—the rich being robbed of their land and possessions by the poor. I often wondered if perhaps history might not have been completely rewritten if all the women in the royal czarist court in Imperial Russia had known how to type. Perhaps the Bolsheviks wouldn't have had a chance. Attending classes, however, I couldn't help but feel a kinship with Princess Ragda. I was certain that her mother, the queen, had given her the same advice that my mother had given me. But when I tried to point that out to Eric, explain that even the very rich worked, either out of necessity or a simple need to maintain their mental health, his response was always the same:

"I refuse to allow my wife to work as some two-bit secretary. Not acceptable—it's just not acceptable."

"But to start out like that . . . just to begin before I could move up to something else . . ."

He glared at me. "If you have some kind of a burning desire to type and serve coffee, I'll let you type out the grocery lists from now on—I'll even buy you a typewriter—and as far as serving coffee is concerned, how about a cup right now?"

Those daily battles with Eric resulted in my sitting in front of the television set for most of the day, eating entire Sara Lee cakes, Stouffer's macaroni-and-cheese dinners, Schrafft's bridge mix, and anything else I could find to stuff into my mouth. Sometime in the afternoon, I would cope with the agony of going to my closet to try and find anything that would fit on my grotesque body

before I made the ritual pilgrimage to the grocery store
to shop for dinner. Dinner—served precisely at seven
o'clock every evening, so Eric Ornstein could watch the
evening news and not be forced to look at or talk to his
miserable wife.

Mother's warnings of obesity if I didn't marry young
confused her because I had achieved just that despite the
fact that I had obeyed her life plan for me. This was just
not supposed to happen.

"Maggie dear." Mother was speaking to me as if I
were insane, the way I imagined psychiatrists talked
manic depressives down from window ledges, the way
policemen convinced psychopaths not to spray their families with rapid-fire machine guns. "Maggie dear, I'm
not being critical, but have you looked at yourself
lately?"

Had I looked at myself? Had I noticed perhaps that my
once large green eyes were now buried beneath several
layers of bloated flesh, my nose had vanished from my
face, just another fold of skin that camouflaged my for-
merly well-defined cheekbones. Had I remarked that my
breasts had become pendulous and my waistline equal in
proportion to my enormous haunches and hips? Had I
looked at my legs lately—once shapely, with slender ankles—which were now so swollen that my panty hose had
increased in size to extra-large? And my friends the san-
itation workers no longer whistled at me when I walked
down the street—the final insult, the ultimate barometer
of my decline into repulsiveness. But there was one pos-
itive thing, which resulted from all my hours in front of
the television set: it only intensified my desire to become
a television journalist. I was totally secure in the knowledge that that was exactly what I wanted to do with my
life. It was only a question of beating this case of terminal self-destruction, so I could launch a career.

"Maggie dear, what's really bothering you? Maybe I
can help," Mother said as she walked over to the mirror.
Pinning up a strand of hair that had fallen from her neatly
rolled chignon, she dabbed dots of lipstick from her
mouth onto her cheeks. "Poor Maggie," she repeated
distractedly. "What's bothering you perhaps I can help?"

How could I explain to Mother—who had repositioned herself at the foot of my bed—why I hated my life, loathed my every move being dictated by a man who believed that the fundamental answer to my problems was a "good shtup." Eric said that to me on numerous occasions when I pointed out that I needed something more to make me happy—something other than gratifying his sexual needs and taking care of him. "I know what you need, Maggie, a good shtup, and then you'll get off my back."

"Carnegie Hall has these marvelous dance classes," Mother said. "Stretching your muscles and toning up would be wonderful for you, but first I want you to see Dr. Feldman. He'll give you little pills that will cut your appetite. I guarantee that you'll lose fifty pounds in three months flat."

Although she was calm, there was a shrill quality to her voice that told me she was bordering on hysteria. This was the ultimate disgrace—if Eric Ornstein banished Maggie Sommers because she became fat, rebellious, and ugly. The doorbell rang at that moment and Mother got up to answer it. It was Cara. I recognized the sound of her permanent appendage—the Silver Cross stroller—as it crashed through my front door, chipping paint off the walls in my foyer for the millionth time. Cara's oldest child was already in school, and she had only to cope with number two, while number three grew peacefully inside her. Waddling into my bedroom, she smiled shyly at me, embarrassed that she was witnessing this display of weakness on my part. Maggie, the sister who was always considered headstrong and tough, was now in the process of falling apart, and Cara, the one categorized as delicate and vulnerable, had fooled everybody and was competently managing a home, a husband, and almost three children.

"False pregnancy," Cara announced, "Steven and I were up half the night reading one of his medical books and he feels it's definitely false pregnancy."

I could just picture Steven, my psychiatrist brother-in-law, and Cara sitting up half the night desperately trying to find a label that would define the reason that I was destroying my life.

"Steven's concerned about you, Maggie," she said. "And coincidentally, he has a patient who has the same problem."

"It's not that," I answered impatiently. "I want a job, not a baby."

"Then why don't you get a job?" she said, exasperated. "If that's the problem, then it's easy to solve: You're capable of getting a job."

"He won't let me," I wailed.

"What do you mean he won't let you?"

"Why are you so surprised?"

"Because I never knew," she said.

"You never asked," I answered.

Cara glanced questioningly at Mother, who just shook her head. "Eric earns enough money; he doesn't want Maggie working."

"That's ridiculous," Cara said, sitting down next to me. "What does one thing have to do with another?"

"Because Maggie's job is to take care of Eric; he's supporting her," Mother said matter-of-factly, and then added, "Look at you: You're perfectly happy taking care of Steven and the children. Why does she have to make all this trouble?"

Cara smiled at me. "Because I'm me and Maggie is Maggie, and if she wants to work, then she should be able to work. If I wanted to work, Steven would be delighted, as long as I was happy."

"You see," I wailed again. "You see, it's not fair."

"Cara," Mother said sternly, "if you came over here to make trouble, then you can just take your stroller and go somewhere else."

"I'm not going anywhere unless Maggie tells me to." She smiled at me again.

"Stay, Cara," I said, holding on to her hand.

"Then tell her she has to lose weight, at least."

"You have to lose weight," Cara said quietly. "But you know that."

I just nodded.

Mother picked up the telephone and dialed Dr. Feldman—Irving Feldman, diet doctor to the rich and famous. His multicolored pills in their little gray plastic box—two pink in the morning, three green in the afternoon, and four orange at night—would get me back down to size six in no time.

"She has this condition," Mother said, cupping her hand around the mouthpiece of the telephone. "My son-in-law, the psychiatrist, thinks it's false pregnancy. Yes, fine, Dr. Feldman, two o'clock tomorrow—and thank you so much."

Hanging up the telephone, Mother clasped her hands together joyfully.

"Tomorrow afternoon is the first day of the rest of your life," she announced triumphantly.

"Will you go, Maggie?" Cara asked gently.

Turning over in my bed so my sobs were muffled against the pillow, I cried, "I won't go unless the conditions are very clear."

"Honestly, Maggie," Mother said, reaching for her purse. "You're being terribly difficult—ungrateful as usual."

"What do you mean, Maggie?" Cara asked softly.

"I mean," I said, turning around to face her, "who's going to convince Eric Ornstein that I'm allowed to get a job?"

"No one," she said, smiling. "You're just going to do it, and the hell with Eric Ornstein."

"And I hope you'll support her when she's out on the street, because I won't." And Mother walked out of the house, angrily but imperious as ever.

Three weeks later, after five sessions with Feldman and fifteen exercise classes, I had lost ten pounds and finished writing up my résumé. As soon as I could fit into something to wear, I decided that I would begin making appointments for job interviews. And when Eric came home from the office that Thursday night, I gave him my résumé to read. Hanging up his coat on a gold-monogrammed hanger in the hall closet, I watched him as he glanced at the typed sheet of paper. Suddenly he turned a ghostly white, clutched at his chest, and gasped for breath.

"What is it?" I screamed. "What's the matter?"

"I'm not sure," Eric stammered, lowering himself into a chair. "I feel sick. Get me a glass of water."

I ran into the kitchen and returned with a glass of luke-warm water, which I handed to my dying husband at the same time that I grabbed his wrist in an attempt to take his pulse. I succeeded in knocking the glass of water out of his hand and spilling it all over his gray pin-striped suit.

"God damn it, Maggie," he shouted. "Look what you've done now."

"You scared me, Eric. I thought it was a heart attack."

"No, no," he said impatiently. "I'm all right. It was just an anxiety attack."

Eric wandered into the living room then and stared morosely out the window.

"Why are you wasting time writing résumés so I have to get upset? Don't you realize that if I'm upset I can't work and support you?"

"I don't want you to have to support me. I want to work and share that with you."

"Let me explain the facts of life to you," he said sternly. "You have so far failed as a wife not only be-cause you've allowed yourself to get so fat and disgusting that I'm ashamed to take you out for dinner but also be-cause you have deprived me of my conjugal rights."

Actually, Eric never used the words *conjugal rights*, but I knew that was what he meant. His exact words were: "You have become so disgusting that I wouldn't touch you with my brother's thing." And because Eric Ornstein didn't have a brother, I clearly understood the gravity of that statement.

"Not only have you failed in that capacity," he con-tinued, "but you also have proven yourself incapable of producing a healthy child."

"Why do you blame me?" I said, tears gathering in my eyes.

He ignored my question, "After that fiasco . . ."

My dead baby was now being referred to as a fiasco.

"After that fiasco, you proceeded to become so gro-tesque that you made my life hell so that I can't even get it up to make you pregnant again."

"Do you think I like looking like this?" I cried.

"Shut up and listen to me, Maggie, because I'm not particularly interested in how you feel right now. I didn't bargain for this. I was prepared to give you a beautiful life, and there are hundreds of women out there who would prostate themselves just for the chance of being Mrs. Eric Ornstein."

"Prostrate, Eric," I corrected him. "You mean prostrate."

"I mean grateful," he shouted. "That's what I mean."

The argument continued well into the night and kept returning to the subject of my dead baby. Finally, I dared to ask the question I had been forbidden to ask.

"Was it a boy or a girl, Eric? Please tell me if my baby was a boy or a girl." Eric looked at me with a combination of disgust and fury. He had always refused to tell me the gender of my stillborn child, having enlisted the support and agreement of my family and the cooperation of my doctor because everyone agreed that it would only "humanize the incident" if I knew. But it wasn't a good enough reason for me: I needed to feel the pain of loss of a real being that I carried for nine months, a being I didn't want but nonetheless would have borne. And I felt responsible for the death of that baby, because of my feelings of rejection that I was sure were transferred through the placenta. But it was all done under the guise of protection, under the banner of "It's best for Maggie."

"What was it, Eric?" I repeated softly.

"If you promise to lose weight," he finally said, "and make an effort to make me happy and give me your word that you'll never bring up the subject of working ever again, I'll tell you." He made it sound so logical, so reasonable, so simple, that if I didn't agree I was clearly mad.

Looking at Eric coldly and speaking in a tone of voice that I had never used before, I said, "No deal, Eric, there's no deal." The discussion was over and I never found out if my baby had been a boy or a girl.

CHAPTER THREE

The living room of Rose and Tony Valeri's white frame house on Hylan Boulevard in Staten Island is a shrine to their son. Several photographs of Joe are displayed on the black-and-gold flocked wallpaper, surrounded by flowers and positioned directly underneath a large wooden crucifix. Joe Valeri is portrayed in various stages of his brief life—a high school graduation picture of a smiling boy in a black cap and gown, a tough-looking older kid glaring out from the frame, a pack of cigarettes tucked underneath the rolled-up sleeve of his white T-shirt, a more mature young man, cuddling a German shepherd puppy.

Rose's arms are wrapped around me as she weeps, her breath coming in short gasps as sobs rack her plump body. Tony is standing next to us, his barrel chest neatly clothed in a red-plaid flannel shirt buttoned up to his neck and his oversize stomach hanging over his shiny blue slacks. He shifts self-consciously from one foot to the other as tears stream down his face.

Rose backs away from me, to wipe her eyes on a crumpled tissue. She stuffs it back into the pocket of her pink flowered apron and shakes her head. "I'm real sorry for crying like that," she says softly.

Tony moves over, nearer to me, and takes my hand in his large callused ones. "Thanks for coming to see us," he says simply. "Joey was our only son, an only child."

They sit down next to each other on the white brocade sofa, covered in clear plastic, the closeness of their bodies giving them comfort in their grief.

"He was a good boy," Tony says, choking back sobs. "He never hurt nobody."

I have to bite down on my lower lip not to cry, not to make Rose and Tony feel obliged to comfort me. They need time to express their own sense of loss right now.

"He was our only son," Tony repeats, blowing his nose. "Rose couldn't have no more; we tried, but Rose lost two." He starts to weep again, and Rose pats his thigh. I want to say something to them, but the words get caught somewhere in my throat.

"Do you have family in the New York area?" Rose asks. "Are you here to spend Christmas with your family?"

How can I explain to this simple loving woman who has just been robbed of her motherhood that I arrived in New York yesterday and haven't even told any member of my family that I'm here? How can I tell these two innocents, these two grief-stricken people who received a gray metal casket as a combination Thanksgiving-Christmas present, that I spent Christmas Day in the business-class section of an El Al jumbo jet, winging my way back to my own emptiness and despair. But the dull ache that I feel inside of me, the longing for Avi, who is now so far away, seems so trite compared with their anguish. Yet I know that even though I share Rose and Tony's pain over Joe's death, there is a limit to what they can comprehend about a more subtle kind of loss.

"Joey said you were going to spend Thanksgiving with us," Tony says shyly. "If we knew you were here for Christmas, you could have spent it with us too, because we were all alone." He is crying again. "No more Joey," he sobs.

Rose cradles his head, pressing it gently to her breast.

If anybody shouldn't have been robbed of parenthood, it is clearly these two people. As I sit with them, watching them trying to cope with their enormous loss, I wonder if a letter to Vera and Alan Sommers wouldn't help— a letter requesting permission to adopt their youngest daughter, Marguerite.

I imagine Father opening the door of the Sommers apartment and stooping down to pick up the Saturday-morning mail, which has been left in a neat pile on the straw welcome mat with "vSa" printed on it. Tearing open the unfamiliar blue envelope with no return address, he reads it before passing it to Vera, who is busy messaging Nivea cream in wide upward strokes to her face and neck.

"Dear Mr. and Mrs. Sommers,

"Our son Joey was killed by a stray grenade somewhere in Lebanon and Maggie came to visit us in our house on Staten Island, which, by the way, has no more mortgage. Tony paid it off last year when he cashed in his veterans term insurance. We own it free and clear. Anyway, there we were, all sitting around and talking and crying, when Maggie came up with the idea of standing in for our boy Joey, maybe it would ease our pain, she said. We agreed because it would certainly make us feel better, less heartbroken and lonely, if we could adopt Maggie, and you people are so busy anyway. You see, our son Joey was killed right before Thanksgiving."

"Um," Vera says. "These are definitely uneducated people, and look, Alan, the paper is so cheap."

"Yes, dear, but they sound sincere enough," Alan answers, burying himself in the financial section of the *New York Times*. "I think it's a good idea."

"Well," Vera finally agrees, "if it's all right with you, then it's fine with me."

Rose Valeri comes back from the kitchen, carrying a tray. She pours three cups of tea from a pot decorated with green Christmas wreaths and offers home-baked cookies from a painted platter of smiling Santas.

"We watch you on television," she says shyly. "Me and Tony, we watch you all the time."

"Are you back for good?" Tony asks.

"No, I'm only on a temporary leave of absence, because my agent and bureau chief felt I needed a break." I almost add that covering death on a daily basis has a tendency to wear one out, but I stop myself.

I want to tell Rose and Tony what I have come to say, but it's still so difficult.

"I wanted you to know how much I cared about Joe and . . ."

They sit forward on the edge of the sofa, because they

have been waiting for this, and they have every right to expect it.

"Joe didn't feel anything," I finally managed to explain. "It happened so fast that he never felt anything." I look up at the ceiling, hoping that gravity will keep my tears in their respective ducts.

"Was he wearing his flak jacket?" Tony asks softly.

"Yes, it's regulation, we always wore them in the field, but . . ."

"But the fucking grenade got him in the head," he finishes bitterly.

There is nothing much left to say.

"Bless you for coming," Rose says, walking me to the door. "It meant a lot to us, you know." She wipes her eyes.

"Don't be a stranger," Tony adds, shaking my hand.

As we hug and kiss goodbye, promising to keep in touch, we all know that this bond we share is brief. It will fade as time heals the shock of Joe's sudden death.

The wind whips through my hair as I stand on the forward lower deck of the Staten Island ferry. Leaning on the metal railing, I wrap my camel-hair coat tightly around myself and shiver in the freezing winter weather. The Manhattan skyline appears in the distance as the battered boat groans its way back to the island where I grew up. A woman with a small child clutching her hand approaches me and asks, "Aren't you Maggie Sommers, ABN News?"

"No," I answer quietly. "Who's Maggie Sommers?"

○

We were in an ersatz French restaurant in Tel Aviv on that last night, neither of us particularly hungry as we went through the motions of eating dinner. I was fascinated by the piece of fried pâté that was swimming around on my plate in a pool of yellow grease.

"Why do you fry the pâté?" I asked the maître d'. "They never do that in Paris."

"What do they know about pâté in Paris?" he said, dismissing me with a wave of his hand.

Avi and I have been inseparable since the twenty-second of November, the day of the gray metal casket, as I had taken to calling it. As I sat with him that night in the restaurant, Vera's words kept reverberating in my head.

"You can't build happiness on someone else's misery."

"But, Mother," I had protested, "Eric is destroying me."

"Better you than him," she had replied. "Let him have the guilty conscience."

I didn't want to remember the days with Avi, walking along the beach in Tel Aviv and sharing our experiences until we were almost able to finish each other's sentences. I didn't want to think about our nights together, making love until we couldn't move anymore, falling asleep limp and moist, only to awaken several hours later to start all over again. I hadn't told him yet that I was leaving Israel the next day for an indefinite period of time. He didn't know that I planned on leaving him forever. The tears I had shed the past month for Joe Valeri had something also to do with my confusion over Avi. He permeated my life, invaded my thoughts so that I was unable to concentrate on the most important aspect of my being—my career.

"Maybe you're not giving your marriage a chance," I said, dabbing at the grease on my plate with a piece of rye bread.

I had suddenly become a marriage counselor, offering my client confidence in his sexual prowess before sending him on home a little more loving, a little more caring. If Maggie Sommers, successful marriage counselor, couldn't make it work for herself, then the least she could do was to make it work for someone else.

Avi looked at me very intently then, suspicious as to why I had chosen to tackle the subject of his failed marriage.

"Look," he said, taking my hand. "It isn't that I haven't given my marriage a chance. I've stuck with it for fifteen years, even though I knew it was all wrong from the beginning."

"Then why did you marry her?"

"Maggie," he said wearily, "we've been through this before. It was the '67 war, and I'd already been seeing her for several months. I needed to know that she was there waiting for me when I came back or if the worst happened and we lost. But it was over so quickly that I didn't have time to think about what I'd done. So I just buried myself in my work, got so wrapped up in the military and the threat of another war that I didn't pay attention to my personal life. It's what governs most of our time here anyway, war or the constant threat of war. You know that."

"You must have loved her," I persisted.

He frowned. "I was twenty-five years old; what did I know about love? I suppose it was partly because Ruth came from South Africa, which made her exotic in Israel, and partly because she had blond hair and blue eyes, so different from the girls I knew on the kibbutz. But what did I know about love?"

What do any of them ever know about love when it's over? They consistently disavow and disacknowledge any feelings they had for a woman once those feelings are dead—as if anything short of forever is a black mark on them, on their ability to make it work the next time . . . And as if I cared if he made an honest error—loved her once and then didn't anymore.

"That's not a good enough reason," I said.

"The reasons don't matter anymore," he answered impatiently. "I don't have to defend a mistake. The point is that she was cold and uncommunicative from the very beginning, and when the war ended in six days, I hardly had a chance to adjust to anything, let alone a marriage."

"What do you mean?"

"Israel suddenly had all this new territory, thousands of Arabs to absorb. We weren't living a dream anymore; we had gotten what we wanted. We were a nation."

"What did that have to do with your marriage?"

"Everything," he said stubbornly. "I was so busy working that I didn't have any time to consider anything else. I went through the motions of being married in between worrying about the borders or training my squad of paratroopers. Personal life was a luxury; what I was doing was serious business—life-threatening business. Israel wasn't an abstraction anymore.''

"Guilty on the grounds of patriotism, or was Zionism the reason for all those other women in your life?''

He smiled slightly at my sarcasm. "I guess,'' he answered slowly, "that I was satisfying a physical need in the beginning, and then it became something more. I needed to feel a closeness with someone that I didn't have with Ruth. And I hated myself for all the times I lied to her, until I began hating her for driving me to it.''

"Why should I believe that I'm different?'' I said softly. "Why should I believe that I'm the one who finally made you really care?''

He pressed my fingertips to his lips and I automatically felt that familiar weakness in the pit of my stomach, that sinking sensation that made me lose all powers of rational thinking.

"Maggie,'' he said, "I don't want anyone else but you. You give me everything. I'm forty years old and I'm tired of leading a double life. I want to build something with you.''

I detected the not-so-distant rumblings of a fatal mid-life crisis, that emotional skirmish where casualties dropped in kitchens and bedrooms. I suddenly felt as the self-ordained protector of the victims, even those whose husbands had penetrated my very soul. I was determined to patch up the last fifteen years of Avi Herzog's marriage before I robbed my lover of what he described as the best month of his life—a month that made him feel alive again.

"Avi,'' I said quietly, "I'm not for you. You need someone who's willing to devote all her time to you, and I can't do that.''

"You are for me,'' he said, gently touching my face, "because I want you.''

And even though I rejected the child who conveniently died at birth, resented a father who sent me to private schools, resisted the teachings of a mother who simply tried to groom me as the perfect hostess, rebelled against the stockbroker husband who only offered me a beautiful life, and was doing everything in my power to alienate

Avi, he still wanted me. Because if they want you, they want you, and you could be Lucrezia Borgia, Lizzie Borden or Medea embodied in one woman and it wouldn't make the slightest difference. If they want you, they want you.

"Your life is about war and mine is about my career," I said, brushing his hand away from my face.

"Your whole life has been about a war, Maggie, your own war."

"And I respect that," I continued, ignoring him, "because having a commitment to your country is very noble, but I don't believe you could ever respect my commitment to my work."

"What I feel about you has nothing to do with my country or my work. It's got nothing to do with the war in Lebanon. You're just a part of me."

Because if they want you, they want you, and that emotion usually ends up consuming every part of them, to the exclusion of everything else that once seemed so paramount. And it begins so innocuously, a disturbing twinge in their groin every time they think of you that suddenly has the potential of reaching catastrophic proportions. Because if they want you, they want you, and everything else becomes expendable.

"Don't misunderstand," I said very seriously. "I respect the reasons that your army went into Lebanon, although you might have to consider other options someday concerning the Palestinians. But I still respect your position."

Avi shook his head sadly. "It's your own position you have to understand—that war inside of you."

But it wasn't the moment, it was only December, and Israel was still fighting in Lebanon, just as Maggie was still struggling within herself.

"Avi, I'm going home tomorrow," I finally said. "I'm leaving Israel for a while."

"I know," he answered, stroking my cheek tenderly. "I've known for the past week."

Tat Aluf Avi Herzog hadn't been trained in intelligence, and trained by the best, not to know the movements of the woman who allowed him to leave several pairs of trousers, shirts, and shoes in her small apartment hotel in Tel Aviv. But I hadn't been trained in manipulation, and trained by the best of mothers, not to be quite capable of twisting the facts.

"Avi, don't even try to stop me," I said, hoping he would do just that. "I can't give you what you need, what you deserve."

He didn't respond, just sat there fiddling with the ashtray, his mouth set in a tight line. He listened to me ramble on about all the things I couldn't do for him, because perhaps, if I admitted I could, I might have been happy, and that would have ruined everything, especially my life plan of misery.

"Then again, Avi," I said, feeling obliged to fill the lull in our conversation, "just because I have a demanding career doesn't mean that I can't be a woman. But maybe it's all wrong. You'd just get tired of me in the end, and there'd be another war, so you'd have another excuse to do to me what you did to Ruth." I took a deep breath.

"Are you finished, Maggie?" he asked, his soft brown eyes studying me sympathetically.

I wanted to hold him. "No," I snapped, "I'm not finished, and by the way, why didn't you ever have children with her? I suppose that was her fault too."

"No," he said quietly. "It wasn't only her fault. It's hard to have children with someone you hardly talk to, but you should know about things like that."

"I only know that I'm not going to go through it again. I'm not going to keep making choices in my life and try to be something that I can't be for a someone who doesn't understand me anyway."

He smiled. "I understand you better than you think you do."

I started to interrupt again, but this time he stopped me. "Let me speak now. I've listened to you." And he put his hand on mine, tracing my fingers as he spoke. "I've understood enough never to mention that we were living together, because it would have made you run away from me. I knew that any invasion into your life had to be kept a secret from you."

"And I'm not going to change, so maybe you'd better just run right back to Ruth." But I already felt the tears gathering in my eyes.

"And I never complained when you worked until two or three in the morning. I accepted your erratic hours because I knew they were a part of your life, your work."

"Don't think for a minute that they'll ever stop being a part of my life," I said, wiping my face with the back of my hand.

"I understood what I was getting myself into the moment I saw you, the moment I fell in love with you, so there were no surprises, Maggie." He pressed my palm to his lips.

"And of course you want to try and change me now—make me into something that you'll end up despising."

"I would never try to change you, and I could never despise you."

"In little ways, putting pressure on me to be home and . . ."

He smoothed a strand of hair from my face and looked at me tenderly. "All I ever did, Maggie, was move over in bed when you came home, so I could take you in my arms and hold you until you finally fell asleep."

I shook my head. "You had to make sure I knew what I was about to miss, didn't you?"

"And what about what I'll miss?"

"Maybe if you had been that way with Ruth, she wouldn't have been so cold and uncommunicative."

He held my tear-streaked face between his hands. "Stop pleading her case, Maggie. I know her attributes better than you do. She never complicated my life, because she was totally predictable."

"And I suppose I complicate you life?"

He was silent a moment as he lit one of his small black cigars, inhaling it deeply. "You certainly don't give me that routine security that I felt with her," he finally said, exhaling a fine stream of smoke.

"Then why do you want me?"

His lips were almost on mine. "You're the most exciting woman I've ever known, and I'm hoping that you'll adjust to the fact that you're in love with me."

"What makes you thing that I'm in love with you?" I said, even though I knew things had already gone too far.

Squinting, he looked at me through a haze of smoke. "If you don't love me and don't intend to make some semblance of a normal life with me, then maybe you had better leave, and I won't try and stop you."

"Oh, I see. If a woman gives you some semblance of that normal life, she ends up boring you, and if she doesn't exactly fit the mold, then she's discarded as a bad investment for the future."

"What the hell does it take to make you happy?" he exploded.

"You'll never understand," I said bitterly. "Just when I had everything worked out, you had to come along and ruin it."

"Stop fighting me, Maggie. I love you."

"Take me home, Avi. I have to pack."

"The trouble with you, Maggie Sommers," he said sadly, "is that you don't know where home is."

We went to bed that night and didn't touch. The following morning we rode in silence to Ben-Gurion Airport, where Avi mechanically helped me with my suitcases and waited while I went through the rigors of the security check. When the flight was finally announced, we walked slowly together to the gate. It was only then, seconds before I was about to walk out of his life, that he took me in his arms and said, "This isn't the end, Maggie. It's not over."

I didn't look back as I strode toward the plane, because I was afraid that if I did, Avi Herzog would be gone, and I wanted to remember him forever like that. I wanted to remember him forever standing there and loving me.

○

The ride is over. The ferry is docking at the Battery Park, and suddenly the thought of going home alone to my Greenwich Village apartment is not terribly appealing. I decided to walk up Sixth Avenue, to reacquaint myself with a city that now seems so foreign to me. The irony is that every corner, every building, every billboard,

holds a memory, yet does little to give me any comfort.
What is familiar to me is somehow painful, and what is
different is almost frightening. I duck through the crowds
on the street, the homeless sprawled in the gutters, the
peddlers hawking their goods on the sidewalks or cook-
ing food on makeshift burners on mobile food stands,
and wonder when life changed so drastically anyway.

It isn't just life that has changed—the outward trappings of a city now overcrowded and a little shabbier. It
is I that am so different; my head cluttered with conflict-
ing options or unfamiliar feelings. It is hard to actually
define that first moment when my life began reeling out
of control, when everything became so confusing. As I
trudge along, my only consolation is that certain people
are still with me, still offering solace and support.

○

I had been seeing Quincy regularly over the past year.
Hurried lunches during the week or relaxing Saturday
afternoons in her loft in SoHo were welcome respites
from the boredom of being Mrs. Eric Ornstein. I was
always hesitant to include Eric, because I instinctively knew that he wouldn't approve of her. She was the
antithesis of everything he admired in a woman—
aggressive, clever, and successful. And the fact that she
even had a happy marriage would have confused Eric and
made him uncomfortable, because he wouldn't have been
able to categorize her as a feminist. Yet Quincy understood that it just wasn't the moment for me to do something else with my life.

"Maggie," she said on numerous occasions, "I know
you're smart enough to realize that I'm here to help you
when you finally decide to face reality."

"As soon as I figure out what reality is," I usually
answered, "you'll be the first to know. Thanks, Quince."

The problem was that reality reared its ugly head all
by itself, or at least along with the systematic destruction
of everything that even vaguely resembled the Maggie
Sommers Quincy knew. And the worse it became, the
more ashamed I was to see her.

"We have this bizarre telephone relationship lately," she complained. "I never see you anymore."

"I'm so busy organizing the house," I lied. "Closets, drawers, working with the decorator. I'm just in a mess right now."

But the silence on the other end of the telephone said that she really didn't believe me, although she was kind enough never to insist. Finally, after losing the first twenty pounds, I mustered up the courage to go to her office for lunch, convinced that the shock wouldn't be that great. I was wrong. Dressed in a shapeless but chic black tent dress that fell way below my pudgy knees, I taxied down to the Art Deco building in Rockefeller Center. I rode up the forty-three floors to her office, feeling only slightly anxious. The plush beige-and-brown executive suite overlooked the ice-skating rink, one of my few happy childhood memories. But as soon as I saw her, I instantly wished I hadn't come.

"I guess we'll skip lunch," she said, hanging on to her desk. "What in God's name have you done to yourself?"

"It was worse," I answered, lowering myself into one of her armchairs. "I just lost twenty pounds."

"Oh, Maggie," she cried, waving her secretary away. "No wonder you wouldn't see me. Why did you do this?"

Crossing my legs at the ankles so my chafed thighs wouldn't rub together, I answered as calmly as possible. "I suppose I was more miserable than I knew. I guess I was afraid of facing it, because then I'd have to do something about it, so I simply sabotaged any chance I had. I kept eating until I had destroyed all my other options."

"Well, if it's any consolation to you, you certainly succeeded in doing just that." Quincy pressed down the intercom button and instructed her secretary to bring in two black coffees, and fresh fruit with cottage cheese from the office kitchen.

"We're eating in," she announced, "so you can tell me everything and so nobody sees you. This place is crawling with television people."

I was becoming more and more ashamed, but the fact that she was even still willing to listen gave me the courage to go on. "You'll be pleased to know that I finally decided what I want to do," I said, in an effort to cheer her.

But she didn't respond, just stared at me in disbelief.

"I want to do documentaries on Vietnam or starvation in Appalachia—you know, serious subjects."

"Nobody in their right mind would let you do anything on starvation," she said. "So let's just forget your plans for a while and concentrate on getting you back to the beautiful woman I once knew. Now, what are you doing to lose this weight?"

"I've been going to a diet doctor, who gives me appetite-suppressing pills. I also exercise every day at Carnegie Hall, so I can firm up as I lose."

"How long has this been going on? The doctor and the exercise, I mean."

"For about a month, and I've already lost twenty pounds. I only have another thirty to go."

"You don't have to convince me of that, dear." She smiled. "What are you eating?"

Our lunch arrived. As Quincy made room for everything on her desk, I described my routine. "For breakfast I usually fight with Eric, so I only drink half a cup of black coffee."

"Good. What about lunch, when he's not around?"

"Lunch is never a problem, because I only eat after I've finished my exercise class. And I'm always with a few people from the class who are also on diets or into health foods. Lunch is usually just yogurt and fruit."

"And dinner—do you cook for Eric?"

"Yes, except on Sundays. I make fish or broil a piece of lean meat. Cara gave me a vegetable steamer, so that helps, or I make a salad with a lemon and vinegar dressing. No desserts, bread, or wine. It's really very sad."

"This is sadder," Quincy said seriously. "And at night, if you get hungry again before you go to sleep, do you pick another fight with Eric?"

"I don't have to," I answered, smiling. "It usually just happens, without too much effort. He's miserable with me looking like this."

Quincy just shook her head. "Not as miserable as *you*

ought to be. And your clothes, Maggie—nothing must fit you.''

"Actually, nothing does, except for Cara's old maternity outfits that she gave me.''

"Oh, Maggie," Quincy said. "Don't let anyone ever tell you that for a fat girl you have a pretty face, because it's not true. You look dreadful, and don't you ever forget it.''

We finished our salads, chatting about other things before I finally asked what had been on my mind for two years.

"Quincy, can you help me? I want to work in television. I don't mean doing documentaries. I want to do anything that will get me in the door.''

She stood up and walked around her desk to gaze out the large picture window. When she finally turned around, she had a very somber expression on her face.

"I have vast contacts in this industry, but I'm not going to introduce you to anyone now—not while you look like this.''

Lowering my head, I knew she was right, but it still didn't change how humiliated I felt. Fortunately, Quincy was not one to linger on an unpleasant subject once the point had been made. She sat down at her desk and began to flip through her overstuffed Rolodex file until she found the card she had been searching for. Picking up the telephone, she dialed. "Nick? Quincy," she said into the phone. "Fine, and you, dear? I've been thinking about what you asked me, and I've found someone just perfect for you. Only there's one problem. She's busy right now; you won't be able to meet her for about"—and then she peered at me over the top of her half-rimmed glasses—"about two months. She's just finishing up another project but definitely wants to get into local news. Can you hold off? Yes, Nick, great. Oh, her name is Maggie Sommers.''

Quincy didn't exactly lie to Nick Sprig, bureau chief of the American Broadcast Network's Local News Division. I *would* be very busy finishing up another project: losing thirty pounds was going to be a full-time job.

"Now, here's what we're going to do," Quincy said,

making it a joint effort. "In approximately two months, providing you've kept up your end of the bargain, I'm going to phone Nick and set up an appointment for you to meet him. In the meantime, give me your résumé so I can send it over there."

"Here," I said, thrusting it into her hand. "I even put down that I could type sixty words a minute."

"If you put that down, that's exactly what you'll be doing," she said as she buzzed for her secretary. "Ellen, come get this résumé and white out the part about typing. Make me three copies."

"By the way, what will I be doing there?"

"Probably starting out as a gofer—doing a little of everything until you learn about the broadcast industry."

"And then?"

"And if you don't admit you can type," she said, smiling, "—because if you do they'll pigeonhole you and hire someone else to do what you want to do—then you'll get what you want."

"What do I want?"

She glanced at me. "You eventually want to be on-air."

I bit my lip pensively.

"Well, don't you?" she asked.

"I guess so."

But Quincy wasn't particularly interested in my opinions. She was just concerned with getting me back in shape. "You're going to check in with me every week so I can see how well you're doing," she announced. "I've got an investment in you now, Maggie Sommers. You just became a client."

But she was also my friend. Bringing her chair next to mine, she said gently, "Whatever happens to you, no matter how great you look or how well you do, I don't want you ever to forget how you feel right now. I want you to remember that you looked so awful that I wouldn't even let you meet anyone. Don't ever try to destroy yourself again, please."

There were tears in my eyes as I asked, "Why are you bothering with me?"

She laughed her throaty laugh as she stood up. "Because you're bright, funny, and obviously self-destructive. We need women like you in this business.''

I checked in with her dutifully every week, although sometimes she was too busy even to talk to me. It didn't matter, as we had developed our own routine. I would poke my head into her office and she would motion me inside. Opening my coat, I would turn around once, lift my skirt to midthigh, and wait for her thumbs-up sign. There were many perplexed directors, production assistants, and assorted ABN executives who never understood my bizarre act or Quincy's pleased reaction. Finally, at the end of two months, I was once again seated in her office, this time with an appointment book balanced on a now-slender leg. I listened as she spoke on the phone to Nick Sprig.

"Tomorrow at ten o'clock," she said. "She'll be there, and thanks, Nick.''

"I'm so grateful," I said, after she hung up.

"Don't be grateful," Quincy answered, genuinely. "Just don't do anything as stupid as that ever again.''

The reception area of the American Broadcast Network had been cited in *Architectural Digest* as "a creative environment.'' Lucite and chrome furniture, and lush potted plants encased in gaily colored ceramic planters, sat on the pastel-gray carpet. Walls were done in muted shades of blue textured fabric, on which hung state-of-the-art graphics—the latest creations of the most trendy artists. Young men resembling department store mannequins, dressed in red blazers with the ABN insignia stitched on the pockets, stood stiffly, their hands clasped behind their backs, only coming to life when a tour group had to be escorted through the building.

A guard handed me a plastic pass with the word VISITOR printed on it in large black letters. "Straight ahead," he said.

"I walked around a long corridor until I found myself standing on a stained yellow linoleum floor, facing a dilapidated elevator that looked as if it couldn't make it up to the third-floor local newsroom. I learned later that everything in the television business looked beautiful on the outside, a facade that lured in the advertisers who paid for the programs, or fooled viewers into believing that television was as glamorous as it appeared on the screen.

The elevator lurched to a stop, and I stepped out. Another long corridor greeted me, this one comprised of nothing but doors with plaques indicating the corporate titles of the occupants of those offices. I also learned later that because the turnover of employees on the executive level was so great, names were never engraved on those plaques. Finally, after what seemed like miles of carpeted hallways, I stood in front of a sliding glass panel on which was stenciled: ALL UNAUTHORIZED VISITORS KEEP OUT. As I walked timidly inside the newsroom, I saw head shots on either wall of the media stars who delivered the news, weather, and sports, and were paid yearly salaries that could have fed an entire African nation for five years. Within seconds of asking for Nick Sprig, I noticed a harried-looking man of about thirty-five, deep circles under his eyes and a cigarette dangling from his mouth, emerge from a cubicle.

"Nick Sprig," he said, offering his hand. "And you must be Maggie Sommers. Follow me." He was tall and sinewy, and moved with an athletic swagger.

The newsroom was cavernous, with desks placed in long rows throughout the area, an obstacle course for those who were unfamiliar with the narrow-access-aisles, which only allowed for minimum maneuverability. On each desk was a phone and a small television monitor illuminated only with image, never sound. All along one entire wall was a large board, which gave the lineup of the nightly news spots, with, written in green crayon, the time and length of each piece as it was slated to appear on the broadcast. "Nothing's sure," Nick said. "It's all subject to change if there's a last-minute-breaking story."

Directly underneath the board was a long table, which seemed to be the focal point of all the hysteria that permeated the room. Eight people sat at the table and controlled what was called the assignment desk, which meant that they were in constant contact with every remote news team, city ambulance, fire truck, and police two-way radio. Information and directions were screeched into telephones and then over microphones in the newsroom, alerting reporters to all the grisly and dramatic stories that broke before, during, and after every broadcast.

Nick walked swiftly, stopping only to answer a random question from someone who would corner him as he weaved in and out of the chaos. I followed directly behind him, stumbling only once, when he failed to warn me of a sudden change of direction. He finally stopped in front of an office, opened the door, and motioned me inside.

"Anybody with a door to their office is either on-air or suffering from ulcers because they've got the responsibility of making sure all deadlines are met and no mistakes are made during the broadcast. I fall in the latter category." He grinned.

He pointed to a seat before walking around a red metal desk that was covered with papers. Lowering himself into a black leather swivel chair, he poured a glass of water from a stainless-steel decanter, popped two aspirins in his mouth, and slugged them down.

"So you want to be in television news."

"Yes," I answered meekly.

Nick picked up my résumé, which had been lying on top of a pile of file folders, and casually glanced at it.

"I need a desk assistant, one twenty-five a week plus benefits, profit sharing at the end of two years, and one week's salary at the end of the first year."

I had absolutely no idea what a desk assistant did, but I was sure whatever it was, I could do it.

"You married?"

I nodded.

"Children?"

I shook my head.

"Want any?"

"Never," I said emphatically, hoping that Eric Ornstein hadn't bugged my pocketbook.

"And don't bother telling me that you can't type," he said, rubbing his eyes. "I already know that routine."

I smiled, suddenly self-conscious under his steady gaze.

"Turn sideways."

I turned my body around.

"No, just your head," he said impatiently.

I instinctively turned my face so the better profile—left side—would be visible.

"Ever think about going on-air? You're a pretty girl."

There would come a time in my life and in my career when I would take great exception at being called a "girl." There would come a point when I would actually tell men with whom I worked that the word was "woman." "Try it," I would say. "Woman. See, it's not so difficult."

This was not yet the moment. My head was spinning, because Maggie Sommers, girl, had just been offered a job. In fact, I was so excited that I even forgot to ask what a desk assistant did.

"You're lucky, Sommers," Nick said.

It occurred to me then that I had used my own name, a good name for television, in anticipation of the time when it would appear on that final credit roll.

"Why am I lucky?" I asked in a tiny voice.

Nick was busy rummaging around in his drawer. "Because," he said with his head down. "I'm the best, and I'm going to teach you all about this lousy business." Belching softly, he unwrapped the two white tablets he finally found and put them in his mouth.

"Go to personnel on the sixth floor and fill out the forms. Monday OK?"

"Monday is fine," I answered, my head still spinning.

My hand was on the doorknob, as I was about to dash upstairs to personnel, when he started to laugh. "Aren't you even going to ask me what a desk assistant does, Sommers?"

I blushed. "I was going to, but . . ."

"You collect the breaking news stories from the assignment desk," he explained, "type them up neatly—sorry, kiddo—and bring them to me. I choose the ones that'll be used on the air and assign them to a reporter, who goes out with a crew to cover them. Get it?"

"I get it," I said, and smiled.

"Nine o'clock Monday morning." He paused. "And

I like my coffee light.'' It didn't bother me that I would be typing and serving coffee, because I was still so busy imagining my name on the final credit roll. I had certainly come a long way since that tombstone. I was now in television news.

Three days later, on Sunday morning, I knew that if I didn't tell Eric about my meeting with Nick Sprig, leaving for work would present a major problem. I had even contemplated lying to Eric, but that would only have postponed the inevitable. And it was the inevitable that frightened me.

Eric listened politely to me now, less out of interest perhaps than because I was back to one hundred and eighteen pounds. However, I was forbidden to mention anything that might conceivably upset him and be counterproductive to the progress he was making with his therapist.

"Anything that causes an incendiary reaction on my part gives me anxiety, and that reduces my ability to advance within the company. Just because it's Dad's business doesn't mean that I don't have to work as hard as anyone else.''

"Is that what your therapist said?'' I asked.

"That's correct. He's concentrating on helping me to control my fluctuating emotions, which only fluctuate when I can't function on an even keel, and that only happens when my ability to perform at work is hampered, and that makes me anxious. It's a vicious circle.''

My life was hell.

While that explanation for his anxiety-advancement was what he gave when slithering into bed with an erection, another explanation emerged with the emergence of his body from mine.

"Why the hell did you put in your diaphragm? I want a child. We're out of step with other couples our age, and that makes me extremely anxious. I won't be able to function at work.''

I was propped up in bed that Sunday morning, watching Eric do his sit-ups on the floor.

"If you get pregnant now, Maggie''—up, down—"it's

only October''—gasp, gasp—''you could have the kid in July''—huff, puff—''which means he wouldn't lose a year in school because of a December birthday.''

''Bang, bang,'' I muttered under my breath.

The day passed, and it was evening. We were preparing to leave for our ritual Sunday-night Chinese dinner, only tonight I had specifically asked to be alone with Eric. Sunday dinners with Eric's parents always gave Mildred an opportunity to criticize me and Harry an opportunity to criticize Eric. They also gave both Mildred and Harry a chance to interrogate both of us as to why we weren't pregnant.

''So,'' Harry would say every Sunday, the grease outlining his thick lips as he devoured his mu shu pork and pancakes, ''why don't you two stop fooling around and start fooling around? I want to be a grandfather.''

During these conversations, Mildred always eyed me suspiciously, while Eric would invariably reply, ''Ask her, Dad. It's not my fault,'' to which Harry would say, ''If she were my wife, I wouldn't have to ask her anything—I'd just do it,'' prompting Mildred to glare at me while tossling Eric's hair with one bejeweled hand.

That particular night we were alone. Eric had already polished off a plate of spareribs and was in the process of eating the last egg roll. Noticing that I hadn't touched a morsel of food from the array of platters that covered the table, he said, ''Not hungry, Maggie, or still dieting?''

''Eric,'' I finally said, ''I want to talk to you.''

He looked up from his plate and nodded, an indication that he could eat and listen at the same time.

''Eric, I got a job at the American Broadcast Network. I start tomorrow as a desk assistant, one hundred twenty-five dollars a week, and I'm really excited about it.''

The words tumbled from my mouth, less out of excitement than fear, because I just wanted to get it over with. Let the dirty deed be done. Or as Harry Ornstein would have said if he had been with us and thought that getting a job was as good an idea as I thought it was, ''God bless. Enjoy.''

Eric put down his fork, dabbed at his lips with the

white linen napkin, chewed the remainder of the food
that was still in his mouth and looked at me through
narrowed eyes. Swallowing, he took a long sip of water,
dabbed at his mouth again, and said, ''You did this without first consulting me?''

I blinked several times but didn't respond. My hand
was wrapped around the glass of water, ready for Eric's
anxiety attack, which didn't happen that night at Mr.
Tong's Chinese restaurant on East Fifty-seventh Street.
We sat in silence while the waiter brought the check. We
left the restaurant and walked up Third Avenue toward
our apartment in silence. The tension was evident, but
somehow I wasn't afraid, because I knew that whatever
happened, I would be at work the following day at the
American Broadcast Network. Yet I was more sad than
victorious at the realization that Eric had already lost the
battle and was suddenly in the process of losing the war.
My marriage was ending, something that wasn't supposed to happen. I had somehow managed to get what I
wanted, but found myself completely unprepared to accept the consequences. A subtle transition occurred at
Mr. Tong's, a small incident that made me want to comfort Eric, to explain that I really didn't plan on this turning out the way it had. But he never would have accepted
comfort from the woman who had plunged a knife into
his groin. And I was acutely aware that I was thinking
groin and not heart, because what happened that night
had nothing to do with anybody's heart.

We entered our dark apartment, still in silence. Eric
switched on the lights and without a word hung up his
own coat in the hall closet—a sign that I had already been
deprived of that menial chore, stripped of that small
honor. He walked into the bedroom, sat down on the
bed, and began unlacing his shoes. I undressed slowly,
folding my clothes meticulously and putting them away,
before I changed into a nightgown. Eric emerged from
the bathroom, wrapped in his beige silk dressing gown,
and stomped over to the bed. Ripping the magazine out
of my hands, he flung it on the floor. ''I have decided
not to forbid you to do this, because I think you should
learn a lesson about life, see how hard it is to earn a

living. You're a spoiled brat, but I intend to see you
through this phase, providing you understand that there's
a limit to my patience.''

I knew that night that Maggie Sommers and Eric Ornstein would never grow old together. I suddenly felt an
overwhelming affection for this man, because for the first
time in my marriage, caring about him didn't cost me
anything. I wanted to tell him that we still had a chance
of salvaging something, but he never would have understood and I was incapable of explaining. Eric Ornstein
was as much a victim of this absurd trap as was Maggie
Sommers—this trap that had been created, this trap that
dictated what was expected of us to be.

I didn't protest as he climbed into bed and shut off the
lights. I didn't resist when he reached for me in the dark
and buried himself inside of my body, making love to me
out of his own anger and frustration. This was new to
both of us. There was finally equality in the Ornstein
house—we were both equally terrified.

CHAPTER FOUR

As I began my tearful stand-up on that exact spot where Joe died, I noticed Avi was behind the camera, his hands clenched in fists at his sides and watching my every move. I had just refused to say the words that had been written for me, the lead-in to the grisly account of Joe's death.

"Good evening, ladies and gentlemen," I refused to say. "This is Maggie Sommers on a dank and dreary night in Beirut."

Throwing the script down, I screamed, "There will be no dank and dreary tonight in Beirut."

Larry Frank, my producer, ran up to me, trying desperately to calm me. His tone was conciliatory as he said, "You're a tired girl, Maggie, and you're upset, so why don't you just read the lines and get it over with, so we can all get some sleep."

"I'm not a girl," I said thought clenched teeth. "I'm a woman, and you're an insensitive fool, Larry, and you bet your ass I'm upset, but I'm still not reading those lines."

"All right, Maggie darling," he answered soothingly. "Then if not dank and dreary, how about cold and rainy or even gray and dismal? Take your choice, sweetness."

But it had nothing to do with choice; it was simply a matter of refusing to reduce this heartbreaking incident to a mere weather report, to measure the level of our grief by the inclement climate in Beirut that night. I intended the stand-up to be a touching account of how one twenty-seven-year-old Italian-American sound man who worked for the American Broadcast Network on assignment in Lebanon happened to be sitting in the wrong place at the wrong time, while I had the good fortune to be sitting six inches to his left.

The crew had gathered around me by then, cups of steaming coffee warming their hands, looks of alarm on their faces. Glancing at them for some sign of support, I only saw those same expressions—relief that it hadn't been one of them, panic that it still could be, if another RPG accidentally landed in our midst.

"Maggie darling," Larry said with an exaggerated calm that eventually escalated to a deafening crescendo, "we're two minutes till airtime, so would you mind, darling, please putting that microphone to your beautiful lips and describing to those nice people out there what happened today to Joe Valeri, because if you don't, Maggie darling, the chances are that it's going to happen again, and I bet you know why—but in case you forgot, I'm going to tell you, Sommers: It's because we're in a fucking war zone, so let's go—*One minute and counting. Thank you very much.*"

Several people gave him a standing ovation,, clapping their hands together slowly, because, after all, he had managed to say it all without so much as taking a breath. Pretty impressive. But there was still no dank and dreary or cold and rainy or even gray and dismal, and it was just unfortunate that Joe wasn't there to witness that ludicrous display, because he would have surely been amused.

"*Good evening, ladies and gentlemen. This is Maggie Sommers from somewhere near Sabra Camp in Lebanon, where someone we all loved very much died tonight: Joe Valeri. . . .*"

Avi came up to me afterward on that tragic and miserable night in Beirut and without a word slipped his worn leather flight jacket around my shivering shoulders and led me to the waiting jeep.

"Now I know why I want you so much," he said softly.

o

The walk from the ferry to my Greenwich Village apartment has exhausted me. Standing in my foyer, I barely recognize the image that is staring back at me in the mirror, a woman with deep blue circles under her eyes, cheekbones that appear to be straining through sallow skin, and hair that tumbles in knotted disarray over her shoulders. That haunted look in my eyes fascinates me, though, an expression that is only enhanced by my wrinkled black dress, laddered stockings, and pumps covered with mud from walking around Rose and Tony Valeri's backyard.

I make a mental note to bathe, change, and put on some makeup before Quincy and Dan arrive later on this evening, at least to camouflage the anguish that I feel. And it still has to do with Avi, alternating between imagining him standing at Ben-Gurion Airport, loving me as I walked out of his life, and agonizing that he has already run back to Ruth, eternally grateful for the boredom and predictability that she offers him. I remember a drive we once took between Jericho and Tel Aviv, two hours of beautiful road bordered by lush terrain that I hardly even noticed from the window of the car. I couldn't keep my hands off him as he tried not to lose control and plunge down an embankment.

"We should never be more than fifteen minutes away from a bed," he said, laughing. Avi, who swerved onto the shoulder and took me in his arms, kissing me and touching me until he finally climbed with me into the backseat. Avi, who pulled me on top of him, over him, until we could resume the drive back to our bed.

My living room looks so abandoned now, with the soot-covered white sheets draped over the furniture and paintings. Flinging them aside, I examined all the precious mementoes displayed on the tables, objects I have collected from years of traveling all over the world. Even the photographs of my family, strangers smiling lovingly at me from their tarnished silver frames, are comforting. It's as if they are welcoming me home, yet keeping my arrival a secret from the real people who posed for those pictures.

I hear Rose ask again, "Do you have family in the New York area?"

The plants are all dead, drooping limply in their pots,

the plants that I had so painstakingly positioned near the windows so they could drink in the morning sun. Poor Joe: how he hated the nights in Lebanon, when the only light came from flashes of artillery and mortar shells.

The Bukhara rug on the floor of the dining area looks so shabby and worn. But, it's been seven years since Eric and I battled over it during our divorce settlement, seven years since he agreed to let me keep it—after I returned all the jewelry his mother had given me.

"Women who choose independence buy their own jewelry," he said.

And for years I believed that independence was never rewarded by anything more than loneliness.

"I chalk my marriage up to experience," I would tell people, until I learned that experience was something I got only when I didn't get what I wanted. Until Joe Valeri, I believed those things, and then it all changed; things that used to mean something suddenly didn't anymore.

My suitcases are still leaning against the wall in my black-and-white bedroom, in the same spot where I hurriedly dumped them last night before falling into an exhausted sleep. That room was never designed to entice visitors into a warm environment of pink lights and soft colors, into the receptive body of Maggie Sommers. Father had summed it up aptly when he said, "Your bedroom makes a statement. You're simply not interested."

Standing in front of my dresser now, I slip out of my clothes and once again study my face in the mirror. Perhaps I look so lifeless and drained because I am suddenly in such unfamiliar surroundings, without the usual backdrop of war and devastation.

"I fell in love with you in Marjayoun that day," Avi said.

Just as I am about to unhook my brassiere and pull on an old, torn T-shirt, I see a familiar face staring at me from across Tenth Street. It's the face that has been watching me for the past six years. I don't know the name of the face, but I feel very close to my disembodied friend. He has seen me undress, dress, speak on the phone, read, laugh, cry, and make love. I have a recurring fantasy about him. At a cocktail party somewhere in

New York, he comes up to me and takes my hand, leads me away from the crowd. Pinning me against the wall in a secluded corner, he gives me a glass of chilled white wine.

"It's been long enough," he says. "We're both finally ready."

I don't even blush when he confesses that he has been using his 20 × 60 binoculars to watch me make love. He only wanted a better understanding of what I enjoy when an unknown intruder plows into my body. The face is too secure ever to be jealous during those moments, too confident to waste time on preliminaries, like drinks, dinner, or trial runs. The face is prepared—prima facie—to offer me a wonderful life in spite of my hectic schedule and peculiar faults, such as strewing papers all over the floor or drinking Evian water straight from the bottle. What we have is very special. Taking my hand, the face assures me that he is completely self-sufficient, that looking out a window is enough to sustain him for the weeks and months when I'm away on assignment. But just as I am about to accept his proposal and finally live happily ever after with someone who really understands, the dreadful possibility confronts me. The face that gazes at me from across Tenth Street is nothing more than a torso propped up at a window, ignored and abandoned by those who grudgingly care for him.

Suddenly, I am brought back to reality by the shrill ringing of the telephone. Racing to answer it, I hesitate for a second, because I'm just not ready to face the crackle of an international cable. Not yet.

"Maggie, I've been trying to reach you all day. I was worried."

I recognize the voice immediately. "Quincy, I'm so happy it's you."

"Where were you?"

I take a deep breath. "I went to Staten Island to visit Joe's parents."

"How sweet, Maggie. It must have meant a lot to them."

"It meant a lot to me," I say simply. "I loved him."

"Well, we love you and we're going to see you at about eight. Do you need anything?"

"No, thanks. I've got everything. I'm just trying to whip this place back into shape, everything's a mess."

"Why don't you just rest today and start on all that tomorrow? Take it easy today, Maggie. You've been through a lot, and you must be jet lagged."

"I'm fine, Quince," I say without much conviction. "I'm always fine."

"I know that, sweetie. That's what worries me."

When I hang up with Quincy, I shower, change, and begin to apply a layer of foundation to my face, concentrating on those deep blue circles under my eyes. My hands tremble as I blush on some rouge and dust on a little powder before I study the final effect in the mirror. It is hideous. The radiant woman I used to see every morning when I was with Avi has somehow been replaced by a shriveled old lady with blue hair and over-rouged cheeks, someone whose self-image has been hopelessly distorted from too many years alone. And what I'm really seeing is the woman I fear I'll become—someone who finishes a loveless and empty life clutching a paper bag filled with bread crumbs, which she flings to the pigeons in a lonely park.

Quincy finally arrives, standing in my foyer, lowering her white wool hood. She fluffs up her short red hair, which has been flattened by the sleet and rain.

"You look tired, Maggie darling," she says. "I'm so glad you're back home."

Dan Perry scrutinizes me, cupping my chin in his hand. "You're still beautiful, Mags, but you look drained."

"Thanks," I answer, linking my arm through Quincy's. "I can certainly count on you to be brutally frank."

Dan maneuvers around us, his perfectly proportioned, compact body disappearing into the kitchen. "I'm going to put the champagne in the freezer."

"I've missed you," Quincy says, sitting down on one of the chintz sofas in the living room. "I felt so damn helpless when it happened. I wanted to do something more than telephone you, but I just couldn't get away. How are you, Maggie?"

"There wasn't anything you could have done. It was awful, and I think it got worse for me since the initial shock wore off because I keep reliving it."

Dan bounds back into the room, his dark eyes twinkling as he looks first at Quincy and then at me. "Did you tell her?"

"Not yet," Quincy says, patting his hand. "I was just about to. Maggie, they want you to host a new magazine-format show that's scheduled to air out of New York this spring."

"Isn't that terrific?" Dan says. "More money, and it's your own show. You'll be all over the world, civilized places where you can really enjoy yourself while you work."

They are watching me, watching for me to exhibit a hint of emotion, to register excitement or even displeasure—anything other than just sitting there and staring at them in disbelief.

"Well?" Quincy says, glancing at Dan.

"Well what?"

"Well, aren't you thrilled?" Dan asks.

"No, I'm not thrilled at all. In fact I'm rather annoyed that you would just waltz in here and assume that I'm going to be delighted with some inane magazine-format show. Don't I have anything to say? After all, it's still my life, even if you do get ten percent of it."

"Of course you do," Quincy says softly. "It's entirely up to you, you know that. It's just that we thought you'd be relieved that you wouldn't have to go back to the Middle East to cover the war. We thought you'd be excited that you finally made it."

"I've already made it," I say angrily.

"If you call doing stories out of Marjayoun making it," Dan quips, "then I guess you're right. But that hellhole doesn't exactly compare with traveling to Paris, London, Rome, and Athens and doing feature reports about topics that you can even think up yourself."

Pacing up and down in front of the window, I can hardly control myself. I am simply panicked that someone is going to take my area away from me—and with it, Avi Herzog.

"Look, thank you both very much, but I love where I am, what I do there, and I intend to go back."

Dan looks deflated as he rubs his eyes wearily with his hands. "I'm going to get the champagne."

"Maggie," Quincy says, "I know this is hard for you because of what happened to Joe, but you can't let it consume you. You're going to have to let go of it at some point, and that's why I thought that a change of scenery would be good for you."

"I only agreed to come back here because there was a temporary cease-fire and now it's only a question of time before Syrian troops infiltrate behind PLO lines. The fighting is going to start again, and when it does they're going to need coverage."

"Maggie, stop it. You're not the only reporter they have to send in there."

"I'm the only one who really understands what's going on. The others just read the copy—they might as well be hosting a magazine show."

Dan is back in the room, carrying a tray with the champagne and three glasses. "I've got news for you, Maggie," he says, popping the cork. "The audience out there doesn't know the difference or care. They wouldn't know a Shiite from an Israeli, an Amal from a Palestinian. They're just interested in knowing if they can travel to Europe without getting hijacked or if there's going to be another gasoline shortage or if the Communists are going to take over the world and real estate prices will go down. Come on, Mags, television is the dumbing of America."

"Well, then, maybe you'd better find a more willing client, a more reasonable piece of flesh to peddle, who'll be thrilled to anchor some meaningless magazine show."

Quincy is stunned. "What's the matter with you?"

"How can you talk like that?" Dan says, handing me a glass of champagne. "You're not just a client; you're a close friend."

But I can't answer either of them, because my head is buried in my hands and I am weeping. Quincy walks over to me just as the telephone begins to ring.

"Please," I say, crying, "will you get it? I can't."

Several minutes later, Quincy comes back. Sitting down, she puts her arms around me.

"You should have told me," she says, pushing my hair out of my face.

"I'm sorry, Quince."

"Told you what?" Dan asks.

Tilting her head to one side, she asks, "Can I tell him?"

"Yes."

"It seems there's a man—with the most wonderful voice, by the way—who's in love with Maggie." And then she turns to me. "Avi wants you to know that he misses you and that he'll be in the field tomorrow but he'll call right after he gets back, which is midnight New York time. Why didn't you tell me that was the reason you wanted to stay in Israel, and is he talking about the kind of field I think he's talking about?"

"So maybe it would be better if I took that magazine-format show."

Dan laughs. "You're the most contrary person I know, worse than my wife. We're delighted if there's someone in your life, and Quincy can march right into ABN and renegotiate your old contract. So what's the problem?"

"He's married," I say dully.

"Oh, shit," Quincy responds.

"Married can get unmarried," Dan says pragmatically. "I still don't see the problem, unless that field he's referring to is a battlefield, and you've gotten yourself involved with a military man."

Quincy is watching me closely. "Have you, Maggie?"

"Yes; no; I don't know. Yes, I'm involved and yes, he's a general, and it's a battlefield; but no, its not the same over there as here; and I don't know what I'm going to do about the whole thing."

"Don't tell me it's different because over there the elite are in the front lines and over here only the poor get killed. Very admirable of them. Maybe you should reconsider that magazine show."

"She doesn't want to do that," Dan says. "She's in love with him; she's just upset that he's married."

"That's not the point," Quincy says.

"Of course that's the point; ask her."

They turn to me, waiting for a response.

"I don't want the responsibility of his marriage on my shoulders," I finally answer.

"Don't flatter yourself," Dan says matter-of-factly. "It wouldn't be because of you if his marriage ends. It never is. His marriage probably has been on the rocks for years."

"Maggie," Quincy says sincerely, "we've got meetings with Grayson in a few days. Why don't you just think things over and not make any snap decisions tonight. After all, you just got back, and you must be exhausted."

"I suppose you're right, Quincy. Maybe by that time I'll know if Avi still wants me or not."

"Since when does your career revolve around a man, Maggie Sommers?"

"Since she fell in love with one," Dan says, smiling. "Isn't that right?"

"Let's just change the subject," I answer, noticing that Quincy is too surprised even to continue the conversation. "How's Grayson? I haven't seen him in months."

"The same; he never changes," Dan says, pouring some more champagne.

Quincy appears to have recovered sufficiently to start laughing over a funny memory. "Do you remember your famous date with him?"

I try to fake a laugh, to appear interested in changing the subject. The truth is that the last thing I want to do is remember that night with Grayson Daniel.

○

By the spring of 1973 I had been working as Nick Sprig's desk assistant for two years. One night while I was in the newsroom on an urgent assignment, I noticed a distinguished-looking man watching me from the doorway of a corner office. He smiled. I smiled. Seven and a half seconds later, I was seated in an executive office facing Grayson Daniel, director of ABN's owned and operated stations located in key market cities throughout the United States.

Grayson was lanky, casual, the quintessential Wasp, with just the right amount of gray in his sideburns and his pin-striped suit to be believable. His tanned face broke into easy smiles, even though his steel-blue eyes remained cold and expressionless. It was his mouth, however, that especially fascinated me, barely moving as he spoke, yet enunciating his words flawlessly. And his cadence of speech and choice of words were vaguely reminiscent of a college boy who had remained just that. "That was a neat piece you did for the Six," he would call out to someone, or "That's a dandy bit of broadcasting, friend," he would say to our weatherman. "I sense you're a gal with a lot of fine potential," he actually said to me while staring directly at my breasts.

I smiled, blushed, and twisted a strand of pearls around my fingers. Although it seemed perfectly logical that on-air talent could be discovered in television newsrooms, especially if starlets were discovered in drugstores, I was nonplussed by all his attention. He was now concentrating his gaze on my gleaming gold wedding band.

"Tell me a bit about your goals, Miss Maggie," he said, propping his long legs up on a desk.

I found myself looking directly into the properly worn soles of Grayson's scuffed brown Gucci loafers as I explained my goals.

"I'd like to be on-air, covering stories that have an international and political impact. I would like to believe that I'm capable of changing the system by making the viewers confront controversial topics such as the Vietnam war, or welfare, or starvation."

I would have continued, had Grayson not cleared his throat loudly several times.

"Your idealism is admirable, my dear," he interrupted, "even if your goals aren't entirely realistic. You see, Maggie, this is a rich man's world, and without the rich, the poor couldn't afford to be idle. So the bottom line is that nobody wants the system changed, because it would only upset the balance that divides the world into the haves and have-nots."

I smiled for lack of anything better to do. It was clear

that Grayson was not particularly interested in my goals after all.

He unwound himself from his position where his Gucci loafers were in my face and walked casually toward the window, his hands clasped behind his straight back.

"What we're considering here at ABN right now is hiring a female on-air crime reporter. We feel that it might just improve the sluggish ratings, as well as give our viewers something pretty to look at." He winked and began to pace back and forth. Suddenly he stopped, whirled around, and pointed a spindly index finger in my startled face. "When I work, Miss Maggie, I work hard, and when I play, I play hard."

I actually laughed out loud but then hastily apologized.

"Are you a team player, Maggie Sommers?"

"Yes, sir," I answered, wondering where the "sir" came from.

"Good," he said, rubbing his hands together. "Now, you're editing a piece with Sprig, and then I guess you'll have to rush right on home to your husband."

It was more a question than a statement, and Maggie Sommers, team player, was no dummy. I looked directly into Grayson Daniel's humorless eyes and said, "Not necessarily."

"Well, then," he said, beaming. "Maybe it would be a good idea if you and I grabbed a bite to eat somewhere and discussed that possibility."

"What possibility, Mr. Daniel?" I asked, because if you're going to play on a team, you'd better know the rules.

"The possibility of hiring a female on-air crime reporter," he responded, clearly pleased that the game had already begun.

And I didn't flinch or blink, just continued to look directly into Grayson's unsmiling eyes.

"You and Sprig have edit room number three," he said curtly. "I'll pick you up there when you're finished, and it was really neat meeting you, M.S."

Nick and I were still in edit room number three at nine-thirty that night, running and rerunning portions of a tape that was part of a three-segment story. The subject concerned the treatment of the city's poor at hospital emergency rooms, and it was critical that we eliminate eight minutes of the piece, as the lineup for the nightly news had been changed. Our first segment was suddenly scheduled to air on the eleven o'clock broadcast, and every frame, each word, seemed so crucial to the story that we were having problems cutting.

"The woman with the kid's got to go," Nick said, downing the last drop of his cold coffee.

"But the kid's delirious, and she's been sitting there and holding him for two hours."

"Yeah, yeah, but the viewers don't know that," Nick said, matter-of-factly, "and the guy with the stab wound is a better visual."

"But we already have a stab wound."

"This stab wound is better," he said, lighting a cigarette.

"Then cut the other one."

"Nope, can't do that, because the guy buys the farm right on the table. It's too good."

"Then cut the other one," I said logically.

"Can't do that, either, because stab wound number two makes it—doctors took him in right away, emergency team really did their stuff on that one."

"All right," I said wearily. "No kid with fever is one minute, and if we cut some of the file footage of the South Bronx, we can probably get rid of another two minutes five seconds."

"Maybe," Nick says slowly, rubbing his chin, "just maybe, but that still leaves us about five over."

Glancing at my watch, I suddenly remember. "Oh, no! I forgot to call Eric. It's almost ten o'clock, and he must be frantic. I'm never late."

Nick rolled his eyes as he shoved the phone toward me. "Make it fast. We've only got another hour before airtime."

I dialed my phone number and waited anxiously for Eric to answer. Finally, on the fourth ring, he picked up. "Eric," I said. "Hello, Eric?" But the only response was dead air and heavy breathing. "Eric," I repeated, "it's me." Again, more dead air and heavy breathing. "Eric, please, I can't hang on the phone. I just wanted you to know that I'm alive and I'm sorry but I lost track of time. I'm still in the edit room—Eric, are you there?"

"Maggie," he said cheerfully. "How nice of you to call. I just finished cutting my finger trying to slice a piece of salami for dinner."

"I'm really sorry, Eric. I don't know what to say. Try running it under the cold water."

"What's that, Maggie dear—my finger or the salami?"

"Eric, please," I whispered into the receiver. "I can't argue now. I said I was sorry."

"Well, well. Miss Desk Assistant, one hundred twenty-five dollars a week plus benefits, is sorry. Tell me, Miss Desk Assistant, do you think you could manage to live on that?" Eric's voice no longer had a lilting, sarcastic tone. He was yelling into my ear at the top of his lungs. "And by the way, Miss Desk Assistant, who the hell is supposed to take care of me while you worry about the poor, sick, and underprivileged for the goddamn evening news?"

Nick was pacing nervously up and down the tiny cubicle, muttering to himself. It was now or never.

"Who?" I screamed. "I'll tell you who, Eric. Your mother, that's who!" And I slammed down the telephone so hard that the ashtray bounced up in the air and scattered cigarette butts all over the stained gray carpet.

"Good evening, ladies and gentlemen," Nick said into his empty coffee container. "Another marriage bites the dust, and it happened right here, live from the studios of ABN Local News."

Sitting in a dimly lit restaurant near the studio, which Grayson had touted as "a nifty place, with a good fry man," I could hardly swallow my double cheeseburger. Grayson kept touching my face as he talked.

"What's happened is that a team of media consultants devised a plan that's guaranteed to increase our ratings and at the same time satisfying the coming trend in America." He paused to take a long sip of his double martini. "Now, what the viewers want or think they want

is a woman reporter, and the reason is this feminist revolution that's gaining momentum all over the country.
With me so far?''

I nodded my head and tried to swallow.

''Good,'' he said, patting my knee. ''Now, what this
means is that ABN will be forced to hire a woman, and
because we want to always be several steps ahead of the
other networks and therefore satisfy what we believe is
the coming trend, we've decided to do something really
extraordinary.'' He paused again, to touch my nose.
''You've got eyes the color of emeralds, Miss Maggie.
Anybody ever tell you that?''

''No,'' I answered, the interested expression still frozen on my face. ''Go on, Grayson; this is fascinating.''

''We've decided to do something really extraordinary,'' he repeated. ''We've decided to hire a woman to
cover crime—not consumer tips or human interest in New
Jersey or weather or anything else that's typically a woman's area. Oh, no. ABN has decided to go all the way
and put a woman where she's never been before: in the
slums, in the drug dens, in the police stations, with the
Mafia bosses, the killers, the rapists—all those terrific
places that our viewers love to see. ABN intends to be
the first network to get a woman out of the kitchen and
supermarket, away from the high pressures and low pressures of a weather map, away from the bake-offs in Se-
caucus, and right in the middle of the dirty disgusting
scummy rat-infested world, where she'll have to rely on
her guts, brains, and good journalistic skills.'' He smiled.
''But,'' he concluded, ''because this is television, she
has to be beautiful and have a great body, or it just won't
work. Right?''

''Right,'' I answered, still reeling from my trip through
the ghettos.

''Now, we've been watching you for several months
now; in fact, I've been aware of you for longer than that.
You're a very pretty girl, Maggie Sommers, and only one
of two girls at ABN who has any working knowledge of
what goes into a broadcast. Unfortunately, the other girl
spends too much of her time distributing leaflets about

that feminist movement to be considered a team player, Clear?''

"Clear," I answered.

"My position on the subject is very simple," he said, signaling the waiter to bring another round of drinks—his third double martini, my second Coke. I had no excuses that I didn't know what I was doing. I was totally sober and completely in control of all of my senses.

"I'm all for equality when it comes to basic human rights," he continued.

I didn't bother to ask him if those basic human rights were limited to eating, breathing, and sleeping.

"However, I don't believe that women should be encouraged to take jobs away from men, the natural breadwinners, the ones who have the ultimate responsibility of feeding the family. It's not even fair to expect a woman to take on that burden, bringing home the bacon and having to cook it too. It defies nature, and it's the old story of the silent majority versus a few frustrated gals who kick up their heels when all they need is a good man around to keep them happy. And it's because of us—the media—that they get any attention: I know that, but that's the way it is.''

By that time Grayson had practically downed his third double martini and had his hand under the hem of my skirt.

"The real truth," he said, leaning over conspiratorially, "is that women are just happy as hell the way they are, pampered, loved, and cherished as good wives and loving mothers, the backbone of this great country. But the name of the game is ratings, and so we do what we have to do at ABN, which brings us right back to you, M.S." and he smiled a big smile, which didn't even come close to reaching his eyes. "How would you like to test for the slot of female on-air crime reporter?—because you seem to have all those attributes we talked about." And then, as though on cue, he hiccuped.

So, in the end, it really boiled down to typing and tits after all. Typing got you in the door, and tits got you in the studio. And while Grayson had been discussing breadwinners and mothers, ratings and feminism, I kept imagining him trapped beneath the spinning wheels of an Edsel, a trickle of blood running down the side of his mouth, his cold eyes glassy and lifeless, because if I hadn't done that, I would have been forced to face the cold, hard truth that had suddenly presented itself between myself and Grayson in that nifty restaurant with a good fry man: sex.

"How would you like to take a little peek at our new ABN corporate suite, Miss Maggie Green Eyes?" he asked, his hand already on the small of my back as he steered me out of the restaurant.

"I'd love to," I lied, following him for parts unknown in every sense of the phrase. Crossing Ninth Avenue, I frantically searched the street for an out-of-control Edsel, but no such luck.

The American Broadcast Network corporate suite looked more like a tony hunt club somewhere in the north of England than a trysting spot for television executives. The living room had a deep-green carpet on which solid English antiques were carefully placed, each with that properly worn look of having been passed down from generation to generation in one colorless sitting room after another. The paintings on the light-green walls depicted scenes from various stages of the hunt—horses and riders soaring over neatly trimmed hedges or hound dogs straining at their leashes in pursuit of helpless little rabbits. In the center of the room was a completely incongruous black-and-gold Formica bar, behind which stood Grayson Daniel, completely at ease and mixing two pink foamy drinks that had green cherries floating around the top. When he was finally satisfied that he had included a bit of everything from every bottle on the bar, he raised his glass and slurred, "To a better America, free of pinkos." And then he raised it a second time, only that time he was already sitting next to me and nuzzling my ear. "To my new on-air crime reporter. Let's screw a little."

The bedroom wall was papered with the Gettysburg Address, and somewhere right near "Fourscore and seven," Grayson was struggling out of his clothes. I was stretching out languidly on the red-white-and-blue sheets, trying not to allow guilt to stand between me and an opportunity to be the first female on-air crime reporter for ABN Local News. There wasn't much time for guilt, however, because suddenly Grayson zigzagged toward me, his boxer shorts balled up and tucked underneath his arm.

"Touchdown," he yelled, diving on the bed.

He was on top of me, squeezing my breasts, scratching my left nipple with his family-crest ring, and murmuring incomprehensible things.

"Feel how hard I am," I thought he said.

I reached down obediently between his legs but came up with nothing.

Just as I thought that I had indeed misunderstood him, he said it again: "Feel how hard I am."

So I thought I was off mark. Moving my hand over a little to the right and then a drop to the left, I still came up with absolutely nothing that even remotely resembled something hard.

I never told him he was drastically mistaken. "Wrong, Grayson," I didn't say. "It's not hard; in fact, it's so slippery and soft that I can hardly hold on to it."

But he was already drooling on my mouth, his version of tongue kissing, which was, hopefully for his sake, attributable to the fact that he was so terribly drunk, which could have also accounted for his flaccid organ.

"Take it," he slurred. "It's all yours . . ."

Grayson never finished his sentence, nor did he actually allow me to take it, because he passed out. Beads of perspiration dotted my forehead and upper lip as I realized there had been no penetration, not even the tip, not even in just a little. Maggie Sommers, team player, was still technically monogamous—she hadn't actually betrayed her husband. As I gathered up my clothes, the only thought that disturbed me was whether Grayson would realize that we hadn't done it. As I dressed hurriedly and raced downstairs to find a taxi, I hoped that Grayson would delude himself into believing that we had done it. Riding home in a cab, I thought about the possibility of Grayson's thinking we had done it but also remembering that in his alcoholic stupor, it hadn't been that terrific. As I let myself into my apartment, it occurred to me that the only thing I really hadn't worried about was if Eric Ornstein might have wondered where I had been until two-thirty in the morning.

The following day I was summoned to Grayson Daniel's office in the executive tower of the broadcast center. He greeted me at the door with an affectionate hug and a knowing wink. "Here she is," he exclaimed, "the sexiest crime reporter in television!" Not only did he think we had done it, but he apparently thought it had been good. And it seemed only logical that after last night, especially since he chose to believe his own revised scenario, crime reporter was the least he could give me. I wouldn't have balked or blinked if he had said chairman of the board or even president of the holding company. I did feign surprise, however, and delight at his news.

"How wonderful, Grayson," I said, with a note of restraint. "When do I begin?"

"Audition in the studio tomorrow afternoon," he said smoothly.

It would be a lie to admit that I wasn't slightly disappointed.

"You'd better get yourself an agent, Miss Maggie Sexy Mouth."

So, if it took typing to get you in the door and tits to get you into the studio, it took an agent like Quincy Reynolds to make sure you had a good contract, so nothing in your life would ever again depend upon typing and tits.

I was sitting in the high barber-type chair in the makeup room the next morning, with Quincy watching. "Do you suppose they think I'd make a good journalist?" I asked naively. "I mean, that's what I've always wanted to be."

She looked at me as if I'd completely lost my mind.

"You must be kidding. This has nothing to do with anything at this point except your cheekbones and husky voice."

I was crestfallen. "So this is how it is in television," I answered, tilting my head back so the makeup woman could brush some color across the cheekbones that apparently got me this audition. It was disturbing to think that anything else that transpired for this opportunity could have possibly been avoided.

"No, this isn't how it is just in television; this is just how it is period, usually. But you'll have the last laugh," Quincy predicted.

"How so?"

"When you're a household word and earning lots of money, everybody will think you were born with a microphone in your hand."

"What if they don't like me?"

"Then we'll go to another network," she said. "Stop worrying."

Quincy wrapped her flowing green plaid cape around her shoulders dramatically and flounced out of the room. "I'll be right above you in the control booth. Good luck, Mags. You'll be terrific."

The three cameras in the studio were aimed directly at me, although I was instructed only to look into the one that had the red light illuminated on top. Someone had clipped a small microphone onto my simple white silk blouse, which tied at the neck in a floppy bow, and someone else had placed a small receiver behind my ear.

The floor director pointed at me. "Ready, Maggie. I'm going to count back from ten, nine . . ."

And when he reached zero, Grayson's voice boomed over the microphone from the control booth. "Take it, Maggie, it's all yours," and I started laughing so hard that they had to begin the count all over again.

I read the copy, slowly at first, something about a fire in lower Manhattan, where a man crawled out onto a window ledge before jumping to safety into a net, to the cheers of curious spectators and relieved fire fighters. In fact, I read the copy at least five times before I didn't smile where "a fire raged" but rather where "Angelo Tarluzzi jumped to safety." Grayson, Quincy, and Nick came down from the booth when the piece was over.

"Great, Maggie," Quincy said, hugging me.

"Good work, kid," Nick said. "Terrific."

"Neat, M.S.," Grayson said. "Just dandy."

And all I could think of saying was, "Thank you, Angelo Tarluzzi and the entire New York City Fire Department, for making this possible."

○

The street below my window is quiet now; the neighborhood restaurants are closed and the cars are no longer honking their horns. The pizza we ordered hours ago is finished, only several clumps of congealed cheese are left, sticking to the greasy wax paper. Quincy is sitting on the floor, her head leaning against the couch, while Dan is stretched out, his head in her lap. We have been talking for hours, remembering all of the incidents and events that are so amusing now, but that seemed so terribly serious when they happened, so long ago. And while I feel more connected to the past, I still fell uncertain of the future and confused about the present.

"It seems like a hundred years ago," Quincy says, stretching.

"It seems like a hundred years ago that I've had any sleep," Dan says, standing up. "I'm beat."

A wave of panic sweeps over me at the possibility that Quincy will be leaving me alone tonight.

"Don't go; please stay," I say.

"I have to feed the cats," Quincy says. "Unless you will." She looks at Dan.

"I'm going to feed the cats," he says with a grin. "And I leave you with my wife."

"Thanks, Dan," I say, hugging him. "I really didn't want to be alone."

"Will you try to get some sleep, you two?" he says, taking Quincy in his arms.

Quincy nods and then turns to give Dan a kiss. "Thanks, sweetie. I'll see you in the morning, which is only a few hours away—it's already four o'clock."

After Dan leaves, I take some pillows from my bed and toss them to Quincy, along with a couple of blankets. We are comfortably installed on my two living room sofas when I say, "It's so strange: When everything started going so well for me at ABN, my personal life started to fall apart.''

"That's not exactly true," Quincy says. ''Your personal life fell apart long before that. It's just that you had other options by that time, and you weren't so frightened anymore. I remember you from the beginning, and you weren't happy with Eric from the moment you married him.''

o

By New Year's Eve 1974, I had been working as the on-air crime reporter for almost two years. Most of my days were spent climbing the stairs of rat-infested tenements, interviewing victims of muggings, robberies, and rapes. I would pick my way through rubble-strewn streets where a lost generation of youth, track marks on their arms symbolizing a losing battle with drugs, would stare curiously at me and at the camera. Sometimes I would just weep with the ghetto mothers whose starving children were exploited by the media—by me—to demonstrate the horrors of the system, to sensationalize the facts, to grab the audience as the lead-in story on the nightly newscast. And other times I would just be furious when the camera zoomed in for a close-up shot of Maggie Sommers holding the hand of a thirteen-year-old rape victim as the child described the shame and trauma of her experience. My director would order a tight shot, left side, of Maggie Sommers sitting on the dirty floor of a cramped apartment while that same child told of the repeated beatings and sexual abuse she suffered at the hands of her own father.

And while I was never sure where the blame actually lay for all that misery, I did feel guilty about the presence of the cameras and the lights. I felt guilty until I realized that they wanted it as much as they out there wanted it. Communication—reached out and touch me. See what it's like here. Help. And Grayson was absolutely right—grisly human drama as reported by a woman gave everybody what they wanted, a subtle combination of sex and suffering. But something was happening to me, something that made my personal life seem so remote. I could only feel emotion when I thought about *them;* I couldn't seem to feel anything where it concerned me. It made it easier that way.

Nick Sprig had kept the promise he'd made to me four years earlier. He was still teaching me everything there was to know about "this lousy business." I was never to nod as if I understood anything anybody ever said because if I looked perpetually confused, they would be forced to repeat their stories over and over again.

"People love to talk," Nick said. "The more you let 'em gab, the more you'll find out. Just let 'em talk, Mags, and look adorable and confused."

Maggie Sommers's career was doing just fine. Her marriage was another story. That particular night, New Year's Eve 1974, Eric and I were due at the Sommerses' annual New Year's Eve party, a lavish ritual that included Mildred and Harry Ornstein, and Cara and Steven Blattsberg. That yearly party was the perfect example of why I was still married to Eric. Breaking the pattern of going year after year was as unthinkable as actually daring to get a divorce. I was simply not ready to take a stand on either issue.

Eric was clipping his black bow tie to his white ruffled tuxedo shirt, while I was sitting at my dressing table, dreading the hours that stretched ahead.

Eric refused to discuss what I did with my time during the day. If people happened to recognize me in a restaurant or on the street because my face was a familiar fixture in their homes every evening, Eric would handle the situation in the following manner: "As you may or may not have noticed, we are in the process of eating our dinner. Would you mind?" or "Would you allow us to cross the street? We pay taxes too, you know."

It was an unspoken rule in the Ornstein household that Maggie was never to bring, as Eric put it, "the streets of New York into my home." The other rule held more serious consequences. Maggie Sommers had been, at Eric's directive, depositing her salary checks into her husband's checking account for the past four years. A monthly allowance was doled out to Maggie for her lunches, car-fare, and any other personal expenditures that did not exceed twenty-five dollars, provided that receipts were diligently turned over to Eric every week. "Deductions are crucial to a family that has two people supporting the welfare system," Eric said on numerous occasions. There was something definitely unfair about the whole arrangement, but I wasn't prepared to confront it yet. And when I was finally ready, it was too late.

"Maggie, hurry—we're going to be late." Eric was marching up and down the bedroom, bending his toes with each step in an effort to loosen his stiff new black patent-leather pumps. "What a waste," he mumbled, sitting down on the eggshell-colored chaise longue.

"What's a waste?" I asked, searching for my dress in the closet.

"Good legs, good bones, and with my mind we could really have terrific kids."

Turning around, I flashed Eric a toothy smile. "Good teeth too, Eric," I said. "You forgot the teeth—never wore a brace—calculated could save us approximately three thousand dollars per child, which means if we had three children, like Cara, we'd be ahead nine thousand dollars."

I had made a vow to myself that night not to react to anything that Eric said or did that would have ordinarily offended and enraged me. My head already ached in anticipation of spending an entire evening with the Sommerses—an evening where guilt was the appetizer, criticism the main course, and generous helpings of painful childhood memories were sprinkled on everything. It all made me wish that I hadn't come each time that I went.

I slipped into my dress, a clinging black jersey sheath that I had worn to several family functions over the last few years—including Cara and Steven's tenth wedding anniversary party, only two weeks before. That was the night when Steven had to perform the Heimlich on Mildred after a meatball lodged in her throat. Eric just stood there, screaming, "Swallow, Mom, come on—show us how you can swallow." He claimed afterward that the episode forced him to face his own mortality.

"That's the dress you wore when Mom choked," Eric said. "Change it; it makes me anxious."

Smiling sweetly, I walked to the closet and pulled out another dress, a beige silk evening shirtwaist, never worn to a choking.

"Wear the pin Mom gave you, Maggie."

I obediently took the pin out of my jewelry box, a gold frog that vaguely resembled Mildred, except for the emerald eyes. Mildred's eyes were brown.

"Pin it on the other side, Maggie."

I didn't react, but merely removed the frog from the right side of my dress and repinned it on the left.

"Wear your hair down tonight."

Nodding my head, I removed the hairpins so my hair tumbled down around my shoulders.

"Put on some more lipstick."

I sat back down at the dressing table and applied more lipstick, pressing my lips together firmly before blotting them with a Kleenex.

There was almost nothing that I wouldn't do for Eric tonight except leave my diaphragm in its pink plastic powdered case so I would get pregnant.

"There's going to be some big changes around here this new year," he suddenly said, "changes that you'll undoubtedly not like very much."

"What kind of changes?" I asked, brushing my hair.

"Changes that include my not sacrificing my happiness for the sake of your whims."

"What whims?" I was determined not to react, not to escalate this discussion into what could easily have become a brawl.

"Whims like your career. This is the last year that I intend to be humiliated when Dad asks when we're having children."

"Then tell him it's none of his business."

"I certainly will not. It's as much his business as it is ours."

"Then let him have your baby," I snapped. And with that, all my good intentions evaporated.

"I'm not going," Eric yelled, tearing off his bow tie

and throwing his jacket on the floor. "I refuse to go and be humiliated unless I have a commitment from you."

Slamming my hairbrush on the dressing table and making an enormous dent in the wood, I yelled back, "You're not interested in me or anything about me. All you want is a child, and I happen to be necessary for doing that."

"Well, well, you finally caught on," he sneered. "So if you're smart enough to know that, then why do you fight me all the time?"

"Because I don't want a baby now."

And then he walked over to me, bent down, and looked into my eyes. And because I expected so little emotionally, I responded instantly to him.

"I need you, Maggie," he said.

The magic words. But it could have been worse.

Eric stroked my body, oblivious that we were already an hour late. For the first time in a long time, I actually felt receptive, wanting him to lower himself inside me to make love to me, and I told him that.

"Make love to me, Eric," I said.

The last thing I heard was his zipper, and then, without warning, he took my head roughly between his hands and pushed it down between his legs.

"Put it in your mouth, Maggie, in your mouth."

I was on my knees between Eric's legs, my tongue flicking over the head of his pulsating appendage.

"Put it in your mouth, Maggie," he commanded again. "In your mouth."

Taking a deep breath, I inserted it in my mouth, approximately one quarter of the way down. I made slurpy noises as I sucked on it, coming up for air only twice before sucking on it some more.

"No, Maggie, not like that," he said gruffly. "Watch your teeth."

Opening my mouth a little wider and swallowing a little more, approximately one third of the way down, I tried very hard to keep it firmly between my cheeks, careful not to catch any skin in my bicuspids.

"No, Maggie," he said even more gruffly, placing his hands tightly around my head. "Like this."

And then he guided my head up and down on him until

I gagged and choked, because the head of IT was grazing against my tonsils. It was approximately three quarters of the way down and plunging. I felt as if I were drowning as Eric moaned, his breath coming in deep sighs, his hands moving my head up and down at a furious pace. Suddenly there was an explosion of liquid inside my mouth. I knocked Eric's hands from my head, surfacing from the sloshing fluid that seemed to be enveloping me, choking me. I was gasping for breath, drowning in Eric Ornstein's sperm, when I suddenly realized why it could have been worse. My diaphragm was still in its pink plastic powdered case.

Happy new year.

CHAPTER FIVE

Quincy is still fast asleep on the living room sofa, the gray down quilt wrapped snugly around her face, when the garbage trucks begin their early-morning clatter in the street below my window. Tiptoeing into the bedroom, I turn down the bed and crawl between the ice-cold sheets. It is ten o'clock in the morning when I wake up again, this time to the sound of the shower running in the bathroom.

I pad to the door on bare feet and knock lightly. "Is that you in there?"

"Who were you expecting?" Quincy calls back.

She is standing in the doorway, a black terry-cloth robe tied loosely around her diminutive frame. "What's the matter, Maggie?"

"I've been doing a lot of thinking. Maybe I've been having second thoughts about that magazine-format show after all."

She slides her arm through mine. "Let's do this over coffee."

Quincy has a concerned expression on her face as she watches me pour coffee beans into the grinder. "Are you sure it's the show you're thinking so seriously about?"

I glance up, but then immediately direct my attention back to the beans as they clatter against the sides of the plastic cylinder. Suddenly the process of making this particular morning pot of coffee is a most serious ritual. I need time to collect my thoughts, to know what I mean, so that Quincy can explain it all back to me later. "It's a tremendous opportunity, and I'm grateful to you for—"

She holds up her hand. "You don't have to be grateful;

it's part of my job and you're a friend. Remember we swore eternal friendship in blood and tears that day in London?'' She smiles.

I smile back. The coffee has stopped perking, and I carefully fill two mugs, handing one to Quincy and setting the other down on the counter for myself.

''The point is that it's a lot more money and a chance not to be under the thumb of producers, directors, or cameramen.''

''That's not true, Maggie. As long as people have to deal with people, you're always at the mercy of others.''

''Not you; you have your own business.''

Quincy laughs. ''You must be kidding. I'm constantly at the mercy of clients and television executives. I can't get away from that.''

There are a few moments of silence before I say in a soft voice, ''I was rough on you last night, wasn't I?''

''No,'' she says. ''You were rough on yourself.'' She pauses. ''This isn't about the show, is it, Maggie? I mean, it's about something else.'' She is watching me, her lips parted, a frown visible, but she doesn't push.

''I love him,'' I say, turning away from her. ''And then he clutters my head, and I have to back off.''

''I should have known,'' she says, leaning against the refrigerator. ''Actually, I did know it.''

''Look, I know it sounds stupid,'' I explain, looking directly at her now, ''because the whole process is going on in my head anyway but sometimes I feel trapped by my own feelings, and that's when I get scared that it's going to interfere with my work. It's nothing that he does—I mean, nothing bad. He loves me; It's that simple, and it sometimes makes me feel as if I want to rip off some invisible chain and just shake myself free of him. So there's where the magazine show began creeping back into my mind. Do you see what I mean?''

She pours milk into her coffee. ''I see what you mean, but I'm not sure that you do.''

I take a deep breath and try to say it clearly—so that perhaps even I can understand what it's all about. ''OK, so here's the point: Why don't I take the show and try something new: not go back into the Middle East and—''

"Maggie, you're already trying something new—loving someone. Why don't you just try one new thing at a time for now?"

"You're my agent; why're you talking me out of this?"

"Out of what? Out of another hundred thousand dollars a year or out of a chance to be happy with someone? Listen to me, Maggie. You're probably one of the very lucky ones: punishing yourself—and Avi, for that matter—equals another one hundred thousand dollars a year before taxes. No, don't interrupt me for a minute; just listen. Now, if we figure in strictly business terms that the show is not a news broadcast—it can be canceled, which translated means that you'll be canceled; and then, if you calculate the additional income after taxes, my share, since I'm going to act like an agent and be selfish, isn't even enough to pay the mortgage on my beach house for a year. Not to mention that if you're canceled, some twenty-five-year-old girl is going to be sitting in your chair on the network news show, and then what? But you know what, Maggie? I'd encourage you to take a shot anyway, if I didn't think you were just using this as a way of running away from a man who's mad about you—if you weren't running into this as a way out. But that's the part of me talking that's not your agent; it's the part that's your friend and wants you to be happy."

"You still don't get it," I say miserably.

"I get it; you don't get it."

"I hate him sometimes, despise him because he's married. I don't trust his intentions, and then I resent him for hurting his wife, for leaving her, and that's when I want to just run away—from him, from Israel, from network news."

"Why not parlay this whole self-destructive kick into something really big?" Quincy says sarcastically. "I mean, why not wait until they offer you anchor on the network news, maybe even two specials a year, like Walters, for a million dollars—then you can really do a number on yourself. Right now you're not important enough to really make that big a dent when you self-destruct."

"You're unbelievable," I say, wondering how I somehow lost control of this conversation. "But what if I really don't want him; what if he really doesn't want me?"

"Then you'll deal with it when you're with him again. You'll work it out, but don't confuse issues and don't make career decisions either because you love someone or because you don't."

"I love him," I say quietly. "I am absolutely mad about him."

"I know," she says, smiling slightly. "That's what this is all about."

The walk across the kitchen into Quincy's arms takes her by surprise almost as much as it surprises me, but then so do my tears.

"Why do I do this?"

"Because you're not used to being happy."

"Maybe it's because of Joe's death."

"Maybe," she says, stroking my hair. "And maybe it's because of Eric and Vera and Alan and everything else."

"Then why," I say, stepping back so that I can wipe my eyes and blow my nose, "do you manage so well in spite of all the grief that you've had?"

"I don't always manage so well. It's tough sometimes and very tempting to just walk away."

"But you don't."

"No, I don't," Quincy says thoughtfully. "And the reason is probably because I'm ten years older than you and more philosophical about life. There's something to be said for mellowing, accepting the love and comfort of someone like Dan."

"Well, then, I've got something to look forward to, don't I?" I smile.

Quincy makes a face. "Yup—getting old like me—right?"

"I've changed, haven't I? I mean, I've changed since we started out in this game."

"Tremendously, sweetie—in many ways. Of course you have."

"I feel very different now, even professionally. Things are easier."

"I remember when you first went on-air and you were

really at the mercy of every line producer and floor director on the set."

"It was hard, but I don't think I noticed it—I was too thrilled with doing it. It was a novelty then."

"Do you remember the day you were covering the funeral of that policeman—the day you almost got fired?"

"I sure do, but there were other reasons—other things that happened that day."

Quincy nods. "I almost forgot those other reasons."

○

Fifth Avenue had been cleared of traffic, with police barricades holding back the throngs of people who had lined up on either side of the wide street. A group of city officials, including the mayor, the chief of police, several congressmen, and a handful of top police brass, medals and ribbons gleaming on their blue jackets, stood in front of the ornate doors to St. Patrick's Cathedral. The cardinal of New York was in the center of the group, his hand holding on to his red hat, while the crisp November wind whipped at his purple robes.

Television cameras and microphones had been set up on the sidewalk in front of the church, and black cable lay strewn on the steps. Technicians and reporters either milled about or paced aimlessly, waiting for the media event that was about to occur. For some inexplicable reason, this particular funeral had been chosen by the city's hierarchy as an example that senseless killings of New York's finest would no longer be tolerated. The murder of one policeman, felled while in the line of duty, was sufficient grist to mobilize the city's press corps into launching an intensive media war on crime. However, and not that it really mattered, Richard Steven Tomaski had not exactly been felled while in the line of duty. It was more a question of his being in the wrong place at the wrong time and compounding that oversight by committing two additional errors. Tomaski happened to be wearing his uniform when he stopped for a beer at the Silver Star Tavern on Chauncey Street in Brooklyn, two blocks from his apartment, and he also happened to reach for his gun when two seventeen-year-old kids burst through the door and announced a holdup. Tragically, that second error proved fatal. Tomaski lay sprawled on the floor within seconds of reaching for his revolver. Several hours later, when the coroner pronounced him dead from multiple gunshot wounds to his chest, groin, and left thigh, Tomaski still had that same baffled expression on his face—a face that would never age more than its twenty-five years.

My crew edged closer to the gutter, a minicam balanced on my cameraman's shoulder, my producer craning his neck in the direction of the two motorcycles, driven by two helmeted policeman, that were coming down the street. Behind them were three black limousines, followed by the flower-laden hearse. Suddenly the other television crews were pushing forward to get an unobstructed view of the six uniformed pallbearers, who had grouped together, waiting to carry the casket of the fallen policeman into the church. As the hearse rolled to a stop, I made a sudden decision to walk around the left of the crowd, toward the curbside door of the lead limousine, in which I was certain would be Richard Steven Tomaski's widow. Several seconds elapsed before the left rear door opened and a pale blond woman was helped onto the sidewalk. She stood still, waiting, until a man emerged from the right front of the limousine, walked around, and handed her the baby he held in his arms.

Stepping closer to the grief-stricken woman, my microphone dangling discreetly at my side, I said, "Mrs. Tomaski, I'm really so sorry about your husband."

My initial approach to the grieving widow was one I would have instinctively used even if Nick Sprig hadn't taught me that the best way to get an exclusive interview was to approach the subject from the human aspect of his predicament. If the subject happened, for instance, to be a mass murderer who had just been struck down by a crack-shot police sniper and was lying in a pool of blood, I might have said, "People annoy me too. I especially hate big parties." Or if the subject happened to be a hit-and-run driver who was handcuffed to a chair in a police station, I might have remarked, "What a coincidence; I had the same problem with the brakes on my Honda.'' At least those were the lines that were tossed around the newsroom to make the actual event, when it really happened, more tolerable, since Nick claimed that Maggie had this tendency to get emotionally involved.

In the case of Rita Tomaski, Nick's opinion of Maggie's penchant for emotional involvement, as well as his description of ''this lousy business,'' was entirely appropriate. Maggie Sommers didn't have to reach down very far to feel that emotional involvement, nor could she doubt the veracity of Nick's evaluation of the television industry. That particular story was especially heartbreaking because the key player was a victim—and victims were Maggie's specialty.

''Mrs. Tomaski,'' I repeated, ''I'm really so sorry.''

She eyed me suspiciously but didn't reply. Instead, she clutched her baby tighter to her breast, her thin hand cupped around the child's blue knitted cap. It was only when Rita shifted the cumbersome tote bag filled with diapers and baby bottles that I made my move. Only when Rita became momentarily disoriented, unable to balance baby and bag, did I tuck my microphone under one arm and gently lift the sleeping child from her arms.

I could see out of the corner of my eye that Kelly Blake and Fred Foreman, my cameraman and producer, were creeping cautiously around the crowd. Fred's hand was clenched in a fist, making tight circles in the air near his head, a sign to Kelly to move in for a close-up shot. He sensed that Maggie Sommers was about to make six million viewers out there cry right along with poor Rita Tomaski.

The baby hardly stirred in my arms as I reached over to hold my microphone. He gurgled only slightly when I said, ''Mrs. Tomaski, I'm Maggie Sommers, ABN News. Will you talk to me for a minute?''

A wild look flickered in Rita's eyes, because she couldn't understand how it had happened that a strange woman was holding the only living memory of her dead husband. A look of desperation crossed her face because she was furious that this same strange woman, a reporter, had somehow trapped her into giving an interview. Rita responded predictably. Lunging for the baby, she cried, "I don't want to talk to you. I don't want to talk to anybody."

But Maggie was quick as she took two small steps to the left and flashed Rita a big smile.

"I'll only take a minute of your time, Mrs. Tomaski," I said rapidly. "Just a few questions, I promise."

The unspoken deal, you give me a minute of your time and I'll give you back your baby. And there was no doubt what the response would be, because it was as easy as taking candy from a baby—or taking a baby from a confused and grief-stricken mother who just wanted to go into a church to pray for her husband's soul.

Rita closed her eyes for a moment before slowly nodding her head. "OK, I'll talk to you," she said dully. "Only, please, just for a minute. I have to go inside."

But I was already counting backward from sixty, not for poor Rita but because the time for this entire segment was only four minutes and thirty-two seconds.

"Did you always dread that this would happen?"

"No," she answered quietly. "I tried not to think about it. Only, when it happened to someone else, I used to get scared."

Forty-five seconds, Rita. More concise, if you please.

"What was your first reaction when you learned that your husband was dead?"

Rita's mouth twisted into an expression of pure hatred, her eyes narrowed into a look of utter loathing. Come on, Rita, I thought, only thirty seconds. Don't fold on me now; I've still got your baby.

"How do you think I felt? I wanted to die. I didn't believe it, and then, when I saw him, I wanted to die." She started crying softly.

"Did you actually go to the bar after it happened?" I asked, aware that Fred was running his finger across his throat—time to finish.

"Yes, they called me," she wept. "They were giving him last rites when I got there."

"Cut, Maggie," Fred yelled.

"Thank you very much, Mrs. Tomaski, for sharing

your feelings with us today," I said, handing back the infant, who had also begun to cry.

Maggie Sommers had kept her promise, only six seconds over the one minute that she had promised and now she had to dash, because there was one final segment to do to fill in the remaining time. I didn't look Rita Tomaski in the eye as I handed back her baby because I didn't want her to see that Maggie Sommers had tears in her eyes too. Rita would never know that Maggie was very ashamed and very sorry for doing that to her, but she had her own problems, and one of them would be made a whole lot worse if she wasn't a good reporter and lost her job. Right then, I had an exclusive with the widow, however, and for the moment things weren't at risk.

I followed Kelly and Fred across Fifth Avenue for a long shot of St. Patrick's Cathedral, a shot that would backdrop Maggie Sommers for the final portion of the piece. Standing in the middle of the deserted street, the camera rolling, I suddenly refused to say the words that had been written for me earlier that afternoon in the studio. That was the moment when Maggie Sommers argued and resisted and decided to take a moral stand after her immoral standup. It happened when I began to read the copy.

"Richard Steven Tomaski is being honored here today in an extraordinary display of pomp and circumstance. His family, friends, and some of New York City's top political officials are mourning him with the kind of love and dignity that makes New York so very special. Richard Steven Tomaski would have been proud; he would have wanted it this way—" I stopped.

"Wait a minute," I said, walking toward the camera. "What does this mean—'he would have wanted it this way'? He wouldn't have wanted it this way at all. He would have wanted to be home with Rita and the baby or finishing that beer or even"—and I paused—"or even standing here mourning someone else with dignity and love. He wouldn't have wanted it this way at all."

"Just read the goddamn copy, Maggie, just read it.

Kelly and I have to go to the Bronx to cover a fire, and I'm hungry. Just read the damn copy.''

"I'm not saying that last part, that part about wanting it this way. I'm just not doing it." And I sat down on the curb, the microphone resting on my knees, and waited.

Fred Foreman knelt in front of me. "Maggie, if you don't read this copy and read it right now, I promise that you'll never read any copy anywhere ever again. Is that clear? Now read the copy."

Though I mulled that possibility over in my mind for a second or two, there was no doubt what the answer would be, because it was as easy as taking candy from a baby or taking a baby from a confused and grief-stricken woman, or threatening Maggie Sommers that she would never work again and be forced to have a baby of her own. I got up, walked back to the middle of the deserted street, held the microphone up to my mouth, and read the copy.

When I finished reading the copy, I threw down the microphone and stomped off across Fifth Avenue, only I never made it more than three steps, for a piece of heavy black cable that had been flung in the street caused me to trip and plunge headlong into the arms of a man. Regaining my balance, I looked up in embarrassment and surprise to see that Paul Newman was apparently attending the funeral of Richard Steven Tomaski. I felt my face getting hot as I looked at the man again: same blond hair cropped close to his head, startling blue eyes, full, sensuous mouth, medium height, compact build, but there was something not quite right. The nose was different, imperfect somehow, as if someone once smashed it with a right hook that permanently knocked it over to the left, which was exactly what had happened to Detective First Class Brian Flaherty during a raid on a heroin den several years earlier.

"I don't think Tomaski would have wanted it like this, either," he said, taking my arm.

I didn't answer right away, even though he had undoubtedly just saved me from doing to my nose what had been done to his. Instead, I was busy examining my broken heel.

"Oh, shit," I said, holding it up. "This just caps a perfect day."

His grasp on my arm was firm as he helped me limp over the steps of the church. "I'm Detective Brian Flaherty," he said, "and I already know who you are—I'd recognize those green eyes and sexy mouth anywhere."

"Um . . . I . . ." I said, pretending to be still engrossed in my shoe.

"I'm just surprised we never met before," he continued.

I looked up, directly into his incredible blue eyes, and couldn't help thinking what a shame it was, a waste. But it was just impossible for me to get by his vulgar cadence of speech.

"Did anyone ever tell you that you look just like Paul Newman?" My head was reverberating: Come here—Go away; Come here—Go away.

"Yeah." He grinned. "Everyone. Except for the nose—right?"

"I hadn't noticed," I replied icily.

"So," he said, ignoring the blinking Go away signal, "if I look like Paul Newman without the nose and you don't look like Ann-Margret, except for the chest, how come we never met before?" His look was seductive; his words were repulsive. "So how come," he pressed, "since we both cover crime?"

I inhaled quickly, a short little gasp that was designed to feign annoyance. Actually, I was mesmerized by his lower lip. "I really don't know," I answered. "I mean, what precinct do you work out of? What area of crime do you cover? Did you know Patrolman Tomaski?"

He laughed and sat down next to me on the steps. "Whoa! One question at a time."

"I'm—I'm sorry."

He patted my hand. I pulled it away.

"No problem," he said. "I cover homicide out of the Seventy-seventh—Bed-Stuy—and no, I never knew Tomaski."

"What kind of homicides do you usually get in Bedford-Stuyvesant?"

He certainly unnerved me, unless Maggie Sommers

had gotten so dependent upon a microphone that without it she could only ask really dumb questions.

He laughed again. "I mostly get the kind of homocides where people end up dead."

"I'm sorry," I repeated. "I didn't mean that."

He patted my hand again—reassuringly—and looked at me very seriously.

"Sometimes, on the weekends, I get the kind of homocides that are called domestics, the poor people's answer to divorce. Those are the kind of homicides where the husband decides to end a miserable marriage by plunging a knife into the wife's heart—you know, the woman he promised to 'love, honor, and obey till death do us part.' "

"Never obey," I corrected.

"Huh?"

"They never promise to obey; only women do that."

"I don't think it would make a big difference, because sometimes I get the kind of homicides where the wife shoots her husband while he's sleeping, because she can't take the beatings or abuse anymore. In either case"—he sighed—"those are the times I'm glad I'm not married. Are you?"

"Am I what?" I asked, transfixed by his tongue each time he ran it over his lips as he spoke.

"Married?"

"Yes."

He frowned imperceptibly, glanced at me openly, and then grinned as if he had decided to continue whatever it was that was going on, anyway, married or not married.

"Do you have to hang around here until the funeral's over?"

"No," I answered. "But I should buy a new pair of shoes before I go back to the studio."

Brian stood while I remained seated on the steps of St. Patrick's, the melodic strains of Albinoni audible in the background, the red and gold crisp autumn leaves swirling around the sidewalk in the brisk fall breeze, delicate cumulus clouds seemingly suspended in the clear blue sky, and the bulge in Brian Flaherty's crotch blocking my line of vision.

"Do you want to come with me?" I asked, as if there was any doubt in my mind what the answer would be.

And he knew it too, because he just ran his tongue over his top lip as he offered me his hand. Standing awkwardly, I leaned on Brian's thick forearm until I was able to balance myself on my broken shoe.

Come here—Go away was still resounding in my head and growing louder and louder. We were walking slowly down Fifth Avenue toward Chandler's shoe store, and all I could think of was the way his arm felt on mine.

"How do you manage to deal with all the violence that you see every day?"

He sighed. "It's an ugly world; senseless sometimes."

It wasn't exactly the most profound statement I had ever heard, but it didn't interfere with my noticing how broad his shoulders were.

"Um," I said, pulling my arm away and pretending to scratch an itch on the side of my nose.

"It took me a long time to stop ducking into deserted alleys or dingy hallways to vomit my guts out."

Glancing at him, I wondered briefly what kind of human being chooses to deal with that sordid aspect of life on a daily basis, until it occurred to me that I dealt with the same things. Only, what I did was probably worse, because I exploited the horrors by adding coherent narrative to the already shocking visuals that flashed across television screens each and every night. The only difference between Brian Flaherty and Maggie Sommers was that she was ambivalent about it, while Brian was accepting. But that had absolutely nothing to do with why I allowed Brian to walk me to Chandler's. In fact, it was only because of his startling resemblance to Paul Newman that it all happened.

I picked out the least expensive pair of plastic-manmade upper soled shoes because I had neither a credit card nor a checkbook—thank you, Eric Ornstein. Spending the last penny in my wallet, I realized that I was forced to walk the twenty-seven blocks to the ABN studio. Miserable, angry, and frustrated, I paid the girl at the cash register and left the store, with Brian trailing several feet behind me.

I was about to turn around and wait for him to catch up, when I heard: "You've got a great ass, Maggie."

I cringed, although there was no ambivalence in my reaction this time. But, again I feigned indignation when I shot back, "I've got a better left-side profile. Why don't you walk next to me and take a look?"

"Nope," he finally said. "You've got a better ass."

I just stood still, biting on my lower lip and wondering what *it* would be like, although I had a pretty good idea, considering that my underpants were already damp.

"Brian," I managed to say, "I've got to hurry back to the studio. I'm late."

"Come on," he said, taking my hand. "My car's only a few blocks away. I'll drive you."

We were already in the car, stuck in midtown traffic, when Brian asked, "What time do you get off work, Maggie?"

I leaned my head back, my face flushed. "Get off work?" I repeated softly. But there it all was. Brian Flaherty "got off" work. Maggie Sommers "finished." However, Maggie Sommers got off on Brian Flaherty, and in the final analysis, that was the big equalizer, albeit a temporary one.

Brian weaved the car through traffic like someone with patrol experience and pulled up in front of the American Broadcast Network studios. Running his finger across my lips, he announced, rather than inquired, "I'll pick you up at seven."

Nodding my head in acquiescence, I realized that dictatorial behavior in a man, directed toward a woman, was acceptable only if the woman yearned for him to be in that special place that he was aggressively also coveting. Life was not fair when there was reciprocal desire; women were somehow put at a disadvantage. However, it was even worse if the damp and quavering woman was repressed in other areas of her life—worse because that kind of repression usually caused frigidity. Sitting in Brian's car that day, I accepted the fact that he did, indeed, have me at a disadvantage, having achieved that position only because I had willingly complied. And I had willingly complied because he was so sexy that there was simply no choice. But there was something else: Brian Flaherty was not in a position to deprive me of a credit card or a checkbook so that I was unable to buy a decent pair of shoes.

I finally finished work and found myself seated once again in Brian's brand-new blue Plymouth sedan.

"We're going to this bar in Maspeth, near my house," he announced. "They serve big drinks and play all the hits from the sixties. You'll love it."

We arrived at the pub, a noisy and crowded room with a gigantic television set suspended from the ceiling at one end of a long knotty-pine bar that was jammed with people. Brian elbowed his way through a sea of bodies until he found a small space at the far end, away from the television. Wedging me in between two men who had greeted him effusively, pounding him on the back and pumping his hand, he ordered a beer for himself and a Coke for me.

After Brian ordered a second beer, I finally broke down and agreed to have a drink.

"Give the lady a Scotch on the rocks, Mac," Brian instructed the bartender, who poured the drink quickly and slid it down the length of the bar into Brian's open palm.

"Aren't you Maggie Sommers?" the bartender asked, walking toward us. Suddenly twenty pairs of eyes were upon me. I smiled and nodded, distinctly uncomfortable to be the focal point of all the attention. It was unlikely that any of Eric's friends or business associates were in Lucky's Four Leaf Clover Tavern in Maspeth, Queens, but I still would have preferred it if no one had noticed me.

"Drink up, Maggie," Brian said, sensing my concern, "and we'll dance."

I took another long sip—made a face because I hated Scotch—before following Brian onto the small dance floor.

We were dancing to "Jeremiah is a bullfrog," only Brian and I were hardly moving to the upbeat tempo of the music. But even though we were hardly moving, I kept tripping over Brian's feet. Each time that happened,

which was constantly, Brian just pulled me closer to him,
holding me so tight that my feet barely touched the floor.
And it was while I was dancing like that with Brian that
I learned something very valuable.

Brian Flaherty was not hard. Brian Flaherty was hard
as a rock. I thought about that for a moment before I was
able to continue my in-depth analysis. Hard and hard as
a rock are both distinguishable through a tight piece of
fabric at the crotch of a man's trousers. But hard is always
surrounded by other parts in that same area, which are
usually soft. Hard as a rock, however, is never surrounded by anything; it is just a solid bulging mass that
extends over the entire crotch, straining underneath the
piece of fabric. And while hard is the end result of the
transition from flaccid to functional, hard as a rock isn't
the end result of any transition. It is simply that—hard as
a rock—and what it was before it was hard as a rock is
completely and totally irrelevant.

As the music played on, I began to feel vaguely heady
and decidedly hungry, since I'd only had a bagel and a
cup of coffee the whole day. It was a mistake to think
bagel, because bagel instantly reminded me of Eric, and
Eric made me immediately feel guilty. When "Jeremiah
is a bullfrog" ended and Brian led me back to the bar,
he whispered, "My house is right around the corner,
Maggie, and tonight's Tuesday, which means that my
brother Denny works late at Seaman's discount furniture
warehouse. He won't be home until about eleven."

I started to say something, but his lips were on mine.

"Unless we leave now," he said hoarsely, "we'll only
have less than three hours to be alone."

o

Quincy is dressed, sitting on the edge of my bed and
sipping her coffee. "Did you feel the same way about
Brian that you feel about Avi?" she asks.

I think about that for a second or two. "No," I answer
thoughtfully. "I believed I loved Brian because he gave
me something I never had before."

Quincy smiles knowingly. "OK, other than an orgasm, what might that have been?"

I smiled. "Nothing—but back then, that was more than enough."

"Well, did you feel the same way about Brian that you feel about Avi?" she persists.

I think about the question and about my feelings for both of these men. I loved Brian Flaherty because he introduced me to sex, taught me about the sexual potential of my body. I was obsessed by Brian because he dulled all of my senses, like time, space, and the ability or even the desire to think rationally. All but the physical senses that I never knew I possessed. At the time, I was unable to define it as unconnected sexual activity— something women have trouble achieving and something men can do with their eyes closed, which is how they usually do it anyway. This was the first measure of my love for Avi Herzog. Brian never held my face between his hands as Avi did and looked into my eyes while he made love to me.

"Ignorance is bliss," I finally answer.

"In what way?"

"Well, I didn't realize it at the time, with Brian that I had successfully managed to separate my heart and mind from my body."

"That's because you were already aware of your heart and mind and just beginning to discover that other part."

I smile. "It's funny, but it never occurred to me then that there was more."

"Was there?"

"Was there!" I say. "Over and over until I could barely move."

"Um," Quincy says, "so that's when you reacquainted yourself with your head: Brian, meet Maggie and make her run for the hills—right?"

"Not exactly."

But I remember how I never strived for that elusive prize that men take for granted and that women assume they're not necessarily going to have—and so judge the act on other variables. Variables like love, respect, and whether they'll be offered that ultimate compliment, marriage.

But it was partially true. Maggie Sommers accepted Brian with few expectations and Brian possessed Maggie with an unspoiled innocence. Orgasm to Maggie was still a mystery and she already had a husband. Equality to Brian was something vaguely to do with blacks in Alabama, and he was not in the market for a wife.

"All right, then what was the reason?" Quincy asks.

"Maybe it was the whole female orgasm thing, and maybe it had something to do with control."

"Well, we did it to ourselves," Quincy answers. "Because we allowed our orgasms to become a debatable issue. It was ridiculous what we did to ourselves."

"Mmm. I remember. You couldn't open a book or a magazine without another new definition assaulting you. And there were constant discussions by experts who somehow always happened to be men. It just ceased being a personal issue anymore."

"But I thought Brian didn't read, so how was he involved in this debate?"

"He didn't read, and he wasn't really involved, but I was. I was getting anxious because I felt obliged to take on this dilemma, get involved in the debate—you know, whether or not female orgasm really existed and worse, if it did, which kind. It was sort of a game—multiple choice orgasm."

Quincy laughs. "Uh huh—clitoral or vaginal, and then someone stated definitively, as an absolute, I might add, that vaginal orgasm didn't exist. So then I began to wonder what was wrong with me, I mean, what was going on with me all those times that something was happening where it wasn't supposed to happen."

"Well, if it was going on with you, and going on with me too by the way, then why wasn't that enough?"

"Who said it wasn't enough? I mean since when is orgasm not enough?" Quincy asks.

"Since . . . ," I answer slowly, "since the moment that you find someone who has something more to offer?"

Quincy smiles. "So it's a matter of compensation, is that what you're saying?"

"More like maturity."

"No more sex just because it feels good?" Quincy sighs. "Oh well, it was nice while it lasted, wasn't it?"

"Of course it was and is, but it's not everything."

"It never was sweetie, even before you discovered that. It only seemed as if it was, at the moment." Quincy pauses. "And you know what? It still seems like it is— for the moment anyway."

Yet, back then, ignorance *was* bliss. At least for a while, I believed that Brian Flaherty had it all and was the ultimate liberated man. The fact was that he was simply unscathed by the feminist movement, which was just as well because the feminist movement was concentrating on clitoral orgasm. And I kept marveling at Brian's "sensitivity," all the while deluding myself that I was in love with him. And Brian just went blithely along doing what felt good and what felt good happened to include making me respond to an uncomplicated and unthreatened Brian who was more than willing to acknowledge clitoral, vaginal and any other kind of orgasm that happened to occur in that general area.

On the other hand Maggie embraced Avi with few expectations because orgasm was the least of her problems and she no longer had a husband nor wanted one. Avi invaded Maggie, loving her but unable to offer her that ultimate compliment, marriage, because he already had a wife. Everything had changed. Avi knew about the things Brian didn't, but that had nothing to do with making Avi do things that somehow included making Maggie respond to an uncomplicated and unthreatened Avi who also happened to be in love with her. Maggie and Avi made love with their eyes open and it was no longer a question of multi-choice orgasm, because it just happened. What happened between them happened because they were both unable to separate their hearts and minds from their bodies. Ignorance wasn't bliss, maturity was.

"Still," I say, "sex is basically unfair."

"For whom?" Quincy asks.

"For women, because it's just not essential that we have orgasms."

"It's essential that I have them," Quincy says, laughing.

"No, that's not what I mean. If it were essential that we have them, then life wouldn't go on if we didn't. The point is that men have to have them or that's the end of the human race. It's much more serious than a little heavy breathing."

"But it was our fault."

"Why?"

Quincy smiles wistfully. "Because we gave away our secrets, discussed our orgasms a little too publicly, if you ask me. I mean, we could have fooled men into believing that it was as essential for us to have them as for them. Maybe then they would have tried harder. Instead, we got very independent about it and there's nothing great about doing it alone."

"That's true, but still Brian was the perfect example of that equation in the seventies—the equation where a man's cultural and intellectual awareness directly affected his prowess as a lover. You know, the simpler the man, the better the lover, and the more aware he was, the more angry he became which usually meant that he ended up not being able to make love anymore or worse, didn't want to."

"So what you're really saying is that doing it with Brian was like doing it alone."

"Maybe, a little."

"Then after all of that, there's still no changing the fact that *they* call the shots—I mean biologically, of course." Quincy laughs. "Which is probably why a man invented the vibrator."

"Well, if he did, it certainly helped to change things in the eighties."

"I guess most of our anger is gone now, compared to how we once were in the sixties and seventies."

"You know, Quince, it's not that Avi is any kind of perfect example of the man of the eighties, either; it's more like I am."

"How?"

"Well, biology aside, women will admit that the physical isn't always everything, unless they choose it to be."

"Is it always perfect with Avi?"

"No," I answer honestly. "But I love him, and that makes it perfect, and I'm so grateful that I'm not responsible that life goes on. I wouldn't want that burden."

Quincy is silent for a few moments.

"I have to tell you something," she finally says. "And I feel so stupid about it."

"What, Quince?"

"I never did the mirror thing," she says shyly. "I never really cared about examining myself in the mirror. I was just never interested."

I remember the mirror, proof to ourselves in the seventies that we were beautiful and desirable and totally aware of our inner beings. Suddenly I understood the difference. Even though Brian Flaherty was the first man in my life to make me feel that special way, it took years before I became totally aware of my inner being, mirror or no mirror.

"You asked me something before, Quincy," I say, "about the difference in my feelings for Brian and Avi."

"And now you know?"

"Yes. Brian made me aware of the inside, the place where that mirror was supposed to help us see. And Avi made me aware of everything else, something no mirror could ever do."

Quincy studied me thoughtfully. "Do you think it's possible that you're really in love with this man?"

"I think it's very possible."

o

The crowd at Lucky's Four Leaf Clover Tavern in Maspeth, Queens, had dispersed by the time Brian paid the check.

"I've got to make a quick phone call before we leave," I said.

"You can do it from my house, Maggie. I have a phone."

"No, it's better if I do it from a booth in case I speak

for more than three minutes—it's better if the time actually runs out.''

Brian looked at me admiringly, because, as a detective, he understood this kind of subtlety—even if he chose not to address the fact that I was married. But that really made no difference to Brian, since the pleasure of the flesh weren't sins in his repertoire of Catholic dogma—unless of course those pleasures included child molestation, sodomy, or rape. And then it was Brian the detective, not Brian the Catholic, who would right the wrong. Excusing myself, I walked to the back of the bar, where the telephone booth was wedged between the men's and women's rooms.

I dialed my home phone number and let it ring seven times before remembering that it was Tuesday—the night that Denny Flaherty worked late at Seaman's discount furniture warehouse and also the night that Eric Ornstein stayed at his office to catch up on the mounds of paperwork that had accumulated over the previous week. Hanging up, I redialed Eric's office number and waited while Mrs. Pierce, Eric's secretary with the nasal voice, finished her little speech.

"Mr. Ornstein junior's office. How may I help you?"

"Hello, Mrs. Pierce," I said. "May I speak to Eric, please?"

"Who should I say is calling?" she responded predictably.

The year was 1976, and I had been married to Eric Ornstein since 1969—seven years—which meant that Mrs. Pierce had been hearing my voice on the telephone, in person, and even on the air for a sufficient amount of time to recognize it, if she chose to. But she apparently chose not to, because she never seemed to know who I was when I called.

I could just picture Mrs. Pierce—her dyed orange hair twisted into a circle that sat on top of her small head, her overly made up face, scarlet fingernails, and spindly legs encased in black stockings with seams—getting great pleasure out of making me say my name.

"It's Maggie, Mrs. Pierce."

She always reminded me of a wily French cashier

perched on a stool in a Parisian *tabac,* counting French franc notes with the aid of a rubber thimble on the index finger of her right hand. Mrs. Pierce, however, didn't wear a rubber thimble, nor was she a wily French cashier. Rather, she was a secretary from the old school, one of the few left who actually took stenography and who still wore those plastic arm shields to protect the sleeves of her many bright green and blue synthetic dresses while she flipped through the wads of customer buy/sell orders that always sat in neat piles on her desk next to the purple lipstick-stained cigarette that burned down in the amber-colored ashtray.

Mrs. Pierce was always adorned with blue or green stones, depending upon the color of her dress, which was usually caught at her thin waist by a wide black patent-leather belt. Earrings, bracelets, rings, and necklaces dripped from Mrs. Pierce's large earlobes, bony arms, skinny fingers, and scrawny neck—those stones a tribute to the late Mr. Pierce, who had been in the semiprecious-gemstone business until his untimely death at the age of fifty-six. Eric Ornstein had inherited Mrs. Pierce from Harry Ornstein, when, it was rumored, the recently widowed Mrs. Pierce went on an active campaign for a new husband, and Harry got scared.

"Mr. Ornstein junior is on another call," she replied icily. "Can you hold?"

I contemplated explaining that I couldn't hold because I was too anxious to hold onto something else—something just as big and just as hard as the telephone receiver but something far more rewarding.

"Actually, Mrs. Pierce," I said sweetly, "I'm in a pay phone, in the middle of a breaking story, and I just wanted to tell Eric that I probably would be late—maybe as late as eleven o'clock." Naturally, I didn't add that I would certainly be home when Seaman's discount furniture warehouse closed and Denny Flaherty returned to the Flaherty's two-family house in Maspeth, Queens.

The concrete walk leading to the semiattached red-brick house was bordered by a neat row of plastic tulips. As I followed Brian toward the door, I thought I saw one of the lace curtains that covered a ground-floor window part slightly and a white-haired head peek between the folds of fabric.

"Is your mother at home?" I asked.

"Yeah; Mom's always home, unless she's at church or playing bingo on Monday nights."

Of course; how stupid of me; just like my mother. Only it wasn't quite like that, since my mother would have been quite surprised to know that her younger daughter was about to enter one of those funny houses that she only passed on her way to the airport. Actually, Mother would have been even more surprised to know that one of the owners of one of those funny houses was about to enter her younger daughter. Surprised was probably not an appropriate word; flabbergasted, perhaps shocked would even be more apt.

Brian unlocked the door and stepped politely aside. I walked ahead of him, grasping the oak wood railing as I climbed up the thirteen black-and-brown-checkered carpeted steps, all the while feeling Brian's hand on what had already been determined was Maggie's great ass. However, this time, instead of suggesting that Brian examine my left-side profile, I walked slowly, swaying my hips seductively until I had mounted the very last step and stepped inside the living room.

A giant aquarium, with blue and green lights and a miniature statue of Neptune lying at the bottom of the red and blue pebbled tank, lined one entire wall. Exotic colored fish of varying sizes swam lazily in the bubbling water. On the other wall was a brown velour sectional sofa with a zebra striped Barcalounger on one side and a carved Spanish lamp table on the other. Separating the living room from the dining area was an enormous television set attached to a stereo system that flashed colored lights in time to the beat of the music. On the green walls were an assortment of posters which gave the social, cultural and political views of the Flaherty brothers. One poster was that of a motorcycle policeman standing next to his bike—backdropped by an enormous American flag—and pointing his index finger, "NYPD WANTS YOU," it read. Next to it was another poster of a long-haired dazed looking man leaning against an overflowing garbage can in front of a run-down tenement. "DOPE IS FOR DOPES" was the caption. And, scattered throughout the entire room were life-sized photographs of Playboy bunnies representing every month of the year. On this particular visit to Brian Flaherty's house, I never got to see the other rooms, except for the bathroom, because before I could even politely decline the beer that was offered to me, Brian Flaherty was gently removing my clothes.

And he didn't just kiss, he chewed, nibbled, bit, devoured and slurped until my attention was only focused on my lips. There was no other part of my body. I was all mouth until Brian decided to concentrate on my breasts. And he didn't just touch, he caressed, sucked, fondled, stroked, and licked until my attention was only focused on my chest. There was no other part of my body. I was all breasts until Brian decided to slip inside of me with that hard-as-a-rock part of him that I had discovered while dancing to "Jeremiah is a bullfrog." And while Brian was exceptionally oral, he was not particularly verbal. It was only when I registered surprise that he was already inside me, by murmuring in a muffled voice, "Brian, you didn't even reach down and put it in; it just went in all by itself," did he utter the first and last sentence he would utter during the entire three hours I spent with him on that plush green nylon shag carpet in his living room. "Guys," Brian said, "who have to put it in have no business being there." I thought of Eric Ornstein and silently agreed with him.

It kept going on and on until, somewhere in the deep recesses of my mind, and while I was still lying underneath the taut and muscular body of Brian Flaherty, a man I had just met several hours earlier, I became vaguely aware of a pain somewhere near my coccyx as well as on my chin. Each time, however, that I was on the verge of asking Brian to identify the discomfort, my body shuddered in response to his and caused me to think about something else, something in the deep recesses of my body.

Brian Flaherty qualified for a new subcategory, one that fell directly underneath "hard as a rock," because he not only was hard as a rock on the dance floor and in

the bed, but remained hard as a rock even after he had
an orgasm. He never even bothered to take it out, merely
stopped moving for several minutes, his head buried in
my neck, arms wrapped tightly around me, before the
motion would simply begin all over again. It was during
one of those brief respites, however, that I did manage
to call his attention to my chin, since my coccyx was
more difficult to see.

"You've got a burn from my beard," he said matter-
of-factly. "I guess I should've shaved."

And then he slipped out of me, allowing me to stand
on wobbly legs.

"Gee, Maggie," he said, "you've got a burn from the
carpet. You're really a mess."

When I managed to hobble into the only other room I
would see that night, which was the green-and-pink-tiled
bathroom, I climbed up onto the sink and noticed a shiny
festering round wound on my chin. Turning my aching
body around, I saw another shiny festering round wound
on the base of my spine—a less visible battle scar from
three unrelenting hours of what could only be described
as the best unconnected sexual activity I had ever had in
my entire life. It was clear that time would heal my
wounds, but it would surely never dim the memory of
what had happened there that night.

I walked back to the living room in the same naked
state I had been in from practically the moment I arrived
in Maspeth. When my eyes finally adjusted to the dark-
ness, I scanned the floor for where I thought I had left
Brian, somewhere between the zebra-striped Barcalounger and the gurgling aquarium. He was nowhere to be
found. Suddenly two figures appeared, one clothed and
one unclothed, both holding cans of beer and coming out
of what I could only assume was the kitchen. I stood
perfectly still, barely breathing and stark naked, the out-
line of my body casting a large shadow on the wall right
between Miss June and Miss November. I clamped my
hand over my mouth, dropped it in an effort to shield my
breasts, and exclaimed, "Oh, Mary, Mother of God."

Now, why I chose to call upon the Blessed Virgin at
that particular moment could only be explained by the

phenomenon that Irish Catholic sperm was so potent that it actually penetrated the speech center of my brain.

Brian was next to me then, an arm slung casually around my trembling shoulder. "Say hello to my brother Denny," he said.

I must have mumbled something, an inaudible and embarrassed "Hello," before disengaging myself from Brian's grasp. Stooping down, I gathered up my clothes, which were strewn all over the floor, and made a hasty retreat to the bathroom.

Minutes later I was back, makeup repaired, hair combed, dressed. I sat down next to Brian, who was still unclothed, and listened as Denny described the two sales he had made that night.

"So this guy comes in and without no hassle buys this Early American maple dining room combo, including the hutch, real nice, with high-gloss finish like the kind you see in those houses where the presidents always died, you know the kind."

"Yeah." Brain nodded. "Down in Virginia."

"Yeah, those ones. So he buys that, and then just before I was gonna go, this broad comes in with a toy poodle, white job with polished nails, and buys this French provincial bedroom set."

"The broad or the dog?" Brian was laughing.

"Huh?"

"Which one was the white job with polished nails?"

"Yeah, that's pretty funny," Denny answered, bobbing his head up and down, which was apparently his version of laughing. "The dog. Yeah, funny."

"Brian," I interrupted in a tiny voice, "I think I'd better go home."

"You leavin' so soon?" Denny said, brushing a strand of red hair from his freckled face. "It was really good to meet you, and I bet we'll be seeing each other again."

That was certainly a fair assumption on the part of someone with whom I already shared a peculiar kind of bond.

I smiled. "I'm sure we will, and congratulations on your two sales."

"Yeah, thanks, and if you or your family ever need furniture, think of Seaman's."

"Oh, most definitely," I said, trying to imagine how sensational an Early American dining room combo with hutch would look in Vera's eighteenth-century-French country house.

"Give me a minute, Maggie," Brian said, "and I'll just throw something on." And then he cupped my chin in his hand and added, "Don't put any cream on it; just let it dry up naturally."

I nodded, wondering how many times he had been confronted with a similar problem in his life. That particular piece of knowledge fell into the same area of expertise as those other things Brian just seemed to know about naturally.

We were in the car, speeding across the Fifty-ninth Street Bridge, away from his world and back into mine, when I decided to be completely clear about what the rules were in our little deception.

"I'm married," I said suddenly when he had exited from the ramp.

"I know," he answered, glancing at me. "You already told me that."

"Doesn't it bother you?"

"No; why should it? I'm not doing anything wrong."

It was amazing but perfectly logical.

The nuns taught Brian that acceptance on any level was proof of a profound belief in the Lord, and the Lord worked in mysterious ways. Brian learned that there were only two ways to live on this earth: a right way, which guaranteed a place in heaven after the visuals of life were over, and a wrong way, which promised that the tortured soul would burn in hell, damned for all eternity to nothing but endless reruns of all those visuals. That black-and-white dogma, however, never challenged Brian's intellectual curiosity, nor did it dampen his spirit. He learned that he could bend the rules just enough to have a good time, as long as his good time didn't hurt anybody.

Brian had spent the interminable hours in catechism waiting for the school bell to ring, so he could run over to the vacant lot on Monroe Avenue and whack his cherished worn leather softball with his smooth autographed bat. And when Brian wasn't whacking softballs on Monroe Avenue, he could sometimes be found huddled behind an abandoned building with four or five other boys, whacking something else—aiming it directly at a shiny silver quarter that had been strategically placed several feet in front of the group. Brian invariably won, hitting the mark, and he pocketed the quarter without any fear of divine reprisal. He wasn't hurting anybody, and he believed he could deal with the punitive measures later—much later, if necessary, in another lifetime, if there was one.

Brian was graduated from high school, resisting the pleas of his parents to become a priest and pressing his own dream of becoming a policeman. While he was prepared to accept the right way and the wrong way and never to question those mysterious ways of the Lord, there were just certain things that Brian Flaherty was not willing to give up. So Brian became a cop and transferred that black-and-white dogma to the streets of New York, where everything was really very simple if you played by the rules. If you obeyed the law, you stayed on the outside, worked a nine-to-five job, whacked a few softballs, humped an Italian girl on a Saturday night—no quarter—eventually got married, had a couple of kids, and made sure to save enough money so someday you could retire to the west coast of Florida, where there was hardly any street scum. If you broke the law, you were packed off to jail, and Brian got to do his job.

Brian Flaherty became exceptionally adroit at questioning suspects in a kindly manner, offering them coffee and cigarettes and making them believe that it was totally understandable why they had bludgeoned other human beings to death. Brian would excuse himself politely, however, at a certain point in their conversation and nod to his partner, who would just be entering the cramped interrogation room to continue the questioning, though not quite as kindly as Brian. After a while, but not too long, in case things went too far, Brian would amble back into the room, feign indignation at his partner's obvious lack of sympathy, and without further ado, get a signed confession from a very frightened but grateful prisoner. Not surprisingly, it was precisely because of Brian's highly successful methods that he had been promoted to detective first class just two weeks before his thirtieth birthday, which had been only a month before his meeting Maggie Sommers in the middle of Fifth Avenue that day.

Brian ran his home life just as smoothly as he did his job. Living in that two-family house in Maspeth, right above his widowed mother, he felt he was doing the right thing for himself, his mother, and God. Every morning at six o'clock, Mrs. Flaherty went to mass at Our Lady of Redemption Church, which was located two blocks from the Flaherty house. Sometimes on Sundays, providing Brian wasn't working, he and Denny would accompany their mother to mass and know that they were doing the right thing. And it worked for Brian, made it possible for him to do those other things.

"You can't ever call me at home," I said, as we headed up First Avenue. "You have to call me at the studio. I'm there every morning between nine and ten, before I get sent out on assignment."

"Deal," he said, squeezing my hand. "But if you tell me when I can see you again, I won't have to call you this week at all." He grinned.

I felt pleased—relieved that he wanted to see me again—but also terrified that I was officially involved in an extramarital affair. Brian Flaherty was not just for one night.

"Unless you shave," I joked, "I'm never going to see you again. How can I go on the air looking like I just fell on my face?"

And then it occurred to me that I would tell Eric just that if he asked what happened to me.

Brian laughed. "I promise to shave. What about tomorrow?"

We were approaching Seventy-second Street when I realized how imprudent it would be if he dropped me off in front of my apartment building. "Brian," I said, "stop here and I'll take a taxi the rest of the way." He understood immediately and rolled to a stop on the northeast corner of First Avenue and Seventy-second Street.

"Goodbye, Brian," I said softly.

"Goodbye, Maggie," he answered, gently touching my bruised chin. Our eyes met briefly before I opened the door of the car. He knew.

It suddenly struck me as I rode up in the elevator, that my broken shoe was an integral part of my excuse for Eric. I tiptoed noiselessly into the apartment, holding my shoes in one hand while I turned down the dimmer switch in the foyer with the other. The door to the bedroom was ajar and the lights were on. Eric Ornstein was awake. Putting on my broken shoe and its mate, I limped into the room and stood at the foot of the bed. Eric was sitting up, propped against several pillows and totally engrossed in the yellow pad and calculator that were on his lap. He was so preoccupied with scribbling numbers that he didn't even react as I launched into my well-rehearsed story.

"Look what happened to me," I said breathlessly. "I was chasing my crew, who were trying to follow the police because a robbery suspect was—"

"Mmm," Eric said. "I'll be right with you."

I shifted uncomfortably from one foot to the other and waited.

"Finished," he said triumphantly, tossing the pencil down and looking at me. "Now, what happened to you?"

Taking a deep breath, I began again. "I was chasing my crew because they were following the police, going after a robbery suspect, when I fell flat on my face, broke my shoe"—I held it up—"and hurt my chin." I jutted out my chin.

"Where did this happen?" he asked, peering over his glasses.

"In Maspeth," I answered without thinking. I could have kicked myself. Flatbush, Kew Gardens, Harlem— anywhere but Maspeth.

But he wasn't terribly interested anyway, and his answer to me only proved that, as well as verifying that age-old adage that guys who have to put it in have no business being there.

"Put some cream on it," Eric said. "But first come here. I want to show you something."

I sat down and looked at the complicated equations on his yellow pad. "What are you so busy doing at eleven-thirty at night?"

He smiled. "I just charted your monthly menstrual cycle for the month of December. I figured out, based on your last period, the times when you're the most fertile."

"Why?"

He smiled again. "So that we'd be sure to get pregnant next month. And just to make double sure, I found your diaphragm and cut it up into small pieces."

I listened, although I really didn't believe what I was hearing. My only victory was that, unbeknownst to Eric, I had started taking the pill three months earlier. I hadn't wanted to take any chances.

"Based upon my calculations, we have to do it on the twelfth, thirteenth, and fourteenth, and just to be extra sure on the morning of the fifteenth, and then, along with this rectal thermometer"—he reached over on the night table and held it up proudly—"because rectal is more accurate than oral—we should be pregnant by the end of the month. Now lie down so I can see what normal is for you before you start ovulating."

I just looked at him incredulously with my hand clamped over my mouth before I was even able to speak.

"Oh, Mary, Mother of God," I finally exclaimed, because apparently Brian Flaherty's sperm were still sloshing around the speech center of my brain.

o

Quincy and I are sitting in the living room now, our coffee mugs on the glass table.

"The horrible part about you and Eric," she says, lighting a cigarette, "is that you never would have left him—it would have gone on and on."

"That's not true; I would have eventually, when I felt more sure of myself."

"No, I don't think so. You have this facility to separate your professional life from the emotional, and I think being sure of yourself professionally had nothing to do with being afraid of actually leaving a marriage.''

"And what if I had fallen in love with Avi at that time in my life instead of now?"

Quincy thinks for a moment. "You wouldn't have looked at him, or if you had looked at him you would have run away and kept right on running. You were a child in many ways then, and he would have terrified you because he would have expected you to act like a woman.''

"I was a woman," I protest. "I had tremendous responsibility.''

"Yes, professionally you always delivered. But that's not the point. What I'm saying, Maggie, is that staying with Eric then was simple in a way: He didn't expect you to be anything more than a wife and mother. Avi would have expected you to pull a lot more—give a lot more. He would have been much more demanding." She pauses. "Isn't he?''

"Yes," I answer softly. "He certainly is.''

"Could you have gotten away with ignoring him, or being unfaithful, or not discussing feelings and problems?''

"No," I say quietly.

"That's the point.''

"The point is also that I happen to love Avi.''

"I know, but you're a different person now, and what I'm saying is that you wouldn't have dared to love an Avi then." She exhales a fine stream of smoke. "But tell me something: did winning that Emmy make you feel more secure about yourself?''

I shake my head. "Truthfully no, but it did make me a little less frightened about having to face life all alone. I mean, I stopped having visions of my eating a cheese sandwich all alone in some hovel—I didn't have poverty or destitution nightmares.''

Quincy laughs. "It was an amazing chain of events, in a way. It was as if the moment you went off to cover that story, everything just began to happen.''

"It's true, isn't it? It was one thing after another.''

"Well, it certainly helped you to see Brian clearly. Were you scared?"

"Absolutely shitless—but there was something worse that I kept thinking about."

"What?"

"Not doing it and letting someone else win that Emmy. I mean, then it would have been cheese sandwiches in some hovel all over again!"

○

I was sitting in my office in the newsroom that day, a beautiful spring morning in April 1975, trimming a stack of family photographs to fill up a brand-new album. There was no particular assignment for me yet, on what seemed to be a slow news day. People were perhaps feeling too good about the weather to bother robbing banks, burning down buildings, or killing each other—the regular occurrences that filled the time slots on the nightly news broadcasts. And that meant I could leave early and spend more time tonight in Brian Flaherty's bed in Maspeth, Queens. The telephone rang just as those visions danced in my head.

"That you, Mags?" Brian said.

"That's me," I answered brightly.

"Listen, Mags," he began in his monotone detective voice. "I've got a problem. I'm in the middle of this hostage situation up in the Bronx—some crazy's got his wife and two sisters at gunpoint in his apartment."

And being a selfish hedonist, I immediately assumed that Brian was calling to tell me that unless the man released his family by the end of the day, we would not be seeing each other that evening.

"He's got a couple of homemade bombs in the apartment; says they could blow the roof off his building."

I was now definitely prepared for the depressing eventuality of having to spend the evening with Eric Ornstein, listening as he tried to muster up the courage to ask me for a divorce. Lately, it had become even more depressing, as he had developed a new routine—one that had begun shortly after the fateful night when he first introduced me to his rectal thermometer. His presenting me with hypothetical scenarios such as, ''If we were to get divorced, which we never would, of course, but if we did, who do you thing should get the Bukhara rug,'' had resulted in our pretty much disposing of the contents of the living room, kitchen, and bedroom. My guess was that tonight was the night for the dining area, which meant that Eric would undoubtedly pose the most costly hypothetical question of all: ''Do you think the Wedgwood china and Baccarat crystal would lose their value if the sets were divided six and six?'' What was disturbing was that out of this entire hypothetical division of property, I had so far ended up with only six pairs of king-size sheets, including fourteen pillowcases but not including the bed, one waffle and grilled-cheese maker that Eric had once seen advertised on television, a set of kitchen knives that he had also once seen advertised on television, and several Mexican tile trivets that Cara had brought back from Acapulco one year. According to my husband, all that the Sommers family ever tangibly contributed to the marriage were theater tickets, two seats in their box at the Metropolitan Opera, and a pressure cooker, which exploded in Eric's face one Christmas Eve when he tried to steam some corn on the cob. He didn't let me forget that he was really being quite generous, since he'd never been informed prior to our marriage that I would need two root canals.

''The guy's name is Hector Rodriguez, a Vietnam vet and former mental patient. Seems he was working in some kind of outpatient rehab program, welding metal. The foreman was riding him for being late all the time, so he just snapped—ran home and grabbed his wife and two sisters, who were all watching television. He's threatening to kill them and then turn the gun on himself. You know, Mags, the same old story,'' Brian concluded in a tired voice.

The same old story about Vietnam veterans who ended up as outpatients in mental institutions but whose anguish and suffering were somehow never of any interest to the police after they inevitably became involved in the drama. But before I could even comment on the situation or even tell Brian how disappointing it was that we wouldn't be seeing each other that night, he said:

"The real problem I've got is you, Mags."

"Oh, don't worry about me," I said, trying to sound cheerful. "We'll see each other tomorrow."

"That's not the problem," Brian said very slowly. "The problem I've got is that Hector says he'll give himself up only if you go in there and talk to him."

"Me?"

"You."

Just at that moment, Nick Sprig dashed into my office, out of breath and obviously very agitated about something.

"Get off the phone, Maggie," he said excitedly. "I've got to talk to you."

"But," I stammered, "I'm talking to Brian, and it seems there's a—"

"Hang up the phone, Maggie," Nick ordered. "You can talk to Brian later. I've got a hostage situation."

"Oh, you too," I said, not getting it. "So does Brian, and the guy says he'll give himself up if I go in there."

"Wait a minute," Nick said, looking puzzled. "Where's his hostage situation?"

"Brian dear," I said into the telephone, "could you tell me the exact location of your hostage situation?"

Brian recited the address, 510 Morris Avenue, which I repeated to Nick, who looked at me in amazement before snatching the phone out of my hand.

"Brian," Nick said, "what do we do? I just got word."

I was sitting in my office in the newsroom on a beautiful spring day and listening incredulously as two men— one a detective, who also happened to be my lover, and the other my bureau chief, who also happened to be a close friend—discussed what they should do about sending me into a hostage situation where a man was holding his wife and two sisters at gunpoint. Not to mention, of course, that he happened to have several homemade bombs at his disposal that could blow the roof off his apartment building.

"Wait a minute," I said to Nick. "I'd like a word with both of you."

Nick signaled me to keep quiet while he listened intently to Brian, making hurried notes on the back of a photograph of Maggie Sommers when she was twelve years old, in the golden era of her daughterhood. Finally, he handed me the telephone and said, "Here, talk to him, and then meet me in my office. We've got to move quickly." And then he dashed away, much the same way as he had dashed in.

Putting the receiver up to my ear, I said in a very soft voice, "Brian, this is crazy."

"Listen, Mags," he answered, still in his monotone detective voice. "Hector gave me his word that he'd surrender if he just got to tell you his side of the story."

One would have thought that Hector and Brian were old friends, bowling partners, drinking buddies, the way he spoke about him—just two old pals who had known each other simply forever from around the old neighborhood.

"His word," I repeated. "And you believe him?"

"Mags," Brian said, "I have certain doubts, but basically yes, I believe him because he's scared shitless."

"Why me?" I asked Brian.

"Because," he answered in a cheerless voice, "you're a good-looking broad who covers scum in this shithole."

Perhaps there were very valid reasons why we hardly ever talked.

"Brian," I said, holding my breath, "if I were your wife, would you let me go in there?"

He chuckled, and actually emitted the same sound that Ralph Kramden used on *The Honeymooners* when he threatened Alice with the moon. "Mags," he said, "if you were my wife, I wouldn't let you be doing this kind of job. You'd be a secretary or a manicurist or maybe a hatcheck girl at a good restaurant in the city."

The overwhelming sadness that enveloped me could only be compared to a man's organ going limp at the moment of penetration, withered into a pathetic mass of wrinkled flesh. Limp with the tragic realization that I was talking to a total stranger, I began to wonder why I had been looking to Brian as the man who would save me from tumbling into a solitary void after Eric Ornstein finally mustered up the courage to ask me for a divorce. Hector Rodriguez had suddenly become more than just a faceless Vietnam veteran who was holding three people hostage somewhere in the South Bronx. Hector was a catalyst. It was as if our futures were inextricably intertwined.

"Brian," I said softly, hanging on to the last shred. "Do you love me?"

"Maggie," he began impatiently, "you're married. I love you like a married woman."

"And if I weren't married," I persisted. "Would you love me then?"

"Listen, Maggie," he replied, sighing, "I've got a hostage situation. Could we talk about this later?"

I wanted to tell him that there would be no later for us, except perhaps several hours of uninterrupted fucking. My stupidity was to have expected that the New York City Police Department would rescue me from my anguish and despair when one of their first-class detectives couldn't even comprehend the anguish and despair of someone named Hector Rodriguez, someone he considered street scum. So joining Hector at his apartment didn't seem like such a bad idea after all. In fact, it seemed more logical than anything else at the moment.

"Maggie, I've got to run," Brian finally said. "I'll call Sprig back in thirty minutes to find out your decision."

I glanced down again at the photograph of Maggie Sommers in the twelfth year of her life and lamented the fact that I never appreciated that golden era of her daughterhood and the simplicity that accompanied it before it all ended so abruptly. The trauma of the particular day the photograph was taken was the reason my face looked so sullen, staring into the camera. I had been summoned out of English class by my headmistress just as my teacher, Miss Hadley, was about to begin an analysis of *The Scarlet Letter*. Vera was waiting for me, sitting primly on a chintz-covered chair in the parent's lounge. Nodding discreetly to the imposing and fearsome Miss Harkness, she took my hand and led me outside onto the lush green lawn that served as the girl's hockey field—one of the main attractions of the suburban private school.

"There was blood in your bed this morning," she stated, not wasting time on amenities.

The first thought that flashed through my mind was that I was being accused of murder. "Why me and not Cara?" I managed to stammer. "We both left at the same time this morning."

"Because," Vera answered, thrusting a neatly wrapped white paper package into my trembling hand, "you bled all over your sheets."

"How do you know it was me?" I wailed. "Why is everything always my fault?"

Tears streamed down my cheeks as Vera sucked in her upper lip and looked at me with an exasperated expression on her perfectly made up face. "You started menstruating today, and you'll be doing it every month for the next forty years."

Sentenced for life. Doomed. Condemned. My introduction into womanhood had transpired quite unceremoniously that day on the girls' hockey field. What exactly was happening to my body on the day Miss Hadley gave the analysis of *The Scarlet Letter*? I watched Vera flee, teetering on her high-heeled Ferragamo shoes—beyond the hockey field, past the red brick science building, near the white stucco cottages that housed the faculty, until she disappeared into a yellow checker cab that had been waiting for her at the bottom of the hill. "Keep your meter running, cabbie, I just have to pop in for a minute and tell my younger daughter about the blood on her sheets."

I stood there, clutching the neatly wrapped white package while my classmates began milling around near the goalpost, waiting to pose for the class picture. Running to the girls' room, I stumbled into a stall, unwrapped the bundle, and discovered three sanitary napkins and one pale-pink flowered elastic belt from which peculiar metal fasteners were suspended. It took only five minutes to figure it all out, suppressing a horrified scream at the sight of the blood smeared on my inner thighs as well as all over my white cotton underpants. It was only after I had recovered from the shock that I came to the sorrowful conclusion that something had changed drastically in my life, which accounted for my face looking so sullen in the photograph.

I didn't know what it was all about then any more than I knew what it was all about on that beautiful spring day when a Vietnam veteran grabbed three people and held them hostage in his apartment in the South Bronx, the day that Brian Flaherty turned out not to be my salvation. The only thing I did know was that it was the last time I would make the fatal error—God, how I'd miss Brian's taut and muscular body with his hard-as-a-rock organ throbbing inside of me—of believing that if my cunt was filled with Irish whimsy, my head didn't need to be filled with Jewish savvy. It was the last time that I would ever assume that just because a man didn't have a long history of Jewish neurosis, which dated back to sometime before the burning bush—and the symbolism didn't escape me— that he still didn't have certain built-in prejudices that dated back to sometime before the potato famine.

Not that Jewish automatically implied brilliant while Catholic automatically implied dull. Eric Ornstein would always dismiss all of that intellectual rhetoric as a big waste of time, claiming that everybody would be "a helluva lot happier if they just stopped reading all that garbage and followed their natural instincts," which brought me to Eric's list of "suitable" jobs for women: motherhood. Brian, on the other hand, would dismiss all that intellectual rhetoric, calling it gobbledygook, as a big waste of time, claiming that everybody would be "a helluva lot happier if they just stopped reading all that garbage and just did *it.*" Easy for him to say. Yet that did not necessarily mean that I could have lived in connubial bliss with a man who talked only about baseball, the latest in handcuffs, or that new stereo system he coveted, which played up to eight cassettes at a time without his having to get up—or pull out—to change tapes. However, it also did not necessarily mean that I could have spent the rest of my life with Eric Ornstein, who made love like a supersonic train speeding between Paris and Geneva without even stopping at Dijon for a whiff of the mustard.

As I contemplated the possibility of spending the last moments of my life with Hector Rodriguez, I realized that spending them with Eric Ornstein in a horizontal position or with Brian Flaherty in a vertical position was an equally horrendous fate. And while I still blamed Vera and Alan for convincing me that Eric was the answer, I blamed myself—God, how I'd miss Brian's expert tongue probing the inside of my body—for never posing certain questions that would have made me see that Brian wasn't right, either. The only irony was that Eric wanted Maggie Sommers single while Brian wanted her married, and Maggie—fifteen years after that first drop of blood appeared on those sheets—still didn't really understand what it was all about anyway.

Walking slowly through the newsroom toward Nick Sprig's office, I had already decided to accept Hector Rodriguez's invitation to join him in his apartment at 510 Morris Avenue. There was really no choice, for he had suddenly become an integral part of the only element in my life that belonged to me—my job.

"Nick," I said, sitting down, "what do you think?"

"I think," he answered, his black eyes sparkling, "that you could win an Emmy for this."

"Terrific," I answered. "But what about my chances of getting out alive?"

"That's what we're going to talk about," Nick said seriously. "Brian told me there's a ninety percent chance that the guy is on the level—he'll surrender if you go in."

"Terrific," I said again. "But we both know about statistics. If he surrenders it's one hundred percent, and if he doesn't it's zero."

"Look, Maggie, we don't have much time, because the guy gave the cops one hour before he blows everyone away."

Nick must have temporarily lost his mind. "Are we talking about the same old Mr. Ninety Percent Reliable?" I asked, shocked.

He looked at me sheepishly. "Maggie, whatever you

decide to do is fine with me. I'm right behind you, and I'll even go in with you. I won't leave you alone.''

Looking at Nick Sprig, I wondered why all the really wonderful men were either married or involved with other really wonderful men.

"Let's go," I said, standing. "Call Brian while I call Eric.''

"Why the hell are you calling him?''

"Because," I answered jokingly, "Eric would never forgive me if I got killed without telling him where the laundry ticket was for his shirts.''

"Be serious, Maggie," Nick said earnestly. "Why are you calling Eric?''

"I guess," I answered truthfully, "that I want him to worry about me—just a little.''

I dialed Eric's private number, because I was in no mood to pass through Mrs. Pierce, who had she been a Catholic, would have surely run out to light a candle to ensure that the bullet would pass right between my eyes in that apartment in the South Bronx.

I counted the rings . . . three, four, five, and finally, on the sixth ring, he answered breathlessly. "Eric Ornstein here.''

"Eric, am I disturbing you?''

"Yes. Gold's going to hell and I'm up to my ass. What's going on?''

Explaining the whole story and hanging on only twice, while he did something with yen and then something else with deutsche marks, I finished by stating dramatically that Hector had given the police a one-hour deadline before he would kill everybody in the apartment, including himself. Silence. There was no doubt in my mind that Eric was rendered speechless because he was so overwhelmed with remorse for all the awful things he ever did to me. He was probably wondering how he could make everything better—perhaps beginning with an equitable distribution of the contents of our apartment. Or maybe, just possibly, he was groping for the right words that would put our marriage back on track, enable us to start anew—anything that would save me from having to face life alone since Brian Flaherty had ceased being a viable alternative.

"Maggie," he finally said.

"Yes, Eric?" I answered, my voice filled with hope.

"What do I do if something happens to you?"

"What do you mean?"

"Well it's pretty goddamn selfish of you to do things and not even consider how a negative outcome might affect my life."

"Eric, I don't—"

"Like for example, where's the grocery store, number one, and number two, where am I supposed to pick up my laundry?"

"The ticket for your shirts is in the second drawer in the kitchen, near the stove." Perhaps I suspected all along what had finally happened: my marriage was over.

As I gathered up my things for the trip to the South Bronx, I began to play a deadly little game with myself. Words like *free, kaput, alone, curtains,* popped into my head. As I rode down in the elevator, that deadly little word game became a deadly little word-association game.

Curtains—No place to live. No home—Not a nickel to my name. Not a single nickel—Divorced. Divorced—Never remarried. Unmarried—Bag lady. Bag lady—Hector Rodriguez.

As the van crawled through heavy crosstown traffic, Nick glanced over at me, interpreting my silence and the beads of perspiration on my upper lip as apprehension about going into the middle of a hostage situation. "Don't worry, Maggie," he said reassuringly. "I'll be right with you." The truth of the matter was that Hector Rodriguez was the least of my problems at that moment, because I was hit by the realization that I had neither credit cards, bank account, nor charge plates—not to mention that my entire net worth was tucked away in my wallet, right in my purse, and was somewhere in the neighborhood of $27.50.

The van turned onto the East River Drive, weaving in and out of lanes until it finally reached Willis Avenue and headed toward Morris Avenue. As we passed several burned-out tenements, Nick said, "Take a right at the next street.'' The driver, a man with a death-defying attitude, swerved the car to the right. ''Roger, chief,'' he quipped. When the van stopped for a light beside a group of addicts who lay sprawled in the gutter, I decided that if everything went according to plan and my head wasn't blown off, I would make love to Brian tonight for the last time before going home and demanding that Eric give me back my money that had been deposited into his checking account for the past four years. My mood was definitely grim as the van finally rolled to a stop at the corner of Morris Avenue and 148th Street. Several police cars were parked lengthwise in the middle of the street as a kind of barricade. Dick Carlson, the cameraman, shoved his enormous shoulders through the open window of the van and showed the police our credentials. The cars were hastily moved to allow us through. The scene resembled a battlefield, with clusters of curious spectators—or blood-thirsty civilians, as Brian always called them—gathered together near an ambulance, three fire trucks, two red emergency rescue wagons, and four unmarked police sedans with portable red lights flashing on their roofs.

Nick helped me down onto the curb after we pulled up next to one of the police cars. Standing in the street near Nick and a new sound man I had never seen before, I became aware that several people in the crowd were calling me.

''Hey Maggie, you goin' in there?'' ''Maggie, gimme your autograph.''

''Welcome to Morris Avenue Maggie, this is no man's land.''

The sound man, a fatally beautiful boy with long eyelashes that swept over his tanned cheeks, poked me gently in the ribs. ''Flash 'em a smile, a little leg, maybe.'' He grinned. ''This could be the high point of their lives.''

Obediently I waved. But I couldn't take my eyes off him, his perfect features, his graceful movements. ''You must be new, I've never seen you before.''

He brushed something from my cheek. ''No, I'm on loan from network—I usually work overseas.''

''What was on my face?''

"Just a speck of dirt."

"Thanks." I pause, "What's your name?"

"Joe Valeri." I smiled. "Hi, I'm Maggie."

He just smiled back.

Two plainclothes detectives approached, walkie-talkies in their hands. "The subject has been informed that Maggie Sommers will be going in," one of them said.

"OK. I want the crew to stay put—don't move," Nick said as he followed the detectives over to a row of police cars that were strategically positioned in front of the building.

"Did you ever notice how real people become subjects or perpetrators to the police as soon as something happens?" Joe observed.

"They cease being human," I agreed.

Before we could say anything else, Nick motioned to us. "Looks like it's a roll," Joe said, sprinting toward him.

There were approximately ten police cars in all, each with two policemen wearing bulletproof vests and crouched behind the open door of their vehicle. The high-powered rifles they held were aimed directly at the entrance to 510 Morris Avenue. Brian was there, standing with his hands on his hips, his jacket off and his tie loosened, while he consulted with two police officials. His muscles rippled against the thin fabric of his blue shirt, perspiration stains making large circles on his back and under his arms, as he stooped down to pick up a clipboard.

"He's your guy," Joe said with a smile.

I feigned innocence. "What do you mean?"

"I mean"—he laughed—"put your tongue back in your mouth."

I was stunned by Valeri's bluntness, unable to respond. But then Nick rushed over to give us our instructions.

Joe followed Dick, who was already panning the entire scene with his minicam. I studied Joe for a few moments, and knew somehow that if we both survived this latest lunacy, we were going to be very special friends. Just as I was about to walk over to Nick to see if he needed me for the opening segment, Brian spotted me.

"Mags," he said, "are you all right?"

"I'm fine," I answered, gazing into his incredible blue eyes and missing him already.

"Hector is waiting for you. Everything's set."

"Great," I lied, wishing we were in his bed in Maspeth, Queens, right that minute—one last time—instead of wasting precious hours here.

Nick was signaling the crew. "Save the rest of the tape," he yelled, before calling out to Brian: "Wait, I want to talk to you."

"What's up?"

"I want to go in with Maggie."

"I'm not sure he'll agree," Brian answered.

While they were discussing the probability of Hector Rodriguez's allowing Nick Sprig into his apartment, Joe touched my arm, calling my attention to the roof of 510 Morris Avenue as well as to the roofs of the adjoining buildings. SWAT teams were standing at the ready position, their legs spread apart, their weapons poised, obviously waiting for instructions to fire. "Poor bastard," Joe said quietly.

"I don't know, Sprig," Brian was saying. "The deal was that Maggie goes in alone."

"I don't want her going in alone, and what's the point of the whole thing if my crew can't go in to film it?"

Brian headed over to the communications table that had been set up in the middle of the street, near the battery of police cars that served as the front line of this bizarre battlefield. "I'll ask him," Brian called to us.

While he was speaking to Hector, who was barricaded up in his apartment, I couldn't help but be amazed at how those intricate communication lines had been set up in a matter of hours, when it took days to get a repairman out to a private home to fix something as mundane as a faulty electrical outlet.

"Look at that," Joe remarked, pointing to the equipment. "I've had a broken phone for three days and the repairman isn't coming out till tomorrow."

"I was thinking the same thing," I answered.

"Why do you wear a wedding band?" Joe asked suddenly.

"Because I'm married."

"You don't look married."

"I don't feel married, but that's another story." I smiled.

"Enter the poor man's Paul Newman. Right?" Joe glanced over at Brian. "He's not for you, kid."

Nick was signaling me. "I want you to do a stand-up with Brian," he interrupted, "describing the whole scene for the viewers—you know, what Hector wants, what you're going to do, the whole schmear."

I nodded, still thinking about what Joe had said.

"And fix your face," Nick added. "Comb your hair so you look sensational."

As I walked toward the van, the shouts of the curious spectators began again.

"Hey, Maggie, you single?"

Waving, I thought to myself, Soon; very soon.

"Smile, Maggie. You afraid of Puerto Ricans?"

Smiling, I thought to myself, Not Puerto Ricans; only Jewish stockbrokers who take my money.

And then, just as I was climbing inside the van to fix my face and comb my hair, one idiot in the crowd began screaming, "Jump, Hector, jump," until the entire crowd was chanting, "Jump, Hector, jump," which provided the missing element needed to turn the event into a veritable carnival.

The crew was waiting for my stand-up to begin, 510 Morris Avenue looming in the background, and getting increasingly anxious with every passing second. Brian was oblivious to everything, engaged in a heated discussion with Nick, and Nick was visibly concerned with organizing the crew so the coverage of this spectacle could proceed without further incident.

"How about thirty minutes after Maggie goes in? Then I go in with the crew. Fair?"

"I don't know. He needs time to talk to her. I don't want to make him nervous, make him feel like he's being rushed or pushed. I want those women out alive."

"How the hell much time does he need?" Nick exploded. "Thirty minutes is long enough for Maggie to be in there alone with him."

"Look," Brian said, "my only concern are those three women."

"Four," Nick corrected him. "Don't forget about Maggie."

Brian was clearly agitated. "Don't get cute, Sprig. I didn't forget."

"So do I get to go in there after thirty minutes?"

"Yeah, yeah, but I want you out as fast as possible after that. The agreement is that he releases those three broads after Maggie goes in—clear? If not, Sprig, I'm going to order backup."

"What the hell does that mean?"

"It means," Brian shouted, "that you'd better not annoy him with your lights and cameras or there's going to be a very big boom in there."

Nick backed off slightly, enough so they were no longer nose to nose. Brian just continued to glare at him, except when he turned to spit on the sidewalk.

"Shit," Nick said, shaking his head, "this is just great. Now I've got to worry about the cops too." He looked directly at me. "Maggie, what do you think? Are you willing to risk it alone in there for thirty minutes?"

Brian was next to me then, his arm around my shoulder. "Don't be so dramatic, Sprig, she's not going to risk anything."

Nick shot him a disgusted look. "He really gives a shit about you kid, really cares."

Brian dropped his arm from around my shoulder. "Cut the crap, Sprig, I've got no time for this bullshit."

"Well, I've got all the time in the world to make sure Maggie's going to be safe." He touched my face gently, "What do you think? I want you to be totally sure and comfortable with this." Brian was watching me intently but I was hardly paying attention. "Sure," I answered distractedly, "it'll be fine."

Nick was organizing the crew now, signaling them to take their positions for the stand-up in front of the building. "Move in closer to Brian," Nick ordered me.

"Give me a sec, huh," Brian responded, "I've got to give one of my men a message from Hector."

While Brian was conferring with a patrolman, an obvious novice who looked even more frightened than we did, Joe Valeri wandered over to me.

"Are you scared?" he asked.

I thought about it for a second. "It's strange but I know that I'm going to be all right."

He smiled. "No, it's not strange, it's gut feeling, I've got it all the time when I'm overseas doing a story."

I studied him a moment. "What do you mean?"

"I cover a lot of action stuff—wars, riots, revolutions, you know, the kind of thing network runs as the lead-in story. And I always rely on my gut feeling right before I go in. If I feel confident, it always turns out all right. If not, then . . ." he paused and shrugged.

"Then what?"

"Then it's over, I guess."

"Yes, but how do you know? I mean, would you refuse . . ." I didn't finish my sentence because Nick and the others were laughing.

"And while you're at it, Brian," Nick was saying, "my wife needs a loaf of bread and a container of milk."

"Very funny, Sprig," Brian said, before turning back to the patrolman. "And one regular coffee and a cream soda. Got that?"

The patrolman nodded.

"OK, now, one hot dog, heavy on the sauerkraut, one ham and cheese on a hero, one tunafish on rye with a slice of tomato, and a pastrami on white, mayo and a large bag of Dorita chips."

"Hey, wait a minute," Nick called out as the patrolman started down the street. "If NYPD's paying, then Maggie should get lunch too."

"Hold it!" Brian yelled to the patrolman. "Maggie?"

It was becoming absurd. "I'm not really hungry," I began but Joe interrupted, "Get a sandwich. You'll want one if everyone else is eating."

"OK. I'll have a BLT on wholewheat."

"Anything to drink?" the patrolman asked.

"Coffee."

"How do you take it?"

"Regular," Brian answered for me.

Joe gave me a peculiar look before he turned away to manage the sound boom.

Brian had already donned his jacket and was running a comb through his hair.

"Ready?" Nick asked everyone. "Let's roll."

"Detective Flaherty," I began, "what's going on here?"

Flaherty cleared his throat. "We have a hostage situation here," he droned. "One Hector Rodriguez is holding his wife and two sisters at gunpoint in that apartment building." Brian turned, pointing to 510 Morris Avenue, as Dick panned the building with the camera.

"When did all this begin?"

"It began at precisely ten-twenty this morning, when we received a telephone call from the perpetrator, who informed us that he intended to kill his wife and two sisters and then turn the gun on himself."

"Did he explain why?"

"Yes, he did, but I'm not at liberty to say."

"Detective Flaherty," I said, glancing briefly at Valeri, "it is now twelve-ten. What's changed in the past two hours?"

"What's changed is this," Flaherty answered, running his tongue across his top lip. "The subject, one Hector Rodriguez, requested that you go in there and talk to him. He wants a chance to explain his grievances to you before he surrenders."

"Let me get this straight, Detective Flaherty," I repeated, for the benefit of any viewer who might have tuned in late. "There's a man up there"—I pointed to the building—"who's holding three people hostage and claims he'll surrender only if I go in and talk to him. Is that correct?"

"That is correct," Flaherty said.

"Well, Detective Flaherty," I answered, with just the right amount of drama, "let's go."

And away we go, Alice—to the moon, because he sounded exactly the same during the interview as he always sounded, only suddenly it bothered me.

Dick followed us, holding the minicam, while Joe leaped ahead, tilting the sound boom toward the entrance. Brian, the blond hair glistening on his thick forearms, held my elbow as he escorted me up to the entrance of 510 Morris Avenue. I waited as the frightened young patrolman handed me two brown paper bags—the coffee and sandwiches—before I walked through the door and began the climb up the four flights of stairs to the Rodriguez apartment.

The name was written crudely in pencil on a white piece of paper and pasted directly underneath the peephole: Apartment number 40 RODRIGUEZ. Balancing the two bags of lunch carefully on my knee, I knocked lightly.

"Who's there?" a man's voice yelled.

"It's Maggie Sommers, ABN News," I answered, sounding not unlike the Avon lady.

Suddenly a woman started to wail, another female voice began to scream, and a third launched into a stream of unintelligible Spanish.

"How do you know you're alone?" the man shouted above the din.

"I know I'm alone," I answered calmly. "What you mean is how do *you* know I'm alone?"

"No," he screamed hysterically. "That's what I said."

"No," I started to answer automatically. "What you said was—"

"I ain't alone," the man screeched. "I know I ain't alone."

One of the brown paper bags began to leak hot coffee on my knee. "Hector," I said, assuming the man was Hector, "I'm alone and we made a deal. Now why don't you let me inside, because I've got your lunch."

The door opened and a terrified and unshaven man about thirty-five years old stood before me. He was wearing a torn pair of baggy brown pants, no shirt, and had an amazing collection of gold chains and medallions hanging around his scrawny neck. Brushing his shoulder-length black hair out of his eyes with one shaking hand, complete with dragonlike curved fingernails, he motioned me inside with what appeared to be an awfully big gun. Pretending that I didn't even notice his weapon, which he seemed to enjoy brandishing around, I walked directly over to a table covered with stained blue oilcloth. There were two women cowering in a corner, their faces streaked with tears, and another woman sprawled languidly next to them on the floor.

"Sandwiches and drinks for everybody," I tried to say gaily, emptying the brown paper bags.

One of the women was fearsome-looking, weighing at least two hundred pounds, the other was anorexic, with a mustache and heavy black eyebrows, and the third woman, who was now standing up, was vulgar and bandy-legged, with hair dyed an incredible red. Unclipping one rhinestone barrette, she fluffed her hair so that it fell over one eye.

Pictures of Jesus Christ in various pious poses, performing some of the better-known miracles of his illustrious career, were plastered all over the light-green walls. Smiling at the sexpot, who was leaning against a huge television set on an ersatz wood stand, I casually appraised the other contents of the apartment. Two overstuffed and torn sofas, one broken rocking chair, and two white tables with photographs of John Kennedy, Robert Kennedy, Martin Luther King, and what appeared to be the entire Rodriguez clan, on a picnic somewhere near an amusement park. And then I noticed, while putting the lunch neatly on the table, the three shoe boxes on the floor near an open window. They were stuffed with twisted bronze wires, white putty, and about eighteen sticks of dynamite.

"Don't try anything funny," Hector said nervously, pacing up and down the room and waving the gun wildly around his head. He spoke with a slight lisp and picked up a stutter as he became more agitated.

The two women on the floor began whispering to each other.

"Shut up," Hector yelled, whirling around.

Their instant reaction was to begin wailing and screaming again, until the redhead, who was obviously the ringleader of the trio, said something in Spanish. They were immediately still. Turning to me, she asked, "Didja bring my Doritos?"

"Actually," I replied, peering into the now empty brown bags, "they must have forgotten them."

"*Puta,*" she muttered under her breath.

I ignored her and turned to Hector. "Put that gun away, Hector," I said, "or I'm not going to serve lunch."

My words were vaguely reminiscent of Vera Sommers on those sunny afternoons near the pool: "Put that dirty stick away and wash your hands, or there'll be no lunch."

Hector, unbelievably, put down the gun on one of the overstuffed and torn sofas and obediently sat down at the table. Turning to the two women on the floor, I asked, "Don't you want some lunch?"

They glanced at each other fearfully, then at Hector, until the obese one, at the mere mention of food, raised herself on her enormous legs and waddled over to the table. The skinny one was still unsure, as she looked at the redhead sexpot for a sign that it would be prudent to join us.

The redhead looked at me. "My name's Estella," she said suddenly. "I'm his wife."

"How do you do, Estella," I answered. "Why don't you tell your friend to come to the table?"

"She ain't my friend," Mrs. Charm School replied. "She's his sister."

"Well, whatever—friend, sister—why don't you tell her it's all right to get up?"

Estella, in a manner worthy of a debutante, jerked her thumb in the direction of the table and screamed, "Get your ass over here, bitch!"

Hector's sister scampered over to the table faster than anyone could say "Luncheon is served."

"Now," I said cheerfully, "who gets the hot dog, extra sauerkraut?"

Had I known that one innocent question would have unleashed a tirade that could have cost me my life as well as the lives of everybody else seated at the table, I would never have asked it.

"Hector gets that," the fat one screeched.

"No I don't," Hector screamed. "I get the ham and cheese."

"No, *stupido*," the one with the mustache shrieked. "You get the hot dog."

"You shut your face, *puta*," Hector shouted, jumping up. "I get the ham and cheese."

"I heard you, *maricón—tu dice* hot dog," Estella yelled.

"*No soy maricón*," Hector wailed, sobbing. "I blow everybody up."

"Over a hot dog!" I screamed.

And the he made a dash over to the three shoe boxes, flung himself down on the floor, and began frantically tampering with the wires. Knocking down my chair, I raced over to him and—God knows how—kicked him over with my foot.

Hector was lying in fetal position near the three bombs, whimpering like an injured puppy.

"It's all right, Hector," I said soothingly, stroking his hair. "It's all right. I know you get the ham and cheese. It's all right, they're wrong, the ham and cheese is yours."

"I no *maricón*," Hector whined.

Glancing up at Estella, who had called him the name that appeared to be troubling him, I asked, "What does *maricón* mean?"

Estella threw her head back, and in an authentic rendition of Teresa Berganza playing Carmen, let out a raucous laugh. "Faggot," she yelled shrilly, "Hector is a faggot—he no can make babies."

"Do you blame him," I muttered under my breath. But before I could gather momentum and really attack this shrew for calling Hector names that were causing him to roll around on the floor and kick his legs up and down, the other two harpies began jabbering and screeching so violently the building could have blown up without the help of those homemade bombs. Holding Hector firmly with one arm stretched across his bony chest, I yelled at the top of my lungs, "ENOUGH, EVERYBODY SHUT UP!"

There was silence. Estella looked stunned, her haughty expression replaced by one of disbelief as she actually stopped twisting her hair around her fingers and stood motionless. The other two just stared, their jaws slack, their mouths open in surprise. But Hector was the most amazed, astonished that someone had dared to defend him against his three tormentors. I had only been in the Rodriguez apartment for less than ten minutes, yet it was very clear that Hector had been browbeaten to the point where any normal man would have snapped long ago.

Before I could say anything else the phone that was hooked up to the communications center in the street began ringing.''

"You OK, Mags?" Brian asked calmly. "We heard you scream."

The man had ice water in his veins, except when he didn't. "Put Sprig on," I said.

Nick was on the line instantly. "What's up, kid? You OK?"

"Everything's under control." I had already decided how to describe this insane situation without the others in the room understanding. "Just listen to me and don't say anything," I instructed him, formulating the words in my head. And although Nick Sprig was black and my command of Yiddish was extremely limited, we had both worked in television in New York long enough to have learned the basics.

"Hector has tsuris because the nafkas are meshuga."

Nick understood immediately. "Go on," he said, trying not to laugh.

"The situation here is shlect because he has been gonifed and nudzhed, and any normal person would have told the nafkas to kish mir in tochis a long time ago—get it?"

"Got it," Nick replied. "So what's your suggestion?"

"A little chicken soup—get that?"

"Got it too," Nick answered, laughing.

Hector allowed me to lead him back to the table, where he sat down and began chomping happily on his ham and cheese sandwich. Suddenly, without warning or maybe because things were too quiet, the fat one suddenly screamed, "Chew with your mouth closed, *cochino*."

And right on cue, the one with the mustache chimed in, *"Loco*, you eat like a pig." Without further hesitation, Mrs. Hector shrieked, *"Maricón, tu no sabes comer, no sabes nada!"*

Naturally, Hector threw down his sandwich and lunged for the gun, knocking over my regular coffee in the process spilling it all over the front of my pale-peach knit dress. It was at that moment that I made a decision.

"Hector!" I yelled, tripping over a chair but managing to tackle him just as he was about to grab the gun. "I want these three *locas* out of here right now—do you hear me? O-u-t! Throw them out!"

He started to laugh, quietly at first, while he kept repeating the word over and over—*"locas, locas"*—until he was doubled over, laughing so hard that tears were rolling down his cheeks. The women, confused about their impending liberation, began chattering again in unintelligible Spanish, until I screamed, *"Shut up!* I have to use the phone."

Brian listened carefully as I explained. "The three women are coming out."

"Can your crew come up?"

Turning to Hector, who had calmed down a bit, I asked, "My crew wants to come in and put you on television. Can I tell them it's all right?"

"Sí, sí," he said, bobbing his head up and down, "I put on a shirt."

"Five minutes?"

Hector held up ten fingers.

"Ten minutes," I told Brian.

The moment had come to allow Hector Rodriguez a shred of his dignity.

"Tell them to get out," I said quietly.

And he did, although not exactly the way I would have suggested, but probably exactly the way I would have done it had I been in his position. They were pushed and shoved out the door, followed by a flood of obscenities shouted in Spanish and English.

"Maricón!" Estella shrieked as her parting shot.

"Putana!" I yelled as the door slammed shut, because it was just too hard not to get into the swing of things.

Hector turned and smiled like a naughty child. *"Sí."*

By the time Hector returned from the bedroom, where

he had washed his face, slicked back his hair with tonic that smelled of coconuts, and put on a clean white shirt, my hands were shaking so badly that I could hardly hold my bacon-lettuce-and-tomato sandwich.

After he finished tucking his shirt into his torn brown baggy pants, he sat down at the table to finish his lunch. He looked with dismay at the ham-and-cheese sandwich that was lying on the filthy braided rug, where he had thrown it in a fit of rage. Suddenly we smiled at each other as if we shared a funny secret. Without saying a word, I handed Hector the hot dog with extra sauerkraut, which he took without the slightest hesitation.

"Good?" I asked.

"I love hot dogs," he said, chewing happily.

When the bell rang, Hector was munching on his hot dog, all the while nervously kicking the table with his foot and staring blankly into space. The gun was lying on the table and the explosives were still activated in the shoe boxes on the floor next to the window.

"It's my television crew. May I open the door, Hector?"

He nodded.

When I pulled the door open, Nick immediately grabbed my arm. "The guys from the bomb squad are here," he whispered. "Do you think he'll let them in?"

Hector was still at the table, eating his lunch when I asked, "Hector, my crew is here. Would you also consider letting some men into the apartment to dismantle the bombs you made?"

He nodded again.

Dick Carlson was perspiring profusely as he set up his minicam. Joe Valeri walked directly over to Hector and shook his hand before adjusting the sound boom for the interview.

"Hi, Hector," he said. "My name's Joe."

"Hi, Joe," Hector answered.

Leading Hector over to the sofa where we would sit during the interview, I noticed that the three men from the bomb squad were already clipping wires and detaching the eighteen sticks of dynamite from the white putty.

"It's all right," I said gently to Hector.

Nick knelt down a few feet away from us. "Hector, my name's Nick, and I'm going to direct this interview."

"Hi, Nick," Hector said, grinning.

"You're going to do real well. Just look at Maggie—don't look at the camera."

"Ready?" I asked.

"Ready," Hector answered.

Pointing to me, Nick nodded.

"Hector," I said, looking into his eyes, "why did you take your wife and two sisters hostage and threaten to kill them?"

Nick suddenly held up his hand. "Stop, Maggie. Cut. What's all over the front of your dress?"

Looking down, I noticed the coffee stains. "I forgot," I said. "It's coffee."

"Go inside and turn your dress around, so the stains are in the back."

I was back on the sofa in less than a minute.

"Pick it up from the beginning," Nick said.

"Hector," I said, looking into his eyes, "why did you take your wife and two sisters hostage and threaten to kill them?"

Tears welled up in his eyes. "I am the hostage. They are no hostages."

"What do you mean, Hector?"

"I work and give all money to Estella. She give me nothing—only carfare to go to factory, and sometimes she make me sandwich. I have no money to buy new shoes."

"Why do you give her all the money?"

"Because she make me feel bad we no have baby. She nag me all the time to have baby, call me names." He looked pleadingly at me, willing me to understand. "How to make baby with someone who yell and scream all the time?"

Somewhere on the Upper East Side of Manhattan, near Gracie Mansion, a working wife named Maggie Sommers sat at her polished oak drop-leaf kitchen table, the light from the stained-glass Tiffany fixture casting shadows on her spinach quiche. She mused over a question a friend has just asked.

"I suppose I resent the fact that Eric only gives me carfare to go to work—not even enough money in case I have to buy a pair of shoes."

"Why do you allow that to happen?" the friend asks. "After all, you work."

"Because he makes me feel incredibly guilty about the fact that we don't have a baby. He berates me constantly, but really, how can I possibly consider having a child with someone who does nothing but harass, criticize, and scream at me all the time?"

The camera followed Hector and me out of the apartment at 510 Morris Avenue. By that time, there were several other television and radio crews waiting to record the dramatic surrender, which was not particularly dramatic after all, just terribly sad. The policemen were still crouched behind the open doors of the cars, their high-powered rifles pointed directly at poor Hector, while the SWAT teams were still on the roof, in position. The curious spectators began cheering as he appeared.

Detective First Class Brian Flaherty greeted Hector Rodriguez with a pair of handcuffs, which he immediately slapped on Hector's thin wrists while reciting his rights to the bewildered man. The ambulance rolled to a stop several feet away, and two paramedics approached Hector cautiously.

Taking one of his handcuffed hands in mine, I looked into his red-rimmed eyes. "I won't forget you, Hector," I said solemnly. "I promise you."

And while flashbulbs popped in his face, the white-coated paramedics led him away silently.

"Can I buy you a drink?" Joe asked.

"No, thanks," I said, glancing at Brian. "I've got an appointment."

He shrugged his shoulders. "We've got plenty of time for that drink"—he grinned—"but I've got a funny feeling he doesn't."

* * *

Mary Margaret Flaherty was all dressed up in a bright-yellow knit suit, a gleaming gold cross resting between her pendulous breasts, and her high black orthopedic shoes laced snugly around her thin ankles. Her white hair was meticulously combed into tight little sausage curls, and her bright-pink lipstick was smeared all over her front teeth. She was walking out of the Flaherty two-family house in Maspeth, Queens, just as Brian and I were walking in. Planting a noisy kiss on her son's cheek, she announced, "Flora Carlucci is picking me up in her car any minute to take me to church. It's my bingo night."

I stood smiling at her while she appraised me from head to toe with a knowing look.

"Where's your hearing aid, Mom?" Brian asked.

"Broke it, Sonny," Mary Margaret answered.

"I've heard so much about you from your son," I said in an effort to make contact. "I'm so happy to finally meet you."

Ignoring me, she talked directly to Brian. "Where're you going tonight, Sonny?"

"We're just going to watch a little television, Ma," Brian said.

"And you must be Maggie," Mary Margaret finally said. "An Irish name, Maggie?"

"No, Ma," Brian said, turning beet red. "Maggie's not Irish."

"Where are your people from?"

"Actually," I answered nervously, "my father's from the Bronx and my mother's from St. Petersburg, Russia."

But the Russia got lost in the air, somewhere above the ear without the hearing aid.

"St. Petersburg," she said wistfully. "The late Mr. Flaherty, may he rest in peace, had people in St. Petersburg. We used to drive down there to visit them every winter for two weeks."

"Yeah, I remember that," Brian said, relieved that the subject switched from sin to sun. "Cousin Tim Riley and his wife. Pop used to love to go there before he passed away."

Why is it that the Irish always "passed away," as in "The late Mr. Flaherty, may he rest in peace, passed away," while Jews "died"—just plain old "Sol dead from a tumor in his esophagus that caused him to choke to death on his own vomit near the eleventh hole, poor bastard."

A car horn honked, and Mary Margaret Flaherty waved one white-gloved hand at Flora Carlucci, who had pulled up to the curb.

"Don't stay up too long, sonny," Mary Margaret said, giving me another knowing look.

But how could she possibly have known that I would only keep Brian up as long as she could stay up, because the moment he was no longer up, there was no reason for me to stay and keep him up.

"Bye, Ma," Brian said. "Have a good time."

The stereo in Brian's bedroom played the same tape over and over—*Strangers in the Night*—because he hadn't yet bought the system that could play up to eight cassettes at a time without his having to get up—or pull out—to change tapes. I was on my stomach on his bed, with Brian on top of me, his hard-as-a-rock organ moving rhythmically, his mouth buried in my neck. Our bodies were dripping, slipping against each other, moving faster until his fluid finally filled me up. Taking several deep breaths, he lay very still on the damp sheets. Several minutes elapsed before he rolled over on his side and pulled me next to him so my buttocks and back were curved into his stomach and groin. He kissed my neck, running his tongue down along my right shoulder.

"Brian," I said, "that's what we are."

"Uh?" he answered.

"Strangers in the night, that's what we are," I repeated.

He didn't respond, but rather reached down and touched those places on my body where he wanted to be again, probing other places open and beginning once more.

"Do you call this strangers in the night?"

I pulled him close, my arms wrapped around his neck. Our lips were pressed together while our tongues danced languidly inside our mouths.

"Brian," I gasped, as he pushed deeper inside of me, "Eric and I are going to get a divorce."

And he stopped then, his erection gone, withered down to something barely recognizable, and the moment was lost forever.

"I can't marry you, Maggie," he said miserably, sitting on the edge of the bed.

"I didn't expect you to," I said softly, hugging my knees up to my chin.

"I mean, I care about you, Maggie, but I've got Ma and the job."

I wondered if I would have felt a more acute loss if somehow Brian had phrased it differently, like "I adore you, darling, but my career is simply too demanding to expect any woman to share in my life. And of course there's Mother."

There was a strained silence until I made the first move, which was actually one of the last moves. Getting up, I walked into the bathroom, washed, and dressed, putting on my pale-peach knit dress correctly, the coffee stain visible.

Brian was ready, waiting to drive me home. I walked up to him and took him in my arms, holding him very close and saying a silent farewell, because it was over.

Twenty minutes later, he stopped the car in the usual place, five blocks from my apartment house on East End Avenue. There was still a strained silence, as there had been for the entire trip from his world back into mine. Once again I made the first move, which this time was the final one. Getting out of the car, I mouthed the words "I love you," because in a way I really did and in another way I was still deluding myself.

The agitated voice of Eric Ornstein coming from inside our apartment diminished to a hushed whisper as I walked through the front door. Dropping my tote bag on the floor, I glanced briefly at the mail lying on the table in the foyer before entering the living room. Eric was seated on the lemon yellow sofa next to his mother while his father paced up and down the room, his hands clasped behind him.

"Hi, everybody," I said, sitting on a white muslin barrel chair.

Harry stopped pacing while Mildred looked at me with an expression of nothing less than consummate loathing. Taking a deep breath, she placed her hand over her heart at the same moment that Eric crossed his lanky legs and glanced expectantly at his father.

"Why, hello, Maggie," Harry said, smiling broadly.

Harry Ornstein's physical appearance had always made less of an impression on me than his slimy personality even if his face was a fascinating study in disproportion, eyes that were small and closely set on either side of a remarkably large nose, thick and fleshy lips positioned over a receding chin. Studying my father-in-law, I recognized that particular smile, the one that usually meant that the snake was about to strike.

Harry Ornstein, who had sold a thriving coat manufacturing business in New York's garment center to buy a brokerage house on Wall Street from a close friend who was on the verge of bankruptcy, was the same man who once explained, "Blue coats blue chips, it's all the same crap. The name of the game is knowing how to shaft people with a smile."

"What's going on here?" I asked, noticing the small black-and-white television set that was usually in the kitchen was now now on the glass parsons table near the couch.

Mildred crossed her plump arms over her chest, a gesture that customarily preceded a rocking motion vaguely reminiscent of prayer time in an ultra-Orthodox home. Predictably, Mildred began rocking back and forth on the sofa, while Harry sat down in the other white muslin chair, rubbing his temples with his pudgy fingers. Eric started to hum.

"Shut up," Harry snapped.

There was something very wrong.

"What's going on?" I repeated, glancing around the room.

"We seem to have a slight problem," Harry said, his enormous teeth peeking out from under his fat upper lip.

"Eric?" I said questioningly.

His only response was to hum that tuneless melody again.

"I told you to knock it off," Harry yelled.

Mildred patted Eric's knee with one hand while she fiddled with the pear-shaped six-carat diamond with the other.

"We watched you on television tonight," Harry said, smiling again.

Perhaps the Ornstein family had congregated in my living room to watch the news and decided that they didn't approve of my coverage of the hostage drama.

"Did the piece interest you?"

Rubbing his hands together so that his star-sapphire ring clicked against his onyx-and-diamond pinkie ring, Harry shook his head sadly. Spittle glistened on his bottom lip as he spoke. "Oh, Maggie, Maggie."

"Look," I finally said impatiently, "would someone please tell me what's going on here?"

Mildred began twisting her gray baroque pearl necklace around so the diamond clasp was positioned directly underneath her double chins.

"Where'd you get that stain on your pretty dress?" Harry asked in a deadly voice.

"Hector Rodriguez spilled coffee on me while I was in his apartment," I replied, totally bewildered.

"Ah," Harry said dramatically, "the magic of television."

"What do you mean?" I asked, even more perplexed.

"The stain never even showed up on the screen," he said, smiling.

"That's because my bureau chief had me turn it around before we began shooting the piece."

Perhaps the cleaning bills had been too high.

"And so," Harry said, sounding like Perry Mason, "you stopped off in Maspeth, Queens, to turn it back around before you came home."

Eric began humming again, frantically, desperately, until Harry threw a pillow at him from across the room.

"That's the last time I'm going to tell you to shut the fuck up!" he screamed.

It was suddenly very clear, but there was nothing I

could do because it was too late. The damage was already done. What was interesting was that my first thought was of Mother and how she would react after learning that Eric's family had apparently engaged a private detective, who had followed her younger daughter and caught her turning around her coffee-stained pale-peach knit dress in a two-family house in Maspeth, Queens.

"How's your fancy-schmancy mother going to feel when she finds out her daughter is a whore?" Mildred asked, reading my mind.

Harry rose, and with a sweeping gesture of his right hand, befitting King Solomon, said, "Mildred, Mildred, is that any way to talk to family?"

My face felt hot, my hands clammy, as I studied the intricately patterned Bukhara rug.

"You had me followed," I whispered over and over. "You had me followed."

"Maggie, Maggie," Harry said dramatically. "Followed, followed—is that all you can say?"

So I said something else. "Eric, how could you have allowed them to have me followed?"

"This is a sorry day in the Ornstein house," Harry said, "and you are responsible for this terrible grief that we're feeling. We loved you like a daughter, and for a daughter to betray is like a knife in the heart."

"Not to mention that she did it with a goy," Mildred chimed in.

"Goy schmoy," he said, in his profound wisdom. "The fact is that my Maggie—like a daughter she was—" But he couldn't even finish his sentence, so distraught and upset was he that his Maggie—like a daughter she was—had betrayed.

"I'll handle this, Dad," Eric said bravely, clutching his mother's hand.

And Harry, in his profound wisdom, still tried to control the situation so there was no unnecessary name-calling or trauma to his loved ones—including Maggie, whom he loved like a daughter. "Schmuck," Harry said through clenched teeth. "You'll do nothing, you schmuck. You couldn't even keep your own wife from spreading her legs for some goy cop."

So what did I have to lose—being banished from Buckingham Palace maybe; or not having to watch Mildred scraping the dinner dishes into the maid's toilet, "not to waste a garbage bag," or hearing Harry tell a waiter, "Stolly on the rocks, no fruit," which I learned meant Stolichnaya on the rocks, no lemon or lime, please"; or never again having to play hide-and-seek with Eric's blasted rectal thermometer?

"Don't you dare talk to me like that," I said coldly. "I simply won't stand for it."

And my indignation seemed to titillate Harry, who looked at me with an expression of nothing less than admiration. "If you were my wife," he said, "this wouldn't have happened."

There was a chance, a slim chance, that Harry might encourage some kind of equitable solution to this problem, if I played my cards right. "Harry, if I were your wife, we would have discussed this problem together and not involved our parents."

He responded predictably, given his monumental ego. "I tried to do the best I could with Eric, but he's not that bright. I tried to teach him basic rules, but he just wasn't cut from the same cloth as his father. The boy's weak."

There might be time later to comfort Eric, my husband the boy, but right then my salary checks seemed more important. "Harry," I said, "why did you have me followed?"

He sighed. "I would rather have cut out my heart than do that, but someone said they saw you holding hands with some guy in a diner in Maspeth, Queens. Believe me, Maggie, my first reaction was shock and disbelief. But then someone else saw you getting into a car with the same guy in front of the studio. What choice did I have? I hoped against hope you'd prove them wrong."

It wasn't so dumb to cry then, because Harry produced a handkerchief with a flourish and handed it to me, as he proclaimed, "I don't want to involve dishonest lawyers in this, because they'll charge exorbitant fees. We'll settle this ourselves, like our forefathers settled things in the times of Moses."

Eric cleared his throat. Mildred hiccuped.

Inspired by Harry's allusions to the tribal rites of the ancient Hebrews, I caught the spirit.

"I promise not to do anything that will hurt anybody any more than they're already hurt. And I swear not to talk to a lawyer."

"You know, Maggie," Harry said warmly, "I still feel about you like a daughter—like blood."

"Dad," Eric whined.

"Shut up," Harry said, without even turning around.

"Perhaps I should stay at Quincy's tonight and let everybody calm down, and then tomorrow, when we're all feeling a little better, we can sit down and talk this out."

"Maggie, you're behaving like Sarah would have behaved. Now remember, no lawyers—yes?"

Quincy was not terribly surprised to see me standing in front of her door that night, although she couldn't understand why the tears kept flowing as I recounted every gruesome detail.

"So it's over," she said pragmatically. "So why are you crying? You've been miserable for years."

"Because," I sobbed, "I feel so guilty, and Harry treated Eric so terribly—calling him a boy."

"He *is* a boy," Quincy answered firmly, "or he wouldn't have called his daddy when he had a problem."

"I can't really blame him, Quincy—I was dreadful."

She looked at me as if I had lost my mind. Standing, she walked to the window and stared for a while before she turned slowly. "Should I remind you of all the wonderful incidents that happened throughout those sensational years with him?" she asked softly.

I shook my head, blew my nose and coughed. "No."

"Why? Because you might forget to feel sorry for him?"

But I was determined to blame myself. And Quincy didn't try to dissuade me when I finally announced at five o'clock in the morning, "My place is with Eric, I'm going home. Maybe I just needed a good cry."

One hour later I was back on Quincy Reynold's doorstep. Eric had already changed the locks. So much for Sarah and Moses and those tribal rites, dating back to

the ancient Hebrews, the ones that discouraged paying
exorbitant fees to dishonest lawyers.

"So much for sentiment," Quincy said briskly, pulling
me inside. "There's a clean glass somewhere. Pour yourself a stiff drink and get some sleep."

CHAPTER SIX

Quincy is aware of my anxiety. My fingers twisting my hair into knots and then ripping them out, my foot tapping a desperation waltz, cause her to watch me with concern. It is the time for procrastination and she senses that and so doesn't make much effort to leave me alone. She does reach for her purse tentatively from time to time or makes another feeble leaving gesture, which affords me the choice of being alone. And there are so many things I could be doing right now: unpacking, cleaning, organizing files, arranging possessions, falling into the trap of trying to work out the rest of my life. But I want her with me, if even for a few more minutes, until some of those thoughts stop bouncing around in my head, thoughts that are confusing and painful. All too soon I'll be forced to settle back into the world of television contracts and unhealed familial wounds, and do it knowing the Avi will not be walking through the door at the end of the day to make it all better.

"Are you up to meeting with Grayson tonight for dinner, or should I postpone it?" Quincy asks as she once again gathers up her things in yet another feeble attempt to leave.

"No, don't postpone anything. I'd better get my contract settled, so at least I have that in my life."

She bites her bottom lip pensively. "Spare me the self-pity, Maggie; it just doesn't become you."

I have to smile, even though I try not to, because she is right—it doesn't become me. But the thought of acting cheerful right now exhausts me. "Go on," I say. "You're dying to list all those wonderful things I have in my life—all the things I should be grateful for."

"I could hardly contain myself until you asked," she responds.

"Well, go on."

"All right. For one thing, you've got someone named Avi Herzog calling you tonight at midnight, and for another thing, you've got a terrific support system, people who love you, including Dan and me, and—let's see— you've got this terrific body and sensational legs, which I'm sorry to say will probably still make an impression on Grayson, which can't hurt." She smiles. "So what else is there? Oh, maybe the fact that your great fear of ending up alone, a bag lady, won't happen now, since as of last year you're officially part of that terrific ABN pension plan."

"And there *I* was, wondering how to parlay my body and legs into an old-age retirement plan. I almost forgot about ABN's policy that takes care of old war-horse journalists."

"Do you want to know who's going to be there tonight, speaking of old war horses?"

"Who?"

"Elliot James, since he's your network bureau chief and, more important, Grayson's whipping boy." Quincy fluffs up her hair in the mirror before turning around to look at me. "Maggie, you need sleep. Why don't you take the phone off the hook and just rest today. You've got nothing else to do that's pressing."

"I thought I'd call Mother."

Quincy takes off her coat and flings it dramatically on a chair. "In that case, I'm staying, because you'll need someone to pick up the pieces afterward."

"You don't have to," I say halfheartedly.

"Come on, let's get it over with," she says, leading the way back into the bedroom. "You must be feeling too good and probably need to be beaten down just a little."

Quincy sits on a chair in my bedroom while I dial the number. She smiles, weakly but encouragingly, as I wait for someone to answer.

It is noon on Tuesday, the twenty-eighth day of December, 1982, and Avi Herzog apparently still wants me;

Grayson Daniel is dining with me tonight to discuss my new contract, so I am obviously still employable; and I happen to be a grown woman. Yet amazingly my hands won't stop shaking.

"Hello."

I pause, hardly noticeably, before I say "Hello" back to Father, who has picked up on the second ring.

"Father, it's Maggie, and I'm back in New York."

Quincy rolls her eyes.

There is a pause, not just noticeable but interminable, on the other end of the phone.

"Well, well," he finally says. "Back in New York and there wasn't even a ticker tape to warn me."

I am drawing little square boxes, rows upon rows of small attached boxes, on a scrap of paper.

"How are you, Father?" I ask, ignoring his sarcasm.

"I'm just fine, but I understand your sound man's not doing so great—got his head blown off by a bunch of dumb Arabs. Serves him right for being there."

One sentence, just thirty words—because I'm counting them as they reverberate in my head—represents everything that ever went wrong in the Sommers house when Maggie was growing up. There is really nothing more to say to him unless I choose to attack, teach, or defend, and I choose not to do any of those things because it is just too late. My eyes fill with tears—a usual reaction, one that almost happens at the mere mention of his name.

"Is Mother there?"

And Father doesn't even bother to answer because he has done his job for today; his mission is complete for the afternoon.

Vera Sommers's voice is charged with anxiety yet tinged with a hopelessness that is both familiar and disturbing. "Hello, Marguerite," she says listlessly.

"What's the matter, Mother? You sound awful."

Quincy shakes her head and lights a cigarette.

"Nothing," Mother says. "When did you get back?"

"Yesterday," I lied.

"Cara's not here, you know; she's in Aruba with her family for the holidays."

"I know, Mother. Would you like to come downtown to visit me this afternoon?"

I am amazed that Vera not only agrees to come downtown, a trip that she is usually loath to make, but also seems to be in a great rush to get there.

"I'll just grab a taxi and be there in about fifteen minutes," she says before hanging up.

"Well?" Quincy asks.

"Well, it's the same old story," I reply, "only this time I heard a hopelessness in her voice that I remember from when I was a child. It reminds me of the day that Father drew that shocking picture on the cocktail napkin at Trader Vic's in the Plaza Hotel."

Quincy looks bewildered. "What are you talking about, Maggie?"

○

That particular summer, 1963, was a relatively pleasant one because I had managed to convince Mother and Father to allow me to go to Camp Chippewa, near Bangor, Maine. It would be the first time that I didn't have to spend the months of July and August at the Sommers country house on Long Island.

I was sitting cross-legged on the floor of my bedroom in the Fifth Avenue apartment, waiting for Jonesie to finish sewing name tapes on my camp clothes. Jonesie, a long piece of white thread hanging from her mouth, handed me neatly folded shorts and shirts, which were to be put into a large steamer trunk on the floor near the window. Jonesie had only to worry about packing me, since Cara wasn't going to camp. She had a job at Lenox Hill Hospital, as one of the volunteers who wore those red-and-white-striped aprons and pushed magazine carts around the hospital so the patients had something to read as they either waited to heal or waited to die.

Mother had said her goodbyes to us several days earlier. She had gone to visit her parents in Milwaukee, we were told, but would be unreachable, as they were heading for a remote lakefront resort in northern Wisconsin, where the infrastructure was as crude as the quaint log cabin in which she would be living for a month. And, Mother in a log cabin was even less believable to Cara and me than Father's nightly excuses as to why he was unable to eat dinner with us. "I'm working my ass off so you two can go to fancy private schools, camp, and college. I won't be home until well after midnight."

Glancing at my watch, I was horrified to see that it was almost five-thirty. I was due at a command performance at six—dinner with Father at his request at Trader Vic's restaurant in the Plaza.

"I've got to go, Jonesie," I said, "or I'll be late."

She nodded as she rose laboriously, her gnarled hand holding on to one enormous hip for support. "Hurry, then, Maggie, so you can look pretty for him."

The bus deposited me on the corner of Fifty-ninth Street and Fifth Avenue, near Grand Army Plaza, where a group of bearded men and long-haired women were singing folk songs in front of the fountain. Dressed in a white pleated skirt, a blue-and-white flowered blouse, and white Pappagallo flats, I certainly looked as if I belonged inside rather than outside, where I would have much preferred to spend the evening.

I walked up the green-carpeted steps and into the lobby, winding my way through the display cases of sparkling jewelry and chic cruisewear until I reached more green-carpeted stairs, which led down to the Polynesian restaurant.

A graceful woman wearing a silk sari greeted me at the entrance and escorted me to Alan Sommers's table. As I approached, Father stood politely and waited for me to be seated before he sat back down and ordered a fruit punch, no rum, for me and another vodka gimlet for himself.

"How are you, Maggie?" he said stiffly.

"Fine, thank you, Father," I answered formally.

"All set for camp?" he asked mechanically.

"Almost, Father," I answered defensively.

"Splendid," he said automatically.

"Why did you want to have dinner with me, Father?" I asked stupidly, and from that moment, everything seemed to fall apart.

There was no further conversation until the drinks arrived and we both had something to concentrate on other than our own reactions to my unforgivable blunder. But then, before I even had a chance to put the straw that was protruding from the ersatz coconut to my lips, Father slipped my cocktail napkin out from underneath my drink. Reaching into his breast pocket, he produced a pen and proceeded to draw a crude-looking face on the napkin, shading the areas around the eyes and chin before making thick lines across the bridge of the nose and the forehead. The drawing began to take shape, resembling a person who had been in a terrible accident and was swathed in bandages.

"This is what your mother looks like right now," Father said, turning the napkin around and sliding it toward me.

I studied it for a moment, distinctly uncomfortable under his steady gaze, until I finally said, "What happened to her?"

He was suddenly in no special hurry to explain further. Taking a long sip of his drink, he leaned his head back, and without any display of emotion watched the tears spring to my eyes and roll slowly down my cheeks.

"What happened to Mother?" I repeated, trying not to cry.

"Your mother didn't go to Milwaukee," he revealed, his lips pursed in satisfaction. "She went into the hospital to have her nose fixed, and when you see her, right after dinner, don't cry because it will only make her feel worse."

Although I felt relieved that there wasn't something terminally wrong with her, I didn't exactly understand why she had decided to have her nose fixed, a perfectly good nose, which looked just fine to me.

"She walked into a wall when she was pregnant with Cara," Father continued, "and the bone calcified over the years. She was snoring so badly at night because of the deviated septum that I couldn't sleep, so she decided to do something about it."

It didn't occur to me then that Mother's undergoing rhinoplasty so that Father could sleep was almost as absurd as Father's cutting off an ear so that Mother could breathe.

"Does Cara know?" I asked meekly.

"She does now. I had her meet me in Mother's room at Lenox Hill right before I came here."

As I think back now, I wish that I had snuck that napkin with the drawing of the bruised and battered face into my pocket so that I could tell this story in later life without anybody doubting its veracity. "Look, everybody," I could say, "look at the napkin. That's why Maggie Sommers has difficulty in cementing healthy relationships—it's all because of the problems she had with her father. See the napkin? It's not Maggie's fault that she can't love you, it's not her fault at all."

I didn't eat very much that night, leaving the egg rolls, breaded shrimp, and spare ribs spread around my plate. Father finally finished, having ordered dessert and coffee, and paid the check. He walked swiftly out of the restaurant, with me scurrying after him, and hailed a taxi. We rode in silence up Park Avenue until we arrived at the hospital.

"Remember what I said about not crying," he admonished me again as we walked down the hospital corridor. Turning the corner, he strode briskly into her room while I lingered timidly behind.

But I could see her lying there and she was swathed in bandages, exactly like the drawing, with bruises and contusions covering her entire face and neck. She resembled a bowling ball, with two slits for eyes where the holes would have been. And even after Father's admonitions about not crying, there was no avoiding my hysterical reaction. I cried, coughed, and sniffled, oblivious to the other drama that was taking place in her bed. It was only when the burly male attendant burst into the room and held Mother down that I paid attention. She stopped crying and thrashing around then, while a nurse jabbed a needle into her arm and the attendant stroked her brow soothingly. Mother's outburst momentarily subsided until she looked at Father and sat bolt upright. "How could you?" she sobbed. "I don't want to live anymore." And then she sank back against the pillows and dozed off.

Cara led me out of the room then and into the visitors' lounge where we sat on a tattered green plastic sofa and talked in hushed tones. It seemed that Cara had been mysteriously paged to Room 1212. She had no idea who the patient was until she entered, and almost fainted from the shock of seeing Mother in that condition. Unfortunately for Cara and probably for everybody else as well, she also arrived at a most inauspicious moment. Vera, despite her swollen eyes and drugged state, spotted dusky-pink lipstick on Alan's collar and handkerchief.

"I stood at the door," Cara explained, "and just listened as Father didn't even bother to deny anything. He just told her that he would do as he pleased and if she didn't like it she could move to Wisconsin or anywhere else she liked."

He never noticed Cara until he passed her on his way out.

"He told me he was meeting you for dinner and that I was to remain with Mother until he returned."

And then he returned, with me in tow, which was the moment that a burly male attendant had been summoned so that Mother could be sedated and not rupture any of her stitches. I hugged Cara tightly when she finished her story, grateful that I had a sister, but still feeling completely confused and impotent. I just couldn't understand why Father had behaved that way.

○

"It's amazing that both of you can walk and talk," Quincy says sadly.

"I suppose so," I agree, accompanying her to the door.

"But then that's probably what made you strong." She hugs me. "I've got to run, Mags—see you tonight at the Russian Tea Room?"

"Yes, and Quincy . . ."

She nods her head. "I know."

I hug her again. "Thanks—for everything."

She holds me at arm's length. "Do me a favor," she

says gently. "Don't let anything upset you today. There's been enough."

After Quincy has left, I brew a fresh pot of coffee and straighten up the apartment in preparation for Mother's visit. The doorbell rings just as I am arranging the cups and saucers on a tray. Vera Sommers, with one nose job, two face lifts, and a slim body from years of grueling exercise, looks quite well for her sixty-four years. Quite well, except upon closer inspection. Her face is visibly drawn and her mouth is twitching nervously as she slips out of her full-length fitch coat. Hugging her, I am not offended that she is unresponsive, standing stiffly with her arms at her sides. She steps back after a second or two and attempts to smile. "You look reasonably well, Marguerite; a little tired, but I suppose that's because of your abnormal life-style."

We are off and running.

Vera walks into the living room, smoothing her long black sweater, which is belted over her tapered black slacks, and sits down.

"Are you back for good or just on temporary leave?"

"Temporary leave, only I'm not sure when or even where I'll be going. I should know more tonight; I'm having dinner with Grayson."

She is silent as she sips the coffee I have given her. Averting her eyes, she nervously swings her leg back and forth.

"What's bothering you?" I finally ask. "I know there's something—I heard it on the phone and now I see it."

She sighs deeply. "I'm just sorry that Cara's in Aruba."

"I already know that, Mother," I say wearily. "But there's something else."

"Well," she says, putting down her cup and saucer, "it won't come as any surprise, because you've known all too much for all too long, both you and Cara."

She could have saved herself the trouble of explaining, because I *did* know, having heard the same story countless times over the years.

"Your father is involved with another woman, and I suppose I should be used to it by now." She sighs. "But

I suppose I'm just getting too old and too tired to keep pretending that I don't know, and''—she sighs again—''I don't want to end up alone.''

''How do you know?''

Vera looks at me as if I am even more stupid than she always claimed.

''How do you think I know?'' she says disgustedly. ''The same way I always know: He's hardly ever home at night, and when he is, the phone rings once, the signal, before he rushes into the den to make that furtive return call.''

It is almost three o'clock in the afternoon and Mother has still not left my apartment. Her ability to cope with Father's careless treatment of her is simply diminishing. The pain grows more acute with each passing year, as time erodes her spirit and introduces a new variable in the equation called fear. She is sitting on the same spot on the sofa, desperately trying to prove to me that her fear of abandonment is greater than the pain of all the indignities she suffers at Father's hands.

''I just can't function by myself; I'd be only half a person.''

''No you wouldn't, not if you started out as one hundred percent instead of only fifty.''

''But I didn't, you see: My life with him was fifty-fifty. Without him, I'm empty.'' How was she supposed to know back then that had she made it one hundred-one hundred and not given away any points over the years, she might have felt only a terrible loss instead of also feeling an enormous void.

''And what is he without you?'' I ask.

''According to him,'' she says, ''a lot happier.''

''Maybe you'd be a lot happier too.''

But she doesn't want to hear that. ''By the way,'' she says, ''your husband had another baby, a second boy.''

Eric Ornstein, remarried for the past six years and now the father of not one but two children, is still forever Maggie Sommers's husband. It would have really been too much to expect from Mother to stop referring to him as my husband.

''How do you know?'' I ask politely.

"He sent us a birth announcement."

How transparent. How utterly blatant that Eric includes Vera and Alan Sommers on the list of people to whom he sends birth announcements. But then Eric always needed to prove that our failed marriage was solely my fault. He needed to show everyone connected to me that he only wanted a normal life and children.

"Maggie," he once said, "you are pathologically without maternal instincts—that's your problem, and it will be the downfall of this union."

"You gave Eric no choice, you know," Mother says, refilling our coffee cups. She has gotten a second wind. Other than being our usual topic of conversation, it gives her an opportunity to deflect her own painful realities. "You drove him to do what he did."

"Why am I responsible for Eric's actions as well as for my own?"

"Your infidelity"—Mother pronounces the word with such distaste that I have to smile—"was uncalled for. The man was worthless."

"And if he had been socially acceptable to you, would that have made it better?"

"It certainly would have made it better for you."

"Impossible," Mother says. "Eric's intentions were honorable; he tried to make a life with you, and when he found it was impossible, he simply moved on to someone who was willing."

There is no adequate response to counter that logic, because to Mother, culpability in any sexual triangle is judged by the level of the man's worth on the open market, while the woman's culpability is judged by the level of her own bad judgment.

"And Ronah—do you condemn her as you do me?"

Mother looks at me incredulously. "Of course not. Eric is a decent man."

"But she had an affair with my husband while I was still married to him. Doesn't that count?"

"No, Marguerite," she answers patiently, as if I were brain damaged. "He married her, and besides, anybody who has an affair with someone who wears a uniform is just asking for trouble."

"Brian didn't wear a uniform, Mother; he was a detective," I say wearily, probably for the hundredth time.

"That's even worse," she says, frowning.

But I understand her logic—the rules and regulations of the cheating game. Infidelity for the sake of lust is condemnable, while infidelity for the sake of ultimately cementing a legal bond is excusable except if one of the parties in question happens to wear a uniform. This is definitely not an appropriate moment to discuss Avi Herzog.

"It wasn't very pleasant for me when I found out."

"I suppose not," Mother says vaguely. "But it was your own fault."

I am on the verge of losing my temper, but with a dancer's precision, I wave my arm, take two graceful steps away from her line of vision, and breathe deeply. "And how was it my fault?"

"You should never have gone to that Valentine Day party. You should have had more sense than to practically catch him red-handed. Not very smart, Marguerite."

My self-imposed pact of silence and control has expired. "How the hell—" I take another deep breath and start again. "How was I supposed to know that he—"

"Women have instincts about those kinds of things," Mother interrupts. "But then you were so busy playing your own little game . . ."

"What I was busy doing was working. Believe me, that was the last thing in the world I needed after a terrible day at work."

○

It all began with the usual frantic rush to finish writing the copy that would accompany a piece I had just shot on the abhorrent conditions of a certain tenement in Harlem. I was all dressed up that particular evening as I sat huddled over my typewriter, dressed to go to a Valentine Day party at Eric's office. And Nick had other reasons for wanting to finish quickly and leave the studio—it was his fourteenth wedding anniversary. He was leaning against the wall near my desk, prodding me on so we could get into edit. But I was having problems, finding this particular story extremely difficult to write. Even though I had been the on-air crime reporter for two years and was used to the fast-paced multiple deadlines of the nightly news, I still couldn't adjust to some of the tragedies that filled those news spots. And that particular Valentine Day broadcast was especially tragic.

"Can I mention the landlord's name?" I shouted over the din of clattering typewriters and general bedlam in the newsroom.

"Why not? You checked—he owns that rattrap, doesn't he?"

"Yes, but I'm listing more than violations; I'm practically accusing him of manslaughter."

Nick looked at me as if I had lost my mind. "What the hell are you talking about?"

I stopped typing, resting my arms on the carriage of the machine, and said, "You didn't even screen my piece, did you?"

"I trust you, Mags," he said, lighting a cigarette. "How bad could it be?"

The expression on my face must have told him that it could be very bad—terrible, in fact.

"What the hell happened?"

"You'll see," I answered, turning back to type the conclusion of my text.

"Did you try and call him or go to see him?" Nick asked, peering over my shoulder.

"Yes, I called three times and he refused to talk, and then I went to his office with a crew, but they slammed the door in our faces."

"Great," Nick said, rubbing his hands together. "We'll run that on the six."

"You'll get better than that," I muttered under my breath as the telephone rang.

Nick picked it up.

"Hi, babe," he said softly. "Me too."

I stopped typing and stared vacantly into space, distracted by Nick's intimate tone of voice, which was reserved exclusively for his Vivian.

"Sure I am. Just as soon as I finish this one last piece," he said, kissing the mouthpiece twice before hanging up.

I shot him a scathing look before banging out the last sentence and ripping the paper out of the machine.

"If you're not too busy," I said, arranging the pages, "perhaps you'd like to hear my text."

"Give me a break, Maggie. Twenty seconds for my personal life isn't going to kill anyone—this is only local news."

"So what should I do, just go into edit cold without you even knowing what it's all about? Fine." I threw down the papers and started to get up.

"Hold on, Maggie," he said impatiently. "Go on, read the damn thing."

I stared at him another few seconds before clearing my throat. I began:

"Sheldon Schwartz owns a tenement in Harlem, where the city pays him approximately one thousand two hundred dollars per month per welfare family. For this amount of money, a welfare mother like Emma Rollin lives in two rooms with her four children on Cates Avenue, where there is faulty plumbing, sporadic electricity, no hot water, and no heat. In the kitchen [camera pans kitchen], the ceiling has caved in on one side, exposing dangerous electrical wires and heavily rusted metal pipes that are held up only by rotting metal supports. The walls have large gaping holes, where rats scamper in and out—"

"Stop a minute, Maggie," Nick interrupted. "It's the same old shit. What's the hook here that makes this story so earth-shattering?" He glared at me.

I glared back. "You mean the part that makes it worthy of a top spot on the local?"

"Maggie . . ." His voice warned me to stop.

I stopped. "OK, the part that makes this story so good is the part about the child."

"Read," he said wearily, "that part."

"Several hours later, ABN rushed back to Emma's apartment. One of her children accidentally tumbled from the six-story window and was killed. [Camera close-up of a body on sidewalk.]"

"Oh, shit," Nick exclaimed, rubbing his eyes. "How?"

"No glass in the window."

"How old?"

"Two."

"Sorry, Mags. Did you get a statement from Schwartz?"

"Should I read? It's in the copy."

"Yeah."

"ABN telephoned Sheldon Schwartz several times, but he was always unavailable. When we went to his office, the door was slammed in our faces [shot of camera being jostled by someone]. Shortly before this, ABN called his office and was informed that he was expected in and would be willing to make a statement. He had just called from his car phone."

Nick was silent.

"Well, what do you think?"

"I think," he said slowly, "that I'd like to shove that car phone down that bastard's throat."

I shrugged, took his arm, and walked with him toward the edit room.

"What a fucking nightmare," he said, shaking his head.

Jack Roshansky, the editor who taught me what should stay in a piece and what should end up on the cutting room floor, was waiting. His big belly spilled over his turquoise-studded Indian belt as he lowered himself heavily into a captain's chair in front of the television monitor. There was silence except for the sounds of the whirring tape as Jack pulled levers and pushed buttons, reversing and forwarding the frames until he was ready to dub in my voice to match the visuals that were flashing across the screen above us.

"OK, Maggie," he said. "Let's go."

I read the text, glancing up every few seconds to make sure I was in sync with the images, or stopping altogether depending on Jack's signal. It was only five-thirty, and for once we were right on schedule to air the piece at precisely seven minutes into the six o'clock broadcast. The final portion, about Sheldon Schwartz calling his office from his car phone, was matched with file footage of limousines, bumper to bumper, creeping up Park Avenue during the usual evening rush hour traffic.

Although Jack Roshansky had spent twenty years of his life in the news business and had seen every imaginable horror of daily life in New York, he was clearly distraught at the image of that tiny broken figure lying in a pathetic crumpled heap in the gutter. Slamming the last switch to the close position, he muttered. "Prick," before getting up.

Nick stood also, a cigarette dangling from his mouth. "They should throw the book at that son of a bitch."

"Life sucks," Jack proclaimed solemnly. "The rich get richer and the poor get shafted."

There were times in the news business, most times, when the on-air reporter had absolutely nothing to do with the impact of the news item being reported or with the reactions of the viewers, and that was one of those times. I gathered up my papers before touching Jack's arm. "Thanks for another terrific job."

"Don't thank me, kid," he said gruffly. "Thank that prick Schwartz." And Jack Roshansky also knew that there were times in the news business, most times, when an expert technician had absolutely nothing to do with the impact of the news item or with the reactions of the viewers. Tragically, that was clearly one of those times, because the visual was just so awful that words or intricate cuts were almost superfluous.

"You leaving, Maggie?" Nick asked.

"Yes; I've got to meet Eric at his office. There's some kind of Valentine's Day party for his staff."

"If you like, I'll drive you," he said, hurrying toward his office. "It's on my way to the tunnel."

"Two seconds," I said, rushing to my cubicle for my coat.

Nick met me at the door to the newsroom just as I was putting on some lipstick and running a brush through my hair.

"Where's Brian tonight?" he asked, steering me toward the stairs.

It had long ceased being a secret between us that I was

having an affair with Brian Flaherty. There had been many lengthy discussions, long after everyone had left the office when Nick advised me to leave Eric and make a new life for myself. There had been endless conversations over countless cups of coffee in the ABN cafeteria when Nick told me that unless I made an effort to begin again, alone, I would never find the right man to make me happy. And there had been numerous talks, as we sat in the ABN van on the way to cover a story when Nick insisted that Brian Flaherty was just not that man.

"Brian's working tonight," I answered. "I talked to him earlier."

I followed Nick down the stairs and out the door of the studio. We walked the two blocks south to his parked car in silence. Unlocking the door, he reached onto the front seat and handed me a bulky pink-and-white-wrapped gift, Vivian's anniversary present, before helping me in and closing the door.

"Does she appreciate you?" I asked, after he was settled behind the steering wheel.

"Of course she does." He smiled and turned the key in the ignition. "We appreciate each other."

I was instantly sorry I had asked, because it only triggered his usual lecture, the one he constantly gave about the merits of a good, solid marriage.

"I'm not going to tell you that you could have the same thing," he said, guiding the car toward the West Side Highway.

"Like you've never said it before," I answered, leaning my head back and closing my eyes.

"OK, so I'll say it again."

"You've got me, Nick," I said, smiling. "I'm a captive audience."

"You should leave Eric and end that ridiculous relationship with Brian, because neither relationship is realistic."

"I haven't reached the point where I contemplate my life in terms of realities."

Nick chuckled. "That's terrific, but someday you will, kid, and then you'll call me up and tell me I was right all along."

"What do you mean, call you up? Won't we still be working together?"

"Probably not. You'll be in network or hosting your own show. You're not going to stay in local forever."

"So it'll take that long for me to face reality," I joked.

He patted my hand. "Not at all. You've got this ambition; the way you drive yourself is frightening to watch sometimes. I feel it when I'm working with you. It's as if you push yourself that way to forget that there's nothing else in your life that fulfills you, nothing that makes you happy."

The same old story, the inevitable end of the evolutionary process that once began with "I know what she needs" but is now phrased differently, to include the strides we have made professionally: "If she was getting it, she wouldn't have this driving ambition."

"I suppose I can't have both?"

Nick exited the highway and turned the car into an alley, a shortcut, before stopping on the corner of a narrow street that led directly into Wall Street.

"Don't start that crap, Maggie. That's not what I meant. I love what I do as much as you love what you do, but I still need to know that Vivian is there waiting for me every night when I come home."

It was still fascinating to me that men needed that security, even more than women, even though it was more acceptable for men to sit alone in a bar or a restaurant. It was less a question of fear of being alone than simply a need to have someone there to listen to the sound of his voice or greet him when he walked through the door. Bizarre that for me the only welcome aspect of being alone was that incredibly delicious silence at the beginning and end of each day.

"Oh, I get it," I said. "What I really need is a wife, because they're the only ones who would be willing to wait until I got home, dinner all ready and my children all clean and scrubbed. What husband would be willing to do that?"

Nick pushed a strand of hair out of my eyes and looked at me tenderly.

"I don't know, Maggie, but all I do know is that I care

a lot about you and that being a great big success isn't
going to be enough someday if you don't have someone
around to share it with.''

"Oh, Nick," I said wearily, "I'm just so tired of
fighting everything.''

He leaned over and kissed me on the cheek. "Sommers, I really do care about you a whole lot.''

"I care about you too, even if you don't have it completely correct.'' I smiled before adding, "And Vivian's
a lucky lady.''

"She thinks you're lucky too," he said, grinning. "She
says you spend more time with me than she does.''

"I know, I know," I said, laughing. "Don't even say
it: I could find a man just like Vivian—right?''

I hugged him again before getting out of the car. Standing on the corner, I watched as he pulled away, honking
once before disappearing down another alley. The Valentine Day party at Eric's office was something I had
been dreading since he told me about it, two weeks before. Bracing myself, I walked into the marble-and-glass
lobby of 63 Wall Street, determined to get through it with
a minimal amount of tension.

The elevator stopped on the sixteenth floor and opened
into a reception area, which had been decorated with red
and white balloons hanging next to pink streamers that
were covered with tiny red and white hearts. In one corner, strung across the wall, was a large gold-lettered sign,
surrounded by cut-out pictures of pink cupids floating on
puffy white clouds, that spelled out "Happy Valentine
Day." Walking around the stainless-steel desk and past
the smoke-colored sliding glass panels, I entered the main
trading room. The furniture had been cleared to one side
and hidden underneath beige canvas drop cloths. Suspended from the ceiling was a tremendous flesh-colored
net filled with more red and white balloons.

Dozens of people were milling around, with dozens
more straining to be heard over the disco music that
blasted from speakers on the walls, as they hung around
a long table that had been transformed into a bar.

I stood on the fringe of the crowd, scanning the room
for a familiar face and realizing how very uninvolved I

was in Eric's life. There was absolutely nobody that I recognized as either an acquaintance or an employee, which was perfectly logical, as that was only the third time in seven years that I had been to my husband's office. The other two occasions were relatively brief—once, when we were newly married, I picked up Eric to go to Chinatown for dinner; and once, when we were newly married, Mildred and I picked up Eric and Harry to go to Chinatown for dinner.

It was only when I finally decided to head over to the bar for a drink that I noticed her. She was standing very close to Eric, gazing adoringly at him, listening with rapt attention to something he was saying. Fascinated, I observed them for several minutes before it struck me—that woman was clearly the next Mrs. Eric Ornstein.

She was very tall, almost as tall as Eric, and very thin, with masses of streaked blond hair that tumbled in meticulous disarray around her bony shoulders. Her kelly-green skirt was very short and very tight, revealing no hips and spindly legs, and her white silk tunic, caught at the waist by a belt made of green seashells that clanked together when she moved, revealed no breasts. One hand, with clawlike square-shaped red fingernails, rested casually on Eric's arm, while the other hand nervously flicked ashes from a pale-green cigarette. There was something vaguely familiar about her, and it wasn't until I felt a hand on my own arm and turned around to face Mrs. Pierce that I realized why.

"Well, Miss Sommers," she said icily, "what brings you here?"

Had I felt completely blameless, innocent of any wrongdoing, I might have answered indignantly that I was Mrs. Eric Ornstein and therefore had every right to be there, and how dare she even pose that question. My own guilty conscience, however, coupled with the possibility that I had driven my husband into the arms of another woman, prevented me from exhibiting the proper outrage at her question. There was no doubt that someone was trying to rob me of something that was not necessarily good for my mental health—namely, my marriage to Eric—and there was also no doubt that it was probably all for the best. But I just didn't feel that February 14, 1975, was the appropriate moment. I simply wasn't ready.

"I told Eric I'd come," I answered meekly, hating her for putting me on the defensive, hating Eric for putting me in that position, and hating myself for being such a hypocrite.

"My daughter Ronah," she said proudly, gesturing to that mass of streaked hair and the clawlike nails that were now stroking my husband's left cheek.

"Um," I said, wondering why I felt as if I had just been kicked in the solar plexus, when this had been a long time coming.

"Why don't you go and meet her?" Mrs. Pierce challenged me.

"Um," I said again, stunned into an inarticulate heap of wounded wife.

Although my eyes were riveted on the two of them, I did manage to give Mrs. Pierce a rather sickly smile before walking away. Tapping Eric gently on the shoulder, I felt an intruder, a voyeur. Ronah's beady black eyes bored into me as Eric turned around, a startled expression on his face. Brushing Ronah's hand away, he was clearly embarrassed.

"Hi, Maggie," he said, blushing.

I smiled. Ronah was appraising me flagrantly, her eyes sweeping over my entire body from head to toe as if she was evaluating the only obstacle between herself and a cooperative apartment on East End Avenue, a membership in a country club in Westchester, and a brand-new last name. Although it was entirely possible that she loved him and this was terribly unfair, I immediately dismissed that thought from my mind, reckoning that there was nothing fair about Ronah Pierce's robbing Maggie Sommers of her options.

Eric shifted self-consciously from one foot to the other and blushed an even deeper shade of red as I reached up to straighten his tie. Don't worry, Eric, I thought. This one won't leave you just because your wife makes proprietary gestures to your tie—she wants your charge cards too much. Eric coughed nervously several times as I picked a speck of imaginary lint from his lapel. Don't be uncomfortable, Eric. Soon she'll be picking lint off your clothes and even doing your laundry, and she'll never run off to do a story without remembering to tell you where the ticket is for your shirts. In fact, Eric, she'll never be running off to do anything, because her only job will be as your wife. Eric took out a handkerchief and mopped his brow as I linked my arm through his. Poor Eric, he was even too flustered to introduce us properly, and Ronah was clearly uncertain of the protocol for wife meets girlfriend.

"Hello," I finally said, extending my hand, which I noticed was covered with ink stains. "I'm Maggie."

Ronah took it gingerly, shook it without any grip, because she must have either been concerned about breaking one of her spectacular fingernails or was loath to touch my less than spotless hand.

"I'm pleased to make your acquaintance," she said in a heavy New York accent.

Charmed, I'm sure. "Eric," I said, feeling nauseated, "get me a drink, please."

"Right," he answered eagerly. "What do you want?"

Hemlock, straight up. "Scotch on the rocks, please."

We were alone, the soon to be ex-Mrs. Ornstein and the soon to be new Mrs. Ornstein. I had this fleeting fantasy of simply telling Ronah that I knew everything and how pointless it was to pretend that nothing was going on when it would really be so much more civilized to sit down and decide upon the most painless way of handling our little problem. Of course, I wouldn't forget to mention how terribly delighted I was for both of them, which would be a blatant lie since I was having extreme difficulty controlling myself from ripping off her false eyelashes. But she was playing for keeps, and I had all I could do to keep up.

"You certainly look different on television."

That was a hard call: Take it as a compliment or fight back? "Thank you. What do you do?" I was really proud of myself for not adding, "in addition to sleeping with my husband."

"I'm a decorator," she said, her beady eyes darting

nervously around the room. "I'm surprised you don't know that. Eric hired me to do your apartment."

This was too much—the sheets weren't even cold and already I was being eased out. "Oh," I said. Brilliant.

"I'm really anxious to begin," she said, fiddling with her lime-green-seashell belt.

Her bobbed nose suddenly caused me great concern for Eric's unborn children, as it was unclear just how bad it had been before she had it fixed. But I forgot about the genetic implications of this union when the anger enveloped me.

"What luck that he found someone to do that," I said, my camera smile frozen on my face, "because we're just not sure what color to do the nursery."

She turned a ghastly shade of green, not unlike her belt, and began tapping her fingernails together furiously.

"But of course," I added, "we should probably wait until after the baby is born, unless we just do it in yellow and be done with it."

Ronah's thin mouth twisted from side to side as she tried to form words.

My eyebrows were raised, my lips parted slightly, as I stood there shamelessly doing nothing to allay her worst fears.

"Are you and Eric," she finally stammered, "are you, I mean, does he, are you having a—a baby?"

I actually tossed my head and laughed one of those "Let them eat cake" chuckles that ladies occasionally emit at cocktail parties in Washington when the Republicans are in office.

"Well, are you?" she repeated, shrill and desperate.

And I felt sorry for her because she was so hungry, so insecure, so afraid that she would lose what she believed was her dream. I could have lied and caused her tremendous anxiety. I could have dashed those hopes of hers with a word, making her angry and miserable. Or I could have continued to feel for her and walked away from this messy situation, allowing her to make a life with my husband. But had I done that, capitulated without even telling the tiniest lie, I would have been forced to make a life for myself, which was terrifying to me. The answer,

I reasoned, was somewhere in the middle of those options: Ronah Pierce should have to suffer just a bit as a small price for the happiness she would eventually find when Maggie Sommers was all alone.

"I'm not pregnant yet," I answered shyly, "but Eric is desperate to have a child." That certainly wasn't a lie—it was merely a question of who got to be first to give him what he so desperately wanted.

Ronah turned a chalk white from her former shade of ghastly green. "But you don't want children, I thought," she slipped.

"What makes you think that?" I asked sweetly, wishing I were still in the edit room.

"I mean," she faltered, "you have your career. I thought that someone like you—I mean, you're busy and everything."

I put my hand on her arm. "You're right, Ronah, but it's very complicated."

She pulled away, her eyes opened wide before she began coughing uncontrollably.

Ignoring her little seizure, I forged on. "Are you married?"

"No, not yet," she choked out.

"Oh, are you going with anyone?"

Her cough had subsided. "You might say that," she said coldly.

Sisterly, sincere, interested: I was all those things. "How long have you been going with him?"

"It's really none of your business." she snapped.

I flinched. She was tough. "I'm sorry; I didn't mean to intrude."

"I just try to keep my professional life separate from my personal life," she said haughtily. "And since I'll be doing your apartment, it's probably best not to get too involved."

This one was positively unbelievable. "When did Eric tell you to begin?"

"Begin?"

"The apartment."

"Oh, anytime I want to, but he did say that he wanted it finished by summer."

Time was clearly running out for me. "I'd like you to take a look at an apartment of a friend of mine. She just had a terrible tragedy, but her house is quite beautiful," I said.

"Why?"

"Why? Because the man she had been seeing suddenly went back to his wife. Of course, he paid for this fabulous apartment and had it decorated, but she's miserable. I like the look of the living room."

"I prefer to do my own work, without any outside influence. I find I get better results. How long was she with him?"

"Who?"

"Your friend and that married guy."

"Oh. About six months, but it didn't really matter, because married men rarely leave their wives."

She was suddenly angry, defending the cause, forgetting that she always made a point of never mixing business with personal. "Yeah, well, they do if the wives are cold fish and the girlfriends hot."

If only we had been having this conversation on an airplane: There would have been a sickness bag. Eric appeared with our drinks before I could respond, a Scotch on the rocks for the exiting cold fish and a Bloody Mary for the entering hot tamale, which was really quite sweet considering he hadn't even asked what Ronah was drinking. And it was that particular action which proved to me that this was probably the real thing—love—since my husband was neither practiced in the art of deception nor known for his thoughtful and considerate behavior.

"Eric," Ronah said sharply, "illuminate my ignorance. *Your wife* tells me that you're still trying to have a baby."

Oh, my God. Not only did this woman want my husband and my apartment with the walk-in cedar closet, but she also wanted her ignorance illuminated.

Eric looked wildly around the room, as if he expected an invisible hand to pluck him up and save him from this horrible situation. But instead of being saved, he managed to make it worse. He moved, an abrupt and sudden jerk to his wrist, causing the glass of Scotch to crash to the floor, but not before the golden liquid splattered all over the front of Ronah's kelly-green skirt. Letting out a squeal, she jumped back and began frantically brushing the whisky away. Eric looked at me beseechingly, but I simply shrugged my shoulders in helpless resignation.

"Here, Ronah," he managed to say, handing her a cocktail napkin. "Take this."

She pushed it away as she fled to what I imagined was the women's room, to clean her clothes.

We were alone.

"She's very pretty," I remarked.

"Who?" Eric asked in an unnaturally high-pitched voice.

"Ronah."

We were both silent, until we began speaking at the same moment.

"You first," I said, laughing.

"No, it was nothing. What did you want to say?" He didn't even crack a smile.

"How did you meet her?"

"She's Mrs. Pierce's daughter, and when she was sick with the flu, Ronah substituted for her. I think it was about two months ago, because she had just moved up from Florida. I think she got divorced or something."

Divorced or something. He probably knew her entire history, not to mention the texture of the skin on her inner thigh. But then she had allowed him that. I forbade him everything.

"She looks like Mrs. Pierce."

"No," Eric said defensively. "She's much better-looking."

It was all so pathetic and pointless, because fundamentally he deserved better than this. I had been a lousy wife—unwilling to give him what he wanted—and Ronah was so well suited to his needs. But those benevolent thoughts didn't last too long because he wouldn't even allow me that.

"I'm not angry, Eric," I said gently.

"About what?" the hypocrite and liar answered.

"About Ronah," I said sweetly.

"Why should you be angry about her? I'm the one who

should be angry at you, for telling people that we're trying to have a baby, for God's sake.''

"Well, aren't you? I mean, don't you keep telling me
that you want one? Isn't that why you keep trying to take
my temperature every morning?''

"Ssh," Eric whispered. "Shut up." He was playing
it very close to the vest: The first one who turned up with
a child got him. Say the magic word, and the duck came
down and gave you Eric.

"Why should I shut up? It's true, isn't it?''

"Look, Maggie, talking about it and actually doing
something about it are two very different things, and we
haven't been doing too much about it lately.''

"I guess we haven't been, have we?'' And then an
overwhelming feeling of despair enveloped me, because
it was all falling apart, ending, and despite everything, I
found that terribly sad.

"And another thing," he continued, gathering momentum. "I'm not happy.''

"Umm, peals of laughter don't exactly echo in our
house, do they?''

"Listen," he said suddenly, grabbing my arm, "if
you're willing to get pregnant, I'm willing to try and
laugh. What do you think?''

It didn't sound that fair to me, a baby for a laugh, a
fetus for a chuckle. "Eric," I said sadly, "I have to go
home. I've got some work to finish up. We'll talk about
this another time.''

He nodded and took my arm, leading me through the
crowd, past the smoke-colored sliding glass panels, and
into the reception area, decorated with pink cupids and
puffy white clouds. We were standing together, waiting
for the elevator, when Ronah appeared, a large water stain
on the front of her kelly-green skirt.

I held out my hand. "Goodbye, Ronah. It was good to
meet you.''

She ignored my hand, glancing at Eric and then back
at me, before shrugging her shoulders. There was a smirk
on her pinched-in face. "I guess it was only a question
of time before you found out about us.''

"For Christ sake," Eric exploded. "That's going to cost me."

The elevator came and left, with me still standing in the reception area, literally caught in the middle of the two of them.

I looked at Ronah.

"Well, I just wanted her to know that if anybody is going to have your baby, it's going to be me," she shrieked.

I looked at Eric.

"I told you I'd handle it," he answered her, through clenched teeth.

I looked at Ronah.

"Oh, yeah, putz—well, you don't seem to be doing such a great job." And then she actually jabbed her finger into Eric's chest. He grabbed it and twisted until she screamed.

"Ouch!"

I looked at Eric.

"Listen," he shouted, "my word is good! All you're supposed to do is play with your fabrics and leave the rest to me."

I looked at Ronah.

"Leave it to you, my ass—after she tells me that you're still trying to convince her to have a baby."

I looked at Eric.

"Look, she's still my wife," he whined.

I looked at Ronah.

"So, schmuck, now you're defending her?"

I looked at Eric.

"I'm not defending her," he hissed. "But do you want to live like a pauper?"

I looked at Ronah.

"You'll be paying alimony for years anyway," she hissed back. "Who would marry her, with ink stains all over her hands?"

"Excuse me, please," I said politely, tapping Eric on the back.

They both stopped screeching and looked at me as if they were seeing me for the first time, which they prob-

ably were since they had obviously assumed I had gone
down in the elevator.

"What do you want now?" Ronah said, her eyes narrowed. "Haven't you caused me enough grief?"

"Ronah," Eric said harshly, "shut up."

And then she actually began to weep, which only
prompted Eric to moan, "Oh, no—will you knock it off."

"I can't help it," she sniffled. "I love you."

And then everything changed. She was the wounded
party, because loving him afforded her a new status that
I could never hope to achieve. She was an endangered
species, an out-of-print rare book, someone deserving of
protection, respect, gratitude. She loved him.

"Maggie," Eric said coldly, "I thought you left. Do
you need bus fare?"

The transition from meriting cab fare to getting bus
fare in those circles could be brutal.

"No, thank you, Eric. I have money."

But he had already produced a dime and a quarter from
his pocket. "Here, take this in case you need change,"
he said, wiping the corners of his mouth with the back
of his hand.

I ignored the small change, suddenly preoccupied with
bigger bucks, namely my salary checks deposited in his
bank account for the past several years. But it was not
the moment.

"Eric, could I talk to you alone for a moment?"

He turned to Ronah. "Will you be all right?"

"Uh huh," she wept.

"What is it, Maggie?" he said impatiently, as he led
me to the far side of the reception area.

But Ronah was right behind us.

"Eric, I'm sorry that this had to happen like this. I
feel terrible."

"What exactly do you think happened?" he asked
sternly.

I didn't quite understand right away what he meant,
but then it dawned on me. "I don't think, Eric. I know."

"Just what do you know, Miss Investigative Reporter?"

I shook my head.

"Well, don't just stand there—you're on. Tell me what you know."

"Eric," I began, "why are you making this more difficult than it is?"

"I'm not making it anything," he said with a sarcastic laugh. "I'm just an innocent bystander."

"All right, Eric," I said, turning to walk away. "Let's just forget it."

He caught my arm. "Where do you think you're going?"

I squirmed out of his grasp. "Home. At least it's still my home until she decorates it."

He laughed a hollow laugh. "Nothing happened here, Maggie, and don't feel terrible about anything. Ronah is just high-strung and can't help herself."

Ronah moved closer to us. "What does that mean?"

"Yes, what does that mean, Eric?" I added.

He looked from one to the other of us. "I'm an attractive guy, a good catch, and a lot of women have crushes on me. It's meaningless."

"What a crock of shit that is!" Ronah shouted.

"Ronah," he said tightly, turning around, "will you go inside and leave us alone for a minute?"

"Never mind, Eric. The elevator is here, and this time I'm getting in it."

The elevator door closed on Eric Ornstein and Ronah Pierce, he bending down to pick up that dime and that quarter that must have dropped when she shoved him, and she tapping her right spike-heeled shoe precariously near his head. Safely inside the elevator was a very relieved Maggie Sommers—relieved because she had finally found out that Eric had been doing to her what she had been doing to him, and ironically it was Ronah who had illuminated her ignorance.

○

Mother shrugs her shoulders, turns, and steps inside the walk-in closet in my bedroom. Sighing deeply several times, she begins to separate my skirts from my dresses from my blouses from my slacks. Although I try repeatedly to coax her out, she persists on attacking, with a vengeance, the rows of clothes that are hanging on wire hangers, while she makes intermittent disgusted clucking noises with her tongue. Sitting on the radiator cover under my window, I am wondering how I can convince Mother that it makes absolutely no difference to me that my clothes are not hung on monogrammed hangers in neatly defined rows, as are Cara's in her walk-in closet in Short Hills, New Jersey.

"Wire hangers are merely another example of why you failed as a wife. Why can't you be like Cara? She's such a joy, conforming to all those standards of normal living."

"Mother, please."

"Don't 'please' me," she says. "It's all part of the same thing and precisely why a perfectly decent man like Eric is busy having babies with another woman. It's the hangers."

It is only slightly disturbing to me that I understand Mother's reasoning in comparing my failure to bear Eric's children with wire hangers.

Carrying a pile of them, which she places in a heap on the floor next to my distressed-oak double dresser, she looks over at me, undoubtedly waiting for me to ask what wire hangers have to do with my reluctance to make a normal life for myself. I ask. She breathes a sigh, which I interpret to be relief, and turns around. "There are certain habits a woman forms when she's still young," she says, opening the top drawer of my dresser and making another disgusted clucking noise. "I tried to ingrain those habits into you from the time you were fifteen. Those habits allow decent men like Eric to be comfortable in their marriages, knowing they are married to women with normal desires." She pauses, tossing my brassieres and panty hose out of the drawer and onto the bed. "Those women don't depend on cleaning establishments for their clothes hangers; they order monogrammed hangers, which indicate to their friends and family that they are indeed part of the system. It's like natural childbirth, something you wouldn't know about."

I turn my head away from the window and look at her. "What do you mean?"

"I mean," Mother says, "that women like us don't have natural childbirth, where their husbands are in the delivery room watching them dilate to the size of a dinner plate."

"Why not? It's perfectly natural."

"Oh, really. Well, that shows how much you know. No man wants to touch a woman again once he sees her dilated to the size of a dinner plate."

I am trying very hard to digest this last piece of information, because somehow it seems to have a great deal to do with Vera and Alan's relationship and perhaps even with my relationship with both of them. "Was Father in the delivery room when you had us?"

"Certainly not," she exclaims. "Why on earth would you say that?"

"I don't know, I just wondered. Maybe it was why . . . I mean, you and Father . . . ."

Mother opens the second drawer of my dresser and continues, ignoring my explanation. "What we should really do is make a list of all the things you need, so maybe you can start living a normal life, if it's not too late." She folds my sweaters neatly, shaking her head and muttering. "You're damaged goods, Maggie," she says, "and it's very doubtful that you'll ever find a suitable man who's willing to marry a thirty-four-year-old woman who is apparently still so unwilling to conform."

But I had already stopped listening, because all I could think of was Avi in the delivery room with me, holding my hand, while I gave birth to our child. He would never consider me a dinner plate, or damaged goods for that matter, just because I depended on cleaning establishments for my clothes hangers. It was impossible to explain to Mother that the reason I didn't choose a man like Avi Herzog in the first place and avoid a divorce was that it was always easier for me to fail, more difficult for me to succeed. So instead I decided to challenge Mother on her whole basic premise.

"You're the kind of woman you describe, aren't you?"

"I certainly try to be," she answers smugly.

"Then how do you explain your own failed marriage, even with monogrammed hangers, pedicures, and all those other trappings of that normal life you talk about?"

"I suppose," she said, biting her lip, "that sometimes even all that is not enough."

There is no warning, not the slightest hint of what is about to happen, except for one muffled sob. Vera stumbles to the bed and collapses in a tearful heap on my black-and-gray quilt. It would be a lie to admit that I don't feel responsible for her tears. But it is obvious they are not due solely to my unwillingness to conform to her standards of living.

Before I can say anything, she raises herself up to a sitting position and says, "You don't even own one navy-blue outfit, Marguerite."

"I hate navy, Mother," I answer, genuinely perplexed.

"Navy-green, navy-red, navy-yellow, navy-white," she sobs. "Oh, Marguerite, I just can't take it anymore."

"Mother," I say soothingly, "please don't cry, and we'll make that list of everything I need to be normal, and I'll even buy a navy outfit, I promise, and I'll never dilate to the size of a dinner plate."

"Oh, yes you will," she sobs. "You'll see."

"Mother, if I knew how these simple things upset you, then believe me I would never have said anything about hangers or not had something navy in the closet. I swear to you, Mother, I—"

"Oh, Marguerite," Vera cries, extracting a white lace handkerchief from the left cuff of her black sweater, "you're so stupid." Blowing her nose loudly, she snivels, "If he leaves me, I'll kill myself."

I put my arms around her and hold her close, feeling her tears on my cheek as she murmurs over and over that she just can't survive without him. The woman in my arms is my mother, someone who has managed to conform to the system and maintain an outwardly normal marriage for thirty-eight years. The irony is that this normal woman with normal desires is being comforted by a woman who is nothing more than damaged goods. Yet if I forget about the details, those minor differences that have created the enormous chasm between us, I can understand why she is in so much pain. She is agonizing over a man she loves, someone who has hurt her throughout the years, a man who also happens to be my father and has hurt me as well.

Vera disengages herself from my grasp and gathers up the hairpins that have fallen from her chignon and lie strewn all over the quilt. She looks so very vulnerable with her long black hair falling loosely down her back, several fine lines visible around her red-rimmed eyes, and traces of lipstick caught in the creases above her upper lip. I can picture just how beautiful she must have been when Alan married her so many years ago. And I'm happy for me, yet sad for her, that this involuntary display of emotion happened now and not with Cara, who is always in Aruba with a faithful husband and the three products of their love.

"Do you remember when you were seven years old," Mother asks suddenly, "and I took you and Cara to the Plaza for brunch that Easter Sunday?" I shake my head. There were so many Easter Sunday brunches at the Plaza Hotel, when Mother dressed Cara and Marguerite up in navy-blue-and-white sailor outfits and white straw hats with blue ribbons that streamed down their straight little backs. There were so many Easter Sunday brunches when Cara and Marguerite sat at attention at the corner table in the Palm Court of the Plaza Hotel and tried not to point at the array of fascinating people that swept by. "Gesture, dears," Mother would say, "don't point." And Cara and Marguerite would giggle as they imitated Mother's sweeping hand gestures each time another extraordinary person breezed by in another fabulous ensemble. Cara and Marguerite would nudge each other excitedly under the table, intent that neither one nor the other of them missed one single sensational sight that paraded before their eyes during those Easter Sunday brunches. And I remember how Mother would solemnly instruct us to chew our scrambled eggs slowly, mouths closed, and no vulgar gulping noises, if you please, ladies.

"Breathe quietly through your nose, Marguerite," Mother would say as Marguerite made snorting sounds because of an acute case of adenoids. And I remember how Mother would pat the corners of her mouth daintily and frown when Cara or Marguerite smeared their napkins across their faces indelicately. I remember all those Easter Sunday brunches from the time Cara was seven and Marguerite was five.

The memory of Alan Sommers at any family gathering always remains more a vague impression than an actual fact, although I can picture him arriving late and leaving early when he did appear. There was one particular Easter Sunday brunch that does seem more vivid than the others, one where Father never did show up at all to share our delight in the assortment of brightly wrapped chocolate Easter eggs nestled on green paper grass that lined the bottom of the yellow baskets we received at the end of every brunch.

"I remember once when Father wasn't there. Was I seven then?"

"He never showed up," Vera says dreamily. "We sat and waited and waited, until finally I ordered scrambled eggs for you and Cara and eggs benedict for myself."

"Now I remember," I say. "That was the day that Cara took one bite of her scrambled eggs and threw up all over the pretty pink tablecloth."

Mother wrinkles up her nose at my graphic description of poor Cara's unfortunate malady that fateful Easter Sunday. "You started to cry," Vera continues, "because the Easter bunny forgot to come to our table and give you the basket of chocolate eggs."

It's all very clear to me now, how traumatic it was when the Easter bunny ignored me and gave all the other children in the Palm Court those yellow baskets filled with gaily wrapped chocolate eggs. It never occurred to me until right now that the bunny probably didn't ignore me as much as he avoided coming over to a table where a child had just finished vomiting.

"I tried to be gay and happy, make light of poor Cara's predicament," Vera explains, dabbing at her eyes with a white lace handkerchief, "so I wrapped a linen napkin around Cara's stained dress and promised you chocolate eggs when we got home. Do you remember what happened then?''

I close my eyes, trying very hard to reconstruct the events after Vera hurried Cara with the linen napkin tied around her neck and Marguerite without her basket of Easter eggs out of the Plaza. ''Yes,'' I say carefully. ''We got home and you put Cara to bed. I remember sitting on the big chair in Cara's room. You let us watch television together.''

Mother sighs deeply. And then it all comes back to me. After Mother took Cara's temperature, sponged her fevered brow with a cool washcloth, produced five gaily wrapped chocolate eggs for me, tucked Cara into her bed with nice fresh sheets, propped me up in a chair in Cara's bedroom, adjusted the television set to a delightful puppet show for her two daughters, kissed Cara and me tenderly on our foreheads . . . it was only then, when all her duties were diligently performed, that Vera Sommers walked calmly into her bedroom, locked the door, and . . .

''I swallowed eighteen Seconal capsules,'' she says calmly.

I am stunned, even though somewhere in the recesses of my mind I knew it all along. But hearing it from her made it more horrible, robbed me of the remote thought I had clung to over the years—that it was possibly all exaggerated.

''Your father spent the day with another woman, someone he had been seeing for several months.''

''Then why did you try to kill yourself on that particular day?''

''Because,'' she answers quietly, ''he asked me for a divorce that morning.''

''Then why did you wait all day? I don't understand.'' And somehow it was more important to understand the irrelevant and inconsequential details of time and place than to be forced to concentrate on the heartbreaking and fundamental realities.

''Because I told him that if he didn't show up at the Plaza, I would know that he meant what he said. And he never showed up.''

"My God, Mother," I cry, "suppose he had gotten stuck in traffic or had an accident or a million other reasons and didn't intend to go through with the divorce—then what? You would've done something horrible for no reason."

"No," she says firmly, "I just knew. I couldn't bear to face life without him, alone with two small children. I thought you'd be better off without me."

"Oh, we would have been just great, the two of us with Father and some idiot," I say furiously.

"She wasn't an idiot," Mother says quietly. "She was a nurse."

I am even more stunned that she is actually defending him, defending his taste in some idiot who might have been our stepmother.

Father finally came home that night and found he couldn't get into the bedroom. He pounded on the door, calling Mother's name, until Jonesie ran out of her room at the other end of the apartment and, together with Father, broke down the door.

"I had already drifted off, I guess," Mother explains. "Later Jonesie told me what happened—how she put cold compresses on my head." Mother laughs. "As if that would help; poor Jonesie. And then Father called an ambulance, and the next thing I remember, I was waking up in a lovely green-and-white room in the hospital after they pumped my stomach. I had such a lovely view of the East River with all the boats and that cute little park near the mayor's house."

She is clearly warped—perhaps even slightly mad. It's not clear because there were reasons, excuses.

"When I woke up," Vera says, "Father was right there with me, sitting on my bed."

"Is that supposed to make it better, knowing that he stuck by you until what was almost the very end?"

"He said I failed, that I drove him to it, and now I had let him down even more by trying to shirk my responsibilities."

I am livid. "And you *believed* him?"

Vera lowers her head as she twists the white lace handkerchief around her fingers. Stomping angrily to the window, I whirl around to face her.

"Listen, Mother, you didn't fail Father. He's just a selfish, egocentric son of a bitch."

"Don't you dare talk about him like that," she says, her bottom lip trembling.

"Oh, my God," I say softly. "Why do you keep defending him?"

"And what am I supposed to do—pick up and leave at my age?"

I am silent.

"You see," she says triumphantly. "It's not so easy when you have nothing else. My career was my marriage."

"So it was difficult then," I say, sitting down next to her, "when you had two little children, but now it would be easier. You have no responsibilities except to yourself, and you certainly don't have financial problems. Why go on suffering when you could be comfortable without him?"

But she doesn't appear to be listening to me, as she gazes off somewhere in the distance.

"He was your lover, wasn't he?" she says suddenly.

"Who, Mother?"

"That man who got killed in Beirut—he was your lover, wasn't he?"

It is surprising that the conversation has suddenly switched to Joe—a sign that it has turned from the insanities of day-to-day living to the insanities of day-to-day dying.

"No, Mother, he wasn't my lover, he was just my friend."

And why did I say "just" in front of "friend" and leave "lover" unqualified, as if it is somehow better to have a lover than a loving friend? And why would I exclude the possibility of sleeping with a friend anyway, unless I had gotten into the habit of making love with my enemies?

"Joe was gay, Mother; he had a lover who dances with the American Ballet Theatre."

She is silent, watching as I sift through the pile of

panty hose on the bed until I find a pair of gray that will match the gray mohair turtleneck dress I plan to wear to dinner tonight with Grayson, Elliot, and Quincy. "And I suppose the Israeli general is gay too," she say sarcastically.

"No, Mother," I say calmly. "He's my lover." I pause. "And he's also my friend."

She nods. There seems to be an unspoken truce, which lasts only long enough for me to pull on my gray panty hose and walk to the closet to get my dress.

"Why do all Israeli men wear those awful short-sleeved shirts without ties even when they're meeting in the Knesset?" She has seen enough television shots of Israeli officials milling around in front of the Israeli parliament in short-sleeved shirts without ties to have noticed their customary attire.

"Israel is a casual country, where formality is less important than practicality, and it's usually warm there."

"I was amazed, Marguerite," she continues, "when I visited Israel and saw that everybody danced to the paso doble, not to mention how appalled I was to see that the men all shoved toothpicks into their mouths after a meal. Does he dance the paso doble?"

"Only if he has a toothpick in his mouth," I answered flippantly, hunting around on the floor of my closet for my gray boots.

The second shot hits me square in the stomach as I lean over to pull on my boots, which were buried under a pile of boxes.

"And I suppose he's married."

Straightening up slowly, I walked over to the bed, sit down next to her, and take her hand. "You're not going to ruin this one; this one is different."

"I'm not ruining anything," she protests. "I simply asked if he was married, and from your reaction he obviously is."

"I know it sounds trite, but his marriage hasn't been a marriage for years, and he's a decent human being, Mother, someone who—"

"Who is too busy dancing the paso doble with a toothpick hanging out of his mouth to bother getting a divorce," she interrupts.

"You're not going to ruin this," I repeat quietly. "Now just stop it."

And she does stop as she watches me brush my hair.

"Maggie," she says suddenly, "do you love this man, I mean really love him, where you feel inexplicable sensations when he touches your hand, or your eyes well up with tears when you watch him from a distance doing some mundane little chore? Do you just automatically fall into his arms every night and forget everything else in the world when you're near him?"

Turning around slowly, I look at her in disbelief. I suddenly want to hold her, to press my cheek against hers. She is my mother, someone I have known all my life, someone for whom I feel many different emotions. Yet there is something more; I am reeling from the discovery I have just made of this other part of her. I am her daughter, not solely because I have her green eyes, black hair, high cheekbones. The bond I share with her at this moment has only to do with passion. It is suddenly understandable why she tried to end her life that Easter Sunday morning, and it had nothing to do with a fear of being alone with two small children. Alan Sommers, a man I find to be cruel, pompous, and unattractive, is the object of Vera's passion. But the kind of chemistry that Mother has just described has nothing to do with sterling character, good looks, or human kindness. It is simply a question of skin, and the only tragedy is that unstable people such as Mother should never know that kind of passion. It can be deadly.

"Do you love him like that, Marguerite?" she asks in a soft voice.

"Yes, but I would never take my own life if he left me," I say firmly.

"When did you fall in love with him?"

"I'm not sure," I say thoughtfully, "but Joe's death had a lot to do with it. His death was so senseless, so tragic, that it made life completely meaningless. I walked around with this overwhelming sadness because every-

thing could end from one minute to the next—so brutally.''

"So you fell in love with him the day your sound man
was killed?''

I smile. "Not really. I fell in love with him the first
time I ever saw him, but I didn't let anyone know about
it, including myself, until that day with Joe. I suddenly
became very frightened that my life was nothing more
than another assignment. And then I got scared of him
and ran away.''

"Why?''

"I was torn between loving Avi and not caring about
my career, and losing my career because I loved him.''

"And now?''

"Now it's easy to say that without him I feel empty—
that I want him and I don't care about anything else. But
I'm here and he's there.''

Vera takes the brush out of my hand and begins running it through my hair.

"When I met your father,'' she says softly, "he already had many women. But I was very independent,
believe it or not; I was teaching school and had practically no interest in getting married.'' She smiles. "I think
he wanted me so much because I was the first woman
who didn't really want him.''

Father pursued her for months before she would even
agree to go out with him. And when she finally did agree
to have dinner with him, that brash, ambitious Jewish
lawyer who wanted to be the best at everything he did
and own the most beautiful of everything he saw—which
is why he wanted Vera—she found him irresistible.

"He proposed on the second date and I accepted,'' she
says, handing me the brush.

"You must have really loved him,'' I said.

"You know, Marguerite,'' she says shyly, "you don't
have the corner on passion, you and your Avi.''

That statement sounds so very familiar, as if I heard it
somewhere not too long ago.

○

Avi was standing at the sink in the bathroom of my small apartment hotel suite in Tel Aviv, a white towel wrapped around his trim waist and shaving cream all over his face. I was standing behind him, his tattered maroon-and-blue-striped terry-cloth robe tied loosely around me, my arms encircling his chest, my head leaning against his broad back. I listened as he explained how the tide had turned in Lebanon, how Syria's position was getting stronger since the assassination of Bashir Gemayel and the mas-sacres at Sabra and Shatilla. I kept hoping that he wouldn't have to go up to the north today, to the Israeli-Lebanon border, because Palestinian terrorists were once again launching Katyusha rockets into the small Israeli town of Rosh Hanikra.

"Millions of men can shave in the morning without their women standing behind them and grabbing the hair on their chest," he said, smiling.

"Millions of women send their men off to work in the morning," I answered, stroking his muscular stomach, "and I'm probably the only woman who's sending her man off to a combat zone."

"Not here you're not, my sweet, not here."

I suppose it was foolish to be so frightened, but it was December 6, exactly two weeks after the day of the gray metal casket, and it was particularly difficult. I tried not to dwell on it as I kissed his back, burying my face in his skin while he finished shaving, splashed water on his cheeks, and patted himself dry with a towel.

Turning around, he took me in his arms. "Just think about the four days we're going to have together," he said, kissing my hair.

"Tell me again," I whispered, my lips pressed against his ear.

"I'll be back around six to meet you on the veranda of the King David Hotel. Then we'll drive to the Dead Sea, where we'll have four days together alone."

"Will it be good?" I asked, burying my face in his neck.

He tilted my chin with his hand and kissed me softly on the mouth. "What do you think?" he said hoarsely.

"Tell me again—I want to hear it." And we both knew

that this was just a ploy, a stalling tactic before his driver arrived to take him to the north.

"Yes," he said patiently. "It will be good."

"And tell me again," I teased, "about the enemy of the good."

Avi laughed. "So now you're making fun of my English."

"Not the English, just what it loses in translation."

Silently, he took my hand and led me out of the bathroom and into the bedroom, where he gently sat me down in a big chair near the window. Kneeling down in front of me, he put his arms around my waist. "Come on," I said, running my hands through his thick hair, "say it." He closed his eyes and smiled. "OK. The enemy of the good is the better." And I understood so well what he meant, the significance of that phrase, representing all that we stood for.

Once in Poland, when Nazis were overrunning towns and village, a mother admonished her daughter, "Be grateful that they have not yet found us, that we still have some bread left to eat and a roof over our heads. Things are good." And then shots were fired, houses were razed to the ground and people herded off to die. Somehow that mother managed to escape to Israel with her daughter. Once in Tel Aviv during a war, she scolded the girl. "A roof over our head and bread in our belly are not good enough. We will die to protect our country, for the enemy of the good is the better. And better is no more war."

It was six-thirty in the morning, a Monday, and he was scheduled to leave at seven. I had an appointment at eight at the Jerusalem Compound to interview an honest-to-goodness bomb-throwing terrorist who had been caught and imprisoned at that particular detention center. This time, ABN had made a point of requesting that the subject not be the usual university-educated smooth-talking preppy killer, the typical media-star terrorist who had been groomed for the Western press. We specifically asked and had been assured by Israeli authorities that the prisoner in the compound would have blood on his hands and no regrets for the crimes he had committed in the name of his revolution.

Just an ordinary day in the life of two people, I thought, watching Avi dress that morning. There were tears in my eyes as I observed him searching in the dresser drawer for a pair of socks, performing one of those mundane functions of everyday life while unaware he was being watched.

"Someday," he said, flinging clothes on the floor, "when life is back to normal, you'll give me two dresser drawers, and then I'll know that you're serious about me, not to mention the fact that I'll be able to find my clothes in the morning."

I wiped my tears and didn't respond.

He smiled, triumphantly holding up a pair of matching socks. And he saw my tears but chose not to react, because there was nothing much he could do or say that would make it better. He was leaving for the north of Israel, the south of Lebanon, where he would be in the middle of falling Katyusha rockets and random snipers with deadly RPG grenades, like the one that had killed Joe Valeri exactly two weeks ago today. Glancing out the window, I noticed the blue water of the Mediterranean and the smooth white sand where the usual group of elderly residents of Tel Aviv were already tossing beach balls back and forth near the water's edge. And it all seemed so remote from the fighting that still raged in Beirut. After six years of battle and in spite of those blasted red lines that indicated noncombat zones, Syria and Israel were once again confronting each other, which meant that the war was clearly not over. Avi was constantly at risk.

He was dressed in his shapeless khaki army pants, clumsy high-laced black boots, and green shirt with the stenciled insignia of a *tat aluf*—a sword crossed with an olive branch—worn only in the field. He looked so handsome in his work clothes, dressed to kill—or worse, dressed to die.

The telephone rang shrilly then, temporarily shaking me out of my morbid mood. It could only be Avi's driver, calling to say that he was waiting for him downstairs.

"It's for you," Avi said, handing me the phone.

Looking at him quizzically, I listened as Gila asked if she could send someone up to our room to change the mattress.

"Fine," I said, "anytime, because we're both leaving in a little while." I hardly had time to put down the receiver when the phone rang again, and this time it was Avi's driver, Moshe Morad, calling to say that he was waiting downstairs.

We walked down the corridor toward the elevator together, our arms around each other, until we stopped, hugging for a few moments. It wasn't terribly glamorous to be wrapped in a tattered maroon-and-blue terry-cloth robe as I sent the man I loved off to the front lines. How typically dramatic of me to think that, except that it was unfortunately true. Taking Avi's hand, I pressed it to my lips. He smiled as he reached over my shoulder and pushed the button with his other hand.

"If you're going to make yourself sick every time I have to do what I do, you're going to look terrible, and then," he said, kissing my nose, "nobody will ever want you but me."

"Nobody ever wanted me the way you do anyway," I said.

If only I looked like those lissome girls right now, the ones who waved and blew kisses to the sailors during World War II when the big battleships steamed off to war, to faraway oceans. I imagined myself standing on one of those piers, wearing wedgie shoes and a yellow dress that buttoned tightly across the bodice, a yellow flower stuck behind one ear and bright-red lipstick on my lips. It was certainly quite different than the reality—standing in a hotel corridor wearing an old bathrobe, with no makeup on and two combs holding back my disheveled hair. But it didn't seem to bother Avi Herzog.

"Everybody wants you," he said, smiling, "and everybody still asks me what I've got that got you."

"What do you tell them?" I asked, slightly surprised.

Avi looked at me mischievously and before I could stop him, he grabbed his crotch. "This," he said. "This is what I tell them got you."

Just as Avi Herzog was holding on to his crotch and just as I was registering mock outrage, the elevator door slid open, and a man clad in a powder-blue leisure suit and a woman wearing a pink and red floral-print dress, with buttons pinned to their clothes that read GOD IS MY BEST FRIEND, stared at us with expressions of horror and disbelief.

Giggling, I leaned against the elevator door. "You are crude and disgusting, General Herzog," I said indignantly, "and I'll thank you not to do that again." He laughed as he pulled me toward him, kissing me on the mouth while the elevator door slammed repeatedly against my shoulder.

"For this we came to the Holy Land," the woman gasped.

"Close your eyes, Gert," the man ordered. "Just don't look."

"Tell me it's not true," Avi said, stepping inside the elevator. "Tell me it wasn't that."

There was no denying it. What could be better than having that, which was impossible to ignore, and hearing "I love you" at the same time? What could be better than knowing it was there, could be called up at a moment's notice, and still being interested in every little mundane detail of his life?

When I reached the door to the apartment, I found it had slammed shut, which meant that I was locked out. I raced up and down the hallways in search of a housekeeper, but to no avail. Finally, I ran to the emergency exit and bounded down the stairs to the lobby for a spare key, so that I could get ready for my appointment in East Jerusalem, which was now less than an hour away. I careened out of the exit door, turned the corner at full speed in the direction of the reception desk, barefoot with my hair flying wildly around my face, and screeched to a full stop in front of Tat Aluf Avi Herzog; Aluf Michne Gidon Levy, a colonel; and Moshe Morad, Avi's driver. But I pretended not to notice them, operating on the principle that they wouldn't notice me.

Standing up to my full height of five feet seven inches in bare feet and with all the dignity I could muster considering the state I was in, I politely asked the girl at the front desk for a key to apartment 608. Herzog, Levy, and Morad were only a few feet away, no longer engaged in what had undoubtedly been intense conversation concerning their trip to the north. I noticed out of the corner of my eye that Levy and Morad were watching me curiously. Herzog, on the other hand, didn't seem to find my appearance in the lobby curious at all, as he sidled up to me and whispered, "What's the matter, sweetheart—did you run after me because you decided I was right?"

My face felt hot. "Please!"

But before I could take the key and discreetly disappear, Mr. Powder Blue and Mrs. Pink and Red Floral with their GOD IS MY BEST FRIEND buttons had rallied other members of their group and were pointing at us. And it was no mystery what they were saying about Avi's crotch and my unnatural attachment to it.

"I got locked out," I whispered. "Go away."

"A likely excuse," Avi said, reaching over my head for the key.

"And anyway," I said, grabbing for the key, "why aren't you gone?"

"Because plans changed," he answered, holding it out of my reach. "I have to report to the prime minister's office in Jerusalem. Come say hello to Gidon and Moshe before you get dressed."

"Like this? I'm a mess."

"You may have just noticed that, my dear, but we already knew." Taking my hand, he led me over to them, obviously less concerned than I that the woman with whom he lived openly in Tel Aviv was in a state of semi-undress and causing a mild sensation.

"Hi, Gidon," I said, genuinely pleased to see the man who was Avi's staunchest support in the field and closest friend in civilian life.

Gidon's personal appearance certainly belied his fierce reputation among the foreign press as an unyielding and uncooperative spokesman for the Israel Defense Forces. Small and slight, with a boyish face and dark curls that flopped down on his forehead, he evoked maternal feelings from most of the women journalists and was shameless about using them to his advantage. He was sweet, tender, and loving to his friends. "I never see you anymore," he said warmly. "Since you started with this one, you're not asking me to brief you on anything."

"It's not because of him," I answered, aware that Mr. Powder Blue and Mrs. Pink and Red were now flanking me. "It's just that they pulled me out of Lebanon. I'm covering Jerusalem."

"Shalom, Maggie," Moshe said shyly.

"Moshe, how are you?" I said, now aware that someone was tapping me on the arm.

"I was sorry to hear what happened to your sound man," Moshe said sincerely. "He was a nice guy."

I nodded my appreciation, ignoring the person who was currently yanking at my sleeve. It was Gidon, however, who inadvertently forced me to respond by acknowledging her. "Did you want to say something?" he inquired politely. I winced.

"Are you Maggie Sommers?" Mrs. Floral Print asked.

Avi edged closer, grinning. Turning around, I shot him a scathing look.

"Yes I am."

"Well, we watch you in Bergen County," she said, "and I'm really so pleased to have this opportunity to talk to you." Who exactly had given this woman an opportunity to talk to me remained a mystery. She seemed to have just assumed that I was easy to approach—and how could I blame her after that terrific display at the elevator. Herzog, I noticed, still had that amused expression on his handsome face as he stood, arms crossed over his chest, just watching the situation develop.

"I can help you change so lust doesn't rule your life."

"Amen," Mr. Powder Blue exclaimed. "Down with fornication."

Gidon had no idea what was going on but at the mere mention of the word *fornication* he visibly perked up. Although my mouth was open in disbelief, I did manage to decline their kind offer by saying, "That's really very nice of both of you to want to help me but I'm not having any problem with lust, at least it's not a problem for me."

It was as if we were on stage, performing a play, because right on cue my best friend in Tel Aviv and the manager of the hotel, Gila Enav, rushed out from behind the reception desk. "Maggie," she said brightly, unaware of what was transpiring in the middle of the lobby, "I'm going to send someone up in a few minutes to replace that mattress—it's pretty worn out." She stopped and looked at me in dismay. "Is that how you're going to work this morning?"

But it was too late.

"May the Lord forgive you," Mr. Powder Blue muttered, while Mrs. Pink and Red thrust a pamphlet at me, one that had REDEMPTION written across the cover in bold black letters.

Gila linked her arm through Avi's and tried not to laugh, because by that time the entire group of Pilgrims from Bergen County, as the other buttons described them, the ones positioned right above GOD IS MY BEST FRIEND, had surrounded us.

Gidon wandered over to Gila and looked admiringly at her breasts before introducing himself. "I'm Gidon Levy," he said with one of his adorable smiles, "and I'm the official tester for all of Herzog's mattresses."

Gila responded predictably. "What a coincidence. I do the same for Sommers, but could you tell me what's going on here?"

My best friend in Tel Aviv, Avi's best friend in civilian life, and the man I loved, the one who had grabbed his crotch at the elevator and started this whole thing, were all standing around the lobby of my apartment hotel in Tel Aviv and having a wonderful time—lusting after each other or just lusting in their hearts. I was humiliated, trying to make an unnoticed escape toward the elevator, when I heard, "Sunday school is over for this morning, everyone. Maggie's got to get ready or she'll be late." Avi took my hands before adding, "Say goodbye, Maggie, and thank these nice people for trying to help you."

"Thank you," I mumbled, allowing him to lead me away. "And I could just kill you. I'm finished in Bergen County."

Avi didn't answer. Instead, he pinned me against the

wall and kissed me. "Did anyone ever tell you that you were a lustful woman?" he said when he released me.

"I suppose you thought that was funny," I said, as the elevator door closed on us.

He was still laughing as we walked back down the corridor together, our arms around each other, the way we had begun the morning. Avi unlocked the door. "Yes, I thought it was very funny, and by the way, where's Bergen County?"

I was brushing my hair standing in front of the mirror, wearing only a pair of black bikini underpants and red sandals on my feet when he came up behind me and cupped my breasts in his hands.

"They're almost too big for me to hold."

"Don't try to make up," I said, reaching down for a black brassiere and a red T-shirt.

"I'm driving you to East Jerusalem, and we'll still meet on the veranda of the King David at six."

Bending over, I hooked my brassiere. "ABN is going to get mail about this, I guarantee; those lunatics are going to write in."

"It won't bother anybody here in Israel to learn that the ABN correspondent is a fornicator."

I pulled the T-shirt on. "I'm willing to bet that grabbing your crotch like that won't do much for the image of an Israeli general."

Avi smiled. "Don't you know the myths people believe about Israeli generals?"

Shaking my head, I stepped into my blue denim skirt.

"They think we wake up in the morning and swim fifty laps in one of our seas, do a couple of hundred push-ups before we make love five or six times. That's just before breakfast, may I remind you. After breakfast we jog out to the orchard and grab a handful of Jaffa oranges. Then we get down to serious business like rescuing a couple of hostages. After lunch we retire to the briefing room, where we solve one of our border problems, fight a quick war, make some more love. Then after dinner we all gather around to dance the hora for a few hours, make some more love and design a new fighter plane before we fall asleep."

I laughed. "Well, you can count on me to tell everybody that it's not true—I never saw you dance the hora."

"Of course, you've probably just ruined any chance you had of covering the Vatican."

"That's for sure!" I said, snapping the clasp on my watch.

"Your eyes are dark green this morning," he said softly.

"That's because I'm still furious," I answered, trying to sound furious.

We were almost ready to leave. Avi began tossing my tape recorder, batteries, extra cassette tapes, makeup, hairbrush, and notepad into an enormous canvas bag. "See, I'm trying very hard to make up."

Grabbing my small weekend suitcase, I collected the two sets of keys that were lying on the table and looked around the room once.

"You're a beautiful woman," he said, switching off the lights.

"You are forgiven." I laughed. "Just don't do anything else on the way out."

Moshe and Gidon had already left by the time we got downstairs. We climbed into the ABN car, Avi behind the wheel, and began the familiar drive between Tel Aviv and Jerusalem. Gazing out the window, I began making idle conversation.

"I wish we had a proper kitchen in the hotel so I could cook dinner sometimes. I hate always eating in restaurants."

Avi glanced at me. "As soon as we straighten everything out, which will be very soon, we'll not only have a proper kitchen, but also a proper bedroom, where I'll have my own dresser. I'm just as tired as you of living in makeshift quarters. We have to plan the future."

A wave of panic suddenly swept over me as I shifted nervously in the seat and stared morosely out the window. Avi tried to hold my hand, but I pulled it away.

"What's the matter, Maggie?" he said. "Every time I even mention the word *future*, you get upset. Why?"

How could I explain to him that every time he talked about "straightening everything out," my first thought was always about the pain it would cause Ruth. I could just envision the scene in the Herzog house when Avi would finally tell her that he wouldn't be living there anymore. Of course, I always forgot somehow that he hadn't been living there already—and for quite some time. Yet the heartbreak of actually hearing that their life together was officially over and he was beginning a new life with someone else would be unbearable for a woman as fragile as Ruth. I always pictured her with pink plastic rollers in her hair and a wooden ladle in her hand. Tears would stream down her plump cheeks as she cried, "Who's going to pair your socks or make you chicken soup when you're sick?" And then scenes from my childhood flashed before my eyes, and my stomach would knot up as I remembered living in constant fear that Alan Sommers would abandon us. I tried to find the words to explain to Avi, and then they just began to tumble from my mouth, everything that had happened to me and everything that could happen to Ruth. As I poured out my heart, he looked straight ahead, his jaw twitching slightly, his knuckles white from gripping the steering wheel so tightly.

"I'm sorry for her," I explained, "and yet I'm afraid that you'll feel sorry for her and leave me, probably because you'll miss the chicken soup and your socks all neatly paired, and even those cute pink plastic rollers she wears."

He swerved the car over to the side of the road, right beneath a hill where several rusted wagons remained as a memorial to the Jews who had lost their lives during the 1948 war for independence. When the car finally coasted to a halt, he turned to look at me. I was hovering in the corner of my seat, leaning against the door, waiting for the explosion that I sensed was imminent. He ran his hand through his hair, a gesture I knew and loved, before he spoke in a very controlled voice.

"Maggie, Ruth never wore a pink plastic hair roller in her life, and she doesn't know how to cook chicken soup, and . . ." He paused.

"And what?" I asked meekly.

He took a deep breath. "And she doesn't want to be married to me anymore."

"Why? I mean, why didn't you tell me?"

He looked at me very seriously. "Because I didn't want to put pressure on you, I didn't want you to think that I only wanted you so much because I didn't want to be alone." He took out one of his small black cigars and held it between his fingers before lighting it. "You're so independent and strong that I was a little afraid that you'd turn me down." He exhaled some smoke before continuing. "I wasn't sure how to handle you. I wasn't used to someone like you, because Ruth was so predictable, so fragile, which is why it was so surprising when everything changed."

"What changed? I don't understand."

He smiled slightly. "She went back to work, in an architectural firm owned by her brother. I was glad because it gave her something to do, something she was interested in and liked." He glanced out the window. "She met him there."

"Who?"

"An old friend, someone she knew when she was a young girl and first arrived here. I believe her when she says there's nothing between them, and I also believe her when she tells me that she wants a chance to make another life for herself, with someone who wants her." He rubbed his eyes. "She knows that I'm not the one, and she's right to feel that way. She's still so fragile, you know," he concluded defensively.

So much for fragility. It was definite proof that the tsk-rake syndrome still existed. If a woman was perceived as fragile and if she was caught having a lover, it would be viewed in the following way: "Poor Ruthie, Avi ran around on her all her life until she finally found someone who was willing to take care of her because he really loved her, it should only happen to my Miriam, tsk tsk." However, if she was perceived as independent and was caught having a lover, it was viewed quite differently: "That whore Maggie after all that Eric gave her took up with some low-life goy, she couldn't shine my Miriam's shoes, I hope he rakes her over the coals." So in the end

it was really all a question of packaging, and not surprising, therefore, that I felt mixed emotions when Avi
told me about Ruth, considering my own tawdry past. So
much for independence.

There was a strained silence in the car that morning. I
wondered if things would have been different had Avi
been free and available the day he drove me back to the
hotel—the day of the gray metal casket. It really didn't
matter what would have been, because this was the way
it was now and I was trying very hard, for the first time
in my life, not to put any obstacles in the way of my
living happily ever after.

I touched his face gently.

"And so," he said softly, holding on to my hand.

"And so," I answered, barely breathing, "what do
you want now?"

"You," he said, taking me in his arms.

"I'm passionate about you, Herzog," I murmured, my
head buried in his neck.

"I have news for you, Sommers," he whispered. "You
don't have the corner on passion."

○

Vera is plucking specks of dust from my gray-and-black
quilt and shaking her head.

"In the beginning of our marriage, your father would
visit me every other night." She stopped a moment to
see my reaction. "Your father is"—she pauses, groping
for another euphemism—"uh, well endowed."

Maggie Sommers is not a virgin. She has experienced
the heights of passion as well as the depths of despair and
knows about those occasional nightly visits by well-
endowed men who make women sometimes forget who
and what they are. And Maggie has done things with Avi
that Vera could not possibly fathom. But this was too
much.

"I'm not a prude, you know," Vera says, "even though
there are certain things I would never do—those things
that prostitutes and perverts do." It is a certainty that
Maggie has done things with Avi that Vera could never

fathom. However, the mental image of her well-endowed father inserting his oversize appendage into her mother is hard to swallow.

There are traces of sadness in her eyes as she tries to explain why Father never wanted children.

"He thought it would interfere with his career," she says, "that we wouldn't be free to travel and entertain. So I really never thought about having them, until one day I found myself pregnant with Cara. I was delighted. After all, I was carrying the child of the man I loved. In those days, you see, birth control was difficult, and I resisted doing those things that perverts and prostitutes do as an alternative, and your father was so demanding."

I knew it, "those" were the things, but something else was bothering me now. "Did he love Cara when she was born?" I ask.

"I think he loved her as she got older and could respond to him."

"And me, Mother, did he love me when I was born?"

She is blinking back tears. "When I got pregnant with you, he was furious—but what could I do?"

"Did you want me?"

"I guess," she says honestly, "that I wanted your father to stop being so angry, so distant, because I felt so terribly alone."

I understood. Vera was confused and frightened during the entire nine months that she carried me. But I had been inside Alan for much longer before he transferred me, although he never actually felt me leave him. I understood that I had one parent who was oblivious to my presence when I was inside of him and another parent who felt so terribly alone when I was inside of her. It didn't make for a terrific start.

"And now?" I say softly.

"And now I'll just hope that he doesn't decide to leave me."

"And if he doesn't—leave you, that is. Then what?"

"Then we'll grow old and perhaps find some comfort in this continuity that we created."

"And if he does leave you—then what?"

"I'll try again," she says, standing up.

"Try what, Mother?" I ask, following her to the front door.

She turns. "Where are you going now?" she asks, ignoring my question.

"To meet Quincy at the Russian Tea Room. Should we share a cab?"

She slips into her fitch coat. "Yes."

After belting my raccoon-lined trench coat, I put my arms around her, but she moves away from me.

"Do you love him, this short-sleeved Israeli?"

"Yes."

"He'll hurt you if you really do, so you'd better just enjoy the time you have with him, because it won't last. It never does, even though the beginning is always good."

"Mother, the enemy of the good is the better."

She looks at me oddly. "Really, Marguerite, I'm surprised at you. That's not even proper English."

CHAPTER SEVEN

The decor of the Russian Tea Room never changes. Gold tinsel is wrapped around the crystal chandeliers, green and red colored balls are strung across the sculptured ceiling, and tiny twisted rows of blinking lights frame the oil paintings that hang one above the other throughout the main dining room. These decorations are never related to the holiday season but are as much a constant fixture of the restaurant as is Vincent, the maître d', who can always be found in front of the large tarnished silver samovar at the far end of the bar.

"Maggie *bella,*" he croaks in his guttural voice. "You've been out of my life too long."

Hugging him with a hug that would ordinarily be reserved for a favorite uncle if I had a favorite uncle, I reply, "I'm so glad to see you."

Vincent "The Lizard" Roccatello, slight and wiry, with a shock of white hair that constantly flops down over his brow, is dressed in his habitual tattered black tuxedo, a loosely knotted black string tie tucked underneath the frayed collar of his white shirt.

"Grayson and Elliot are already here, and they're delirious about your Emmy nomination for that Beirut piece," he whispers, his tongue darting nervously in and out of his mouth, the mannerism that accounts for his nickname.

I am completely stunned. "What Emmy nomination?"

"The one you're getting for the piece about Joey's death—didn't you know? It's going to be announced tomorrow."

It is pointless to ask how he knows, because Vincent the Lizard knows everything that goes on at every table

227

of his domain. What is astounding is that an Emmy nomination is the reward for my standing bloodstained and rain-soaked somewhere near Sabra Camp that night, weeping in front of twenty million viewers soon after Joe was killed. As if I had planned my reaction. And although Quincy always disagreed with the rule that in television it is only the image that counts, never the feeling, she will be pleased to have an additional bargaining chip before the negotiations begin.

"Where are they?" I ask, scanning the room for a glimpse of the two ABN executives, who have something in common, each of them having shared intimate moments with me in different periods of my life and for very disparate reasons.

"Turn around, table number five, first banquette on your left," Vincent says, scribbling his initials on a bar check that a waiter thrusts at him.

"Let's hope he doesn't notice me. I'm not up to facing them alone."

Vincent strokes my face. "I'll protect you, kid."

I've seen it a million times, how Vincent would stand unobtrusively behind Grayson's chair during those interminable business dinners when Quincy would pick apart every point in one of those deal memos while I picked miserably at the blinis that would invariably remain untouched on my plate. And although Vincent had a reputation for playing the Italian lover, he always treated me protectively, almost paternally. He would wink discreetly at me as I squirmed self-consciously in my chair during one of Quincy's baby-voiced tirades that left Grayson red-faced and trembling and unable to enjoy his chicken Kiev with extra cherry sauce. He would squeeze my arm encouragingly as he pulled out my chair, after Quincy gave me the look that meant I was to get up and walk out. And Vincent would speak in soothing hushed tones while I waited for Quincy to appear with the checks for our coats, assuring me that everything would work out in the end, which it somehow miraculously always did.

Vincent nudges me now, calling my attention to the row of round banquette tables that line the long mirrored wall, where Grayson is standing and waving, a fresh white linen napkin still tucked into his brown alligator belt. There is no longer any choice but to leave Vincent, who is already embracing another client, a little less paternally, and head over to table number five.

"Well, well," Grayson exclaims, unaware that his fresh white linen napkin is still tucked into his brown alligator belt. "Here she is, the Beirut Bombshell."

I have matured. I no longer have an uncontrollable urge when confronted by this silly and insensitive man to knee him in what I know to be his limp and useless organ.

"Hello, Grayson," I say politely, looking directly into his humorless eyes.

"Maggie," Elliot says, getting up. "You're more beautiful than ever."

"Even better off the air than on, if that's possible," Grayson says, pinching my cheek.

Elliot James, boyish and adorable, his bespectacled face framed by a mop of prematurely gray hair, embraces me. After several pleasant moments, I step back, one hand still resting on his shoulder, the other instinctively straightening his red-and-blue-striped bow tie.

"Everybody can't stop talking about you and that piece you did from Beirut," he says, pressing my fingertips to his lips.

"Elliot," Grayson interrupts, giving him a warning look, "why don't we order Maggie a drink?"

"I wish I felt as good about that piece as everyone else does," I say, sitting down.

"Scotch, Maggie?" Grayson asks, signaling the waiter.

I nod.

"They should have given you an ABN umbrella; your hair was soaked. One Scotch and another vodka martini for me. Elliot?"

Elliot shakes his head. "You made everybody feel just how horrible it was," he says, taking my hand.

"No one really thought about umbrellas, Grayson," I say quietly.

"How the hell did you make yourself cry like that, Maggie? Really a super shot, you standing there all soaking wet and covered with blood. Goddamn, that was good," Grayson says, brushing his left elbow against my right breast.

I move away, closer to Elliot.

"Feelings," Elliot says. "She didn't *make* herself cry; she really cried."

Grayson laughs nervously. This man undoubtedly pays a heavy price for the tremendous power he wields: perhaps an inability to experience any real pleasure or pain. But perhaps that is precisely what makes him the incisive, calculating, and heartless professional he is as head of the American Broadcast Network News Division.

"Quincy's a little late," he says, pressing his right leg against me.

I inch away. "She'll be along any minute."

"I'm looking forward to working with you again," Elliot says warmly. "They've given me executive producer of the magazine show because it was my brainchild."

"I didn't know that, Elliot," I answer, genuinely pleased. "Congratulations."

"Yeah, I created it one night when I had nothing to do." He winks.

And then Grayson launches into a lengthy and boring explanation of the severe budgetary problems that the ABN News Division is supposedly experiencing this season.

"How's Frances?" I ask, ignoring Grayson.

"She's all right; making lots of money," Elliot answers, looking decidedly morose.

"How nice for her; I'm so pleased," I say, which is a blatant lie, because Frances James is the most despised agent in the television industry, and nobody would be pleased about anything she ever did except if she were just to disappear.

"She may be making a fortune peddling flesh," Grayson interjects, "but she still won't let our boy here buy bird feed during the summer months—says she can't afford the crumbs, that the little buggers can find their own food." He laughs.

Elliot blushes a deep shade of red as he picks up his shot glass of vodka, which is nestled on a bed of crushed ice in a silver-trimmed compote dish. I watch him down his drink miserably, and wish there were something I could do that would make it better. But I have matured. I no longer have an uncontrollable urge, when confronted by a sensitive, adorable, anguished, and very married man, to try and undo the damage his wife has done over the years, because it never works anyway.

"And that's not all," Grayson continues, still laughing. "They were driving on the freeway in L.A. and Frances spotted a pile of empty soda cans on the side of the road." He pauses to wipe his eyes. "She made old El here stop to get them so she could cash them in—right, El, old boy?" And then he slaps poor Elliot on the back.

But Elliot doesn't exactly give the impression that he is terribly amused. He looks so pained sitting there, staring down at his hands. And it's just as painful for me to remember that it was precisely because of those birds and those crumbs and those discarded soda cans on the side of the highway and those awful insults that were hurled at him in front of shocked guests at chic dinner parties that I felt safe running to him for solace one night.

○

I had worked for Elliot for three years by then, as the on-air crime reporter. He was executive producer of the ABN nightly news. It always made me feel particularly happy to see him sauntering into the newsroom in the morning, swinging his squash racket in one hand and waving to me with the other. Elliot never forgot to compliment me when there was an especially good report or to criticize me when something could have been done better. But regardless of the quality of the news piece, he always gave me one yellow rose on mornings after we had worked well into the night to finish a story, usually after everybody else had given up and gone home.

It was bound to happen with someone; it was that kind of period in my life. I had recently moved into my own apartment in Greenwich village after separating from Eric Ornstein and breaking up with Brian Flaherty and I wasn't having too much success stopping that constant ache somewhere deep down inside me. There was the usual procession of nameless and faceless men who materialize when a woman is alone—drinks, dinner, theater—but one was more boring than the next. Elliot was familiar, a man who understood the pressures of my job, a man who was there each and every day. It began with the early-morning briefing sessions, when he would sit with his legs propped up on his cluttered desk and discuss new ideas for the broadcast or just gossip about people we both knew. It was during one of those sessions, before the hectic morning routine began, that he mentioned the accident. Elliot stirred his coffee thoughtfully for a while before he told me how they had been on their way to a ski resort in Vermont one winter when the car skidded off the road and plunged down a thirty-foot embankment. He looked at me over the rim of his coffee mug and described the horror of regaining consciousness and seeing a shattered windshield and an empty passenger seat. Nothing registered immediately, not until he staggered out of the car and found Frances lying on the frozen ground in a pool of blood, her face in shreds. He blamed himself, wished it were him lying there. He sobbed, screamed, and wanted to die for causing that accident. But that was exactly what Elliot didn't understand—it had been an accident.

Elliot leaned back in his chair then, his arms behind his head, and recalled how the doctors had assured him that his leg, broken in three places, would eventually heal but that Frances would need extensive plastic surgery to reconstruct her face.

There were six operations, performed over a two-year period by a team of the best plastic surgeons in the country, that left Frances with nearly invisible scars, a perfectly straight nose, and one eye that wandered only slightly to the left, which everybody said was a miracle, considering that she had risked losing the eye entirely. Elliot stopped talking at that point, buried his face in his hands, and just sat there. "The irony of it all," he finally said, "was that she had asked me for a divorce only moments before the accident happened. It was because I was so shocked that I missed that curve—cemetery curve I think it was called. The car just skidded off the road and plunged down thirty feet.''

There wasn't very much to say after that, because it was very clear why he had stayed and continued to take Frances's abuse. I thought about it though for the rest of the day and into the evening and decided that he was more of a victim than I was, which made him all the more appealing. By the time that day's piece, on the homeless, was edited, I had already made up my mind. And when Elliot took my hand and asked very tentatively, ''Do you think we could have a bite to eat somewhere near your apartment?'' there wasn't the slightest hesitation.

''I'd like that,'' I answered.

Things were already happening between us in the restaurant when he inquired, rather shyly, if it would be at all possible, after we finished our onion soup and fried mozzarella cheese balls, for us to have sexual intercourse. And it was precisely because he said it that way, using those exact words, sexual intercourse, that I found myself in bed with him, trying to have just that.

Elliot was so painfully shy and so unbelievably naive, spreading a clean towel on the sheets, turning off all the lights, undressing under the covers, and using the word *vagina* as it pertained to where he was trying to be, that it was impossible not to have warm feelings for him. Elliot touched me that very first time, a little here and a little there, as a child who meticulously licks every speck of icing, a little here and a little there, from a large wooden bowl. But he always stopped me from touching him, because there was not very much to touch—Frances had seen to that. Still, I managed to get through that night by trying very hard to arouse Elliot's very soft organ, until it just got too late and he had to leave. When I finally climbed back into bed, after scrubbing the kitchen floor and polishing the copper kettle, I realized that it must have happened after all, very quietly and very quickly, because the towel was very soggy.

I lay awake for most of the night and thought about the words Elliot had used, *sexual intercourse* and *vagina*, and came to the conclusion that they were the root of the entire problem. It was clear that no one had ever taught

him that the word *vagina* should never be used unless it
ended in an *l* and was followed by the word *canal,* as in
the exact location of a breech baby given to a group of
first-year obstetric residents during hospital rounds. It was
also clear that Elliot didn't understand that the word *vagina* should never be used, under any circumstances, by
either one of the two people actively engaged in what
should never be called *sexual intercourse.* I dozed off for
several hours but awoke with another realization. While
the word *cunt* could certainly be ugly and pejorative if
yelled by someone leaning out a car window while stuck
in the middle of a traffic jam, it was clearly the only
appropriate word to use during those moments when sexual intercourse was called fucking, which usually meant
that it was worth the time it took to get undressed. Ironically, it was Avi Herzog who proved me right, because
he somehow had no problem using the right word at the
right time, even if English wasn't his native tongue.

It turned out that the root of Elliot's problem had little
to do with vocabulary, much the same as my reasons for
allowing him inside of my body had little to do with
desire. It was something I needed at that moment, and
when it was over I thought we could both forget about it
and go on with our lives. But the roles reversed somehow, and Elliot became attached, sentimental, clinging.
And in his ardor he believed I resisted only because he
was married, when the truth was that had he not been
married, I never would have taken him in that night at
all.

"I'm in love with you, Maggie, and I don't know what
to do."

"Why do you have to do anything, Elliot?"

"Because I can never leave Frances."

"I don't want you to leave her for me, Elliot, but you
should think about leaving her for yourself—she treats
you so shabbily."

"Never; not after what happened to her eye. I could
never leave her."

I tried to help him, calmly arguing that an eye for an
eye seemed logical enough, but not an eye for a life. It
just didn't seem fair. But Elliot didn't understand my mo-

tives. Several weeks later, he wandered into the news-room late one night while I was busy cleaning out my desk, having just been reassigned to the Middle East.

"I'm sorry," he said quietly, handing me a yellow rose. "I'll probably regret doing this to you."

"I'm sorry too," I replied evenly, "for the whole thing."

And I was, but it was too late.

o

"Speaking about money," Grayson says, still chuckling over those bread crumbs and those soda cans, "is corporate going to pick up the cost of shipping that body back from Lebanon, or does that come out of your division?"

Clutching my throat, I gasp audibly.

"I never thought about that," Elliot says, noticing my reaction.

"Well, damn," Grayson says. "Your division is technically responsible; you sent the poor bastard in there, which means you're covered."

Elliot winces. "Oh, God, Grayson."

It occurs to me how utterly incomprehensible it is that one human being could be so devoid of feeling, even for someone who was now so devoid of life.

"Another Scotch, Maggie?" Elliot asks, giving Grayson a disgusted look. "I think we could both use one after that."

When Pedro—his name pinned on his red cossack jacket—finishes taking the order, I ask, in a tiny voice, "Just exactly how much does it cost to ship a body back from Lebanon?"

"Now, Maggie," Grayson says, putting his arm around me, "that's a corporate problem. Don't you worry about it, although you're sweet to be concerned, since every extra expense affects those salary cuts we're forced to make."

"Oh, for Christ sakes, Grayson!" Elliot yells. "You're too much."

"Wait, Elliot," I interrupt, aware that my voice sounds shrill. "I want to know the cost."

Grayson shrugs his shoulders and reaches inside his breast pocket for a small notepad and a pen. Without a word, he makes quick calculations on a page of white paper.

"About three thousand dollars," he says, flipping the notepad closed.

Pedro is serving the drinks, fortunately making it impossible to continue the conversation. It's so tempting to attack Grayson, point out how callous he is, which is probably why his body doesn't even function. It would have been a disaster, though, because had I done that, my own body, live or remote, would never again be covering the Middle East or working on a new magazine-format show or even doing bake-offs in Des Moines.

"You do have another alternative," I say, giving Elliot a meaningful look.

"What's that, Miss Maggie Tousle Head?" Grayson says, in an attempt to be playful.

Although it is probably safer ducking bullets in Beirut than playing war games with one insensitive television executive who is in the process of making painful but necessary budget cuts, I forge ahead. "Well, Grayson," I say, smiling sweetly, "you might try reclaiming the cost from the El Fateh branch of the PLO, since it was one of their members who launched the RPG that hit Joe. Or if ABN isn't entirely comfortable in dealing with a terrorist organization like El Fateh, they might consider going directly to the Libyans or the Syrians, since they supply the weapons, and simply ask them to reimburse ABN for the cost of shipping Joe's body back from Lebanon. After all, it was one of their RPGs that severed his head from his body." And then I begin crying softly, which makes Grayson so flustered that he knocks over his water glass, which brings Pedro scurrying over to mop up the water from the soggy tablecloth and remove the damp bread basket.

Raoul—his name pinned onto his red cossack jacket—hands Grayson another napkin before stepping aside for Quincy Reynolds. She looks sensational, swathed in

Blackglama mink, although the expression on her face is anything but pleased.

She zeros right in on me. "What's the matter, Maggie?"

"Nothing's the matter with Maggie. Grayson just never learned the meaning of the word *tact*," Elliot says, standing to give Quincy a kiss on her cheek.

"I'm all right, Quince," I say, dabbing at my eyes.

"Oh, bullshit," Grayson says, also standing. "The guy carried minimal insurance, and I was just discussing ways to save the division money so that our on-air people wouldn't have to take such enormous cuts, that's all."

"Deduct the three thousand dollars from my salary, Grayson," I say tearfully. "I'll take the cut."

"Well," Quincy says, sitting down next to Elliot, "at least we know that Grayson will never have a heart attack, because he doesn't have a heart."

"Well, at least I could get a brain tumor—unlike some people I know," Grayson retorts, looking directly at Elliot.

"I've personally chosen a coronary, Grayson," Elliot says. "I feel that as long as I work for you, I have a good chance of getting the illness of my choice, and coronary it is."

"Good one, Elliot." Grayson chuckles. "So let's not get this celebration dinner off to a bad start now."

"Celebration?" I ask innocently.

"You've been nominated for an Emmy, darling," Quincy says. "I meant to tell you."

"How did you know?" Grayson is visibly crestfallen.

"I have my sources," she says, winking at me. Vincent.

"What are you drinking, Quincy?"

"A vodka, Grayson," she answers, fumbling in her purse for a cigarette.

"Well, well, what's the latest news?" Grayson asks, rubbing his hands together.

Quincy settles back in her chair. "Nothing much, except that this Emmy nomination comes at a terrific time, right before we negotiate Maggie's new contract."

Elliot leans toward me then and whispers, "I haven't stopped thinking about you, Maggie."

"There're going to be severe budgetary cuts," Grayson says, "in case you haven't heard. The negotiations come at a very bad time."

"Budgetary cuts or not," Quincy says, exhaling a fine stream of smoke, "Maggie's up for an Emmy—her second—and that means a bigger salary for a program that I happen to know has a budget of six hundred thousand dollars per episode."

"You're talking about a budget that includes everything—soup to nuts. We're even pulling two people off the nightly news to work along with a host, so we don't have to bring in new talent."

Patting Elliot's hand, I say quietly, "I'm glad to see you. You look wonderful."

Elliot squeezes my hand. "I'm glad you're back in New York because I really missed you. Can we spend some time together?"

"Actually, Grayson," Quincy says, making room for the vodka that the waiter is serving, "I've been thinking about Maggie's leaving ABN. She just may be stagnating there."

"Leaving ABN is ridiculous, and you know it," Grayson explodes. "It's her home, and she's never going to get a better deal anywhere else."

"I'm not sure, Grayson," Quincy says, fiddling with the stirrer. "Not if we're talking major budgetary cuts that will directly affect Maggie."

"Look, Quincy, we don't even know if Maggie's going to win that Emmy. She's up against tough competition."

"Elliot," I whisper, "I'm involved with someone in Israel, so the sooner I get back there, the happier I'll—"

"Are you in love with him?"

"Yes, Elliot, I am."

"She'll win it, Grayson," Quincy says firmly, "and you know it."

"I don't know about that," Grayson says slowly. "That piece NTC did about that poor crippled guy in Queens who couldn't even afford a wheelchair . . . Real human interest the way his neighbors rallied around, got him out of that wheelbarrow his wife was pushing him around in, and chipped in to buy a real honest-to-goodness motorized chair—pretty goddamn touching.''

''It was a good piece,'' Quincy agrees, ''but it doesn't compare to the horror of one of the crew getting killed in the middle of a war.'' She stubs out her cigarette.

''I'm not happy,'' Elliot says sadly. ''Things are worse with Frances, and I just can't seem to find the right combination to stop these waves of depression.''

I touch Elliot's cheek. ''I hate to tell you this, but probably the only right combination would be to leave her and find someone you could be happy with.''

''I found that person once, but I couldn't leave then. I thought I was doing the right thing.''

''The problem,'' Grayson says, ''is that we didn't even see an actual shot of his head being blown off.''

''You are a heartless boor,'' Quincy exclaims.

''There's no point in name-calling,'' Grayson whines.

''I guess I sometimes forget that you judge good reporting by how good the visuals are,'' Quincy says disgustedly.

''Oh, Elliot, you're making too much out of that, of us,'' I say quietly.

''It could be again, Maggie,'' Elliot persists, ''if you gave me another chance.''

''I've got warm feelings for you, Elliot, but that part of it is over. I'm sorry.''

''Let's face it, Quincy, I'd be a helluva lot more confident if the Emmy nomination was for a cut of Joe actually getting hit. Now, that's good television.''

''Grayson!'' Quincy gasps.

''Christ, Daniel!'' Elliot explodes.

''I don't believe this whole thing,'' I say, looking around the table.

Quincy is horrified, Elliot is shocked, and I am just plain furious.

''First you try to find a way of not paying for the cost of shipping Joe's body home,'' I say, looking directly at Grayson. ''And then you complain because the footage wasn't gory enough for you.'' I pause. ''Let me tell you what it was like that day, Grayson, in case you didn't hear, because the camera wasn't running and we were just all too stupid to think of turning it on, I guess, and of course a second take was out of the question, since Joe didn't have a head anymore and so wasn't exactly in a position to accommodate us.'' I pause again and take a deep breath.

Elliot puts his hand on mine. "Stop, Maggie. It's not worth it.''

"No,'' Quincy says firmly. "Let her go on.''

Thanking her with my eyes, I continue. "It was just an ordinary day in the war zone near the camps, and I had just finished helping a Palestinian child sift through the rubble, trying to find him a pair of shoes because he had lost his whole house and needed his shoes to walk to Gaza Hospital, where his sister was being operated on because she had lost her legs.'' Grayson looks sick, but I don't care. "Ringler was with three Israelis then. You remember Ringler, Grayson, our cameraman who got wounded ten days earlier but kept right on working? Anyway, he was with these three soldiers; two of them were wounded, one pretty badly, bleeding from his head, and the other with a broken leg. You see, Grayson, the medics were busy trying to patch up another soldier, who had gone into shock.'' The tears are rolling down my face, into my mouth. "The crew from the Irish television station were having their own problems, because their on-air reporter was hysterical, and I didn't really blame him. He was new and had just seen that bulldozer, the one that swept the ground every day picking up the bodies, dumping a new pile of human trash—that day only a hundred dead bodies—into a big ditch so they could be identified by the survivors.'' Quincy holds my hand, her jaw set firmly, her eyes glistening.

"Things were just getting quiet. I was sitting with Joe and trying to tell myself that the day was almost over, when all of a sudden there was a lot of commotion, yelling and screaming, and I suppose I was in shock or something, because all I saw was a clump of bloodied flesh next to me. But that's the kind of super visual stuff that's great for the viewers, so I guess I shouldn't have gotten so goddamn upset."

"Maggie," Elliot says, "enough."

"For who?" Quincy asks. "For you or for her? She needs this; let her alone."

Grayson is silent, his head buried in his hands.

"The point is, Grayson," I say, touching his arm, "I'm not even sure if I should accept that Emmy if I win it, because it still hurts too much and quite frankly it wasn't for ABN, that stand-up, it was for Joe and for Ringler and for me, because I wanted everybody out there—and you know where the *there* is, Grayson, where you get those ratings from—to see just how pointless and screwed up this world is and how poor Joe just happened to get caught in the middle of everything and how I just happened to be there when it happened, a microphone in my hand, a camera on me but I promise you, Grayson"—I can hardly speak; my sobs are uncontrollable—"I didn't do it for you or for ABN."

Quincy hugs me, while Elliot takes out a handkerchief and blows his nose loudly. Raoul and Pedro appear and, without any reaction, mop the table and remove the damp bread basket seconds after Grayson knocks over his water glass again. Elliot takes a swig of his vodka, swallows it, and waits for Grayson to say something, anything, to relieve the tension. Quincy lights another cigarette and winks at me. And Grayson clears his throat several times, removes his drenched napkin from his brown alligator belt, flings it on the table, and looks directly at me.

"That's what I love about you, Maggie, what makes you so damn good. It's your perfect timing."

"You're the one with the perfect timing," Quincy retorts. "You started this whole thing by discussing the cost of shipping the body back; not very smart."

"You know, Grayson," Elliot begins, "she's right. You should think about the human—"

"Shut up, Elliot!" Grayson snaps.

"In my opinion," Elliot persists, "there's more to life than that bottom line."

"Who asked you?" Grayson says angrily.

"Nobody has to ask me. I'm the guy who sent him in. Remember, it's my division that's responsible."

"Well, maybe you should have thought about not sending in a crew where they could get themselves killed."

Elliot looks pained. "I thought about it plenty, but there wasn't any choice, and at least I'm not sitting around lamenting the fact that the camera wasn't running when the disaster happened."

"Look, Elliot," Grayson says, raising his voice, "I'm in television. I'm not a nurse or a shrink or a kindergarten teacher or running some two-bit radio station in the boonies. I'm always going to think about the best possible shot and the highest ratings and the most Emmys, or there's no profit, and if that happens, then you and Maggie and everyone else are out of a job, including me." He glares at Elliot.

Elliot's reaction is to take a long drink of vodka, run his hand across his mouth, and study the table as he speaks. "Then if that's what it's all about," he says slowly, "and you don't give a damn about how anybody feels, you can count me out, take your profit margin, and shove it up your ass."

"What do you do for an encore, Elliot—work for your wife?"

"Look, I don't want any part of this," I say, putting my hand on Elliot's arm, restraining him from talking himself out of a job so he would be totally dependent upon his shrew wife.

"Maggie sweetheart," Grayson says, taking my hand from Elliot's arm, "you're upset, Elliot's upset, we're all upset."

"Why don't we all just stop talking about it, then?" Quincy suggests. "What do you think, Grayson? Let's pick it up another time, when we're all calmer."

"That's very rational, Quincy, but I just want my Maggie to know that I care about her as if she were my very own family, and she is, like everybody is at ABN, my own special little family. Believe me, Maggie, I didn't sleep nights when you were in Lebanon, and then that awful tragedy happened and there wasn't anything I could do that would make it better, so I began thinking about the best way to make it work for all of us—for our little family at ABN—for your career. And then I thought about doing something for poor Joe—like setting up something in his memory. We're not animals, but I also wanted the best possible shot so that my Maggie would win an Emmy for her family.''

"Now I've heard it all," Quincy says.

Elliot starts to speak. "Grayson—"

"No, wait," I interrupt. "Let's get back to the part about setting something up in Joe's memory."

Grayson looks bewildered for only a moment. Recovering almost instantly, he grins and pats my hand affectionately. "That's my girl—always thinking, always listening. Well, perhaps we should set up a scholarship fund in his name at the audiovisual department at New York University."

"See that, everyone," I say, smiling. "Grayson does have a heart."

"You still can't convince me about the brain," Elliot mutters under his breath.

"Now will you accept that Emmy if you win?" Grayson asks me.

"I'm not sure about that," I answer.

"Look, Grayson, I understand how Maggie feels," Quincy says calmly. "So why don't we just have a nice dinner and postpone any talk about contracts or Emmys or anything like that until Maggie and I have a chance to talk."

"Nonsense," Grayson says, turning red. "I want to get that magazine-format show finalized, and we need Maggie for that—she's our best choice."

"Relax, Grayson," Quincy says casually. "There's no rush, and you probably couldn't afford the price I want anyway."

The moment has arrived, as it usually does during every one of these ghastly business dinners, when amenities and old business are dispensed with, ground rules are set, players are in place, and every single word is taken seriously. Not only am I squirming self-consciously on my chair in dreaded anticipation of this event, but I am also breaking up matches in tiny little pieces and constructing tiny little houses on the tablecloth. Vincent is standing behind Grayson. Winking at me, he reaches over him to drop a fresh white linen napkin on his lap.

"Look, Quincy," Grayson says, turning around to glare briefly at Vincent, "let's not be rash. I could probably cut from another area."

"I'll have the chicken Kiev," Quincy says, ignoring him.

"And I'll have the blinis," I say, prepared not to touch a morsel.

"I'll have you," Elliot whispers.

"I'll have the chicken Kiev too, with extra cherry sauce," Grayson says. "And stop hovering over me, Vincent; you make me nervous."

Quincy has already launched into one of her baby-voiced tirades, when Elliot decides on the beef Stroganoff.

"I wouldn't want to put you in an uncomfortable position with your board, who have obviously told you to make these cuts." She smiles an adorable smile, her green eyes sparkling.

"Let me worry about my board," Grayson says gruffly.

Quincy glances at me then, gives me another version of the look, and continues. "I'm not sure if Maggie is even willing to take on this magazine-format show if it means she's based in the Middle East. After all, she put in two years in Lebanon. Maybe it's time for her to come home and settle down."

Elliot rolls his eyes and I mouth the words "thank you" for his much appreciated silence.

"Whether it's New York or Tel Aviv, she won't be covering the battlefront, so we're already talking about a whole other thing. She was there right in the middle of it. No more. Now she'll be doing only human interest stories, heads of state, soft stuff. That would be the extent of her political coverage. But naturally I'd want her based out of Israel, because she's our best correspondent in that area. The viewers have grown to trust her."

Quincy shakes her head. "That's the point, Grayson— she'd probably be willing to do it if she could stay in

New York." Turning to me, she says, "Would you be willing to go back to the Middle East?"

"I'm not sure," I answer on cue, avoiding Elliot's eyes.

"Obviously, Grayson," Quincy says, "if Maggie isn't certain about going back there, then we can't even discuss the possibility of her doing the show. I think we should wait, because it's pointless to go over everything now."

"Maggie," Grayson says, leaning forward, "the thing is that I need you more in the Middle East covering those segments than staying in New York and just doing news. I can get anybody to do that. I originally thought about a substantial salary cut, but I might change my mind if you agreed to go back there—do our little show out of Israel. What do you say, Mags?"

"I don't think so," Quincy answers.

"Maggie," Grayson continues, ignoring her, "for me?"

I shrug my shoulders.

"OK." Grayson laughs mirthlessly. "You win. Top billing, same salary as before, and no cuts."

Elliot laughs and looks at Grayson. "I don't think you understood this entire conversation."

The manipulation at this table was shameful. Fortunately, however, the master manipulator was on my side, and Quincy Reynolds was unquestionably the master.

"Who asked you?" Grayson snaps.

"Nobody asked me," Elliot says wearily, "but I'm the producer of the show, and I listened very carefully to what Quincy Reynolds didn't say."

"Will you accept that Emmy if you win?" Grayson asks, missing Elliot's whole point.

"That's not a bargaining chip," Quincy says, putting her hand on mine before anything else is said.

Vincent wanders back to our table. "There's no more beef Stroganoff, Mr. James, but I've got a wonderful piece of pepper steak," he says to Elliot.

"Take the Emmy," Vincent mouths to me.

"Why?" I mouth back.

"I wasn't making it a bargaining chip—I just wanted

to know where we stood, that's all," Grayson says, giving Vincent a dirty look.

"Why don't you get specific, Quincy?" Elliot says. "Yes, I'll take the pepper steak."

"Because he would have wanted you to," Vincent suddenly says out loud to me.

"What the hell are you talking about, Vincent?" Grayson explodes.

Quincy is speaking so softly now that Elliot is forced to lean very close to her. "I'm talking a twenty-five percent salary increase plus a bonus of fifty thousand dollars at the end of six months if the show runs and then another fifteen-percent salary increase at the end of the first season if we have a renewal—and she'll do Middle East."

"Impossible!" Grayson yells.

"How do you know he would have wanted me to?" I ask Vincent.

"I told you we should have postponed this whole discussion," Quincy says, smiling up at Pedro, who is serving her a steaming plate of chicken Kiev.

"Because he was Italian," Vincent says quietly. "I know."

"What the hell is going on here?" Grayson shouts. "Who was Italian?"

Quincy pierces her chicken Kiev with her fork and says, "Mmm," as the butter runs all over the wild rice.

Raoul uncorks the bottle of white wine, pouring some into Elliot's glass. He swirls it around several times. "Very good, but not quite chilled enough." Raoul puts the wine back in the ice bucket.

"Valeri," Vincent says. "Joe Valeri was Italian."

"What does Valeri's being Italian have to do with the price of everything? And frankly, Vincent, I've had just about enough of your interfering when I try to do business. It's been going on for years."

Pedro reappears, carrying my blinis and Grayson's chicken Kiev with extra cherry sauce. Standing aside, he waits until Raoul serves Elliot his pepper steak.

Quincy pats her mouth with her napkin. "Is your steak rare enough, Elliot?"

Cutting into it, he answers, "Perfect."

Grayson is stirring his cherry sauce distractedly, deep in thought, while I'm picking miserably at my blinis.

"OK, Quincy," Grayson says suddenly, dropping his fork into the cherry sauce and splattering the front of his blue shirt. "I'll give you a ten-percent salary increase, plus a bonus of twenty-five thousand dollars at the end of the first year and then another ten-percent increase if the show is renewed, but she's based in Israel."

"No deal," Quincy says, swallowing a piece of chicken. "And look what you've done to your shirt."

Elliot rolls his eyes. "What a piece of work she is," he whispers.

"What about that scholarship fund in Joe's name?" I ask, ignoring Elliot.

Grayson is busy dipping his napkin into his glass of water, trying to clean off the front of his shirt. "Yes, yes, yes," he says impatiently, "a scholarship fund for Joe Vatucci."

"Valeri," Vincent says quietly, winking at me.

"Why aren't you eating your *blinis*, Maggie?" Elliot asks.

"I'll accept the Emmy if I win," I say, looking directly at Vincent, "and I'll go back to the Middle East if you insist."

Smiling, Vincent backs away.

"What a number *you* are," Elliot mutters, shaking his head in wonderment.

"Well," Quincy asks, smiling, "do I get my terms?"

Grayson hardly moves his mouth as he speaks. "And if you don't?"

"I go somewhere else." She flashes him another adorable smile. "Tomorrow morning."

Grayson slams his hand on the table. "Deal," he says miserably. "And I certainly hope you enjoy your dinner, because I can't." He leaves the table.

Elliot calls after him. "I'll be right there, Grayson." He remains only long enough to try one more time. "I've got mixed emotions about working with you, baby. I'm sorry you won't be living here, but I know the show will be successful with you covering the Middle East." He kisses me on the forehead. "Change your mind, Maggie; at least think about it."

"Oh, Elliot," I say softly, "I want you to be happy— I really do—but I can't do anything for you. It just wouldn't work."

"Elliot," Grayson bellows.

"Coming, Gray," Elliot yells, scurrying after him.

We are finally alone. Quincy orders coffee.

"Whew," she says. "That was tough, no? And you think I'm not at the mercy of anybody." She laughs.

"You're unbelievable. Now what?"

"Now we just have to meet one more time, to sign, finalize everything, and get the spring lineup. The show is scheduled to air March first."

"I'm really looking forward to it."

Quincy looks concerned. "Did I do the right thing for you—I mean, negotiating you back into Israel?"

"Why do you say that?"

"Mainly because of your ambivalence about your general."

"I'm not really ambivalent, Quince. Just nervous about him because he doesn't fit into any category."

"What do you mean?"

"He's unlike anybody I've ever known and I get frightened about him leaving me. It's funny, but I just talked about this with Mother."

"You talked about Avi leaving you with your mother?"

"No. We talked about Father leaving her and how she couldn't survive if he did. I got furious because she was so weak, so pathetic. I wanted to shake her, to make her realize that even if he left her, she was still a whole person."

"But she's not, Maggie. With or without him, she's not a whole person."

"I know and it's so sad. Yet, I wonder if I'm a whole person. Sometimes I feel that without Avi, I couldn't survive."

"But of course you could and you know it. It would be painful but human beings can endure the most horrendous pain." She pauses. "I have."

I reach over and touch her hand. "I forgot for the moment, Quince, I'm sorry."

She clears her throat. "Thank God I forget sometimes too."

We are silent for a few seconds until she asks. "Why would he ever leave you anyway, Maggie?"

"For all those terrific reasons that men leave women—you know, maybe because of a terminal attack of guilt about his wife or maybe just because he would get up one morning and decide he's had enough. I don't know—does it always have to make sense?"

Quincy smiles. "You know, whenever I used to feel that vulnerable and insecure about Dan in the beginning, I would try to focus on something about him that absolutely drove me crazy."

"I already tried doing that, with those ridiculous short beige socks of his."

Quincy laughs. "That sounds fascinating. Did he actually wear them?"

"Oh, yes, and it's something that's ingrained in them. Israeli men think their socks should match their shirts, and their shirts are not so great. Anyway, I tried focusing on those beige socks."

"I'm not so sure that's a good one to zero in on, because men who wear terrific socks usually make lousy husbands."

"Who made that study?"

"It's the Reynolds Report," she says, smiling, "based on personal experience. My first husband wore those knee-high black wools—perfect socks—and look what a bastard he was."

"Well, it never worked with him anyway, because when I tried to kill it over those socks, he was too smart for me."

Quincy looks bewildered. "When did you try to kill it over the socks?"

"At the Dead Sea," I answer, perfectly seriously.

Quincy shakes her head. "Grayson is right about you. Your timing is perfect."

"I've got to run, Quincy. Can we leave now?"

Soon we are walking down Fifty-seventh Street, arm in arm, and looking for a cab.

"You've got plenty of time to get home. Your general is calling you at midnight."

A taxi screeches to a stop several feet away. "You take it, Quince," I say suddenly. "I feel like walking for a while, so I can think about things."

"What things?" Quincy asks, her hand on the taxi door.

Wrinkling up my nose, I answer, "Oh, I don't know. Maybe about beige socks."

○

The wailing melodic sounds of Arab music coming from the inside of a nearby restaurant almost drowned out the bleating of the sheep that wandered along the dirt sidewalk. Avi stopped the car several blocks away from the building that housed the right-wing PLO newspaper, *El Hoqq*, as it was inadvisable for a Western journalist to be seen in East Jerusalem with an Israeli government official.

"Let's try to start out for the Dead Sea as close to six o'clock as possible—before it gets dark."

"How do I kiss you goodbye?"

"Wait until the sheep pass, and then we'll figure it out," Avi said, removing his gold-rimmed aviator glasses and placing them on the dashboard.

"Ah," he said, "that is your first mistake—you are not security conscious. What you don't realize is that they could be PLO disguised as sheep or sheep disguised as Mossad. We are very clever, my dear." Reaching across the seat, he pulled out a green ribbed crew-neck sweater from his bag and slipped it on over his army shirt.

"You're certainly prepared for everything."

"Battlefield initiative is endemic in the Israeli army," he replied with mock seriousness. "That's why we win wars. Now kiss me."

My cheek brushed against the rough wool, and then my lips were on his. He kissed me gently at first and then more passionately, until he just held me tightly against him.

I felt the familiar weakness in the pit of my stomach. "Is kissing like that also endemic in the Israeli army?"

He stroked my hair. "I love you and I want to marry you—that's endemic with me."

He waited for me to balk, to pull away, to retreat into my usual insecurity.

"It's all right," I said. "I'm getting adjusted to it."

Avi put on his gold-rimmed aviator glasses, "Why are you going to *El Hoqq* if your interview is at the Jerusalem compound?"

"Ah," I answered, "you are not as security conscious as you think, my dear. The Palestinians asked that I speak to Mr. Ahmed, the editor of the paper, so that he can arrange a meeting with the prisoner's brother."

"Ah yes." He smiled. "There's always a brother somewhere in the background."

"I love you," I said suddenly.

And he pulled me close again, kissing me tenderly. "You're an unpredictable woman and a lunatic person, and I love you too. Be careful today."

"You too," I said, getting out of the car.

A narrow alley led to the entrance of the *El Hoqq* offices, where Mr. Ahmed was waiting. He was my link to what was called a freedom fighter in the eastern sector of this ancient city that was so soaked with religious meaning, political history, and bitter dissension. Several women dressed in flowing black robes, heavy baskets filled with bread and fruit balanced on their hooded heads, sat on their haunches and chattered in high-pitched voices. An old man was running after his flock of sheep, one hand holding up the hem of his skirt, the other waving a crudely carved wooden stick, as he made the familiar palatal *rrr*.

I pushed open the intricately designed heavy black wrought-iron door and stepped inside the shabby entrance hall. The walls were decorated with photographs of a beaming Yassir Arafat making the V-for-victory sign triumphantly above his head, the black-and-white checkered *kafiich* draped around his face. A man waring tight-

fitting blue jeans and a pink T-shirt with WELCOME TO
MIAMI BEACH stenciled on the front, between two palm
trees, was sitting on the edge of a desk and leafing
through a copy of *People* magazine. Several other men,
also wearing exceptionally tight-fitting pants but with unnecessarily evil glints in their eyes, began making hissing
and clucking noises as I approached.

"Hi," I said. "I love your T-shirt."

He flashed me a big smile, revealing two gold front
teeth. "You are Miss Maggie, ABN News, and I am
Bashir."

"How do you do, Bashir," I said, smiling back.

"I do very well, thank you," he replied, "and Mr.
Ahmed is expecting you."

Bashir motioned for me to follow him through the curtain of brown beads that hung behind his desk. Having
been through this routine countless times, I was perfectly
prepared to wait the two or three hours until Mr. Ahmed
would emerge casually from his office as if he were right
on time for our meeting. The hissing and clucking noises
followed me a I walked through the curtain, caught my
tote bag on several strands of beads, got my hair tangled
in one of my gold hoop earrings which almost caused me
to rip my pierced earlobe in half as I tried to extricate
myself, right before slamming my right knee into a sink
that had been propped up directly at the entrance to the
small and airless room.

"Shit," I muttered under my breath.

Chris Ringler, my cameraman, was already slumped
down on a torn blue plastic chair, his long legs extended,
his tanned and muscular arms folded across his chest. He
wore a broad-brimmed Indiana Jones hat pulled down
over his forehead and a pink T-shirt with WELCOME TO
MIAMI BEACH stenciled on the front, between two palm
trees.

"Hi, beautiful," he said, tilting back the hat. "That
must have hurt."

I nodded, staring first at his shirt and then at Bashir's.

He laughed. "I brought a bunch of them back for the
boys here; thought it would help get us in quicker."

Nodding again, I sat down on a torn yellow plastic chair.

"I'm about to read *The Rise and Fall of the Third Reich* while we wait," Chris said, gesturing to the thick book that lay on a carved brass tray that was balanced on a black teakwood stand.

Putting my tote bag on the floor, I propped up my injured leg right next to Chris's book.

"Leg down," Bashir said sharply. "We don't show soles of shoes."

I looked at him in disbelief. "Bashir, in case you didn't notice, I just slammed my knee into a sink that should never have been left there in the first place."

"Soles of shoes show disrespect in Arab world."

Removing my leg from the table, I replied, "Hissing and clucking at women show disrespect in Western world."

"You are in occupied territory now."

"That's odd," I said. "I thought this was Miami Beach."

Chris jumped up and slung an arm around Bashir's thin shoulders. "Hey, pal, next time I'll bring you a T-shirt with an alligator on the front. Deal?"

Bashir stopped glaring at me. "Deal," he said. "You want some green tea and dates?"

"I don't think there's time," I said, once again trying to incite him. "We wouldn't want to keep Mr. Ahmed waiting."

Bashir glared at me again. "Mr. Ahmed very busy now. You have green tea and dates," he ordered, disappearing through the curtain of brown beads and managing not to slam his knee into the sink.

"That makes me furious," I said indignantly.

"You only make it worse by acting like that," Chris said, slumping back down in his chair, "and if you do, I'll not only be able to finish *The Rise and Fall*, but also the Koran and the complete works of William Shakespeare, and I probably won't see my three-year-old again until he's ready for college."

"I'm sorry, Chris, but it might be nice just once to

cover a normal area, where grownups give us interviews.''

"Come on, Mags," he said, suddenly very bitter. "Don't you know this is prime territory? War is sexy." Sitting up straight, he pulled up his T-shirt so his abdomen was exposed, revealing a thick red scar that ran the width of his stomach.

I touched it gently. "You're alive, Ringler; at least you're all healed."

He yanked his shirt down and leaned back. There were tears in his eyes. "Yeah, only a little shrapnel. Valeri should have been so lucky."

Bashir reappeared, carrying a tray with two glasses of green tea and a plate of sticky dates. "Mr. Ahmed says you are most welcome and he will see you very, very soon."

I didn't even bother to look up, pretending to be totally engrossed in my notes for the interview. Bashir put down the tray and left.

Three and a half hours later, at exactly twelve o'clock, after each of us had consumed four glasses of green tea and a dozen sticky dates, had made several trips to the bathroom, and had paced up and down alternately in the small and airless room, Bashir appeared. "Mr. Ahmed not busy now. Come, come quickly. He will see you."

The temptation to yawn was almost uncontrollable—to stretch languidly and mutter something about no longer being interested in the interview. Christ jumped right up, slipped his knapsack across his back, and hoisted his minicam up onto his right shoulder. I stood also, my red T-shirt sticking to the back of the plastic chair, and followed Chris and Bashir into the main reception area. The door to Mr. Ahmed's office was open, and he was walking toward us.

"Miss Maggie," he said, "I do my very best for you today because all Western press are my very good friends."

Shaking his hand, I noticed his pallor was even grayer than usual, his voice more raspy than the last time, when he had coughed and chain-smoked throughout the meeting.

He ushered us into his smoke-filled office. "Come in, please."

Chris placed his minicam and knapsack on the floor. He appeared visibly disturbed by one of the photographs that adorned the walls—one that depicted twelve- or thirteen-year-old boys posing with Kalishnikov AK 47 rifles and hand grenades. But the photograph that was most distressing was the one right over Mr. Ahmed's desk—a large poster showing maimed bodies scattered on the ground near a burned-out bus at the side of the road, the after-math of what was considered one of the most glorious efforts by the PLO freedom fighters to liberate Palestine. It was taken the night a civilian bus was hijacked on the highway between Haifa and Tel Aviv.

"You will meet him," Mr. Ahmed said, watching me closely.

Startled, I turned. "Who?"

He gestured to the photograph. "The man who made this military action—he is the one in the prison."

Chris's eyes were narrowed. "Holy shit," he said.

Mr. Ahmed smiled. "His brother is waiting for you now."

"Where?" Chris asked, his eyes still fixed on the photograph.

"He is waiting for you in the cocktail lounge of the American Colony Hotel."

"How will we know him?" I asked.

"He is small and dark and answers to the name of Rashid," Mr. Ahmed replied.

I glanced at Chris. "Oh, great."

Ringler smiled as he fiddled with a cartridge of film. "Piece of cake," he muttered.

Mr. Ahmed stood with considerable effort as he attempted to walk us to the door. But he was felled by an uncontrollable coughing seizure, which left him trembling and gasping for breath. Finally, he managed to straighten up by hanging on to the wall for support. "Please send me a copy of the interview tape," he wheezed.

"I'll take care of it, Mr. Ahmed," I said. "And thank you very much."

"Small and dark and answers to the name of Rashid," I mumbled to no one in particular.

Chris followed me back into the reception area, where the same young toughs were still lounging around in their exceptionally tight-fitting pants, with those same unnecessarily evil glints in their eyes. And once again they began making hissing and clucking noises at me. Suddenly I stopped and lifted up my foot so the sole of my shoe was directly in their faces. Chris collapsed against the wall. "You're too much," he roared. "This isn't a Dracula movie."

We trudged down the alley and up the narrow road toward the American Colony Hotel, an interesting Moorish-design structure that had been the headquarters of the British command post during the 1948 war of independence but was currently the meeting place for the many Palestinian and Arab notables who came to East Jerusalem. The lobby was furnished with Moroccan leather chairs, heavy carved oak tables, and white-and-blue tiles that covered the walls. Walking under several stucco arches, we approached the reception desk and were directed down three steps to the cocktail lounge. Chris was right behind me as I entered the dimly lit room, barely able to distinguish the figure of a small and dark man who seemed to be sitting alone. Signaling to Chris to wait, I walked up to him.

"Hello," I said, extending my hand. "I'm Maggie Sommers. Can we talk here?" He stood politely, glancing furtively around the room. "No, not here. I'm expecting someone."

Perhaps it was because my knee throbbed. Perhaps it was because of the young men at the newspaper who had hissed and clucked at me. Perhaps it was because I was anxious to begin those four delicious days with Avi at the Dead Sea. Or perhaps it was suddenly tedious to hear the same rhetoric spouted over and over and see those same horrendous photographs of limbless torsos, charred babies, and dismembered corpses that ended up that way in the name of freedom. Whatever the reason—and there was no excuse—I simply snapped.

"Look, I don't understand," I said. "Why not here and why not now?"

"Because," the man answered, his left eye twitching nervously, "I have made other arrangements; someone else is coming."

I was livid; ABN had been promised and exclusive interview not only with the prisoner but also with his brother. And it had all been arranged and approved by Israeli government officials as well as Palestinian leaders, specifically Mr. Ahmed. Determined to find out what had gone wrong and resolute about doing the interview first, I continued questioning him. "Does this other person speak English?"

The man looked at me with a puzzled expression. "What difference would that make to you?"

"It makes a big difference to me," I answered impatiently, "because I want to be the first American to do this."

He smiled slightly. "Ah, that is what I like about you American women—you are so very aggressive and feisty. I like that."

"Look," I answered, glancing over at Chris, who was leaning against the bar, "I also want to do it while there's still light."

"Ah, that too," he said, fingering his mustache. "The night not possible?"

I was exasperated. "No, it is not," I said, pointing to Ringler, "because he needs light to film it."

The man looked absolutely horrified. "You want to film it?" he sputtered.

Running my hand through my hair, I tried to remain calm. "Look, I've got a job to do, and I don't like this any more than you do, but we're wasting time. Yes or no—do we do it now or do I just leave and tell everybody that your word isn't any good, that you broke your promise?"

"No, no, never—only I cannot do this."

"Chris," I called, "come here, please."

He sauntered over. "What's up?"

"Our friend here is not keeping his word; he's refusing to let us film him. Now what?"

"Please," the man said, now perspiring profusely. "I don't want any trouble. I promise we'll do it tonight, here's some money but no film." He reached into his pocket and extracted some crumpled bills.

Chris put a restraining hand on my arm. "Maggie, stop. I think—"

"No, Chris," I snapped, "I won't stop." Pointing my finger in the trembling man's face, I said angrily, "I don't want your money, and you can just forget the whole thing, but I won't forget this, Rashid."

"Rashid," he repeated. "Who is Rashid?"

That was when the black-haired woman teetered up to him on black stiletto heels, linked her arm through the arm of this small and dark-haired man who apparently did not answer to the name of Rashid, and said in a husky voice, "Mustafa, are you ready for a little fun?"

"Oh, Chris," I said, sinking down in a chair, "I'm really losing it."

But he was laughing too hard to console me. There was hardly any time anyway for me to recover, because just then a small and dark-haired man tapped me on the shoulder and said, "I am Rashid."

He looked more like George Hamilton than Rashid, dressed in a blue blazer, gray slacks, and a powder-blue button-down shirt, open at the neck. His full head of thick black wavy hair and his perfect white teeth could probably have earned him in the area of $100,000 a year in residuals had he chosen a career in Hollywood doing toothpaste commercials instead of working for the PLO.

"Does this mean I won't see you tonight?" Mustafa whispered to me as soon as his companion had strutted out of the cocktail lounge.

Looking up wearily, I said, "Not unless you blew up a bus, Mustafa."

Rashid appeared to be typical of those media-star terrorists who were specifically groomed to tug at the heartstrings of women viewers all over the world. Taking out a cigarette from a slim silver case, he lit it with a heavy gold lighter, observing me through his spectacular heavy-lidded blue eyes. It was essential that he understood exactly what ABN expected.

"Look, Rashid," I explained, "ABN instructed us to film a real freedom fighter who actually fights and doesn't just spout the rhetoric of the cause in some university on the West Bank."

Rashid smiled seductively, exuding confidence that because of his great clothes, fabulous looks, and terrific teeth, he would not be subjected to the usual "we need sensational visuals for our blood-thirsty viewers so could you please look a little more vicious" speech that Western correspondents were known to make.

"Look, you're interviewing my brother," he answered in flawless English, "and it is because of me that he has agreed—I have permitted him to talk to you. Now, if you don't want to interview me for, as you say, background, that is fine. Just say so."

"That's not it, Rashid. What I'm trying to say is this," I said, reaching for one of his smooth hands. "I need someone with blood on his hands—someone who is acting for the revolution, not just talking about it."

Rashid was silent.

"In other words, I want someone who has killed for his cause—like your brother, so quite frankly, I just don't think that it would be helpful to use you today. I'm sorry."

"Why don't you stop beating around the bush, Sommers," Chris said sarcastically, pulling his Indiana Jones hat down on his face, "and just be more blunt."

We strolled outside, into the glorious sunlight, walking along the dirt road that led toward the Old City, while Rashid talked about his life.

"I was recruited into Ashbal, a Palestinian youth organization, when I was fourteen. They taught me how to use an RPG: I was an RPG kid."

Chris gave me a meaningful look. He knew about things like that, kids who were sent to the front lines to launch those rocket-propelled grenades that killed anyone standing within a one-mile radius of the deadly charge—like Joe Valeri. But I knew about those things too.

"How do the parents feel about their children doing that?"

"They're prepared to sacrifice even their children for the sake of our homeland."

We found an empty bench near Dung Gate, close to the Wailing Wall, near a group of French tourists who were sprawled on the grass.

"What do you do now, Rashid?" I asked.

"I teach chemistry in Ramallah on the West Bank," he answered, tilting his face toward the sun.

"What kind of chemistry?" I asked, feeling sick to my stomach.

He smiled. "I teach that sodium mixed with nitric acid makes sodium nitrate."

"What does that do?" My heart was thumping away in my chest.

"With a detonator," he explained patiently, "my students can blow up a building or a few cars or even a military installation."

"Or even a civilian bus between Haifa and Tel Aviv," Chris said softly. "Right, Rashid?"

Shrugging his shoulders, he tilted his face toward the sun again.

"Is that true," I pressed. "Did you supply the explosives?"

He didn't budge, hardly moved his lips as he spoke. "I am here in the sun. I have been convicted of no crime—so why do you accuse me of something?"

"I'm not accusing you, Rashid, I simply wondered if you . . ."

"If I supplied the explosives that blew up the bus," he finished. He was looking directly at me now, his blue eyes unblinking, his mouth set.

My head ached. "Well did you?" I asked in a voice that was barely audible.

His response was only to smile. "Give my regards to my brother," he said, standing. He started down the road then, strolling aimlessly away. But suddenly he turned around and raised his fist in the air. "To the revolution," he proclaimed. "Till the death."

The Jerusalem compound comprised single-story stone huts surrounding a rather large yard. It was the central police station where all accused criminals, both civil and political, were held before trial.

Moud, Rashid's brother, sat in one of the small interrogation rooms, his hands cuffed in such a way that he was able to chain-smoke his cigarettes during the interview. Chris filmed while Moud recited various slogans of his revolution, almost totally ignoring any questions that were asked.

"The Israelis are killing our babies."

"Did your brother supply you with the explosives that blew up the bus?"

"We will not stop struggling until Palestine is liberated."

"Do you feel it's unfair that you're in prison while your leaders are living in villas on the Riviera?"

"Marxism is the teachings of our leaders."

"Is there any chance for a peaceful solution to this problem?"

"We will die for our homeland—make military actions until there is no more occupation."

"Is there any hope for your release?"

And that was the only time he stopped spouting the rhetoric of his cause and looked directly into the camera. "Yes," he said, enunciating very precisely. "The Israelis tell me I may be released in a trade, an exchange of prisoners."

Moud was taken back to his cell, leaving Chris and me feeling vaguely uneasy.

"He scares me," I finally said.

Chris was packing up his equipment. "He's no worse than his brother who's roaming the streets."

We went back to the studio, and spent the remainder of the day editing the piece down to what Ringler so aptly described as "seven minutes of sheer terror from seven hours of sheer hell." It was almost six-thirty when I finally arrived on the veranda of the King David Hotel and saw Avi sitting under a yellow-and-black-striped umbrella at a corner table.

Tourists were everywhere. Women wearing broad-brimmed straw hats, and brightly colored espadrilles peeking out from underneath tie-dyed cotton skirts, held tightly to toddlers' hands, mindful that they didn't tumble over the side as they gazed at the beautiful manicured gardens below. The men all looked bedraggled somehow, as they either guarded purchases or dutifully snapped photographs of their families romping around the famed hotel. Walking past them all, I smiled at the musicians playing violins in the center of the floor and practically fell into Avi's arms.

"What's the matter?" he said. "You look terrible."

I sat down, holding my damp hair away from my neck, and tried to smile. "Should I tell you about my day?"

He nodded.

"Well, first I knocked my knee against a stupid sink at *El Hoqq*, where a bunch of young toughs clucked and hissed at me. Then after waiting three hours to see Mr. Ahmed, Ringler and I finally went to the American Colony to meet this small, dark guy named Rashid, the terrorist's brother, only I thought Mustafa was Rashid, and Mustafa thought I was a hooker. Then it was all downhill in the detention center, where the prisoner spent two hours explaining why he wanted to kill you—and then, of course, after all that, we managed to edit the damn thing down to seven minutes, forty-three seconds, which was only thirteen seconds over."

Avi's brown eyes twinkled as he took my hand. "There was a time when I would have needed an interpreter to understand what you just said. What disturbs me is that now I know exactly what happened to you today."

"Let's get out of here," I said suddenly. "Let's just leave right now and forget about everything.

Avi walked behind me, his hand on the small of my back. "Just one question," he whispered. "How much did Mustafa offer you?"

It was already dusk when Avi maneuvered the car onto the winding road, bordered by rocks and barren hills and surrounded by vast expanses of dusty, dry, and deserted terrain, past Masada on the right and approaching Sodom straight ahead. The air was thick with the sickly smell of sulfur from the Dead Sea, and except for the occasional stone that knocked against the bottom of the car, there was total silence.

"Nothing moves here," Avi remarked. "Everything's so still."

"Will you be bored?"

He glanced over at me as he guided the car around a curve, past an Israeli military base, whose only marking was a soiled light-blue-and-white flag that hung limply from a rusted pole. Speeding past the barbed-wire fence, the car slowed down as it climbed the incline leading to the circular driveway of the hotel.

"I certainly hope we'll both be bored," he said, kissing the tip of my nose. "We need that."

Later that night we sat on our terrace overlooking the Dead Sea, the flickering lights of Amman reflecting on the clumps of salt that floated on the surface, like chunks of ice bobbing in and out of the water. My legs were propped against the railing, my head resting on Avi's bare shoulder.

"Tell me more about Ruth," I said quietly. "Are you upset that it's over?"

He looked straight ahead, smiled slightly, and said, "It fascinates me how predictable you are in certain ways even though you are the most unpredictable woman I've ever met. I was certain that you'd ask me that."

"Does it bother you that I want to know?" I asked, raising my head.

"No," he answered carefully, "because I want to know everything about everyone who was ever in your life." He smiled. "But I'm not American and so not quite as direct as you."

"It's different with my other involvements." The gentle wind whipped through my white silk caftan as I stood.

"It's only different because you're sure how you feel about me and still not exactly sure how I feel about you."

I despised the fact that he knew me so well. "Are you upset that it's over?" I repeated.

He looked at me tenderly. "Maggie, I've never loved a woman the way I love you, and I never will again. We're going to spend the rest of our lives together, because I'm probably the only man who could ever make you happy. I'm convinced of that."

I was listening very carefully, not daring to take a breath, waiting to hear the words *but* or *on the other hand*—words that usually follow a pronouncement so seemingly devoid of any negatives.

"Don't look so apprehensive," he said gently. "There is no catch; it is simply that, nothing more."

"Tell me about her. I want to know everything."

"Come back next to me and I'll tell you—only it's not very interesting."

Sitting down next to him again, my legs propped up, my head leaning against his shoulder, I took several deep breaths.

"I live a week with you in several hours," he said, stroking my face, "a month in several days, and a lifetime in several weeks. I feel you and sense all the energy you have because things happen between us." He pauses. "And nothing ever happened between Ruth and me."

"Never?"

"I was married to her for fifteen years, so it would be a lie to say that I don't have any feeling for her—of course I feel something."

"What?" I fidgeted slightly.

"I never had this closeness with her that we have, but there is a certain loss of something very familiar even if that familiarity was never enough."

"Are you happy that she has someone else?"

"I wouldn't use the word *happy*."

"Are you jealous?" I asked, holding my breath.

Avi's mouth was suddenly tense, his eyes narrowed as he seemed to choose his words very carefully. "I feel betrayed," he finally said.

It was shocking, outrageous, that the man I loved, who loved me more than anything in the world, turned out to be such a hypocrite.

"How can you say that?" I screamed, jumping up. "How can you feel betrayed?"

"How can you be so stupid?" he answered very calmly.

"Stupid!" I shouted. "You think I'm stupid, when

you've just made the most stupid and irrational statement in the world.''

Avi was infuriating, because he refused to get upset. ''You must have temporarily forgotten that you're in love with an Israeli, not an American.''

There was some semblance of truth in what he said. He didn't function in that pseudocivilized world where former husbands and wives give each other perfunctory pecks on the cheeks when they play tennis or cards together. He wasn't one of those spouses who tried to appear natural and relaxed at a cocktail party given by mutual friends, after bitter divorce proceedings were distant memories, children were safely in analysis, and new marriage vows had already been exchanged in small but tasteful wedding ceremonies in someone's garden in the Hamptons.

''What makes you think that Americans are any different?'' I said through clenched teeth. ''Maybe we're just more civilized than you.''

''Because,'' Avi said, reaching for my arm. ''There's nothing civilized about love and passion.''

''Maybe there isn't, but you can't even face the possibility that Ruth may have actually had an affair with this man.''

''I can face it,'' he answered carefully. ''And if she did, there is nothing civilized about my wife sleeping with a strange man, if she did, which I am not at all certain is the case.''

''But you were sleeping with me,'' I cried, twisting away from him.

''It's different,'' he said simply. ''I was never *sleeping* with you; I love you. And besides, there is a double standard.''

I was wild, wanting alternately to repack my suitcases and run back and pummel Avi until he understood the meaning of the word *civilized.*

''Relax,'' he said calmly, taking one of his small cigars from the metal case that was in the pocket of his blue shorts.

''Maybe I don't understand what you really mean,'' I

said, wrapping my arms around my breasts and pacing up and down the narrow terrace.

Avi lit his cigar. "There's bad and there's good with an Israeli," he explained, with an amused expression on his face. "The bad is that we don't consider women to be like men, and the good is that we don't consider women to be like men."

"And," I interrupted, waving my hand in a pretense of getting the smoke away from my face, "you would undoubtedly feel no qualms about doing the same thing to me that you did to her."

"No," he said, trying to trap my leg between his. "Being an Israeli doesn't mean that I am incapable of being faithful to a woman I really love."

"And," I answered, still outraged, "if I did it to you?"

"Then," he said, flipping the cigar over the side of the terrace, "I would kill you." He reached for me then, catching me by the arm, and pulled me onto his lap.

"I love you more than anything else on this earth, so stop being so silly."

"What's the difference between loving me and not loving Ruth if you still feel betrayed she's with another man?"

"The difference is that I wouldn't kill Ruth for that," he said, kissing my neck, "because to me she's already dead." He held me very tightly, his lips barely brushing against mine.

"Would you do it to me?" I asked softly.

"How could I do it to you when all I do is do it to you?" he answered, nibbling on my left earlobe.

"And what about my friends and my career?"

"What does that have to do with anything? I'm proud of everything you do, but I'm really a very simple Israeli," he said, reaching under my caftan and cupping my right breast in his hand. "You're body is mine."

"Avi, I want you to promise me something."

"Anything," he said, putting my hand on his erection.

"I want you to promise me that you'll never say what you just said about Ruth and that double standard in front of any of my friends. They'll think you're a caveman and

I'm an idiot." But deep down I really didn't care, because I was so filled with him.

He nodded and raised his right hand. "Our little secret is safe with me," he said, tilting his head to one side.

Without saying anything, I walked slowly through the open doors of the terrace and into the bedroom. He stayed outside for a while, gazing across the water. I lay on the bed, my white caftan spread out around me, my head resting on my arms. And then he was standing next to me, his hands at his sides.

"Take off your gown," he said softly.

I shook my head slowly, my eyes never leaving his face. He raised an eyebrow, almost imperceptibly, before reaching down to unfasten his shorts. He sat on the bed, took me in his arms, and slipped off the white caftan. Pulling me up gently to my knees, he held my face between his hands. "I love you, Maggie," he said. "I love you."

We both made sounds when he entered, clung urgently to each other, and then yielded to something that had already transpired with the first kiss.

"So quiet," he murmured afterward.

"Because sometimes you knock my breath away," I answered, drawing him into me again.

And I fell asleep thinking that without this man there would be nothing, that without him I couldn't survive. But when the sun streamed through the open terrace doors, I realized that last night was last night and this morning was this morning.

I climbed out of bed quietly, careful not to wake him, and tiptoed over to the dresser where he had put his clothes. Rummaging around in the drawer, I tried to find those ridiculous short beige socks, the antidote for this extreme case of vulnerability. But there were only three pairs of white sweat socks and two pairs of black knee-highs. And he startled me when he wrapped his arms around me and whispered in my ear, "I threw them all out."

"What?" I asked innocently.

"Those ridiculous beige socks," he answered, kissing my neck.

"What ridiculous beige socks?"

"The ones you always use as an excuse to start an argument when things are going too well with us," he said, taking me in his arms.

○

It is almost midnight when I enter my apartment after my walk down from Fifty-seventh Street. The pile of wire hangers that Vera tossed on the floor near my distressed-oak double dresser is still there. Just as I am about to stoop down to gather them up, the telephone rings shrilly. It crashes to the floor as I trip over the wire, lunging for the receiver.

"Hello," I say, hearing the oceanic sound of the international cable in my ear.

"I miss you," he says without even saying hello.

Closing my eyes, I lean against the wall. "I miss you too."

"It seems like months since you left."

"It's only two days," I answer, as if it really matters.

"Well," he says, in his familiar lilting accent, "it won't be much longer now."

"You know about the show?" I ask, amazed that Avi already knows about the dinner meeting with Grayson, Elliot, and Quincy. The first thought that crosses my mind is that Israeli intelligence is unquestionably the best and most effective, for there is no other way he could possibly know, unless Pedro and Raoul were actually Mossad agents.

"I don't know about a show," he says.

And I can picture him, his head tilted to the side, eyes crinkled up, as he exhales a stream of smoke from one of his small cigars.

"I'm coming back. I'm going to be doing a magazine-format show based out of Israel."

"I had no doubt that you were coming back, darling, with or without a job. You belong to me."

A wave of relief floods over me. "So how did you know it wouldn't be much longer until we saw each other?"

"Because," he says, pausing only slightly, "I'm arriving in New York the day after tomorrow and staying one week."

I can hardly speak.

"Happy?"

"Yes, very happy," I say, wishing he were here right now. "But why are you coming?"

"The official reason is to attend meetings in Washington concerning the withdrawal of our troops from Lebanon. The unofficial reason is to be with you."

"How long do you have to stay in Washington?" I ask, already greedy about every moment with him.

"I'll have to spend several days there at least, but I intend to shuttle down and back ever day, that is, if you don't mind me staying with you." And then he adds lightly, "So if you're not busy, I thought we'd spend your New Year's Eve together."

I am again reduced to an inarticulate heap of joy. "Avi, Avi" is all I can manage to say.

"It's flight number three three nine three from Tel Aviv, arriving on the twenty-ninth and I love you more than you love me."

"What makes you say that?" I ask, scribbling the flight number on a piece of paper.

"Because unlike you, I've already accepted the fact that we're going to spend the rest of our lives together—for several very good reasons."

CHAPTER EIGHT

There is the usual early-morning chaos in the studio, a sign that another news day is about to begin. Telephones are already ringing incessantly on the assignment desk, and people are scurrying around to gather the bits and pieces of information that are stacked high in the metal-mesh out boxes. The teletype machines, near the entrance, are clicking away, spewing forth reams of white paper filled with almost indecipherable pale-purple print, which will be miraculously transformed into cogent reports for tonight's broadcast.

A folding table is set up, with a large stainless-steel coffee urn, dozens of paper cups, a jar of powdered cream, a bowl of sugar cubes, and a cardboard box filled with glazed doughnuts.

Wrapped in my beige coyote coat, with oversized sunglasses shielding my face, I stand away from the commotion, wondering why I woke up this morning feeling vaguely nervous, slightly hostile, and somewhat frightened.

My decision to wander up to the studio was made after Cara called to say that she had returned from Aruba late last night with the residue of the flu that had contributed to one of the worst vacations she'd ever had, and to ask if we could meet sometime today for lunch. And even though it was only eight o'clock on a beautiful snowy morning, I was already awake and feeling terribly anxious because Avi was arriving in New York tomorrow.

Cara didn't respond when I pointed out, rather harshly, that anyone who was married to someone named Dr. Steven Blattsberg and who had three healthy children and a sprawling house on four acres in Short Hills, New Jersey, had no right to complain about her life, even if she did return from Aruba with the residue of a flu. And it didn't matter that Steven Blattsberg had thinning brown hair, a slight build, and a nervous habit of puffing on his unlit pipe since he was there to nurse her back to health. Granted Steven was anything but exciting and handsome, and sometimes he even infuriated Cara when he stalked through their house at night making grocery lists. But he loved her and would have been miserable had he known that he did anything to cause her the slightest annoyance. But it was also so typical of my sister not to say anything to him, just as it was typical of her never to remain angry at him for more than a day. Cara simply harbored everything inside herself, except when it just got to be too much, and she exploded. And her explosion was never anything more than a need to talk to me. Today wasn't exactly the perfect day for that, but I agreed to meet her at the studio cafeteria for lunch because of that hurt silence on the other end of the telephone line, punctuated by several pathetic sneezes. But that wasn't all that was troubling her. Right before we hung up, she tearfully confessed that she was pregnant again and couldn't face another extended belly, pendulous milk-filled breasts, six months of midnight feedings, and two years of dirty diapers and I felt like a monster—much worse than vaguely nervous, slightly hostile, and somewhat frightened.

It all came back to me then, slowly, the words Avi said that night at the Dead Sea when he was still inside me: "I want to have your baby," and suddenly I knew that there would never be another man, because no other man would have said it quite like that. There had been other moments in my life when desperation or passion made it tempting to take out the diaphragm or flush the pills down the toilet or rip out the coil. But when the others said, "I want you to have my baby," passion always waned and just in time. The diaphragm stayed snugly in place, the pills didn't end up swirling around the bottom of the bowl, and the coil remained tightly wrapped around the cervix.

All of these thoughts filled my head after I finally hung up with Cara, making me decide to wander up to the

ABN newsroom. It just seemed like the most natural way to get back in touch with reality, whatever that was.

A young girl, the heels of her feet carelessly crushing the backs of her black Capezio ballet-slipper shoes, her pelvis tilted forward, her shoulders slumped down casually, shuffles toward the folding table. There is a pouty expression around her full mouth, a vapid look in her enormous brown eyes as she asks an inane question in an adorable voice of a bearded associate producer who looks at her in awe—as if she had just recounted her own personal experience concerning life after death. Vera's words suddenly ring in my ears: ''There's a new crop coming up every year.'' That phrase was expressly designed to reduce my level of self-confidence, to conjure up old fears and insecurities, to force me to remember that having a successful career would never compensate for not having a successful marriage. Vera would describe how those fresh-faced young women poured into New York by the droves from all over the country in search of a husband, only to diminish my chances of ever finding one for myself. Strange that it never occurred to me to ask Mother why she obviously spent a good portion of her day hanging around the Port Authority Bus Terminal.

The girl is fascinating as she shuffles like that, carelessly crushing the backs of her eighty-dollar Capezio ballet-slipper shoes, tilting her pelvis forward so expertly, slumping her shoulders down so that her breasts are merely vague but titillating impressions against the thin fabric of her blouse, asking inane questions that evoke expressions of wonderment on a grown man's face. And this one would unquestionably be willing to bludgeon her own mother to death for a crack at my job.

Miss Pouty Mouth glances over at me and whispers something into the ear of the bearded associate producer, who looks over at me and nods. And for some reason, inexplicable yet clearly connected to Dawn—someone just called her that—it suddenly seems crucial that I put things back in their proper perspective. It is absolutely necessary to convince myself that I don't want to have a baby with someone who wouldn't even know how to conduct himself in New York. In childish succession, the images

flash into my head—Avi in various typical situations that
could happen to anyone visiting New York, which only
proves that he was right after all. I haven't yet accepted
the fact that we would be spending the rest of our lives
together. But I can't help it. I see Avi arriving at Kennedy
Airport with a cardboard suitcase. Avi hailing one occupied taxicab after another until he finally manages to
win a fight to the death with a little old lady who is
clinging valiantly to the cab door. Avi undertipping the
driver so a stream of obscenities follow him down the
street. Avi accepting Canadian coins from a blind vendor
at the newsstand who can tell, even blind, the tourist
from the native. Avi waiting docilely in line for a table
at a restaurant that boasts a salad bar and cute sayings of
famous drunks, before overtipping the maître d' when he
is seated somewhere in the back near the men's room.
Avi wandering around the streets of New York, gazing
up at the skyscrapers, not watching where he is walking,
until that final pathetic image of Avi hanging onto a
twisted metal streetlamp, desperately trying to scrape the
dog shit from the sole of his shoe. I am amazed at how
smoothly I managed to make the transition from wanting
Avi's baby to dog shit on the streets of New York.

Miss Pouty Mouth is gushing at me, shaking me out
of my irrational reverie. "It's really you—Maggie Sommers. I just can't believe it."

Of course, I have no intention of making it easy for
her, partly because she has absolutely flawless skin and
can't be more than twenty-two, and partly because I don't
and I'm not. Standing perfectly still and expressionless,
I allow her to sputter on about how wonderful it is to
meet me (did someone introduce us?) and how she has
been watching me on television since she was a little girl.

That does it. Removing my sunglasses, I run my tongue
over what cameramen have been telling me for years are
my terrific teeth. It is unbelievable that she instinctively
knew where to plunge the knife into one somewhat anxious woman who simply wandered up to the ABN newsroom to find a little peace of mind.

"What do you do here?"

"I'm a desk assistant."

"Are you trying to break into production?"

"Oh, no. I want to be on-air, just like you."

Bingo.

"Then perhaps you should think about having that mole removed from the side of your mouth."

Her baby fingers flutter up to the side of her mouth, briefly touching the mole, as she continues the conversation as only an uninhibited child can do, without the slightest trace of self-consciousness.

"Thank you so much for telling me that," she says. "And I love all your reports from the Middle East."

And then, while Dawn launches into a monologue about the merits of a course she is taking at The New School ("There's a new crop coming up every year"), my mind becomes filled again with thoughts of holding him, feeling him, touching him, and "I want to have your baby."

"You have the most perfect nose," Dawn is saying, "so straight, and then it sort of tilts up like Vivien Leigh's did in *Gone With the Wind.*"

Does that mean that Vivien's nose stopped tilting after *Gone With the Wind* was in the can? I'm not feeling especially sympathetic today.

"Thank you," I say instead. But my mind is elsewhere, contemplating the advantages of having a spinal block as opposed to natural childbirth.

"Could you tell me the name of your doctor?" she asks.

"What doctor?" I answer, still in the labor room.

"The doctor who did it—fixed your nose, I mean," she whispers.

"I never had my nose fixed," I reply sweetly.

She is clearly flustered. "I'm so sorry."

"Not at all," I say graciously. "I take it as a compliment."

Definitely a spinal block, with Avi in the delivery room watching me dilate to the size of a dinner plate.

There is a temporary lull in our conversation, while Dawn tries to think of something to say that will fall into neutral territory.

"What tape recorder is the best, in your opinion?"

"For what?"

"For doing interviews."

Perhaps I could give this all up, allow Dawn to take a crack at my job, and simply do the occasional endorsement for tape recorders while caring for Avi's child.

"Try using paper and pen," I snap. "There weren't any outlets in cornfields when I started out."

I am instantly sorry for being so harsh. I realize that at her age I was too busy hating my marriage to want a baby. At thirty, I was too busy enjoying my career to want a baby. Suddenly it occurs to me that I don't want to find myself in my forties regretting that I was either too busy hating my marriage or too busy enjoying my career to have had that baby. And when was the last time I did an interview in a cornfield anyway? And it isn't only because Avi said it that way while he was still inside me that makes me so sure. I am simply in love with him, and dog shit or no dog shit, having his baby seems the most logical thing to do.

"Is Elliot James in yet?" I ask, suppressing an insane desire to hug her. It would probably be a lot healthier for me not to go from one extreme to the other in life.

"No, I don't think so," she says timidly. "But would you like to wait in his office? You'll be more comfortable there."

Dawn slips her feet back inside her black Capezio ballet-slipper shoes and walks toward Elliot's office. Suddenly three people who have worked with me since I took my ovaries for granted are crowding around, all saying the same thing. "Poor Joey—what a tragedy."

Agnes Farley, all two hundred pounds of her stuffed into one of those pastel-colored polyester pants suits, is the woman who did my makeup each and every time I went on the air for local news. "I prayed for you, Maggie," she says, pushing a strand of over-bleached blond hair out of her eyes.

"Oh, Agnes," I answer, genuinely touched. "Thank you."

Peter Templeton, tall and thin, with a narrow face and long nose is still wearing that same ratty blue sweater vest. He was my first floor director, back in the days when I covered crime.

"Maggie," he says, embracing me. "I thought about you so often."

"I know you did," I answer, squeezing his hand.

And Jack Roshansky, who resembles Mr. Clean more and more with each passing year, his shiny bald head and enormous stomach always visible across the newsroom, hugs me. "Life stinks," he says sourly.

Dawn is straining to catch every word, as if she is about to uncover a crucial secret about people who have been together in this business for years and have just suffered a common loss—the death of someone who was also in this business for years, with them, part of them. Perhaps she will learn something about that inexplicable solidarity that no course at The New School could ever teach.

"What a scene," Jack says. "It was bedlam here when the news hit."

"How did you manage to get word out?" Pete asks.

It is clear that while I am their only link to the actual event, the one person in the group who can provide the graphic details of those horrible moments right before it happened as well as those terrible hours that followed, they are my only link to the reactions of those people here who loved Joe as much as I did. They need to understand another perspective of the tragedy to fill in the blanks, so they can accept it in its finality. And I need to understand if my sense of loss seems more acute only because I was there when it actually happened. Dawn moves closer to us, waiting to hear both versions of a horrible story that doesn't yet seem real and that concerns one of us who lost his life. "One of us got killed," Chris Ringler wept that day. "One of us got it."

They tell me that the scene in the office was pretty chaotic.

"The call from the Jerusalem bureau was put through directly upstairs to corporate—Grayson's office, I think," Peter explains. And it was only because Peter happened to be sitting with Elliot that he learned that the ABN crew in Lebanon had been caught in some kind of ambush.

Corporate received a confused message that several people had been wounded.

"Nobody was really very sure of anything at that point," Peter continues. "We were just told to stand by until further word came in."

Grayson called downstairs immediately after receiving the news and instructed Elliot to monitor all telex and teletype machines in the newsroom in case anything came in downstairs first.

"It reminded me of that day when Joey took yards of teletype paper and draped it across every desk in the newsroom. We almost didn't get on the air that night," Jack says, smiling sadly.

Shutting my eyes, I try to reconstruct the sequence of events, beginning with Ringler riding inside the Israeli Mikerva tank next to the remains of Joe Valeri, leaving him only when forced to climb out as it approached the outskirts of Beirut. Joe's body was transferred at that point to an armored personnel carrier, which took it the remaining distance across the border. Chris rode the rest of the way into Beirut in the jeep with Avi and me. When we finally reached the Commodore Hotel, we all raced inside in search of a telephone. Chris screeched at the bewildered desk clerk, explaining that there had been an accident and there wasn't any time to run all over the city looking for an open line in one of those public phones that never worked anyway. The clerk was hesitant, his eyes fixed on the blood that was splattered all over the front of my T-shirt, until Avi spoke to him in Arabic, ordering him to provide a phone. We waited for what seemed like an eternity before the clerk finally informed us that it was impossible to get through to Jerusalem, as there had been several bomb blasts in the area, which had knocked down most of the telephone cables. What we didn't know until much later was that the Irish television crew that had been in the area of Sabra Camp at the time had already notified ABN Jerusalem. The problem was that nobody really knew the extent of the casualties, and extracting information from the Israeli army unit that had been in the field was virtually impossible, which was why Grayson received the initial ambiguous report.

"I got a picture from Joey once," Agnes says, wiping her eyes, "of him with a couple of Palestinian children. So sweet."

"The children were the hardest part for Joe," I explain. "He used to bring them food and spend time talking to them." How can I tell Agnes that right before he was killed, he had said a final goodbye to one Palestinian child who was dying of meningitis. And it was then that Joe ran over to me and begged me to read to him, talk to him, anything to help him stop trembling and weeping. How could any of us have known that in only a few seconds, we wouldn't have a chance to say our final farewells to him.

"I was in edit trying to get a cassette ready for Elliot to view before the evening broadcast," Jack explains. "When I went back into Elliot's office, he was sitting on the edge of his desk with a telephone to each ear, barking orders to three secretaries. They just kept racing in and out answering phones or relaying messages that were filtering down from corporate."

"Finally, Grayson came downstairs after about two hours with a telex message in his hand," Peter says. "He handed it to Elliot to read. Grayson just kind of collapsed in a chair, while everybody else in the room were glued to their seats, too shocked to leave."

"I'll never forget how Elliot just hung up those two phones and started to sob," Jack says, shaking his head.

"Everybody was stunned. No one said a word until Grayson finally asked who should notify his family and if he had a wife and kids."

"Elliot was pretty calm by then. He told Grayson that Joe wasn't married, but that he had this friend—that Joe was gay."

And unbelievably, Grayson Daniel had the decency, after grasping the facts concerning Joe's private life, to suggest that someone go to the American Ballet Theatre rehearsal hall and break the news to Joe's friend, Garry Wainwright.

"How did you get the telex out?" Peter asks.

And before I can answer, Jack adds, "When did the Jerusalem bureau actually find out what happened?"

"Everything happened so quickly at that point," I answer. "It was almost a blur."

The atmosphere at the Commodore Hotel was chaotic, with Lebanese civilians fleeing inside to take refuge from a brigade of Amal militiamen who had just opened fire in the streets. Chris and I eventually gave up trying to get through to the Jerusalem bureau by telephone and followed Avi's advice about going next door to send a telex directly to the States. We waited until the spurts of gunfire subsided before dashing out of the hotel. Hugging the sides of the buildings, we crept cautiously down the street until we reached the telex office, which was still open since they couldn't leave the area either. The message was sent directly to Grayson Daniel, ABN News, New York, the one he handed to Elliot to read, with a copy sent to the Jerusalem bureau.

JOE VALERI KILLED BY RPG NEAR SABRA CAMP STOP NO OTHER CASUALTIES STOP WILL CONTACT AGAIN WHEN RETURN TO JERUSALEM STOP SOMMERS AND RINGLER.

Agnes, who has been taking everything in, with a pained expression on her face, begins to talk, to let go of what has been pent up inside her since it all happened.

"I was in the makeup room when I heard over the loudspeaker that someone had an announcement to make."

Agnes describes how she wandered back into the newsroom and watched in amazement as Elliot climbed on top of a desk, raised his hands for silence, and said in a voice that was choked with emotion that Joe Valeri had been killed approximately five hours earlier in Lebanon.

"Then he just knelt down on the desk and started to cry," Agnes says softly, and adds, "I didn't believe it; I don't think anybody really did that first moment. The whole newsroom was quiet. Nobody dared to move. It was as if time had simply stopped. And then we all cried—everybody."

Squeezing Agnes's hand, I feel the tears gather in my own eyes, because it is still so fresh.

"By the time I came out of Elliot's office," Peter says,

"people were either hysterical, pressing poor Elliot for more information, or just too numb to move."

"Where were you when it happened?" Agnes asks me suddenly.

"Next to him, but I didn't see it. I heard something, but when I looked up it was over."

There is nothing much left to say. Dawn looks a little less adorable as she backs away, realizing that television is not always what it's cracked up to be.

"When did you get back, Maggie?" Peter asks.

"Two days ago."

"And for good, I hope," Agnes says, blowing her nose.

"I'm not sure."

"I heard they're shipping you back in," Jack says. "There've been a lot of rumors flying around here."

"I'm probably going back to Israel but not Lebanon."

"There're meetings scheduled in Washington between our administration and the Israelis, beginning the day after tomorrow," Peter offers. "We ran the story last night. Are you covering them?"

Only when he comes home to me every night. "No, I'm not, Peter."

"Another goddamn Vietnam, that Lebanon," Peter says, shaking his head. "Here comes Elliot, and I'd better get back into the studio." He kisses me goodbye before adding, "Stop in to see me before you leave, Mags."

"Don't forget to see me too," Agnes says, hugging me.

"I put a copy of that cassette away for you," Jack says sadly. "I ran it over and over."

"So did I, Jack, over and over in my mind."

Rubbing his mouth thoughtfully with his hand, he walks away.

Maggie Sommers's Emmy nomination was never even mentioned, and for that she is grateful. To the three people who worked with her since the very beginning, it was irrelevant to what was being discussed and what was being discussed were feelings, which never have anything to do with television or Emmy nominations anyway.

Elliot raises his eyebrows in surprise and smiles delightedly when he sees me standing in front of his office. Without saying a word, he takes my hand and leads me inside.

"Did you come here to tell me that you want me?" he asks, closing the door.

"I never stopped wanting you as a friend, Elliot. You'll always be my friend." He pressed down on the intercom button as I amble over to the window to watch the steady fall of snowflakes, which are now sticking to the sidewalk below.

"Gladys," Elliot says, "will you bring in two coffees and a couple of doughnuts, please." He looks at me. "What's the matter, baby? You look upset. What is it?"

I am tempted to tell Elliot that it was because of what happened to Joe, but that isn't exactly the truth right now. I am mourning something else, the loss of my innocence, having misplaced it somewhere within the confines of this newsroom a long time ago.

"I'm frightened," I say truthfully.

"Of what, babe? You've got it all."

I shake my head, tears welling up in my eyes. "I'm frightened because this doesn't mean the same to me anymore—my job, the excitement of a new assignment. It's just not the same for me. I'm only happy when I'm with him, but I'm not sure that it's the right thing to do, because ABN has been like my home."

Elliot waits for me to finish before putting his arms around me. Gladys walks quietly into the room, carrying the coffee and doughnuts.

"Welcome home, Maggie," she says shyly.

"Thank you," I answer, pulling away from Elliot.

I smile. "You see, even with all of Grayson's stupidity and insufferable ways, he's right. Everyone here is like my family. But then, since I fell in love, other things began to matter, not just ABN."

"I'm jealous of him."

There is an awkward silence as we sip our coffees. Glancing over the rim of my mug, I notice a photograph of Frances James, with her wandering eye, still prominently displayed on Elliot's desk. He follows my gaze and shrugs his shoulders.

"I'm still married to her," he says apologetically.

"And you always will be," I say softly.

"It was a mistake, I know that now, but—"

Touching his lips gently with my finger, I say, "Don't, Elliot, not again."

He sighs. "I suppose I should be happy for you, that you found someone."

"Aren't you?"

He smiles and walks to the window. The snow is falling more heavily now.

"I suppose I am even though I always imagined that you'd end up with some preppy executive type—certainly not someone who lives halfway across the world."

I am listening to Elliot while I'm trying to find the right words that will explain Avi Herzog. "Distance has nothing to do with it, Elliot. He's part of my life, more than anyone else ever was."

Elliot looks surprised. "But he's Israeli, I don't understand."

"I love him, he's inside of me, a part of me. It's as if I've known him all my life, maybe even in another life," I add, smiling.

Elliot laughs. "That bad, huh?"

"That good."

"Then if that's the case, I'm happy for you Maggie, not happy for me, but what are friends for if . . ."

But Elliot doesn't finish his sentence because the telephone rings.

"It's for you," he says, handing me the receiver.

Cara is practically incoherent as she tries to explain, between her sobs, sneezes, and the piercing screams of two of her children, what has happened. Finally, she calms down sufficiently to say that Jonesie called several minutes before, just as she was about to leave to meet me at ABN. It seems that Alan Sommers didn't go to the office this morning, but instead stayed home to pack his clothes. Jonesie told Cara that when he went downstairs to the basement to get several more suitcases from the storage room, Vera locked herself in the bedroom. Remembering what had happened the last time she did that, Jonesie got frightened. When Alan came back upstairs and found he was unable to get into the room, he ignored Jonesie's pleas to break down the door and simply stormed out of the house. Jonesie didn't know what else to do but call Cara.

"Did Jonesie call the police?"

Elliot looks at me questioningly.

"She's waiting for instructions," Cara answers.

"I'm on my way," I say. "Tell her to call the police. How long will it take you to get there?"

"In this weather, probably an hour."

My heart is pounding as I hang up the telephone.

"What happened?"

"I take a deep breath. "I think Mother may have taken an overdose of pills."

"Why?"

The deep breath doesn't help. "Oh, Elliot," I say, burying my face in his shoulder and beginning to sob. "Because she doesn't believe she can survive without Father. He's leaving her."

Elliot is ashen. "Maggie, what can I do?"

"Nothing. I have to go."

"Do you want me to come with you?"

"I don't think so. I—Cara—we'll be together there."

Elliot helps me on with my coat. "Will you call me if you need anything?"

I am numb, unable to comprehend what is happening. "Yes, thank you, Elliot. Yes, I will."

Whatever we are as a family, we are survivors. Huddled in the backseat of a taxicab on my way up to Mother's apartment, those words keep reverberating in my head. The ride seems endless. The snowfall, which has now reached blizzard proportions, is causing the cab to crawl at a snail's pace, slipping and sliding on the slick pavement. A yellow tow truck, barely visible in the blinding downfall, suddenly looms ahead in the middle of the street, blocking traffic as it removes a stalled car.

"Can't you back up," I ask the driver anxiously, "get off Fifty-seventh Street?"

"Listen, lady," he growls, turning around, "do ya

think I got a thing for Fifty-seventh Street? If I never saw it again, it wouldn't be too soon."

There is no point in arguing, because judging from the commotion around the two trucks, it's apparent that everybody's nerves are frayed today. My mind wanders instead to our family and the irony of it all. To be so far away from them and this city, so remote in every sense of the word, for months on end, and then suddenly to be in the middle of a snowstorm en route to a potential disaster is at best unnerving. It is as if Mother's apartment is as distant as Beirut right now.

As we exit from the park, Temple Emanu-El looms into view, the bastion of God's tolerance of the borderline believer, the capitalistic approach to Judaism, where generous donations make up for not so steadfast faith. Father would attend services there once a year on Yom Kippur, the holiest of all Jewish holidays. It was the only day when he paid tribute to his past and all he had embraced before money became his only ethic. He would rarely include us. Instead, he would invite us to the Deosophy Center, where abstract and ambiguous lectures on religion were offered to people similar to Father. The soul-searching was impressive, the discussion, boring. Once Cara summed it up succinctly after an especially dull lecture on the Concentric Circle Theory, or the Compartmentalization of Life. Cara decided that it was merely an exercise in keeping everybody from the old neighborhood from ever bumping into anybody from the new neighborhood. But Father described it even better the same night when someone asked him if he was a Jew. "My children are Episcopalian," he said, "my wife's Russian Orthodox, and I'm a lawyer. Here's my card."

Cara was mortified. I was enraged. Father was furious at our reactions. "If you don't like it around here, you can go out and earn your own living," he yelled at me. "Shape up or find someone else to support you," he threatened Cara.

And in the end, we both followed his advice.

The traffic light has now changed six times from red to green without our having moved an inch. Looking at my watch, I see it has already been thirty minutes since Cara's phone call.

"Please," I say pleadingly, "I'm in a terrible hurry."

"Lady, the world's in a hurry." The driver yawns. "Just relax and I'll get you there."

"Do you have a cigarette?" I ask nervously.

"Sure," he answers, offering me a cigarette. "Smoke."

As the cab finally lurches forward, I realize that Cara and I took it for granted that ours was an average family. The angry outbursts that came from behind Vera and Alan's bedroom door were as usual as the nightly clattering of the dinner dishes. But when the fighting subsided, which it always did, life was never any different. Perhaps children simply expect very little. Perhaps it was enough to know that our parents' traumas would never affect us.

"I was so poor that I lived on chocolate bars," Father would complain bitterly.

"The Bolsheviks urinated all over Grandmother's Oriental rugs," Mother would say repeatedly.

We knew that our lives would never be invaded by thugs relieving themselves on our wall-to-wall carpeting and there would always be food on the table. For me, unlike Cara, however, poverty and starvation ceased being abstractions when they became a daily part of my work.

Perhaps this latest incident with Mother is just one more example of Vera's continuing effort to prove how much she suffers over Alan. But if it isn't, I wonder if Cara especially can survive it. Maggie is the strong one, or at least that's what everybody always believed. If only Cara and I were closer, if only they hadn't driven a wedge between us because of their fear of strength in unity. One disruptive child, and they were still considered blameless. Two disruptive children, and people might have wondered. We started out in life instinctively close, emotionally linked, even if we went through the normal stages of sibling rivalry. We screamed hateful words, destroyed each other's toys, and sometimes even envisioned each other dead. But as we grew older and Alan's abuse became more flagrant and Vera's neuroses more evident, we tended to retreat into our separate worlds to cope in our own ways until the outbursts subsided.

Alan convinced Cara that she was mediocre, unattractive, dull, and that nothing was expected of her other than obedience. Blond, blue-eyed, with the delicate features and rounded body of a Botticelli female, she was the epitome of classic femininity—anything but unattractive. And she was interesting, grounded in the classics from an early age because of all the books she constantly devoured.

"They fill a void," she would explain. "They allow me to escape into a better place."

It was understandable why she gratefully accepted Mother's dependency.

At least Vera feigned an interest in Cara. At least between them, the bargain was clear—support for sympathy.

"I made the honor roll," Cara said proudly one night during dinner.

"You're brilliant," Mother answered.

"I bet everybody made it," Father said, without even looking up from his plate.

"Why can't you ever say something nice?" Cara cried, fleeing from the table.

I never dared to pose that kind of question, because there were so many other problems with Father. He tormented me for being different, rebellious, and seductive. When the dentist put his hand on my breast while he filled a cavity, I told Father.

"You asked for it," he said harshly. "You have that look."

At fifteen, his statement baffled me. Dr. Levy's hand had been on my breast while the saliva dribbled from my mouth. What look? Yet when Cara ran home from the park and reported that her bicycle had been stolen, Father interrogated her for hours, until he was convinced that the thief hadn't abused her. Vera claimed later that it was only because Cara was so defenseless. Father disagreed, insisting that it was only because the hoodlum was a Puerto Rican. The pedophile periodontist was a Jew, and how could a Jewish dentist possibly violate a child unless he had been provoked?

My adolescence was like a prison sentence, days and months simply being wished away while only dreams of being grown up and free enabled me to survive. And there was always so much going on in my head—plans, ideas, hopes—that the days and months passed quickly and my youth was suddenly gone. Still, Cara and I would constantly meet in our secret place, the bathroom, where the running water would drown out our furtive whispers.

"I can't stand it," she would complain, "but it's better to act the way he wants."

"I can't stand it either," I agreed, "but I'm not going to let him demolish me!"

"Lady," the cabdriver says, "you should stop smoking. You cough too much."

"I don't smoke," I answer, choking on the cigarette.

"She doesn't smoke," he mutters. "That's why she's smoking."

"I mean, I usually don't smoke," I snap. "I'm a little nervous."

"Life's too short to be nervous," the driver says philosophically.

How short is short on this snowy morning?

Mother once explained to us, in a feeble attempt to justify Father, after a particularly horrible scene, "A man's desire is like a physical pain that has to be satisfied at all costs."

"Is that an asset or a liability?" I dared to inquire.

"It's just the way it is," she replied.

It was then that I realized that whatever it was for them, it was somehow our responsibility, since we drove them to heights of sexual frenzy. It was our obligation either to relieve them or to simply accept their relieving themselves elsewhere.

"It's as meaningless for them as stopping for a drink after work," Mother would say.

And she tried to believe it, because somehow it kept her alive.

"Haven't I seen you before—maybe I had you in my cab?"

"No, I don't think so," I reply, pulling my muffler up to my nose.

He temporarily forgets about me as a cacophony of horns sound. Leaning out his window, he yells, "Whaddaya want me to do—fly? Life's too short to get yourself in an uproar, fella."

"If you say that one more time, I'm going to scream," I scream.

He stretches. "I've got news for you, lady—you're screaming. Why don't ya have another cigarette and relax?"

"Because I don't want another cigarette," I answer, fighting back tears. "I just want to get to Fifth Avenue and Eighty-third Street. Please just get me there."

Chickens and diamonds always come to mind when I think of how Father controlled Mother.

At countless dinners at the Sommerses', he would fling a roast chicken from the table if he detected a speck of blood under one wing.

"You can't even cook a chicken," he would rant. "And I give you everything."

Mother would run from the table in tears, rush into her bedroom, and toss her diamonds out the window. "This is what I think of your everything," she would scream.

And Jonesie would calmly clean up the chicken, while Cara and I would race downstairs to retrieve the diamonds.

"The chicken was undercooked again?" the doorman invariably asked, shaking his head.

Today, the doorman's face at 1014 Fifth Avenue is ashen. Helping me out of the cab, he says, "The ambulance and police are upstairs. . . ." It is more a question than a statement as he waits anxiously for me to explain.

"Thank you," I answer, walking directly into the lobby.

In the elevator, Father's words echo in my ears: "This kind of drama has ceased to impress me. It is all an act."

So why did Vera Sommers swallow thirty digitalis capsules, each unit containing .25 milligrams, which are routinely prescribed in small doses to slow the conduction from the atrium to the ventricular valve and to stimulate the heart muscles in incidents of coronary failure? I find this out from one of two burly paramedics immediately upon my arrival at the apartment. The discovery of what Mother had taken was made after Jonesie called the police.

The emergency rescue team arrived, with all the appropriate paraphernalia used to save lives. They found the empty bottle of pills lying on the floor next to Vera's bed, clearly labeled for Keith Robinson, Jonesie's husband. Jonesie swore that Keith never touched the medication after suffering a heart attack several months earlier, as he had left for Alabama to recuperate and seemed to be doing just fine. But none of that matters now, because nothing remains of the digitalis except for an empty vial and a wad of white cotton.

The answer to the question of why Vera swallowed the pills is undoubtedly explained inside the elegant pink linen envelope marked "To whom it may concern," which has been propped up against the bottle of Joy perfume that sits on the hand-painted eighteenth-century commode reserved exclusively for her lingerie. Slipping the letter into my pocket, I watch this hideous scene in disbelief.

Only minutes ago, Vera was being hauled up from the bathroom floor, where she had been found clutching the toilet bowl, making retching noises that defied all description.

"Mother!" I scream, rushing toward her. "Mother."

Shoving me aside in their haste to save her, the paramedics assure me that digitalis in inordinately large doses—"lethal," I think they said—causes nausea as well as other things.

"What other things?" I cry, hanging on to the wall. The room is spinning around me.

The paramedic, the one cracking his gum, doesn't answer. Instead, he flings Mother down on the bedroom rug, frantically inserting a needle, which is attached to a brown rubber tube, into her vein.

"What are you doing?" I scream, hovering over them.

He doesn't even look up. "Quinidine," he answers breathlessly. "An antidote." I have to restrain myself from covering her, because her housecoat is open and her breasts are exposed. Waves of nausea envelop me. Jonesie, perspiration dripping down her anguished face, rushes into the room and clutches my hand. "There ain't no man livin' worth dyin' for," she sobs.

"Mother isn't dying, Jonesie," I say firmly. "She'll be fine."

"Not this time," she wails. "No siree, this time she's gone and done it for sure."

"Shut up," I cry. "Just shut up, Jonesie."

She puts her enormous arms around me and whispers, "Poor child, poor child."

A policeman tilts Mother's head back as he gives her mouth-to-mouth resuscitation. The other paramedic, the one with the Afro, is busy connecting two electric wires together directly over her heart. "I'm trying to get a heartbeat!" he yells to his colleague. "I'm losing a pulse."

"Keep breathing into her!" he shouts. "Keep breathing."

Everything is a blur—arms, legs, metal, wires, tubes, even Mother's pathetic crumpled figure lying on the floor is hazy. Swaying against Jonesie, I feel faint.

"Give her two shocks and then use the suction!" someone yells.

"Is the vein open?"

"Open—ready for an IV of Verapmil."

"Get it into her fast—let's try and stop the arrhythmia."

"Keep pounding, we've only got three minutes left. Let's go."

Her body flops up and down like a rag doll as it is pulled and pushed by four men who are desperately trying to pump life back into her. But even through my tears I can see that it is useless. The life is seeping out of her so quickly that the race is already lost.

"Breathe!" a policeman shouts, "breathe."

"Please," I cry, feeling so helpless, "please."

The paramedic who has been pressing in and out on her chest in regular intervals moves aside as the other one jars her with a suction cup.

"Press it again, keep it up," he orders, "heart's jumping around like Mexican beans—I'm losing her."

"God in heaven," Jonesie wails.

"No!" I scream. "Please don't lose her."

"Now I've got no pulse," he cries.

"You've got brain damage here," the paramedic says. "It's been fifteen minutes."

"Forget it," someone else mutters.

"No!" I scream, running toward them, "don't forget it."

"She doesn't look good," a policeman says, restraining me.

Her features are barely distinguishable, and her face is bloated and blue. Several people seem to be lifting me off the floor, looking at me with expressions of pity as they hold me up. Cara stumbles into the room, snowflakes still clinging to her eyelashes and blond hair, tears streaming down her full cheeks. She takes one look at Mother and moans softly, her delicate hand covering her mouth. Throwing herself into my arms, she sobs, "I love you, Maggie. Let's not fight anymore."

"No, Cara," I murmur, dazed. "Life's too short."

It is over. There's nothing left to do except remove the tubes, detach the wires, and replace everything neatly in the red box marked ARREST. The policeman who had been breathing into her mouth is now sitting on the floor, trying to catch his own breath.

"I'm sorry," he says softly.

The beepers on the hips of the paramedics are signaling another emergency in progress somewhere else—some other place where there's still hope. They appear so ill at ease as they stoop down to collect their things that I want to comfort them, to assure them that they really tried. And although they are linked forever to me in some macabre way, I just can't find the words right now. Perhaps if I started this day all over again, walked out of this room, came back in, she would be sitting up in bed and reading the Russian-language newspaper, the one she devoured each and every morning of her life. If I closed my eyes, opened them very quickly, maybe none of this would be happening.

There are certain losses in life for which there is no consolation. Cara is crying, her head buried in my shoulder, her fingernails digging into my back. Jonesie runs out of the room, emitting a piercing scream that will reverberate in my head for years to come.

"The deceased," the policeman says. "Was she your mother?"

It takes me fully a minute to grasp what he has said. The deceased he is speaking about is indeed my mother, even if she is already being referred to in the past tense. If only the transition from life to death were a question of grammar, then perhaps only a slight correction would suffice to reverse the entire process. Then I could politely say, "Excuse me, but you've made a grammatical error. She *is* my mother."

Glancing at my face, his own face contorts into an expression of pain. "I'm so sorry, but I need her name and age to fill out this form. Suicide is a police matter."

How bizarre that Vera Sommers—who never even got a parking ticket—has committed a criminal act. Her last deed on earth is felonious assault upon her own body—punishable by what? Death? And why should anybody care anyway, when bodies are sprawled on the streets of New York and corpses are dumped unceremoniously in open graves in Lebanon?

The paramedics are gently lifting the rag doll, its arms and legs dangling limply from its sides, onto the unmade bed. They are covering her with the white-eyelet sheet, one of the ones she bought last year at the January White Sale at Saks Fifth Avenue. How odd to think of that now, and how ironic that only one year later it is being used to cover her lifeless body. Do I detect a look of surprise on her face, or am I imagining it? Is she astonished that she actually did this horrendous thing? Say you're sorry, Mother, and you can have another chance. Just apologize and you can get up—remember, that's what you used to tell us when we were little and believed that ours was just an average family. Burying my face in my hands, I try to block out the screaming words that are bouncing around in my head. They say that when a person drowns, his entire life flashes before his eyes. They never say that when a parent dies, everything he ever said echoes over and over, until the screeching silence becomes more devastating than the words. I am doomed to nothing more than memories of her from this moment on. All forward motion has stopped. Taking a deep breath, I whisper to Cara, "Where's Steven?"

She can't turn around. Her face is pressed against mine. She weeps as if her heart will break. And it will, just as mine will, but right now there are other things we have to do.

"Hospital," she manages to gasp.

"Can you please come with us into the other room?" the policeman asks.

"Cara," I say softly, "I'll help you, but let's go into the living room."

The other policeman steps forward to assist me. We can do this alone. Cara sniffles. Leading her down the hallway as if she were blind, I gently steer her into the living room where she collapses into a chair.

"I love you, Maggie," she says, wiping her eyes.

"I love you too, Cara," I answer, wondering why it took a catastrophe of this magnitude to unleash all this emotion between us. "I just want to check on Jonesie. I'll be right back."

Jonesie is on her knees in the kitchen. The sight of her enormous body in prayer position near the dishwasher is startling. But then everything that is happening around here today is startling.

"Oh, Maggie," she wails, "what now?"

"I don't know what now, Jonesie," I answer, stroking her face. "come sit with us in the living room."

She gets up laboriously. "Maggie," she says, "I ain't gonna work for him and that Loretta woman."

"Who's Loretta?"

"Your father and that woman of his—that's who. I ain't stayin' on in this house," she says firmly.

I put my hands on her bulky shoulders. "Tell me what this is about. I don't understand." But I do understand, only too well.

"The past few years, every time your mama went away or even just stayed overnight at your sister's, he brought her here. He thought I didn't care, but he was wrong. I never said nuttin' 'cause I was afraid this would happen, and now it did.'' She is crying.

"Why didn't you tell Cara or me?'' I ask, feeling sick to my stomach.

"Cara has all them children to worry about, and you was never here.''

This must be the one—the one who put the final nail into the coffin of what was their marriage. But to bring her home to Mother's house—to Mother's bed. What kind of man does that?

"My wife's away,'' a married man once said to me. "Spend the weekend with me in my house in the Hamptons.''

And I went because he was devastatingly attractive and I was hopelessly optimistic. It was ruined from the moment the car drove up his private road and that adorable sign that was etched in the stone assaulted me—LEBO. Leah for her, Bob for him. It only got worse. Sitting in the kitchen while the suffix of LEBO mixed drinks, I was guilt-ridden by the sight of her pots, pans, aprons, cookbooks, and dish towels. By the time I climbed into her side of the bed, I was as difficult to penetrate as the open lips of Leah's dried tulips that sat on her dressing table amid the creams, lotions, and perfumes. But the invasion of my body was nothing compared to the invasion of her privacy. And what kind of man does that? The level of his insensitivity was exceeded only by my own level of desperation. I needed someone—if only for a moment and even if he wasn't really mine.

"My marriage is on the rocks,'' he said blithely.

But his marriage was as solid as a rock—LEBO etched in stone.

Cara comforted me then. "You should never get involved with a man who can't give you his home phone number,'' she said wisely.

I loved her for that, even though it hurt. So how can I blame Loretta, whoever she is, for whatever she may have expected from Father? I shouldn't, but I do, and I will for the rest of my life.

The floor is suddenly opening up, sucking me down

into an imploded black hole, or at least that's what it feels like right now as a voice I hardly recognize explains to the paramedics that it is unnecessary for them to transport the body to the city morgue. "We'll call our physician and have her taken directly to the funeral parlor," I say.

"Pick up by funeral parlor," one of them says into a walkie-talkie. The other one is near the front door, folding up the stretcher, preparing to drag all the equipment out to the elevator. "Sorry we couldn't do more," he says, "but she really wasn't kidding, with thirty digitalis."

"Excuse me," a policeman interrupts, "but I've got to fill out this form."

Of course he does, and yes, I am Maggie Sommers, and thank you all for your concern, and this is a terrible shock because she was our mother—past tense again—but *please* don't put down suicide.

"Can you give me her name and age, please," he says.

Why is it so difficult to tell him her name and age?

"Vera Sommers," Cara answers. "October 7, 1918."

The tombstone flashes before my eyes: BORN OCTOBER 7, 1918—DIED DECEMBER 29, 1982. Would it be acceptable to confide in the engraver that she died a thousand deaths during her lifetime? Would it be too absurd to request that each and every date be included on the monument—in small letters, of course—until this final one, which could simply go at the very bottom? Oh, Mother, if you had only waited one more day, you could have met Avi. Avi, arriving in New York tomorrow and already one day too late. He would never meet Mother, and for some reason, the thought of him suddenly makes it very difficult for me not to weep.

Cara pats my hand. "Try to hang on, Maggie," she whispers.

Officer Ghorty is a nice man. So is Officer Rambusto. "Your attending can mail in the death certificate. I'm sure he knows the routine. In the meantime, I'm going to put down cardiac arrest on my form."

"Thank you," I say, blowing my nose.

"That's very nice of you," Cara says, her voice breaking.

"We'll leave now, if you're sure you don't need us," Officer Ghorty says.

"No, we'll manage," I answer, wiping my eyes. "Thank you again."

"I'll see you out," Cara offers, always the perfect hostess. Jonesie follows her.

By the time they return, Cara resembles a wild animal, her tiny nostrils flaring and her eyes glinting like two blue stones.

"Jonesie just told me about Loretta," Cara announces.

"Are you surprised?"

"No, just furious because he didn't have the decency not to bring her home. He didn't care enough to keep things separate. His succession of women killed her, and I'll never forgive him for that."

"There wasn't no 'cession," Jonesie says firmly. "Jest this one since you was both little."

So this one has a history with us. "I wonder if she was the reason for that Easter Sunday or for that night in the hospital."

Cara looks concerned. "Maggie, you look positively green!"

"Maybe I have the flu on top of everything else. Do you think she's the same one?"

"Which one is that?"

"You know, the one he had since we were little."

"I imagine so," Jonesie says. "The same one since I can remember."

Cara beings to cry again. "I'll never forgive him."

"Oh, Cara," I say, rushing toward her.

"You better call Dr. Mandel," she sniffles, "and I'll call Steven." But as I turn to go, she grabs my arm. "Oh, Maggie," she cries, "what do we do now?"

"What do we do now?" is not a simple question. It encompasses a wide range of possible replies. For the moment, however, I am trying to concentrate on the pragmatic aspect of that query, since we happen to be facing a rather specific situation—namely, Mother lying in her bed, a relatively normal occurrence even if it is two o'clock in the afternoon, except that today she also happens to be dead. Having worked in a profession that has allowed me to see that sordid part of life, I have a perspective of human nature that is occasionally at odds with the prevailing concept of what is considered to be civilized behavior. In other words, the worst is yet to come. And it would be useless and imprudent to warn Cara that the next phase of this nightmare will be even more unbearable than the first.

"We've just got to hang on and get through this," I answer.

"Maggie," she says, a peculiar expression on her face, "we forgot something."

"What's that?"

"Someone should tell Father, don't you think?"

It is not surprising that neither of us has not done it yet and even less surprising that neither of us wants to do it now.

Cara has located Steven at the psychiatric wing of New York Hospital. At first he was rendered speechless by the news but then recovered sufficiently to voice his first concern, which was about us.

"I'm pretty lucky," Cara says thoughtfully. "He's really so devoted."

"Why were you so angry with him in Aruba?"

"Because I blamed him for my getting pregnant again, which was stupid."

"Did you want another baby?"

"Yes, no," Cara says, smiling slightly. "I wanted something to do, since the kids were all in school. I guess going to work terrified me. And anyway, why should I change jobs, when I do this one so well?"

"What about changing jobs the other way?" I ask. "Doing a job well outside and then deciding to be a mother."

Cara looks at me curiously. "Interested?"

"Maybe," I say, lowering my gaze.

"Well, women who do it that way usually do it when they're in their thirties, which means they really want to. They've made a choice."

Dr. Mandel was equally shocked to learn the news and assured me that he would arrive within the half hour.

"He practically wept on the phone. I would have never imagined that he could break down like that."

"Well, he's known her forever," Cara says.

"I know, but still, he has that chilly manner."

"What did he say?"

"That's the point. He could hardly speak, just mumbled something about having Loretta cancel all his appointments for this afternoon."

Cara's eyes narrowed. "Loretta? Who's Loretta?"

"His nurse." It hadn't even occurred to me.

Dr. Hyman Mandel, immaculately attired in a beige tweed sports jacket, tan slacks, and a vicuña overcoat, enters the apartment with a mournful expression on his perennially tanned rugged face. Mandel, who grew up with Father in that unmentionable neighborhood, stopped off long enough in London during his post-graduate years to acquire a clipped British accent, a penchant for warm beer, and a curious reverence for monarchy. Hy is the professional guest, the sought-after, never-been-married bachelor, who once remarked, "It doesn't matter how old a man is as long as he's single."

He never endeared himself to us, to the point where we usually declined weekend invitations in the country if we knew in advance that he would be there.

"I hate how he calls Mother Verushka and how he makes a pretense of only being interested in the Arts and Leisure section of the *Times*."

"And I hate how he reeks of Aramis and talks about the Royals as if they were all so close to him," Cara and I would complain.

Yet there was always a tacit agreement between us and Hyman Mandel to maintain a polite and friendly facade. In spite of everything, he remained crucial to our peace of mind—crucial because he was so devoted to her, so willing to relieve us of any burden concerning Mother.

"Cara, Maggie," he says in his best Prince Philip voice, "I'm devastated." And even with his affected manner of speaking, it appears to be so for he is weeping unabashedly.

"Thank you," I say.

"You're dear to come," Cara adds.

And even though he appears sincere, his overstated display of emotion is most bizarre and definitely out of character.

"Where is she?"

"In there," Cara answers, stepping aside.

He hands me his overcoat before striding into the bedroom.

Cara is obviously also baffled by his peculiar behavior because she shrugs her shoulders and shakes her head. Suddenly there is a wail, followed by a piercing scream, before we hear a succession of muffled sobs.

"Maybe we should stay with him," I say.

"I can't go in there, Maggie," Cara says. "You go."

"Are you all right, Hy?" I ask, standing next to him.

"It's so awful. I just saw her yesterday."

Nodding, I watch as he uncovers Mother before cautiously placing his gleaming stethoscope on her chest and two trembling fingers against her carotid artery.

"I'm afraid she is gone," he says, once again dissolving into tears.

A brilliant diagnosis. "If this is too much for you, perhaps we can—"

He interrupts me with a wave of his hand. "No, no, it's all right," he says, sniffling. "It's just that she's so blue."

Aren't we all. "Why don't you fill that out in the other room," I suggest. It is obvious that the act of writing, of filling out the death certificate, is simply too much for him. Flinging down his pen, he buries his face in his hands and weeps. "I'm so sorry. Maybe we'd better go inside."

He stumbles out of the bedroom without waiting to see if I am following. In the living room, he heads immediately for the collection of Baccarat decanters on the credenza near the window. Cara watches him closely as he pours a generous amount of sherry into a large brandy snifter that he finds on one shelf of the breakfront.

"The policeman put down cardiac arrest," she says meekly.

"Jolly decent of him." Mandel booms, "She certainly has enough problems."

Since when was death a problem for anyone except the living?

"Do you want me to call Regency?" he asks, looking much better since he has downed his sherry.

Regency is the Harvard of funeral parlors and conveniently located right in the neighborhood. There is Gristede's that delivers the groceries, Irving's Prime Meats for the standing rib roast that is served every Thursday, and Antoine's Bakery that specializes in chocolate mousse and low-cholesterol cheesecake. There is Deluxe Cleaners that charges almost as much to clean a dress as the dress cost and certainly twice as much to pleat a skirt than to hang the draperies after Labor Day. There is Saigon Laundry, run by two Vietnamese brothers, who still wear United States Marine combat jackets and who put Father's shirts on those pretty white plastic hangers that fill up my closet. Permanently Potted, responsible for the weekly arrangement of fresh flowers that adorn the Sommers' apartment, painstakingly arranged by the good-looking Greek man and his equally attractive son. But, as vital as these merchants are to the residents of this affluent area of the city, they don't evoke quite the same reaction as Regency. There isn't anybody alive who resides in that twenty-block radius who doesn't know that the ultimate purchase, the very final delivery, will be of their body directly to that funeral parlor.

"If you would call them, Hy," I say, "that would be so helpful."

"And anyway," Cara says, pulling me by the hand, "we have to go to the bathroom."

Mandel gives us a peculiar look as he picks up the telephone.

We are teenagers again, whispering furtively in the bathroom while the running water drowns out our words.

"Why do you think he's so upset?" Cara asks, sitting down on the closed toilet seat. "Do you think he knows about Loretta?"

"I don't know," I answer, leaning against the sink. "I just wonder why we're not falling apart."

Cara brushes a few wisps of hair from her face as her huge blue eyes fill again with tears. "I expected this would happen sooner or later. I somehow knew it would."

"How can you say that?"

"Because it's true," she answers matter-of-factly. "You weren't around to see how totally insane she had become these last few years."

"You're angry at me."

"No," she says wearily. "I'm not angry anymore, but I suppose I was. You got away from her, you insulated yourself. She used to call me every morning at seven o'clock, crying and complaining about Father. I don't know how Steven took it, because she was insulting and horrible to him most of the time. It wasn't easy to cope with her, and I had the kids and the car pool and the house and Steven. It was a lot."

"Why didn't you call me, ask me to help?"

Cara laughs. "Where was I supposed to reach you? I hardly ever knew where you were."

"You could have always found me through the bureau."

"And what was I supposed to say, ask them to have you paged at some Islamic Conference in South Yemen? Come on, Maggie, there wasn't any way because you made it that way."

"So you are angry, why don't you admit it?"

She throws her hands up. "OK, I'm angry. So what difference does it make now?" She shakes her head. "The horrible part is that I'm more angry at myself for being such a fool, than I am at you."

"Why do you say you're a fool?"

"Because I was the good guy all these years, at the expense of my own life."

I am stung. "And what does that make me—the bad guy?"

But she has no intention of restraining herself. "No Maggie, it makes you the smart guy because you just did what you damn pleased and didn't bother to think that maybe I was stuck with all the problems on the home front.''

"It might have been nice if you talked to me once in a while because you know I called all the time but every time I asked about Mother or even your children, you just reported that everybody was fine. It was if you intentionally wanted to exclude me.''

"We were never close,'' she says vaguely, "maybe that's why. Or maybe I thought that you were so strong that you'd take over and then I'd have . . .'' She stops.

"Nothing?'' I say softly. "Is that what you thought?''

Briefly we both smiled, although not at each other.

"They loved you, you know,'' she says defensively.

"Oh did they?'' Did they really love me all the years we were growing up? "It was always Maggie's fault—no matter what happened—even if they caught you red-handed, they always managed to blame me, to claim that I had influenced you to be bad.''

An icy calm descends over Cara's manner. "Why do I always end up feeling sorry for you?'' she asks in a small voice. "I mean, why should I when you ended up with the great life?''

"Are you angry at me for that too?''

The moment is tense, as it always is when we touch on this subject. And it is a rather long moment in which we both fear that we have gone too far, lost the ability to continue—continue to feel even this hostility. But then it takes the form of a straightforward stare as each of us tries to find a way to begin again. Cara walks to the sink and splashes water on her face. She looks at herself in the mirror before her eyes settle on me. "I guess it's not fair to blame you.'' She pauses. "I guess it's not fair to allow my jealousy to confuse things.''

"Why—how could you be jealous of me? You had the same opportunities, only you chose to do something else.''

"I suppose,'' she says slowly, "that I began to feel that I eliminated those opportunities the more successful you became. I suppose I forgot what I had.''

I am trying to find a way to shake aside the curtain of delusions that cloud her vision, to make things clearer.

But clarity was never the basis of our relationship. So why should it be different now? "Cara, you can do other things any time you feel like it and still have your family. I suffered from something that you didn't."

"What?"

"Loneliness."

Cara puts her arms around me. "It can get pretty lonely surrounded by the finger-painting brigade too, you know."

"I need a sister," I answer, hugging her.

Her shoulders lift and she lets out a long breath, as if there was never any other choice for either of us all along. "Me too," she says.

There is a knock on the door. "Who is it?" Cara calls out.

"Steven."

Pulling open the door, she falls into her husband's arms. "I'm so glad you're here."

She picks up her head from his shoulder and our eyes meet. A certain look passes between us, an understanding of our respective joys and agonies.

Steven stares in puzzlement at the sight of us, our tear-streaked faces and disheveled hair. He is not entirely satisfied, but then, he always did lack imagination. "Are you ill, Cara, or just upset?"

She glances at me. "No, just upset and the bathroom has always been our special place—right Maggie?"

He is unprepared for this, feeling as an outsider among us. "And you, Maggie," he says dutifully, "are you holding up?"

"Yes," I say, splashing cold water on my face. Cara is still standing, wrapped in his arms, and somehow being in that position makes her seem smaller, more fragile.

"Did Mandel call Regency?" she asks, moving away from him.

"He's in pretty bad shape, so I called. They want a family member to go over there and make the arrangements. Do you want me to do it?"

We both answer at once. "No, we'll go."

My hands are clasped together now because I feel I am

losing control of my gestures. I am suddenly exhausted, so tired that only five years of sleep could make it better. "There is something you could do," I say.

"What's that?"

"You could call Father and tell him what happened."

Steven is surprised. "You mean that nobody did that yet—he doesn't know?"

Cara shakes her head. "We were too upset."

Steven looks at me, his hand rubbing his chin thoughtfully. "You really didn't do it." As if he expected more of me.

"No," I answer, already halfway out the door. "I guess I just don't like him enough to give him such good news."

Cara giggles. "She really doesn't mean that."

Steven looks petulant, as if he has already missed something, been left out of the game. "Do you?"

I keep walking. "You're the shrink, Steven, do I?"

Regency Funeral Home looks like anything but a mortuary with the pastel-blue carpeting, crystal chandelier, and Queen Anne reproductions scattered casually around the reception room. It looks like anything but a mortuary except for the grief-stricken expressions that are etched on the faces of the attendants and the somber organ music that can be heard coming from behind a series of closed doors. There is no smell of formaldehyde, as we follow the small, fair-headed man downstairs, no glimpse of those rooms in the basement that drain the remainder of life from the dear departed. It is eerie, though, to imagine what is behind each and every closed door as we wind our way through several long, thickly carpeted corridors and into a large and sunny office.

"May I offer you my heartfelt condolences," says Mr. Lance, as he bows slightly from the waist. "Which of you is bereaved?" Now if there were an award given today for the most stupid question, this one would be the winner—no contest. Cara, her face puffy and her eyes swollen into tiny slits from weeping, looks as if she has just forged the Tigris River and lost her entire crew to a group of man-eating alligators. I, on the other hand, can't stop hiccuping, a new development that began when the two attendants from Regency arrived to remove Mother's body on a ghastly black stretcher. The short little gasps that I inhale are expelled in the form of nervous burps.

"We both are," I say, hiccuping.

"My profound sympathy," he says, bowing again. "She was your mother. Of course. Now I can see the resemblance. And naturally you want to give her a farewell befitting someone as truly elegant as she was."

Cara sinks down in her chair in a show of contented apathy. "My sister will handle this," she announces.

Thanks for the privilege, I think, secretly wondering at the endless facets of being a sister.

"Now then," Mr. Lance says, licking one slender finger with his pointy little tongue before turning a page of a glossy catalogue. "Here are some coffins with the prices, and right below is the cost of the entire package, which includes embalming, the viewing room the night before, ceremony room, including music, and of course three limousines to transport Mother and the immediate family to the cemetery, calculated by the mile and not to exceed fifty-five miles or there's an additional charge, and all tolls are included." I feel myself overtaken by feelings of unequivocal hostility, but like a well-bred woman, I hasten to assure Mr. Lance that his explanation is very helpful. "Thank you," I say, "it's all perfectly clear."

He takes a breath, flicking a strand of silver hair out of his steel-blue eyes before continuing. "Gravediggers are provided by the cemetery and now if you'll follow me, I'll show you some of our caskets."

Standing, I have to hold onto a chair to regain my balance.

Mr. Lance adjusts his gold pocket watch, holding it up to his ear. "Shall we?"

"I suppose you'll wait here?"

"If you don't mind, Maggie," Cara answers meekly, "I don't feel very well."

"I owe you this, don't I?" I say, patting her head.

Another wave of nausea envelops me as I follow him into a dimly lit room that smells of cedar and pine and that is filled with a variety of caskets. It is suddenly a grim reality, the realization of a finality unlike anything I have ever known. Mother is dead and I am here choosing a suitable coffin.

"Mr. Lance," I begin.

"I understand," he says kindly, taking my arm.

We walk slowly back to his office, the strength of his arm and a pleasant sensation on mine.

"Should I?" I ask, sitting down next to Cara.

"Yes," she answers, barely moving her lips.

Taking a deep breath, I say, "Will you do it, please, Mr. Lance, make all the necessary arrangements and—"

"The arrangements have already been made," he says, looking slightly perplexed. "All that was left to do was to choose the casket. You see, there wasn't time that day. It was a Tuesday, if I recall correctly. She said she had an appointment."

Cara's eyes are wide with fear, a fear of comprehending something she doesn't want to have to face.

"Don't," I say, touching her hand gently.

Mr. Lance nods. "I'll send you the invoice."

Cara holds tightly to me as we trudge back to the apartment, taking small steps over the icy snow that now covers the streets. The gusts of cold wind blowing in my face make me feel less faint, stronger, as I push on to confront the next phase of this nightmare.

"She made all the arrangements for herself," Cara says softly. "Why?"

"Because she obviously planned this, and you know Mother—nothing was ever right unless she did it."

Jonesie greets us at the door. After we ask a few questions, she explains about the funeral arrangements. "I sent her white brocade dress with the rhinestone cluster buttons." Cara pales as Jonesie goes on. "They wanted a photograph of her—to see how she looked . . ."

"Stop, Jonesie." Steven comes to the doorway, takes his wife by the arm, and leads her into the living room.

"Did you call Father?" I ask, following them.

"Yes, he's on his way."

"What did he say?" Cara asks.

"He was shocked, had trouble believing it."

Cara is gathering momentum. "That's all? He didn't say anything else?"

"Like what, Cara?" Steven asks gently.

But she falls quiet then.

"What can he say, Cara? There's nothing to say," I conclude.

There are telephone calls to make, lists to prepare, the newspaper to notify and the obituary to compose. There are a thousand things to do before the funeral, which is now less than twenty-four hours away. Cara and Steven are sitting on the couch with yellow pads on their laps, making notes, while I sit cross-legged on the floor and leaf through Mother's address and appointment books. There is a recurrent entry, a single "H" every Tuesday and Thursday between the hours of five and seven in the evening. But before I can comment, the letter comes to mind. Reaching into my pocket, I take it out. "I almost forgot," I say. "She left this."

And just as I am about to open the envelope and read Vera's last missive entitled TO WHOM IT MAY CONCERN, which I assume concerns her family, Father storms into the apartment.

He is red-faced and visibly agitated. "What the hell is going on?"

"She's dead," Mandel says matter of factly. "Didn't Steven tell you?"

He sits down, looking better than he's looked in years, trim, fit, and youthful. "I find this difficult to understand," he says, glancing around the room. "I only left her this morning."

"We heard," Cara says coldly.

Father is obviously surprised by Cara's attitude. He seems to have lost his only ally. Someone stole it from him. "I meant," he begins, stumbling over the words.

"We know what you meant," I say.

But then he brightens oddly, becomes dangerously in control. He has found his target. "You were always my biggest source of grief. Do you see what happens when you decide to come home and Mother spends an afternoon with you?"

Steven's reaction is swift. "Alan, everybody's upset to put it mildly. But it's senseless to pick on Maggie. You'll only feel worse in the end, believe me."

"Spare me your wholesale analysis."

"Steven's right," Mandel interjects. "We're all devastated."

"I wonder if *everyone* is," Cara says.

Father's shoulders seem to sag under the weight of Cara's obvious disdain. "Cara," he begins, "please."

"It won't work this time, Father," I say, my hand on hers, "because we all know what you've done, how you drove her to this."

He leans forward, his hand slicing the air as he speaks. "You are nothing to me, nothing you say means anything and she felt the same way. It was the only thing we agreed on—that you were nothing to us."

It was the end of the line. It was the worst place I had ever been, and there was no excuse except for some kind of tremendous energy that had suddenly become unleashed, something that had been pent up inside of me for thirty-four years. It was a marriage to Eric that had no end, terrorists with RPGs killing Joe over and over, stalking Avi Herzog so he would be lost to me forever. It was Mother's senseless life, which caused her death to hold so much meaning. And it was all erupting now, uncontrollably, with little thought of my ever being able to make it better again.

Lunging at Father, I actually slap him hard enough across the mouth to draw blood. "You bastard!" I cry, "you did this to her." But what I'm actually mourning is my power of reason, because we all did this to each other.

And then Steven is next to me, pinning my arms to my sides. For a slightly built man, he is incredibly strong as he holds me in such a way that it is impossible for me to strike again.

"Maggie," he says soothingly, "it's not worthy of you."

Father wipes the trickle of blood from the corner of his mouth with his little finger. "I'm sorry you did that, Maggie," he says softly, "because you're going to feel

worse about it than I do.'' Taking out a handkerchief,
Father dabs at the blood that is still oozing from his lips.

Thanks for the absolution. "I'm sorry," I say, weeping.

But there is a vengeful ally in the room. "She's right,"
Cara says calmly. "You killed her—you and your Loretta.''

Father's reactions pass swiftly—a slight, almost imper-
ceptible twinge of his jaw, several rapid coughs, and then
the denial. "I don't know what you're talking about."

"What's the point," I say to Cara, "leave it."

Steven releases his grip on my arm, guides me over to
the sofa and seats me. "Read the letter, Maggie," he
says gently.

Brushing a strand of hair from my eyes, I nod.

"Do you want me to leave?" Hy asks in a shaking
voice.

"No, please stay, Hy," Cara answers tearfully.

Father gives her a scathing look, making it apparent
that for the first time in our lives, he feels equally about
us. "I'm sure what she has to say is of great interest to
the good doctor."

I take a deep breath, my stomach turning over and
over. "Now?"

Hy starts to say something but stops.

"Go on, Maggie," Steven says, "read it."

'' 'Dear Cara and Marguerite,

'' 'You are the only ones this letter really concerns and
the only ones who might understand how difficult it is to
write. Actually, Marguerite might understand how difficult this is; Cara will be too hysterical to think clearly.
This life—I cannot do this life and so I have chosen—no,
let me begin again, since scratches on a letter are taste-
less. I have not chosen, yet I can't seem to find the
strength to continue this life and so feel it best if I do
not. I could list a million reasons, but they would all be
misunderstood or judged to be irrelevant should you decide to judge me and them. It began with the kitchen
knives and the pharmacy and the fact that the knives were
dull and the druggist wouldn't accept my check and that
times generally had changed. When I was a girl there

was a man who would come around and this man had a
bell and he would ring the bell and wait for the windows
facing the courtyard to be flung open, like so many dom-
inoes falling over on a board, and then he would go from
apartment to apartment sharpening all the kitchen knives
and scissors. Yesterday I wept over those dull kitchen
knives and mourned that little man and his progeny, who
are undoubtedly manning computers in the bowels of
some vulgar corporation. And so I went to the pharmacy
to try and refill several prescriptions, and there was a
young man with dirty fingernails, grimy skin, and an
unctuous manner who refused to accept my check because I didn't have a driver's license. Now, why on earth
would I have a driver's license when I have never driven
a car in my entire life? And what does that have to do
with my bank balance? Are those reasons to choose not
to live any longer, you might ask yourself. But they are,
and they all have to do with the empty tube of dipilatory
cream I found in the wastebasket in my bathroom and the
one missing scarab button from the aqua-colored silk
duster I bought in Paris, France, thirteen years ago, which
brings me to Loretta Buonvista.

    " 'Your father woke up this morning and announced
that he was leaving me. He then informed me that not
only was he leaving me but he was in love with another
woman. I was less shocked by his admission of infidelity
and his intention to abandon me after thirty-eight years
of marriage than I was by his poor taste in finding it
necessary to impart this information to me at seven-thirty
in the morning. I looked at this man, this man whom I
loved more than life itself for so many years, this man
who gave me so much pleasure and so much pain, this
man who fathered my two daughters, and I wondered
whom he had become. I studied his few strands of hair
swept over to one side of his balding head, the medallions
he wore around his neck—one cross, one star of David,
one ankh, and one hand of Fatima, I believe—and wondered when he had started looking like that, as well as
wearing turtleneck sweaters, blue jeans, and elbow-
patched tweed jackets to the office. But the most excruciating realization came when he explained that he wanted

a divorce so he could "seek gratification and fulfill his liberation fantasy." I almost fainted. Of course, I didn't need to find the empty tube of dipilatory cream to know that he had been having an affair with Hyman Mandel's nurse for years (she had a very heavy mustache until recently, about the time I found the tube in my trash basket). And of course I didn't need to notice my scarab button sitting in the shell ashtray on her desk at Hy's office to know that she had worn my aqua silk duster and, I am certain, accidentally ripped off a button. Your father had been bringing her to this house for years whenever I went away, in this house and in my bed. Which brings me back to the dull knives and my unacceptable check and the fact that times have indeed changed.

" 'Tuesdays and Thursdays with Hyman Mandel were wonderful, and oh, how I tried to "get with it" and do what everybody else seemed to be doing. But I simply wasn't constructed to love two men at the same time, and I loved your father more than life itself. Hyman was dear, making me feel young and beautiful again, but passion kills, and your father had already killed me. So let's first dispose of the realities before I end this letter and my life.

" 'I am leaving all my furs to Jonesie, because Cara already has furs, Marguerite would only lose them, and Jonesie would never in her entire life have an opportunity to have things like this. Just don't wear them on the subway, Jonesie, and don't flaunt them at church—you know how dangerous that could be. I am leaving the apartment, which happens to be in my name, to Cara, because it is about time her rather boring children imbibed some of the culture that New York has to offer. To Marguerite I leave all of my monogrammed hangers, satin lingerie pouches, and $200,000 in cash, which happens to be in a joint savings account in your name and mine. The bankbook is in the top drawer of my eighteenth-century lingerie chest—which you may have also, in case you decide to keep your things neatly. I am sure you can buy a decent apartment in Israel for that sum, since I suppose that's where you intend to live (far be it from me to comprehend your penchant for uniforms). To my beloved Hy-

man I leave my gratitude and love for every Tuesday and
Thursday. And as for you, Alan, I leave you your freedom—something you really never wanted, or why Loretta? And, Cara, one more thing: You'll never be thin
enough to think about finding someone more exciting than
Steven, so don't harbor any illusions that things could be
better. He's good and calm and adores you. It's not easy
to maneuver through life with a bunch of children.

" 'Jonesie, I used up all of Keith's pills and I never
would have done that if things hadn't become so complicated, but then we're back to the beginning. Had they
accepted my check at the pharmacy, I could have refilled
my own prescriptions, or had the kitchen knives been
sharp, I could have exercised another option. I was desperate. Forgive me—and please, do not, whatever you
do, bury me in that God-awful white brocade dress with
the rhinestone cluster buttons.

" 'This is my last adventure.' "

My voice breaks at that point and I bury my head in
my hands for a moment so I won't begin crying. Cara is
leaning against her husband, biting down on her lip, also
trying not to cry. Hyman Mandel blows his nose loudly
before getting up and, without a word, walks out the front
door. Father juts out his chin, his mouth trembling, and
says, "Well we all got exactly what we wanted, or at least
what we thought we wanted, including Vera. She's really
gone." He rises slowly and walks wearily into the bedroom, quietly shutting the door behind him, firmly shutting us out from sharing our grief with him. But then I
notice my sister, a tiny smile playing on the corners of
her mouth as she brushes Steven's hand from her arm and
moves next to me. "Finally, in her final moment, she
was fair about distributing her criticism."

I am perplexed only for an instant before I smile. There
is a pleasant and comfortable sensation that passes between us, a complicity.

"Finally," I answer.

Steven offers to return alone to Short Hills tonight to
stay with the children. "I'll bring them in tomorrow for
the funeral," he says, clinging to Cara, kissing her good-

bye over and over. "You and Maggie need to be together."

Cara and I are holding hands. We glance at each other, having already made that decision. We will remain in what is now Cara's ten-room cooperative apartment on Fifth Avenue—our childhood home.

The house is quiet as I lie in one of the twin beds in Cara's old room that night. Quiet, except for Father's sporadic sobs, which are audible through the wall.

"Maybe he's capable of feeling something after all," Cara says softly. But it is impossible for me ever to give him the benefit of the doubt.

"Avi's arriving tomorrow," I say.

"Do you want me to come to the airport with you?"

"No, it's better if I go alone."

Setting the alarm for six o'clock, I fall asleep, holding tightly to Cara's hand.

"I love you," she whispers.

"I love you too."

○

A man is walking through the automatic sliding doors from the customs area. His sand-colored hair falls down on his forehead as he searched the crowd for a familiar face. Dressed in a pair of gray slacks, a blue oxford shirt, and a navy blazer, with a gray herringbone tweed coat slung casually over his broad shoulders, he carries a brown leather attaché case. It takes me a moment to be absolutely certain before I push through the mass of people who are waiting for arriving passengers from El Al flight 3393 from Tel Aviv.

Avi is here.

He kisses my tears, holding me close to him and repeating over and over, "I love you. Never again away from you, never. I missed you."

His hands are on my shoulders as he studies me intently. "Maggie, why are you crying like this? Something happened. What is it?"

"I'm just so happy you're here," I lie.

"This is happy?" he says, brushing away my tears.

He pulls me close to him again, holding me tight as he leads me out of the waiting area and toward the baggage claim.

"Mother died yesterday," I suddenly blurt out.

He stops, shaken, seemingly unable to comprehend my words.

"She committed suicide."

"Maggie, I'm so sorry," he says, stroking my hair. "What happened?"

"It's too long a story now; it's just too long."

His face is etched with pain. "I'm here for you, I'm here."

"Avi, I love you. If anything ever happened to you, if I lost you, I couldn't survive it."

"You're not going to lose me," he says, still holding me. "I'm yours. Try to tell me what happened, Maggie."

As we walk arm in arm toward the baggage area, I tell Avi the whole story, beginning with Mother's other attempts, continuing with Loretta, and ending with the announcement that the funeral is this afternoon.

Avi's driver, who was sent by the Israeli consulate in New York, piles the suitcases on a luggage cart and heads for the waiting limousine. There are no cardboard valises or frantic skirmishes for taxicabs or any of those other images I conjured up in the newsroom only yesterday. Avi is here and completely in charge of getting us home.

"I'm going to the funeral," he says firmly, helping me into the car.

"I knew you would want to," I answer, settling back in his arms.

"We're going to Tenth Street and University Place," he instructs the driver, before turning to me. "You're never going to be alone again, Maggie. You're going to be with me."

"That's all I want," I say softly, my lips on his.

And when he stops kissing me, he holds me against him before kissing me all over again. "My divorce is final in three months, so maybe you'll consider marrying me in March."

My eyes fill with tears. "She'll never know you," I say sadly. "Mother will never know you."

"No," he answers, holding my face between his hands. "And she'll never know our baby."

There is a lump in my throat, which makes it difficult to speak.

"Is it still our secret?" he asks, his eyes twinkling and a tiny smile beginning to form at the corners of his mouth.

And so my life has found its natural solution. "Ours," I manage to say softly. And then those words begin reverberating in my head again: *Whatever we are as a family, we are survivors.*

CHAPTER NINE

The funeral was brief and devoid of histrionics and tension. There were only a few awkward moments that might have intensified into unpleasant scenes. Father arrived at Regency surrounded by an aura of injured virtue even though he wasn't sure what had transpired between Mother and Hyman Mandel. When he finally came face to face with Cara and me in front of the open casket, he played the chords of the bereaved spouse valiantly.

"I'll be at Round Hills resort in Jamaica, trying to put my life back together," he said dramatically.

Cara shocked me by her immediate retort. "Off to Round Hills with round wheels."

Furrowing his brow, he shot me a disgusted look as if it were my fault that Cara had finally stopped pretending.

"Did you see the look he gave me?" I whispered to Cara when he disappeared into the chapel.

She giggled. "He was probably afraid of your right hook."

Jonesie behaved surprisingly well until the moment when she mustered up the courage to peer inside the coffin. Inching her way up to the gleaming mahogany box with its shiny brass handles, she leaned over, almost nose to nose with Mother.

"Lord," she wailed, "they made Missus Sommers look just like Carmen Miranda."

A shocked silence fell over the room as several guests walked discreetly over to see for themselves.

Mr. Lance was standing near the organ.

"Please," I said, cornering him, "please close the coffin right away."

"Pity," he protested. "She has such a lifelike quality,

don't you think? Almost as if she's just going to get up and walk away.''

I hardly bristled. ''Just close the lid, please. She wants to be alone.''

Avi never left my side, from the moment that he stepped off the plane and was greeted by my shocking news. ''Welcome to New York, darling, and don't make any plans for this afternoon because we have to bury Mother.'' Even if it hadn't happened that way, it ended the same. It was certainly a bizarre introduction into the Sommers family or what was left of us considering that Mother was dead, Cara was dazed, and Father was so determined not to miss his plane that he didn't stay to talk to him.

Although Avi's reactions were measured, his entire countenance was dominated by his eyes. They observed everything, with expressions that ranged from sadness to surprise, amusement to rage, and were invariably correct in their appraisal of everybody who approached to offer their condolences. It was only when Eric Ornstein cornered me that I held my breath out of fear that Avi would finally lose his temper.

Except for gaining some weight, Eric hadn't changed since the last time I had seen him, which was seven years ago, in his lawyer's office. Moving instinctively closer to Avi, I shook Eric's clammy hand.

''Maggie,'' he said, with an embarrassed grin, ''I've wanted to bump into you for years, and now this is the way it has to happen.''

''Thank you for coming, Eric.''

There was an awkward silence as Eric glanced at Avi expectantly, waiting for an introduction.

''Eric, this is Avi Herzog,'' I said, after a few seconds.

It was as if he had stumbled on someone from another planet. ''You must be the Israeli general,'' Eric said, shaking his hand.

Avi smiled graciously. ''Yes, and you must be Maggie's former husband.''

Eric frowned slightly. ''We're thinking of spending a month on a kibbutz. What's it like today?''

Avi didn't hesitate for an instant. "It's like summer camp with the fear of God thrown in."

"Funny, I always wanted to take Maggie to Israel, but she never wanted to go, and now it's too late," he said wistfully.

"Congratulations, Eric. I heard you just had another baby," I said in an effort to change the subject.

His face broke into a proud smile as he reached into his breast pocket for photographs. "Here he is, fifteen minutes old, and here he is again, after they cleaned the little fella up."

It wasn't my baby, and it wasn't exactly that I regretted that it wasn't. So why were there tears in my eyes? It was something else, even though he was happy now and I had Avi. It was something about all those wasted years when each of us could have done so much better.

"He's adorable," I said, showing the pictures to Avi.

Avi couldn't have been more charming. "You're a lucky man."

"So are you," Eric said, looking directly at me.

It was then that Ronah elbowed her way over to us, linked her arm proprietarily through Eric's and glared at me. Her fingernails were the same, long and scarlet red, but her hair was cropped so short that it only accentuated the angular lines of her face. She still appeared so self-conscious as if she weren't the wife. Yet, there was something different about her, something that made her hard. That little bit of vulnerability she once had was gone, that drop of insecurity that made her just the slightest bit fragile was missing. She had achieved all her goals and now reeked of smugness. But if she only knew how much I didn't want him back, she might not have bothered to glare at me the way she did.

"Hello, Ronah," I said softly. "Thank you for coming."

She acknowledged my words more as an intrusion than as a greeting, or perhaps she was so uncomfortable that she didn't know what to say. Whatever the reason, it escalated when Eric took my hand.

"We heard she committed suicide," he whispered. "Did she leave a note?"

Avi decided to run interference. "I understand you're thinking of going to Israel," he said.

She was straining to hear our conversation. "Yes, maybe," she answered distractedly.

"Yes, she left a note," I said quietly.

"Have you been before?" Avi asked.

"What did it say? Did it explain why she did this?" Eric pressed.

"How could you ask what the note said, Eric? It's a little private, limited to the family, don't you think?"

"You're still my family," Eric said softly. "I'll never forget that we were once married."

And then the tears began again, and this time I *knew* it was because of all the wasted years, my wasted years, before Avi came into my life. But they were also for Eric, who never knew to be any different than he was.

Avi put his arm around me, while Ronah just stood quietly next to her husband.

"I guess there's always a heavy price for success," Eric said in an effort to fill the silence.

"What do you mean?" I asked, drying my eyes.

"Well, first your sound man and then your mother. What's next?"

"Why does something have to be next?" I cried. "How awful, Eric!"

But he was completely nonplussed by my reaction. "Well, tragedies usually come in threes, don't they?"

Avi was charming. "Why don't we consider Maggie's divorce from you as the first great tragedy, so we can all feel safe."

And then Eric chuckled, although Ronah looked more bewildered than amused. I hugged him, the man who had once been my husband, feeling warm and forgiving and sad and sorry and every other emotion possible, even though I had promised myself not to turn this occasion into a seminar dealing with old wounds.

"I'm happy for you," I said tearfully.

"I always wanted children," he answered, "and you just didn't."

Avi had a peculiar expression on his face as we walked away. "How do you feel about it now?"

"There's happy and there's happy, and he's happy and I'm—"

"Going to be with me and happy for the rest of your life."

Hyman Mandel's graveside confession occurred at the most inauspicious moment. As the box was being lowered into the earth, he clutched my arm.

"I swear I never touched her," he wept. "It was always just drinks and talk every Tuesday and Thursday. I wanted to, but she kept telling me that Alan had killed her from the neck down."

"Why didn't you say something yesterday?" I asked, already knowing the answer.

At that very moment she disappeared forever, right before my eyes, and a weakness enveloped me, making it almost impossible to concentrate on what Hy was saying.

"What difference would it have made?" he said bitterly. "It's good for him to think that she had someone who loved her, and I did love her. She was infuriating, unreasonable, and totally crazy, but she had this charm, a kind of magic, that was so seductive and irresistible that it was hard to . . ." He couldn't finish his sentence because the gravediggers' shovels were clanking against the frozen ground. But it was clear what he meant; his words held more meaning than those spoken by the rabbi from Temple Emanu-El, who had been recruited at the last minute to deliver the eulogy. He had never even known Mother. Father had hurriedly filled him in on certain details of her life—charities she favored, music she loved, and even several amusing anecdotes about the early days of their marriage. And because the rabbi had never known her, had only seen her after she ceased to exist, I was left with the distinct impression that he was speaking about someone else. The woman Hy spoke of was someone very close to me, someone I felt deep down inside.

Right after that, I saw Father again. His eyes were red, and it was apparent that he had been crying.

We stared at each other for a few seconds before I put my hand gently on his arm. "I'm sorry for all of us, because we were all too stupid to make things different."

He lowered his head. "You can blame me for the rest of your life, but it's not fair."

At least we were talking, something so rare that I didn't want to let go of this moment. "She wasn't easy," I said quietly.

"I made mistakes," he said simply, avoiding my gaze.

"Why, Father, why didn't you know better?"

He shook his head. "I'm tired; I'm so very tired."

Tears were rolling slowly down my cheeks. "I loved her."

He looked at me in surprise. "So did I!"

"Then why?"

"I was entitled to something too."

We walked toward his limousine, which was parked under a cluster of trees, near the entrance to the cemetery, oblivious to the rain and sleet that had begun to fall.

"Your sister hates me."

"Do you care?"

He didn't respond.

"Do you care how I feel?" I asked, wiping the downpour from my eyes.

He glanced at me. "Not really," he said honestly. "Because you were never a part of it; you bowed out long ago."

I stopped then, held his arm so he couldn't walk off. "Father, it's not too late . . ."

He nodded wearily. "I can't try anymore. I'm just too tired of the fighting. There are too many things you'll never understand." Taking out a handkerchief, he wiped his eyes. He looked so old suddenly, so beaten down from years of Vera and whatever else he wouldn't talk about.

"Father . . ." But my own tears prevented me from explaining.

"You can't either," he said, with a wry smile. "None of us could ever talk about anything."

And then he turned and walked away, weighted down by an unseen sorrow. He stopped at the limousine, watched me from a distance for a moment or two before he climbed inside. My fingers moved slowly, almost waving, long after his car had sped through the stone gate.

Something else was happening that day that was curious. With an apologetic grin, Avi would help me in and out of cars, on and off curbs, through doors, and he would inquire every few minutes, "Are you all right?"

It was so out of character that I had to smile. Alufi, my general—the man who habitually left me standing in the rain outside a locked car while he raced around to open his side first, or crossed streets, oblivious that I was stranded on the other curb while cars whizzed past—was suddenly preoccupied with my safety and comfort. It was not that he hadn't cared before, it was simply his way of behaving, which was perhaps cultural; and I had learned to accept it as part of him. But something else was happening.

We rode back from the cemetery with Cara, Steven, Quincy, and Dan. Avi was so protective of me, holding me close every time the car rode over a bump in the road, that Quincy finally blurted out, "You act as if she's pregnant."

Everybody looked stunned as they waited for me to deny it.

"I am," I finally said.

And Cara broke the shocked silence by squealing with delight, bursting into tears and saying, "I should have known. Oh, Maggie, why didn't you tell me?"

"We were so involved in other things," I answered, with more than a trace of irony.

"I'm so happy," she said, hugging me.

"Why?" I asked, laughing.

"Because now you'll be human like the rest of us." She was sorry the moment the words left her lips, even if there was a certain wisdom in what she said.

"When?" Quincy asked, pressing her cheek against mine.

"In August."

Dan shook Avi's hand, while Steven pounded him on the back. There was still that special bond that seemed to exist between men when one of them made one of us pregnant.

It was rather unnerving for me to be the center of all of that joy, although Avi hardly seemed fazed by the attention. He handled himself so well, answering questions, smiling, and holding me close to him as we rode back into the city. By the end of the trip, everybody shared the same opinion of Avi, whispering to me that he was charming, kind, handsome, and madly in love.

But I already knew those things about him. What I was beginning to realize was that there was nothing I could ever do to change my feelings for him. I loved him, belonged to him, and that was that.

When we returned to our apartment—it seemed as natural to think "our" as it did to accept that I was now a "we"—the telephone began to ring incessantly. It was either people calling to express more sympathy or it was various Israeli and American government officials who needed to discuss urgent policy changes regarding the meetings that were scheduled to take place in Washington.

Grayson's call came between the Israeli prime minister and the American assistant secretary of state.

"Maggie," he said warmly, "I never could handle funerals ever since my own mother died, but I wanted you to know that I'm here for you if you need me, day and night, and don't worry about your contract."

The argument started shortly after that, although Avi refused to refer to it as anything more than a difference of opinion, preferring even to view it as a discussion or perhaps a misunderstanding due to a language barrier "What's the latest word on the troop withdrawal?" I asked, while brewing some coffee.

"The Americans want a unilateral withdrawal from Lebanon," he explained, reaching for the cups and saucers, "yet they're afraid of letting the Syrians gain a stronger foothold because of Soviet involvement."

"So what's going to happen?" I pressed.

"No easy solutions," he said, handing me the milk. "What did Grayson Daniel say?"

"He was sweet; wanted me to know that he was there for me and not to worry about my contract."

Avi put down his cup and reached across the kitchen table for my hand. Looking at me with a tender expression on his face, he said, "Maggie, I want you to be especially careful now, because of the baby."

"What do you mean?"

He touched my face gently. "You're thirty-four years old, and it's more difficult than if you were in your twenties. I want you to take it slower until the baby is born and not go near any shelling areas or war zones."

Although so much had changed in my life, my work had never been a subject of debate, with parameters being set that would be acceptable to someone else.

There was only one answer that would have satisfied him, and that was the one answer I was not prepared to give at that moment. I did glance up and smile when he added, "I love you, and I don't want anything to happen." But he was too clever to expect instant capitulation, especially when it concerned this pregnancy, which was so new to both of us.

"So the Americans are not taking Soviet involvement seriously, or if they are, they're not willing to take a firm stand," he continued.

I tried not to smile.

He was kissing my neck by then. "Assad will never negotiate with Israel."

"Make love to me," I whispered.

"This isn't some kind of trade," he said quietly.

The Israeli version of compromise was so transparent to me that they could have sent me to Washington to negotiate. I would have fared better than any American government official. Avi's eyes burned into mine as he held my chin in his hand.

"I want you to promise me that you'll slow down and not go near any dangerous areas."

"I know you do, and I can't," I answered, my lips practically on his as he pressed me against the refrigerator in the kitchen.

"Try to adjust to this in a little better way," he said, "and I will too."

"How?" I asked, pulling away from him. "Will you stop doing what you do?" It was the classic Israeli offensive of turning the tables, using whatever weapons were handy, feigning compromise and then adding just the right amount of guilt to confuse the opposition. His response was smooth and predictable.

"This isn't a job for me; it's a question of survival, a permanent commitment."

What do you say to a man who has subtly accused you of wanting him to throw away everything he believed in? "I love you," I said, allowing him to lead me into the bedroom.

And there wasn't any more discussion just then, because somehow—and the details are vague—he was kissing me, and then my clothes were all over the floor next to his and we were lying together on the cool sheets. I do recall that he made love to me so tentatively, hardly moving, that I finally remarked, "You're so afraid of hurting me."

"I love you," he said, burying his face in my breasts, "and I don't want anything to happen to you." And then he added, "Ever."

The argument had ended, although nothing had been promised that was more concrete than spending the rest of my life with him. It was so obvious why he felt the way he did, and had I been more reasonable, I would have made it easier for both of us. It was the first time in our life together that we were expecting a baby and one of us had to stay behind. I ended up weeping, and the reasons weren't completely clear to me, even though I wanted it very much to be because of Mother. Avi kissed away my tears and never allowed me to say anything more, because somehow—and the details are vague—he was kissing me again and again, and then we were making love as if it were for the very last time, no longer tentatively and no longer gently.

"I love you," I whispered, after catching my breath.

"Promise me," he said, before covering my mouth with his.

And still I refused.

New Year's Eve 1983 was spent in a small neighborhood restaurant on Bleecker Street. We were both dressed in jeans, heavy sweaters, ski jackets, and boots, because the weather was still so cold and miserable. Avi blended

into the casual atmosphere of Greenwich Village except
when he pulled out a small card from his pocket that gave
the good years for various wines in Hebrew. It didn't
bother me, although it was amusing to watch him, biting
his lower lip as he studied the card so intently.

"I shouldn't do this," he said, looking up. "It looks
funny to do this here?"

And I just wanted to hold him, because he was occasionally so vulnerable and unsure of everything. The
flame from the candle flickered, casting a shadow across
his handsome face.

"You can do anything you like always," I said, and
then added, "even if that includes telling me not to go
into dangerous areas." I smiled. "Because you're right,
and I was stupid to make things so difficult. Nothing
means more to me than you and this baby."

His eyes filled with tears and he was unable to speak.
Instead, he concentrated on the wine list so that when
the waiter approached the table, he was ready with his
order of some obscure label that I had never heard of.
And when it was uncorked and poured into our glasses,
Avi settled back to sip it, pretending it was exactly what
he had had in mind.

He was several different people during dinner. But
he was especially the innocent child who left Russia in
the dead of one winter night, false papers stuffed into the
breast pocket of his father's long black overcoat, the
mother's quick step that forced him to scamper along,
tripping and stumbling until they finally boarded the train
that would take them across the border into Austria. I
ached to hold him, to draw him into me and make his
memories mine. But he was too quick. His expression
changed after several minutes of silence, his eyes shining
and a tiny smile playing on his lips as he traced my fingers with his. Our baby would be safe, spared the traumas that he had endured, for his impending fatherhood
was vital, the responsibility already essential to his life.
And the transition was natural, although slightly jarring,
when he touched again on the harsh realities that permeated our lives.

"I'm afraid for us sometimes," he said soberly, "be-

cause I've seen so many insanities lately. I just don't want
to tempt fate anymore—not now.''

"How am I supposed to feel then, every time you leave
me?''

"You're supposed to worry but believe that I'm very
careful—that I know what I'm doing.''

"And those insanities? Can you control those uncontrollable elements?''

His eyes held mine and he stroked my face tenderly
before he leaned over to kiss me. "No, not always, my
darling, but you know just a little too much. It makes it
difficult to lie to you.''

I felt a momentary terror. "What do you mean?''

His expression changed then and the Israeli general
appeared, eyes squinted in concentration, mouth set
tightly and tone of voice incisive as he began. "Maggie,
I'm going to tell you something that worries me.''

I glanced sideways at him and at that instant, remembered his powerful body, the brush of his hands, and how
I possessed a part of him that they never could.

"Those six soldiers who were captured from the security zone almost eight months ago—the ones who were
patrolling the area near the UNIFIL outpost. Well, that
wasn't supposed to happen—we missed that one. Three
terrorists simply came along, infiltrated the area and just
plucked them up. And now they are not going to adhere
to any rules of the Geneva Convention. Do you understand what I'm trying to say?''

"Not really.'' But I did—only too well.

"There are no rules anymore. Lebanon has become a
supermarket of hostages.''

I heard the phrase, even repeated it, "a supermarket
of hostages,'' but refused to go further to accept the endless possibilities.

"They'll probably be released eventually in some kind
of trade, and that's part of what we'll be discussing in
Washington. But, it's only the beginning.''

"Of what?'' And suddenly there was another risk.

"Of a different kind of warfare.''

We walked home slowly that night, stopping to look in
windows, anything to divert our attention from all those

confusing possibilities. The snow had tapered off to a
light downfall and the Village streets were practically deserted, except for several groups of people who reeled up
to us, boisterously wishing us Happy New Year. What
struck me was how isolated and far away we were from
what was always referred to as the "Mecca of the revolution." Yet, it was a false security, for whatever happened there inevitably affected everybody here, even if
most people weren't aware of it.

"Wars should be fought only by people who want to
fight them," I said to Avi as we walked.

He stopped and took me in his arms. "Somewhere in
a specially designated field where there is never any
sun."

The rest of us should be exempt. "I'm frightened," I
said softly.

"Happy New Year, baby," Avi murmured later that
night when we were in bed.

It was unclear to whom he was talking, although I answered for both of us. "Happy and peaceful New Year."

It was a dream we shared for almost the same reasons,
but neither of us, knowing what we knew, was particularly optimistic. And the ringing of the telephone
throughout that night only confirmed that the situation
was becoming increasingly critical.

New Year's Day was especially difficult. There was no
doubt that my tears were over Mother for they would
come each time her face appeared so vividly before my
eyes.

"Why?" I cried at one point. "Why did this have to
happen?"

Even Avi Herzog, who was always able to provide rational explanations for everything, couldn't supply a suitable reason, anymore than he could give valid answers
for the senseless terrorist attacks that were escalating in
Lebanon. The war was supposed to be over, everybody
had agreed, but it was as if they forgot to tell the Israelis,
the Palestinians, the Syrians, and the Lebanese. Every
cease-fire was repeatedly broken and Avi's prediction of
"a different kind of warfare" seemed all the more viable.

I was curled up next to him on the bed while he tried to reach the Defense Ministry in Tel Aviv. "Is there any chance that you'll reach some kind of an agreement—a peace plan in Washington?"

I could read the answer in his eyes, the possibility that the truth would only make it worse for me.

"Yes," he finally said, "perhaps we'll reach an agreement. But, who's going to explain it to the Hizbollah and all the other factions that are running wild over there?"

The calls didn't stop. Avi was on the phone throughout that night also, discussing the consequences for Israel, while I was busy having what was erroneously termed morning sickness. In my case, the waves of nausea enveloped me at any hour of the day or night.

"Leave the door open in case you need me," Avi called to me while talking with the minister of defense.

Splashing cold water on my face, I wondered if the entire Israeli cabinet now knew that I was pregnant. As I walked out of the bathroom, Avi was explaining to someone in Washington about the SAM 5's and SAM 6's, the Syrian surface-to-air missiles, that had been recently emplaced in the open trenches. The possibility of direct confrontation between Israel and Syria had now become a very real threat.

"Oh, great," I said when he hung up the phone.

"I did this to you," he answered tenderly, stroking my face. "I made you sick like this."

"You certainly did," I said, lying down.

"You look positively green."

"I feel fine," I lied, feeling positively terrible.

"I'm not sorry, you know," he said, kissing me.

An extraordinary calm descended over me then, a lucidity of feeling beyond anything I had ever known. The fact that he had asked me to stop doing what I had always done in his part of the world didn't deter me; to the contrary, it fortified my resolve. He was my partner, he was my lover, and we were already married to a common cause.

"Neither am I. All I want is you and this baby." I paused. "And an end to this war."

* * *

It is the morning of January 2, and Maggie Sommers and Avi Herzog are each going off to engage in their respective negotiations. Avi is taking the eight o'clock shuttle to Washington to begin the first round of talks at the State Department, and Maggie is due at the ABN studios at nine for a meeting with Grayson, Elliot, and Quincy to finalize her contract.

The same thought keeps coming into my head, that there is something very special about this baby, other than it is I who am carrying it and Avi who put it there. I am certain that whatever happens on this earth, this child will be born and be a part of me and this man who is now standing in front of our mirror in our bedroom, knotting his tie. This baby has already survived so many obstacles, the least of which was my leaving its father at Ben-Gurion Airport in Tel Aviv, loving me while I tried not to love him back. And this is one accomplishment that I didn't do alone, didn't have to fight to achieve and can share with someone for the rest of my life. And then that familiar terror overtakes me, the same gripping fear each time I feel too secure. A very tangible reality since the time I sat on the ground somewhere near Sabra Camp in Lebanon and then rode up to Mother's apartment only several days ago.

"Where will we live?" I ask Avi, trying to focus on something relatively inconsequential.

"In a house," he answers simply, combing his hair.

"How will we find the house?"

His endless patience is astounding. "We'll go to a real estate agent."

"And suppose there's another war?"

"Then we'll win it the way we won all the others," he says calmly. "Only, maybe we'll be able to finish this one before you think us into another one." Avi looks pained as he sits down next to me on the bed.

"And suppose you lose this war? Then what?" I say, nervously shredding a piece of Kleenex between my fingers.

"Then we'll immigrate to New York and I'll open a falafel stand."

Avi stands and walks to the foot of the bed. Dressed

in a dark-blue three-piece suit, a white shirt, and an elegant blue-and-red-striped silk tie, he looks like anything but an Israeli general who just happens to be the prime minister's special adviser on Lebanese affairs. In fact, he resembles an advertising executive or the chairman of the board of a major investment banking firm. But what difference does it make what he looks like? I know who he really is and where he'll be going after he leaves the States.

"There's a good corner near Rockefeller Center. You'd make a fortune selling falafel there."

He smiles as he takes my hand, leading me to the front door.

"OK," I say, waiting for the elevator to arrive, "so maybe a falafel stand isn't that great an idea. How about military attaché in Washington?"

"It's not that easy," he answers. "And this is what I do best."

"Let someone else do it, so I don't have to worry about you all the time."

"Someone else is doing it," he says. "In fact, a lot of people are doing it."

"It's not fair; you know how I feel."

I can almost see the black cloud that invariably descends over his head whenever we have this discussion. He bends down to kiss me goodbye, and we cling tightly to each other, trying to dismiss any negative thoughts until the next time.

"When this is over," he says, disengaging himself from my grasp, "I'll be back at the ministry at a desk, doing an eight-to-six job, and then you'll be bored having me around all the time."

There is another lump in my throat, making it difficult for me to speak without bursting into tears.

"Sommers," he says, stepping into the elevator, "this is the last time we're going to have this discussion. You should have thought about it before. It's too late now." Gesturing to my belly, he blows me a kiss as the doors slide shut.

And then he is gone.

Grayson Daniel reeks of stale alcohol as he leans over

to kiss me. His sorrow over Mother is genuine, even if his way of expressing it makes him sound foolish. Quincy is bending down in a corner of his office, wiping the snow from her brown leather boots with a soggy Kleenex. Elliot stops shuffling through a sheaf of papers and looks up.

"Death is a tragedy, Maggie," Grayson says, tucking my arm under his and leading me toward the picture window that overlooks the Hudson River.

"Why don't we take a look at the contracts?" Elliot says. "Maggie knows how sorry we all are."

But my mind is not on this meeting, which is so crucial to my career. My thoughts are on Avi and what is happening right now in Washington. And I didn't even want to come here this morning.

But as Cara said when I telephoned her right after Avi left, "Life goes on, Maggie. What difference does it really make anyway if you're at a meeting? Mourning is something very private, and quite frankly, I never intend to visit her grave, because she's not even there."

"Where do you think she is?"

"Probably somewhere with the Czar and Grandmother, playing with Fabergé eggs and nibbling on shashlik. Go to the meeting, and good luck."

It was impossible to explain to Cara that it was the whole world that concerned and worried me because it sounded so dramatic.

"They look fine," Quincy says, peering at everybody over her half glasses. "Except Maggie can't do anything really strenuous for a while."

"Why's that?"

Quincy hesitates and glances at me.

"Because I'm pregnant," I answer, "and if everything goes according to schedule, I will be for the next eight months."

"Pregnant!" Elliot shrieks. "My, my, haven't we been busy."

"How the hell did you get pregnant?" Grayson cries.

They are both not exactly thrilled by my news.

"Well," I say, trying not to laugh, "I'm sure you're not terribly interested in how it happened, Grayson. The point is that I can do everything right up until the last few weeks except go into war zones. But we agreed that I wouldn't be doing that anyway, so what's the problem?''

Grayson recovers first. Walking toward me with his arms outstretched, he says, ''Well, well, this is good news.''

Pale and trembling, Elliot is very close to tears.

''I'm so happy to see how happy you both are,'' Quincy says sarcastically.

''And do you intend to get married, or do we have a potential scandal on our hands?'' Elliot asks smugly.

At the word *scandal*, Grayson turns white. ''Maggie,'' he says evenly, ''you do intend to get married, don't you?''

Once again, I am more a property to them than a human being or a friend.

''In March, when his divorce is final.''

''Well,'' Grayson says jovially, ''we can just keep shooting higher and higher until the happy event. Right, Elliot?''

Elliot's response is a scathing look. ''Why don't we get back to the contract?''

''So,'' Grayson says, ''we don't seem to have any extraordinary problems, except that we'll keep the segments easy until Maggie is in . . . uh . . .''

''Better shape,'' Quincy offers. ''So until then she'll stay put in Israel and not be run from place to place.''

''She should have thought of all that before she decided to go and get herself pregnant,'' Elliot whines.

''Now, El,'' Grayson says, holding up a hand. ''I'm sure Maggie thought long and hard about it.''

''Long and hard is all she probably thought about,'' Elliot mutters under his breath.

''Thanks, you're really a good friend.''

''Maggie,'' he whines again, ''how could you?''

''And the father,'' Grayson interrupts. ''Where is he?''

''Washington,'' I answer, shooting Quincy a warning look.

''Look, we'll all cooperate,'' Grayson says, ''as long as Maggie agrees to stay on and do this magazine show.''

"Of course, Grayson," Quincy says, smiling.

"Then it's settled."

But, before anybody can say anything else, Peter Templeton and Jack Roshansky race into Grayson's office and fling several reams of white paper, ripped from the international teletype machines, across Grayson's desk. Without offering any explanation, Jack turns up the volume on one of the two television monitors encased in the wall. When an image flickers on the screen, he explains, "We've got an internal hook-up with Ringler in Lebanon. This is slated to air tonight—the shit's hit the fan."

"What the hell is going on?" Grayson mumbles as he scans the papers. "Turn up the volume."

We all listen in stunned silence as Ringler speaks very distinctly into a hand microphone, backdropped by what appears to be the aftermath of an explosion. It takes me fully a minute to grasp the implications of his report and comprehend the horrors that are flashing across the monitor.

Ringler's hair is blowing in the strong wind as he walks directly in front of a totally demolished building. "This was a hospital—a Red Cross facility that had approximately 287 patients—some Israeli, some Lebanese, and two Americans." He whips the microphone cord around as he walks toward the rubble. "About one ton of dynamite, maybe two thousand pounds of explosives— packed into a truck and driven by one suicide bomber." A siren can be heard shrieking in the background. Ringler waits until an ambulance rounds the corner and speeds out of the compound before continuing. "The site of the blast was this massive eight-story building located just over the Green Line in East Beirut. The reason the structure was so strongly reinforced was because it used to be the Iranian Embassy—ironic, huh?"

Ringler holds up his hand to the camera as several journalists cluster around him.

Quincy looks pale. "I don't understand. Why? What happened?" Elliot tosses some papers aside on the desk. "What's there to understand—those bastards really went and did it this time."

Grayson is sitting on the edge of his chair, his eyes glued to the monitor. "Quiet."

"I've got an update on that death toll," Ringler says, glancing down at a piece of paper. "Three hundred and six—Jesus H. Christ. I'm going live with this tonight, guys—are you getting this?" He cups his hand to his ear, head cocked to one side, before he makes a thumbs-up signal. "I'll have more updates by air-time—Ringler signing off."

Quincy clutches my hand. "I thought the war was supposed to be over."

"Well, someone forgot to tell the Hizbollah," Elliot snaps.

"So El," Jack says, motioning to me, "she going back in there?"

"Not on your life," Quincy interrupts. "That's not the deal."

"It'll be all over by the time we get her back," Grayson answers in a tired voice, "until the next time." He stands. "Maggie can do a special on the whole bloody mess—the aftermath. Shit." He turns to Elliot. "Start it rolling."

Nodding, Elliot begins barking orders in rapid succession to Peter and Jack. "Get the Jerusalem bureau on the phone and tell them to stay put. Run a teaser on this— thirty seconds of Ringler with someone reading in the studio here—preempt whatever's on and let's start with that."

It is difficult to believe even though I can hear in my head every explanation ever given for this insanity that is Lebanon. Only now it all seems less abstract somehow.

Someone from the newsroom pokes his head in the doorway. "We've got Ringler coming up again," he announces before bounding across the hall to another office.

Jack adjusts the monitor which immediately brings Ringler back into focus, this time standing next to a nurse. The woman can hardly contain her tears as she describes the moments right before the blast.

"I saw a green pick-up truck circling the parking lot just outside of the hospital gates." Her voice catches.

Ringler prods her on. "Where were you then?" he asks gently.

"I was just walking up the sidewalk to the side of the road, coming to work. All of a sudden the truck gathered speed and headed right for the checkpoint. As soon as I saw him do that, I knew he intended to crash the gate."

"Did you get a look at the driver?"

The woman nods her head. "Hizbollah, he was Hizbollah."

"How did you know?" Chris raises his voice, so he can be heard over the din of screeching tires and sirens.

She smiles sadly. "The bandana he wore and the look in his eyes, I knew he was going to blow himself up along with everybody else. It was . . ." she gropes for words. "It was like the fourth of July . . . the sky lit up like the fourth of July."

"You're American," Chris says.

"New Jer . . ." she starts to say but doesn't have a chance to finish. Somebody is running up to Ringler now, handing him a slip of paper. "Hold it!" he yells, "I've got more." He scans the sheet, and emits a low whistle before balling it up and flinging it on the ground.

Ringler is speaking directly into the camera now. "Ten minutes after this hospital was bombed and while everyone's attention was zeroed in over here, another kamikaze-type attack occurred down the road at the French Embassy. Another car, laden with explosives and driven by a nut. This time, the whole building just blew over on its side like a concrete deck of cards. Sixty-five civilians are listed as dead." He pauses. "So far."

My hands are clasped tightly together as the screen finally goes black. I am sitting on the edge, my head forward between my knees, shaking. One of ours, one of theirs. What difference does it make when it is clearly all over now? I can feel it and what anybody says to the contrary doesn't matter anymore. The war has entered a new phase—Avi was right. Jack Roshansky moves to adjust the screen, illuminated once more with static and snow. The image of the ABN studio in Jerusalem comes into focus with Dick Swanson sitting behind my desk, about to begin the final recount of this nightmare. "It's confirmed," Elliot says, cupping his hand over the receive. "It *was* those crazy Iranian Hizbollah."

But I'm not even paying attention, my eyes riveted to the monitor as Dick speaks. "Within minutes of the double blast, an anonymous caller reported to a Lebanese news agency in Beirut, saying and this is a direct quote here pulled from the tape, 'We are not Iranians, nor Palestinians, nor Lebanese. We are the soldiers of the revolution, the oppressed on earth, who follow the teachings of the Koran. Allah Akbar—in the name of Allah, we shall die for our homeland.'"

"Every time those fuckers do something in the name of Allah, people end up dead," Grayson says, shaking his head.

"Is that a wrap, Dick?" Elliot says into the phone. "Good, thanks."

Hanging up, he turns to look at each of us in quick succession.

Quincy jumps up then, a tinge of hysteria in her voice, "Maggie's not going anywhere near there, not until things calm down."

"Right," Elliot responds, "and when do you suppose that will be, Reynolds, in the year four thousand maybe?"

I am staring past them all, at some imaginary enemy and suddenly the silence in the room is excruciating. I have a vision of Joe Valeri, as remote as that of a world magically restored to peace, and for a moment I feel the connection between him and all of this chaos. Perhaps the memory of Joe is the only thing that could remove all my choices. But something else is driving me on, something too powerful to ignore as Joe's image fades as swiftly as the room comes alive again.

"I've got a crew covering the meetings that'll be taking place in Washington," Grayson is shouting into a phone, "and I've got only minimal coverage in Lebanon."

"Get someone over at the Iranian Embassy in Paris to make a statement," Elliot says, the receiver balanced between his chin and shoulder.

Quincy looks bewildered. "But they said they weren't Iranians."

"Right, Quince," Elliot says impatiently, "and you

believe that crap! The Iranians are the only ones crazy enough to blow themselves up—the Hizbollah are their brain child.''

"Who do we have?" Grayson calls out.

"I've got Sommers going back in," Elliot responds. He turns to me and snaps his fingers. "Right, Sommers?"

Elliot is completely professional, having forgotten all previous emotional outbursts—or feelings for that matter. "How fast can you get yourself together," he presses.

Quincy's hand is on mine, trying to restrain me from answering too quickly, trying to prevent me from answering at all.

But it's useless, and we both know it. "Now, tomorrow, anytime," I say automatically, without any more thought of choices.

"Get her the same apartment hotel in Tel Aviv," Elliot orders. "And she'll be arriving the day after tomorrow— that means she leaves tomorrow, the El Al flight out of Kennedy." Looking at me, he makes a thumbs-up gesture and nods. And it's as if nothing has changed since I left, nothing much except for one dead parent, a pregnancy that is no longer a secret, and a lover who is undoubtedly going back into an area where crazy Hizbollah are intent upon blowing up the world. But there's something else that hasn't changed: My adrenaline is flowing just as it always does when there's a breaking story.

"You just can't do this," Quincy cries. "You have other things to think about now."

"And Avi," I say quietly. "What about Avi?" I have no life but this one and no loyalty to anyone but him.

Another phone rings. Grayson answers and hands me the receiver, raising an eyebrow.

"Where are you?" I ask, before he even has a chance to speak.

"In the car in Washington, on my way to the airport. I'm flying directly back to Israel because our bases are at risk. Everything fell apart here."

"I know," I answer, crying now.

"When are you coming back, Maggie?"

"I'll be there the day after tomorrow, and I'll bring

your things, and we have the same apartment in Tel Aviv.'' Details. Anything not to have to confront the pain.

''I love you,'' he shouts over the crackle of the phone wires. ''And I'll be at the airport to meet you.''

''I love you too,'' I shout back. ''Promise me that you'll be careful.''

''I can't hear you,'' he yells, as the final crackle cuts us off.

The phone is dead. And there are no promises.

CHAPTER TEN

The El Al jumbo jet is somewhere over Greece when there is a sudden flurry of activity in the front of the plane. A security guard, dressed in the typical tan leisure suit with the obvious bulge of a shoulder holster under one arm, walks swiftly up the aisle. He might as well be wearing a fedora and trench coat for all his lack of subtlety. The steward, Shlomo, a familiar face from the countless flights we have made together on this New York–Tel Aviv run, listens intently to something the copilot says, while several stewardesses stand nearby, their faces reflecting worry.

Avi hasn't called me since his abrupt departure the day before yesterday, although I didn't really expect him to. He was undoubtedly in areas of Lebanon where it was difficult to find open telephone lines. The nightly newscasts were upsetting enough, watching the continued horrors of the aftermath of those two explosions. American and French soldiers, aided by Israelis and the multinational UNIFIL forces, were shown digging out more dead from beneath the rubble. But now instinct tells me that something else happened, that a bulletin was received over the cockpit radio.

Shlomo, with the deep cleft in his chin and expressive black eyes, stops talking as I approach. He smiles and shakes his head. ''I should have expected you up here.''

''What happened?'' I ask, glancing from one to the other.

''Would you like a cup of coffee?'' Shlomo offers, turning around.

I make no move to leave. ''Thank you,'' I say, studying the face of the copilot.

"What makes you think something happened?" he asks, glancing briefly at Shlomo.

"Maggie Sommers is the Mideast correspondent for an American television station," Shlomo explains, as he hands me a cup of coffee, "so she thinks she can smell a story—right?"

A passenger squeezes past me on his way to the bathroom. "You look as if you just received something over the radio," I say.

The copilot shrugs his shoulders, silently instructing Shlomo to deal with the problem, before he turns and heads back into the cockpit.

"Maggie, go to your seat," Shlomo says firmly. "You're not supposed to be up here."

"Look," I argue, "if it's still censored, there's no danger of my calling it in. I'm just concerned from a personal point of view."

"I can't tell you anything."

But his expression is so troubled. "Shlomo, please." And perhaps it is because mine is even more troubled that he finally relents.

"We're being tracked into Ben-Gurion," he whispers, looking furtively around.

My hands begin to shake. "Why?"

"I really can't say anything else. Please don't ask me."

The plane hits an air pocket as I stumble back to my seat, certain that a civilian Israeli aircraft is tracked by military radar or fighter planes only if there has been an attack on Israeli soil or if there is a threat of war. There is nothing to do except speculate for the next hour and a half, until the pilot finally announces our descent into Ben-Gurion. It is with a sense of relief that I gather my things from underneath the seat and step off the plane. And if there is some state of siege or other crisis, Avi will tell me, right before he'll undoubtedly have to dash off to cope with it. But then it is more than likely that ABN will expect me to report immediately to the studio.

The heat in the terminal is unbearable, a drastic change from the freezing temperatures that I left in New York a mere eleven hours ago. Shifting my tote bag from one shoulder to the other, I approach passport control and wait until my passport is stamped. The procedure is lengthy before numbers are punched into a computer and clearance is finally received by the guard. The first security checkpoint is ahead, and it is there that I begin looking for Avi among the throngs of people waiting behind the red line. There is something peculiar registering in my head, although for the moment I still don't understand. Gila and Gidon are standing there, next to someone wearing a military uniform, a man I don't recognize. The second security checkpoint is straight ahead, the guard meticulously scrutinizing the passengers and collecting the blue slips of paper that signify passport control has been cleared. They are only several feet away from me now when Gila whispers something to Gidon. He nods and steps back, turning his head so he is no longer looking in my direction.

Gila's eyes are red-rimmed, her blond hair tumbles down from the clip that still holds a portion of it on top of her head. Her face is pinched and tired, as if she hasn't slept the night, and her expression is so mournful that I have to force myself not to run from her. I can't survive this. I can't go through any more. It's not fair, not this. She takes my face between her hands, the tears rolling down her cheeks. "Maggie," she whispers. "Maggie."

I have suddenly lost any consolation of security; it has been stolen from me, and all that is left is the task of going back to the beginning of the story. I shake my head from side to side, trying not to faint as the room spins around me. The tears are running down my cheeks, into my mouth.

"No, please not Avi, not that," I plead.

Gila tries to respond, but she can't, because it's just as hideous to tell as to receive the words—a succession of blows.

Gidon is next to me, standing near the other man, someone I still don't recognize but who seems to be holding me up.

And then it dawns on me who he is, the military psychologist who is customarily sent when news of this nature is broken to the family. Gidon's arms are around me, steadying me on the other side. My sobs are audible, but then so are Gila's, as they all try to explain.

"Our base in Sidon was attacked by a Hizbollah suicide bomber last night," Gidon says.

But I don't want to hear it, the pain of knowing the details when the story is already so clear. Pushing him away, I just stare into his eyes like a wounded animal, willing him not to go on. His huge hands are on my shoulders and his jaw is clamped so tightly shut that a muscle is pulsating on the side of his face. Discipline and control prevent him from breaking down, but it is too unbearable for me to survive.

"Avi was on his way from Tyre, where he was inspecting another base."

The pain is too acute. Gila pushes the hair from my face, as the army doctor tightens his grip on my arm.

"There was a charge set on the side of the road by a group of terrorists. We found the remains of the jeep, and there was a lot of blood. He's either dead or captured, Maggie. We just don't know at this point."

Dead or captured. Take your choice—one from column A, please, and two from column B. Dead or captured. The words click off like a computer, trying to shake me back to the reality of the situation, somewhere between Tyre and Sidon, a jeep that is badly damaged and a roadside charge.

Gidon glances at the doctor, as if to check with him that he can continue. They are very practiced at this here, only an Israeli can dispense this kind of news so efficiently, a briefing concerning one *tat aluf* who is either dead or captured. It is a subtle process which begins with the initial shock of realizing Avi is not here followed by the cold reality that he won't be coming here or anywhere else for a very long time. Or maybe ever again. It is slowly sinking into my head, there were too many other heartbreaking stories not to know the eventual outcome. I can read it in their eyes now as my hand gently strokes Gidon's unshaven face.

"Please," I whimper, "please," as if somewhere in every disaster there is a miracle.

He looks as if he'll burst into tears, but of course he

doesn't. Once again that controlled expression appears, but this time a trace of anguish is visible.

"Are you sure?" the doctor asks, this stranger who has one of the most horrendous tasks imaginable, helping others to pick up the pieces so life can go on—somehow.

Taking a deep breath, I say, "Yes, please."

"Avi tried to find Moshe," Gidon explains, "and when he couldn't he decided to go on alone. He jumped in the jeep, heading toward the base in Sidon." He pauses. "One of our patrols found the jeep, or what was left of it, on the side of the road, next to a detonated charge."

It exploded apparently later than intended, probably a good three minutes later which provided the miracle, if there was such a thing in this twisted world.

"There was a lot of blood. He was thrown out of the car, which could have saved his life. But his injuries were obviously very severe, so he could have died afterwards."

It is difficult for me to breathe, to close my mouth and take in air because my lips are so parched. They lead me over to the side of the terminal, away from the crowd of people who are kissing and hugging the other arriving passengers. The doctor gently seats me in a chair while Gila's hand remains on my shoulder. My knees are shaking so badly that I have to hold them still with my hands. "Thirty-five Israelis were killed, seventeen Lebanese soldiers, and forty Palestinians who were being held in a jail on the base." As if that is supposed to make me feel better to learn that all those people are confirmed dead, while Avi's fate is still somewhat of a mystery. But it could be worse, he could have been taken prisoner by a group of irrational fanatics who could murder him at whim, force him to die a slow and agonizing death.

The doctor hands me a cup of water, watching me closely as he holds it to my lips. Again that passive expression, the training that permits no trace of emotion that might cause me to crack.

"Which group set the charge?" I manage to ask.

"We believe it was Abu Ibrihim's Revolutionary Council Group."

And it is so obvious that this particular piece of information has already been confirmed by Israeli intelligence. Tat Aluf Avi Herzog was either killed or is now in the hands if Ibrihim somewhere in Damascus, in what might loosely be called a hospital, or, worse, a prison.

My head is pounding so hard that it is almost impossible not to collapse under the pressure. Gila rummages around in my bag for the claim checks for my luggage. The doctor hands me another cup of water. Gidon has the tickets in his hand.

"I'm going to run outside to make sure Moshe is there, while Gidon gets the bags," Gila says.

Gidon touches my face tenderly, a single moment of something more than duty, a caress back into the past, when we were friends and there weren't regulations to follow.

"Are you feeling faint?" the doctor asks.

"No," I answer, leaning on him as I stand.

"Maggie, if they have captured him, they won't harm him. He's an officer and worth too much to them alive."

My fingers grip his sturdy arm, a sign of my gratitude for his trying to make it better.

"How equipped are they to care for him if he is badly injured?" How disciplined am I to skirt the issue of death, the possibility that it is irrelevant anyway.

"The medical care is not as bad as you think," he says. "After all, Assad survived three serious heart attacks."

"They probably flew in a Jewish doctor," I say, wondering how absurd it really is.

He smiles. "Avi's loved. I know, because he was my commanding officer during the Yom Kippur War."

"Even if he's alive in Damascus," I say bitterly, "is he loved there too?"

My sarcasm is inappropriate; he makes that judgment. "He wasn't an elite commander," he continues. "He grew up in the ranks, which is why his men love him so much. He's part of all of us. This is an enormous shock for everybody."

It doesn't surprise me, this communal grief in a country where there are no locked doors and everybody knows everybody else. The one place where the death of one soldier pierces the heart of the entire nation, the invisible thread that connects them all. But why Avi?

"My name is Shimon," he finally says, "and I'm here for you, Maggie. It's very hard, I understand, but you're strong."

"How do you know that?" I ask. And suddenly my anger sweeps over me like lava, lifting me, and I suddenly do feel strong as I embrace it as my one true ally in this whole unbelievable nightmare. He is momentarily taken aback by my question.

"He's not easy to love, is he?" he says. "He's unyielding, stubborn, a man's man, but you managed to keep loving him, and he you. You're still together." At least for the moment, nobody is speaking about him in the past tense.

Moshe bursts into tears the moment he sees me. "I'm so sorry, Maggie," he says, "but I was only in the barracks for a few minutes when he just left. I didn't know he was looking for me."

Touching his face, I press my lips to his damp cheek. How can I possibly blame him, this boy who is so devoted to Avi?

"Avi never said 'Forward,' Gidon once said. "He always said 'Follow me.' " Only this time, he didn't even say that, he simply went on alone. And then that rage envelops me again, making me flail about somewhere inside and then rally and then flail with a kind of desperation that allows me to begin again, rationally. How could he have done that to me, to us, when he knew the risks?

"It's not your fault, Moshe," I say. "You couldn't have stopped him anyway." He wipes his face with the back of his large hand and opens the car door.

Gila is there, next to me, as I climb inside. "He's strong, Maggie," she says. "If he's alive, he'll get out of this."

"And if not?"

She bites her lower lip, unable to respond, her eyes filled with fear. And who is she trying to convince anyway, how does anyone really know what the outcome will be when all that was left was one bombed-out Israeli army jeep in a pathetic heap on a patch of blood-soaked ground somewhere between Tyre and Sidon?

The trunk of the car slams shut before Moshe and Gidon appear on either side. They are seated in the front now as I lean my head against Gila's shoulder. My tears have begun, impossible to control, when Gidon turns around.

"Look, if he's alive, they'll try to orchestrate a trade."

"Do you think he's dead?" But saying it doesn't help.

"I don't know," Gidon answers, one of them again.

"A chance—what are the chances?" For Christ's sake, just one chance.

"Not good."

"What happens now?"

Gidon starts to answer, but the doctor, seated on my other side, cuts in like a tank forging across the Sinai. "We have to wait for them to make the first move—to orchestrate a trade," he repeats.

But Gidon knows the answer better than the others. "There are people now who are in contact, trying to get the body back or establish his condition." He is talking about his best friend, a man he has known for twenty years, fought next to in three wars. It is amazing that he can separate the personal side of this drama from the professional. But it is because they know how to do that here that there *is* a here.

"I'm pregnant, you know," I say to no one in particular as the car speeds through the final security checkpoint, at the exit of the airport.

"I know," Gidon says softly. "We all know, and you won't be alone through this, I promise you. We'll all be with you."

It is exactly as I thought in New York, that no matter what happens on this earth, this baby will be born and be a part of me and of that man who is possibly not here anymore. And even though Gidon assures me that I won't be alone, a beneficiary of that kibbutz mentality, it somehow doesn't assuage the pain of not having Avi with me now and forever.

"Maggie," Gila says, "I'm so sorry about your mother. We heard." There is silence, as if the burden is on me to comfort them, to assure them that is just another shocking piece of news that will be better as time heals the wound.

"You're home now, Maggie. You'll be all right."

Courage. We're with you.

"Hazak Veheimatz," Gidon says simply.

Be Strong, Be Brave. The entire philosophy of the Israel Defense Forces in one thin volume. As if that could possibly ease the pain.

I am in my office at the ABN Bureau in Tel Aviv, sipping a glass of milk and leafing through the piles of magazines and newspapers that are shipped each week from the States and that I never have time to read. Chris Ringler is with me, preparing for an interview with Ahmed Hassan, one of the notable Palestinian leaders from the West Bank city of Jenin and an alleged direct link to Abu Ibrihim.

ABN has been doing exactly what Grayson said they would, shooting higher and higher as time passes so that the American television audience is not aware of my condition. Now, in my sixth month of pregnancy, only my head and shoulders are visible.

The waves of despair envelop me mostly at night, since I manage to keep sufficiently busy during the days to avoid feeling sorry for myself. And there are already too many people pitying me anyway. Quincy calls twice a week faithfully to find out how I am and to distract me with amusing anecdotes about mutual friends in New York. But there is always that moment of hesitation when she starts to ask, to wonder if perhaps there is any news. Cara also calls but usually breaks down somewhere in the beginning of the conversation, before she can even pretend to discuss other things, so that I end up comforting her.

There is still no news of Avi. The six Israeli soldiers who were captured within the UNIFIL buffer zone, now almost a year ago, have still not been released. What is happening, however, is that the Israeli negotiating team is optimistic that their ordeal is almost over. Gidon just told me last night that the Red Cross was permitted to visit them, languishing in a jail in Damascus, and reported that they were relatively healthy and in reasonably good spirits.

Ahmed Hassan has refused to talk to any member of the Western press since the Israeli soldiers were captured. There is no doubt that he knows exactly what is going on, however, from his close friend Ibrihim, but he has also been very reluctant to make that alliance known. The fact that he has now agreed to meet with ABN News must mean that he has something important to place with us—a message from the Palestinian leader.

"We'd better push off," Ringler says, "or we'll be riding around there when it's dark."

"I'd welcome a little company at night," I say, smiling sadly.

Chris hugs me. "Maggie, Maggie," he says, stroking my hair, "it's tough, isn't it?"

I pick up my head and look at him, tears glistening in my eyes. "So tough," I answer softly, "that even you wouldn't believe it if I tried to explain."

Chris pulls me close to him again.

I back away slightly. "No pity, remember?"

He shakes his head, his voice strangely choked. "I remember."

As we drive through the arid hills of the Jordan Valley on the way to the West Bank city of Jenin, I wonder just how far I can go with Hassan. Heading farther and farther over that invisible green line that separates Israel from the territories that were captured during the 1967 Six Day War, my level of optimism rises and falls with each passing mile. Unless we can get Hassan to tell us something concrete, it is another wasted interview. Unless it is in the interest of the PLO to communicate something to Israel via the Western press, it is the same slogans and rhetoric. But, whatever is Hassan's intent, we have to play it out very carefully, including making my interest in one missing *tat aluf* all part of the charade.

It is fascinating how this particular region resembles more of an Arab country than the irrigated terrain that is so prevalent in Israel. Stretches of barren land extend for miles ahead, while rocky mountains border one side of the road. Construction cranes lie idle on the dusty ground near the isolated villas that dot the countryside, and workmen squat underneath makeshift huts, trying to find shelter from the blazing afternoon sun. Ironically, even the unfinished villas all have miniature Eiffel Towers on their roofs, powerful television antennas that beam in signals from as near as Amman and as far as Damascus. Finally, we approach the entrance to Jenin where the pungent smell of bougainvillea petals greet us as we turn up the winding road toward the opulent villa of Ahmed Hassan. The pomela and orange stands that line the makeshift sidewalks are already closed for the day. The merchants are heading home. It is simply too hot to work.

The electric gate that surrounds the house has a small intercom next to the bell. Pushing the button, I hear a heavily accented voice.

"Who, please?"

"Maggie Sommers, ABN News," I answer.

The response is a long buzzing sound that automatically releases the lock. Pushing the gate open, Chris and I walk along the beautifully manicured gardens that lead up to the marble veranda.

He beams broadly, sitting in his usual position in the wheelchair, his white gown hiked up around his thighs so that the twisted stumps of what were once his legs are visible to us. Hassan, the victim of a bombing by a group of Jewish terrorists who didn't care for his politics, is a martyr for his cause and proud to display the scars of his beliefs.

"Welcome," he says, rolling himself forward to greet us. "Welcome to my house."

"Thank you, Mr. Hassan," I say. "I'm glad to see you again."

"You are quite pregnant, Miss Sommers," he says, accentuating the *Miss*, or perhaps it is my own paranoia. "Are you feeling well?" he adds.

"I'm feeling very well," I answer, smiling.

I lower myself carefully into a black wrought-iron chair, watching as Hassan maneuvers himself from his wheelchair onto a porch swing that is suspended from high wooden beams on the ceiling of this outdoor sitting room. When he is comfortably ensconced on the seat, a butler appears, carrying a tiled tray on which are small glasses filled with Turkish coffee. We each take one and sip silently for several minutes, before Hassan finally says, "It is unhappy for you that the father of this child is not here." There are no secrets in this part of the world; all the intrigues are known by both sides except when it concerns internal security of the state and even then, nothing is sure.

My silence offends him.

"Aren't you going to speak of it with me?"

But my response is interrupted by the static sounds of Chris's hip beeper, signaling that there is a message for us.

Standing, Chris says, "We've got a message from the bureau in Tel Aviv."

"Yes?" Hassan answers.

"May I use your telephone please, sir? I have to check in."

"Please," he replies graciously. "In the house. Walid will show you."

He waits for Chris to leave before he continues. "I know that you are very distressed."

It is not difficult to imagine that I would be distressed, upset, or even grief-stricken that the father of my baby was dead or at best half dead in some filthy terrorist den. Yet why would he summon me all the way out here just to offer his heartfelt condolences?

"Yes I am," I say quietly, my eyes never leaving his face.

He takes another sip of coffee, watching me intently over the rim of his cup. He swallows rather noisily, wipes his mouth with a Kleenex that he produces from the sleeve of his gown, and nods. "It's a great tragedy for all peoples that innocent children must suffer because there is no resolution to this problem." Are there other fronts to fight, other targets to destroy before that point is fully understood?

"It is always the question of occupation," he continues, "the rights of the Palestinian people." Nothing against the Palestinians or other innocent victims of this struggle, but still, certain people attract persecution. The Jews did for two thousand years.

"The exchange of prisoners will take place tonight," he says suddenly, massaging his stumps with the palms of his hands.

"And what of this baby's father?"

He has said enough perhaps, his expression is now blank, he has trained his eyes away. "There is nothing," he finally offers, gazing off in the distance.

Chris is on the veranda, an anxious expression on his face. "Maggie, I've got to talk to you a minute."

"There is no need," Hassan says, "she knows from me."

Chris conceals his surprise as he pulls up a chair and sits down.

"The Israeli soldiers are on their way to Geneva now," Hassan says, his eyes glistening, "and the Palestinian martyrs are being processed out of Lebanon for transport into Israel and then to the diaspora."

"How many Israelis will be exchanged tonight?" I ask. I was halfway there now; he could offer me the resolution to all the disconnected components of my life. Please, Hassan, just this one time, and for the sake of one more innocent child. But that was a lie, for it was more for me. Help me to be whole again, please, after all that has already happened.

"There are six Israelis being released for 1,034 Palestinians and Arabs."

"Chris?" I ask, lowering my gaze to the table to avoid Hassan's scrutiny.

"That's what I hear too," he says softly.

I can't protest, which makes my silence as some kind of tacit submission.

Hassan is maneuvering himself back into his wheelchair, a sign that the meeting has come to its conclusion. Grimacing with pain, he finally settles back, placing his hands on the wheels of his chair. Just as he is about to roll himself into the house, he turns.

"We are not barbarians, Miss Sommers," he says. "We are just fighting for our homeland."

Ringler grabs my arm and whispers, "Don't, Maggie."

Hassan is at the door, almost inside. "Many have lost fathers, brothers, sons, children—it is nothing new here."

It is not possible to restrain myself anymore. "But if I only knew if he was dead, then I could be at peace. Like this, it's torture. Please, if you know, tell me so I can go on." My face is buried in my hands.

And I knew even without looking at him that he didn't intend to answer me.

The phones are ringing off the hooks at the studio. Dick Swanson, a veteran newsman who usually has the bored and cynical demeanor of someone who has seen too much, is now animated and vibrant. He is alternating with Chris Ringler, speaking to the ABN New York bureau, the Israel Defense Forces Manpower Division, and the Defense Ministry. Confirmation came through officially just one hour ago that the exchange of 1,034 Palestinian prisoners for those six Israelis captured almost a year ago in the UNIFIL buffer zone will take place tonight.

Miriam Rabai, one of the more vocal and militant mothers of one of the Israeli prisoners, has agreed to be interviewed here at the studio in fifteen minutes, before she is transported to the airfield to wait for her son.

Dick hangs up a telephone and leans forward in his chair. "I want her to explain what it felt like all these months, from the moment he was captured to the moment she found out he was going to be released. I want every man, woman, and child in America to feel her pain and her joy—something completely human, no politics."

Ringler glances up at me with the same expression that has been on his face every time this subject is discussed. Pity.

"Maggie," he says softly, "are you going to be all right? Can you do this thing tonight?"

"Is it too much?" Dick chimes in, as if he suddenly remembered.

There is no time to console them, assure them that if

it weren't for my job, I would have fallen apart a long time ago. Miriam Rabai is being ushered into the studio.

She is an attractive woman of about fifty-five, a survivor of the Treblinka concentration camp, with the world-weary eyes of someone who has simply seen enough, though the inner fire is still visible. She sits demurely on the sofa, her hands folded in her lap, her expression expectant yet calm.

"How do you do, Mrs. Rabai," I say, sitting across from her, "I'm so glad that you agreed to talk to us and so very pleased for you."

She smiles, tucks a strand of her natural blond hair, flecked with silver, into a bun that is twisted at the nape of her neck. "I would have recognized you by your teeth," she says, staring at my stomach. "You have wonderful teeth."

She's tough, brittle even, yet somehow still vulnerable.

"Thank you," I laugh. "Are you ready to begin?"

Chris is already aiming the camera directly at her, the back of my head at the side of his lens for the first segment of the interview.

"I'm ready," she says, her eyes glinting in anticipation of telling her story.

And it is only her pain that I share now, just one half of the ordeal, because her son is coming home and it is almost over for her.

"How did you feel when you learned that Dani was captured?"

"As if someone had killed me," she says simply.

A familiar feeling that never ends, over and over until it depletes me, causing me to die a thousand deaths. "What kept you going, gave you hope?"

She smiles sadly. "I made up my mind one morning, turned over his photograph and promised myself that I wouldn't look at it again until he was home. I talked to him, explained how sorry I was that there would be no more tears, that now I would fight for his release. That was when I began to push the officials here and even offered myself to Abu Ibrihim in exchange for Dani."

I know it all in generalities and am perhaps too frightened now to receive all the details, preferring to remain at a respectable distance from this joyous ending.

"It's almost over now," I say, leaning forward. "Do you believe it yet?"

"Yes," she answers, her reluctance still evident, "almost, but there is still no feeling in my heart—not until he is here and I can touch him."

And listening to her makes me realize that it is this very insanity of gaining and losing, the ruthlessness of this situation in playing with human emotions, that keeps me sane. It is the drama I relive again and again, until there is nothing left inside me except his child.

The interview is over. Chris seems pleased: good visuals, poignant responses. Dick is bending down, gathering up some papers and equipment we need to take with us to the airfield, for the coverage of the exchange tonight.

Miriam is on her way out the door, walking slowly, when she turns. "I admire you, we all do," she says quietly.

I am only mildly surprised. "Why?"

"Because you chose to stay, to remain with us in spite of your tragedy."

It is as if a knife has sliced through my heart. My tragedy. Those words alone have killed me so many times, and now again. "How did you know?"

"This is Israel," she says simply. "There are no secrets."

Dick is touching my arm, diverting my attention toward him, allowing her to leave without further comment or conversation.

"Maggie, Gidon is on the phone for you."

My heart is pounding as I dash to grab it, forgetting even to say another goodbye to her.

"Gidon," I say breathlessly into the receiver.

He takes a deep breath. "Maggie, I'm not sure it's good for you to be there tonight, to cover this exchange. It might be too much for you."

"I thought you were calling because maybe . . ."

Another sigh. "Maggie, it's no use hoping; don't do it to yourself. I just wanted to be sure that this wasn't too much, that I'm here if you need me. I'll come there, but—''

"But nothing," I finish. "There is no news, then."

"Listen, I don't want anything to happen to you. I'm worried, for the baby. You're very important to us."

A communal child, a part of everybody who was ever part of him. Only, he's not here to participate in this event, not available for the moment.

"Dick feels you can do it," Gidon continues, "but I wanted to be sure."

And for all the arguments against it, it is nonetheless the most logical thing for me to do. "I can't," I answer, "I want to. Maybe not for much longer, but right now I can."

But then, after hanging up the phone, just seconds after convincing Gidon that it is not the moment for me to fall apart, I fall apart. Burying my face in my hands, sobs rack my body, tears of despair, until Chris is beside me.

"Maggie," he says, his voice soothing and gentle, "I'm so sorry."

I press his hand to my damp cheek.

"It's just because of Miriam, the exchange tonight, the shock of it. I'll be fine."

He wipes my eyes with his fingertips. "Maybe Gidon is right."

"No! Where do we have to go?" I start to weep again but catch myself in time.

"To the ministry at eleven, and from there we're being transported with the rest of the foreign press corps to Ramat David airfield. It might help if you did this more often—let go like this."

"I try to sometimes, but there's never enough time; we're always so busy," I answer, smiling through my tears.

"You're right," Chris says. "This is the only place where local news makes headlines all over the world."

I am silent, while Chris tries to make more idle conversation. "Your hair's a mess, and since we only shoot your head and shoulders, maybe you should comb it."

It is suddenly the most fraught time, the loneliest moment of my entire life, as I prepare to leave to cover this news piece, the return of six Israeli soldiers.

Every foreign correspondent based in Israel is milling around the tarmac of Ramat David military airfield in the north of Israel. Giant spotlights are beaming light on three gleaming white jumbo Air France transport planes, each with red crosses pasted on their sides, that are sitting at the far end of the runway. They look eerie and almost surrealistic under the star-studded sky.

It is midnight, and the prisoner exchange is about to begin at any minute, with the arrival of the first busload of Palestinians from the Ansar detention camp in Lebanon. They are being brought here as the initial step in a complicated process that will culminate in the release of six Israeli soldiers.

A carnival atmosphere prevails among the foreign press, as journalists joke, chat, and sip coffee from Thermos jugs that are passed around from one to the other. I feel completely alienated from everyone, just not up to participating in all this gaiety. Glancing from time to time over to the cordoned area where the families are anxiously waiting, I wish that my place were with them, counting the minutes until the nightmare was finally over.

Dick is standing next to me, his hands jammed into the pockets of his khaki trousers, and craning his neck in the direction of the barbed-wire fence that encloses the airstrip.

"When the Palestinians arrive," he explains nervously, "they'll board the planes immediately and fly out fast. We'll be here for about four hours in all, because the plane carrying the Israelis will be arriving from Geneva only after these have taken off. So there are two separate segments to cover."

"How many Palestinians are actually leaving from here?" I ask, pacing alongside him.

"About three hundred fifty from here and the rest by boat from Lebanon." Chris is running toward us, out of breath. "Wait," he calls out.

We stop, watching as he bounds up to us, panting. "I just got word that the Israelis are coming in on two separate aircraft, three soldiers on one and three on the other, so we might have an additional fifteen-minute delay between segments.''

A sudden hush falls over the crowd as the buses appear in the distance, making their first turn through the gate.

"Stay put," Dick orders, "and stick this in your ear. It'll be simultaneous translation in case one of them makes a statement. You'll repeat it in English for our audience as they say it.''

"Who really cares?'' I mutter to myself, slipping the wire around my neck and the tiny receiver in my ear. They always say the same thing, over and over, it's been going on for years. At this point, the rhetoric of their revolution or their pleas for a homeland have become as meaningless as the Israelis' promises of finding a solution to the bitterness over this tiny contested strip of land. And I am almost immune since becoming a casualty of this struggle, since sustaining my own loss.

Ringler elbows his way through the crowd, aiming his minicam in the direction of the buses. There are definitely certain advantages to being a pregnant journalist. My spot is assured, no pushing or shoving to rob me of the best vantage point.

"Now, Sommers."

And the camera is aimed at my head and shoulders as I begin my report.

"This is Maggie Sommers at Ramat David airfield in Israel, where the celebrated prisoner exchange of 1,034 Palestinians for six Israelis is about to begin.''

I feel as if I am entering insanity by degrees.

"The Palestinians are jumping off the buses, wearing brand-new green-and-white track suits. As they step down, one by one, onto the tarmac, their plastic handcuffs are cut from their wrists by waiting Red Cross officials. The prisoners are singing the PLO fight song, their fists clenched in the air as they file in an orderly fashion toward the waiting planes.''

There are suddenly no more illusions.

"Among those being set free tonight are half a dozen women, members of the PLO who were also captured in Lebanon during the war and who are being taken on board the planes along with several hundred men. The others are being shipped by boat from the Lebanese port city of Jounié. As soon as this first stage is completed and these planes are airborne, the first three Israeli soldiers will arrive here by a special Swissair carrier, immediately followed by a second Swissair plane, carrying the other three Israelis."

I am grieving, angry, determined not to weep, when suddenly there is a voice coming over the receiver that is in my ear, alerting me that a translation is about to begin. Dick is apparently receiving the same information, because he is motioning to me to move closer to one woman prisoner, who is making a statement for the press.

"My name is Leila and I was in Beirut, where I was taken prisoner for operating RPGs, making military actions against Israel. My husband was killed before my eyes, the day I was captured, and my baby was born in captivity, in an Israeli prison. I was sentenced to fifteen years, but now I am leaving my homeland, free to go to Libya."

And when I finished repeating her words in English, I catch another glimpse of her as she runs to freedom, almost to the plane. She turns, her head held high, a familiar fervor in her eye. We are different, one day in Amman, one in Damascus, a training camp in the Bekaa, prison in Lebanon. We are the same, swallowing grief so only a pride and dignity are visible to the world.

"Cut," Dick yells. "Let's try to get a statement from the chief of staff."

Whipping the long microphone cord around my legs, I head toward General Ehud. The deafening roar of the plane's engines makes it difficult to be heard. Dick cups his hands around his mouth, shouting over the din of the crowd and the noise of the powerful propellers, as the second aircraft begins to taxi slowly down the runway.

"Now," Dick yells. "Before anyone else gets him."

Chaim Ehud, affectionately known as Concrete Man among the foreign press, watches as the last of the Palestinians board the plane, a taut expression on his face while he views the final result of almost twelve months of intense negotiations. My skirt is blowing up above my knees in the brisk wind as I hold the microphone to his mouth.

"General Ehud, it's good to see you."

"Hello, Maggie," he says warmly. "How are you?" But his eyes belie any friendly greeting.

"Well. Will you talk to me for a moment, tell me how you feel right now, watching all of these Palestinians flying out to freedom in exchange for only six Israelis?" You are all culpable.

He doesn't reply immediately, searching instead for the proper words that will justify, explain, ameliorate, and above all, not offend me. He clears his throat which does little to change his gravelly voice.

"I feel very good about this. I believe it is our responsibility here in Israel to bring back every soldier who was sent to war by this government, even if the price is high."

But it is not enough. "If there is any controversy or debate about that price," I continue, "how will you answer your critics who say that you shouldn't have released so many terrorists and convicted killers for only a handful of Israelis?" And if they released every murderer in captivity for one *tat aluf*, would I have taken a moral stand, would I have cared, or would I have bent the bars apart with my hands?

Ehud appears immune. "I would like to answer those people who are saying that. What would they do if they were in a position of authority and were forced to tell the soldiers of Israel, their parents, wives, and children, that these men would go on in jails or terrorist camps without our doing anything. We've done it like this in the past, it is our way, and we will do it in the future."

The policy remains. It is merely a question of luck. Dropping my microphone limply at my side, I wait until Dick and Chris are next to me to register grief.

"Maggie," Ehud says, "I'm so very sorry."

I am staring at him, a flood of tears clouding my vision, rewarded only by his expression of concern and caring, several philosophical words of comfort.

"You know, Maggie, you wish for life and health, and then you find out that he is dead or captured, and so you wish for captivity. Life is strange."

There are times when it is almost comical, when others don't even realize how ludicrous it is.

"You were terrific, Maggie," Ringler says, kissing me. "Really good."

"We've got three hours with nothing to do," Dick says. "There's a lounge set up for the press in one of the hangars—coffee and cake."

"Wonderful," I say sarcastically. "A party, a celebration."

Dick slings his arm around my shoulders. "Come on, Mags," he says. "You're not going to stand up for three hours."

So I allow them to lead me to the hangar, to eat and talk and discuss the first part of this spectacular news event, waiting with the others until the second portion gets under way. And then I can go back to the apartment hotel in Tel Aviv and cry myself to sleep for a change.

The sun is just peeking over the hills of the Golan, daybreak is here, when word filters in that the first Swissair Boeing 707, carrying three Israeli soldiers, is circling Ramat David. My head is resting on Ringler's shoulder when Dick races over to us. He stands still, offering me a paper container of coffee. "Here, Maggie," he says excitedly. "Come on, we have to roll."

The families of the Israeli soldiers are clustered together, separated into private groups, every eye riveted on the plane as it makes its descent onto Israeli soil. Suddenly what begins as a smattering of applause escalates into wild cheers and shouts of joy as it touches down, brakes screeching, and speeds along the runway. People are pushing forward, running toward the craft as it rolls slowly to a stop. Dick hands me the microphone, while Chris clips the cable around my ankle so that I am attached to the sound box. The families are in a frenzy, laughing, clapping, and whistling, while military police try to restrain them from storming the craft.

"I can't do this," I shout over the noise, tossing the microphone to Dick.

"Yes you can," he yells, tossing it back to me.

"No I can't!" I scream, tears rolling down my cheeks.

"Maggie," Ringler suddenly says, "the doors are opening. Move."

But I'm too busy playing catch with Swanson to pay attention. And then Miriam Rabai is next to me.

"My son is on this plane," she says, her face flushed with excitement.

"Maggie," Swanson says, standing between us, "we'll get an exclusive statement from Dani Rabai. Come on, get going."

And Miriam squeezes my hand and nods, this woman who has endured so many things but who now has the most wonderful reward of all, better than even her own life reclaimed so long ago.

Maneuvering expertly through the crowd, I position myself almost at the bottom of the steps of the plane. The first soldier, a young boy of no more than eighteen years old, begins to weep as he falls into the arms of his waiting parents. The second one appears then, tall and thin, and is immediately embraced by his wife, who hands him his infant daughter, obviously born while he was in captivity. This is almost too much for me to bear.

"You're doing great," Chris calls to me, sensing my pain. My face is clearly visible in his lens, undoubtedly etched in agony. I feel numb.

The third soldier is walking slowly down the steps, seemingly dazed in the face of all this commotion. He is Miriam's son, Dani Rabai, so very much like her, with his blond hair and that determined set of the jaw. Miriam runs forward, followed by the father, who clutches Dani to his chest. I move near them, my microphone picking up the end of a prayer of thanksgiving that Dani recites, grateful to be back home in Israel, safe and alive.

"You're up, Sommers," Dick instructs me in a voice strangely charged with emotion.

Moving closer to Miriam and Dani, I wait until several people stop embracing them. Dick points to me and I respond, so practiced from years of doing the same thing that the dazzling smile on my face appears automatically. "You said today that you would feel it in your heart when you finally saw your son. Can you describe how you're feeling now?"

"I feel wonderful," she says joyfully. "I knew it would happen, and I love him." She kisses him. "He looks great, doesn't he?"

"Dani," I say, holding the microphone up to his mouth, "how does it feel to be home in Israel?"

"I can't describe the feeling," he says. "You have to experience it to know."

"Dani," I say, taking a chance, "tell me about those months."

A woman is beating a hand drum nearby, while several others are clapping their hands and dancing together in a circle.

"I met the lonely cell," he says over the bedlam, "and I knew that my biggest enemy was myself."

"How did you stay sane?"

"I only had my memories to keep me alive. And then I thought of my mother and how she was fighting for my release."

"How did you know?"

"Because Abu Ibrihim told me. He said that she was doing his job, pushing the Israelis to make the trade."

"Did you see him—Ibrihim?"

"Yes, I saw him."

"And?"

"And sometimes you read in books that someone has a twinkle of madness in his eye, and he had that."

"Did he ever talk to you?"

"Only to tell me that one of us had died in captivity— to make me feel grateful that it wasn't me."

Miriam pales. My body feels as if gallons of ice water have spilled over it, drowning me in freezing liquid. Trembling, I try to form the words.

"What other one?" I barely whisper.

He is clearly upset, shaken that perhaps he has spoken out of turn, information that could possibly jeopardize the security of the state, once again the primary concern.

"What other one?" I screech, and Dick and Chris are there, holding me up, because it is the end of the line.

"I'm sorry," Dani says, leaning against Miriam. "I don't know. They didn't tell us."

"Dani," Miriam says, imploring him to understand,

more concerned for me suddenly than for him. "Did one soldier die?"

"I don't know. He only said that, he never said any more. It was perhaps to frighten me that he told me, to make me cooperate."

The other craft, another Swissair 707, is circling above the airfield now.

"I'm so tired," I murmur to Dick. "I can't anymore, and maybe it's better just to know, because then it is over."

"Ask Ehud," Dick says, near tears. "Press him to tell you."

Chaim Ehud is engaged in intense conversation with Defense Minister Yariv, away from the crowd and surrounded only by their closest aides.

Shading my eyes from the new sun, I can barely make out the silhouette of the aircraft as it descends onto the field.

"General Ehud," I say, "please, one moment of your time."

Chris is there, holding my arm, as Dick walks to the other side of Yariv. Ehud glances at me, shakes his head, and says, "Just let them get off the plane, please."

"But someone said there was a casualty in prison, that one Israeli died in captivity. Is that true?"

His face twists into an expression of annoyance. Ringler is pressing forward, almost menacingly, pushing past Yariv until he is almost nose to nose with Ehud.

"The family has to be informed first—the family, you understand. I can't release that kind of information to the press."

The noise of the giant motors is deafening.

"But I'm more than press," I cry. "If it's Avi, I should know. I have the right to know."

Defense Minister Yariv turns his back, watching the portable steps being pushed up to the entrance of the craft.

"There'll be a press briefing in hangar three as soon as they deplane," Ehud says mechanically.

Miriam's words echo in my head. "This is Israel. There are no secrets." Except when there are.

"Tell her," Ringler says. "If it's true, tell her."

Ehud has had enough. His expression now has a locked-in glower, and his voice suddenly has changed. "Am I supposed to take the word of a murderer, who sends me messages that one of my men is dead? Can I say that to the press before things are confirmed?"

And so life is as strange as Ehud said before. You wish for the survival of your own even if that means the death of another.

There is nothing left for me, not even to partake in the comfort that is being offered by this family that is Israel. My grief is irreconcilable, defiant though against the memory of once having loved here more than anywhere on earth. Nobody can take that from me. Ringler's eyes shine with fury, his hand still on mine, his touch possessive yet reassuring. Dick looks sick, white and chalky, as if he is crumbling under the weight of sheer tension, suppressing an urge to smash it by smashing someone in the face. And I suddenly feel that terrible yet serene peace that goes along with living among the world's victims. I feel as if I have joined the ranks of those who have been waiting all their lives. Joe Valeri all over again, only now I am a seasoned veteran.

The door to the craft swings open, and seconds pass before two soldiers walk down the steps together, one holding the shoulders of the other, until they are separated by the joyful hugs and kisses of their families. And then a third soldier, tears rolling down his cheeks as a young girl rushes forward to be swept up in his embrace. There are no casualties here. Six were promised and six were delivered.

The Israeli journalists are suddenly pushing forward, followed by a confused and baffled foreign press corps, unsure why there is more commotion at the door of the plane. Flashbulbs are exploding, and cameras are focused directly on the steps leading to the craft.

He is walking slowly, broad-shouldered, still beautiful in spite of the pallor of his complexion of prison. At the bottom of the steps, he turns to his right, his hand raised to salute his chief of staff, who pulls him near, pounding him on his back. He shakes hands with Yariv, who laughs out loud at the sheer joy and surprise of seeing him again. And then he looks around, seemingly oblivious to the cheers and applause of the crowd.

I am short on grace now, merely three feet away, experiencing a bizarre sensation of levitation and embarrassed that my tears and laughter are all mixed up. His left hand reaches up to touch the side of my face, to make sure that I am real. And then I am weeping, filling my mouth with his, obliterating any memory of before, the pain of not having him near me like this for so many months.

Somewhere vaguely in the background there are more cheers, flashbulbs, and then microphones being thrust in our faces. He is holding me against him, smiling broadly and answering the questions that are being fired at him. I can't speak.

"How does it feel to be back home in Israel, General Herzog?" a reporter calls out.

"Great," Herzog answers.

"What was it like there?" another voice asks.

Avi shrugs his shoulders, a wry smile crossing his face. "Interesting," he says, pulling me even closer to him.

"Who captured you?" Another brilliant question. Do I ask questions like that?

"Abu Ibrihim's Revolutionary Council Group," he answers.

"Why were you released in this exchange when only six Israelis were promised?"

"I didn't discuss it with Ibrihim."

A ripple of laughter goes through the crowd.

"Did the Syrians make other demands for your release?" another journalist persists.

"I can't comment on that," Avi says. "The Syrians never consulted me concerning the negotiations."

"How were you treated?"

Avi leans toward me, his lips on mine. "I love you," he whispers.

More flashbulbs explode in our faces.

"How were you treated, General?" the reporter repeats.

"The doctors were very good, my captors were not as

pleasant, but I'm in good shape." And then he kisses me again. "You're very pregnant. Did I do that to you?"

I still can't speak.

"What happened and how were you captured?" It occurs to me how very inane this is.

"I don't remember very much, except that I was driving, and then there was an explosion, and the next thing, I woke up in a hospital where not too many people spoke Hebrew."

Everybody chuckles.

"I missed you so much. You kept me alive," Avi says softly.

"Is the war in Lebanon worth it?"

"That's not for me to say," Avi answers smoothly.

And then some smart-ass in the back of the crowd yells out, "Is Maggie going to get the exclusive to this?"

Avi looks at me and grins before responding. "She already got her exclusive."

My face is burning as everybody begins cheering, whistling, and applauding again.

Dick Swanson is right in front of us now, the microphone in my face, while Chris's minicam is shooting every single inch of my face and body.

"Maggie," Dick says, smiling, "this is a personal moment for you, and the millions of people out there who love you want to know how it feels to have Avi back home."

After all of these years, I am about to have the privilege of being on the receiving end of the microphone, at a moment when my power of speech has temporarily vanished.

"How do you feel, Maggie?" Dick says again, inching closer.

There is suddenly total silence as everybody waits for my response. Looking up at Avi Herzog, I am only certain of one thing.

"I feel," I answer very softly, "an absence of pain."

ABOUT THE AUTHOR

Barbara Victor, a former Middle East specialist for the State Department, has worked in television and radio for many years. Currently a freelance journalist, she has interviewed such notable Middle Eastern leaders as Menachem Begin, Ariel Sharon, Yitzhhak Shamir, Col. Muammar Quaddafi, the Ayatollah Khomeini, and Abu Iyad of the PLO. She lives in Paris, where she is a contributing editor to *Elle* (France). This is her first novel.